ALL OR NOTHING

"Lanigan knows her genre well...peoples her yarn with likable characters as well as several endearingly loathsome ones."

—*Publishers Weekly*

A PROMISE MADE

"As a storyteller, Catherine Lanigan is in a class by herself—unequaled and simply fabulous."

—*Affaire De Coeur*

"Catherine Lanigan is a master storyteller!"

—*Rave Reviews*

AT LONG LAST LOVE

"Catherine Lanigan continues to polish her marvelous gift for storytelling with this emotional and compelling tale of risk taking and divided loyalties."

—*Romantic Times*

BOUND BY LOVE

"Lanigan succeeds in spinning a highly suspenseful, romantic tale!"

—*Publishers Weekly*

SWEET SEDUCTION

"My God, I have never met one like you," he breathed hotly into her ear, where he strung a necklace of searing kisses. Again his lips returned to her demanding mouth.

Valentine's hands left his head, skimmed over his mask and explored the regions of his jaw, throat and chest. She did want all of him, she realized. Her hands traveled down the flat plain of his hard stomach. Just as she was about to move farther, a warning bell clanged in her head.

"I must stop," she moaned.

"No, never," he groaned. "You are my wanton...." His hand splayed across her full breast. "God in heaven, are you harlot or angel?"

SEDUCED

CATHERINE LANIGAN

LEISURE BOOKS   NEW YORK CITY

A LEISURE BOOK®

April 1996

Published by

Dorchester Publishing Co., Inc.
276 Fifth Avenue
New York, NY 10001

Printed in the United States of America.

This one is for my dream team:
Charlotte, Kimberley, and Alicia.

Chapter One

"I have to marry a toad!" Valentine St. James wailed to her twin sister, Victoria, and her Aunt Cherise as they rode in the Countess Cioppoli's rococo gilded carriage to the Mardi Gras Ball at the countess's villa.

Valentine barely noticed the silver velvet upholstery or the burgundy liveried and masked footman and driver. Nor did she take note of the four snowy horses bridled in silver and the enormous silver and gold plumes on their heads. She did not see the sterling silver vases spilling over with white hot-house roses to the right and left of their heads. Tonight marked the official betrothal of Valentine St. James to Lord Justin Hawkeston, and Valentine couldn't have been more miserable.

"You don't know that he's a toad," Victoria countered, her black onyx eyes flashing in her beautiful heart-shaped face. She folded her dainty hands demurely on the billowing yellow satin overskirt of her costume in the French court style.

Valentine frowned at her sister, whose ball gown was identical to her own. Valentine's fingers anxiously toyed with one of the yellow satin rosettes that pulled the overskirt into festoons, revealing the white satin underskirt. The yellow satin and white lace overbodice complemented Valentine's black-as-night eyes, pale ivory skin and pale moonbeam-colored hair.

Valentine folded her arms across her chest and slumped back in the seat. "He has to be as old as Papa and probably ugly to boot! Do you suppose he is bald like Papa? I'll bet he's even got a wart on his nose! Or on his mouth! Ugh! I'll have to kiss him!"

"You'll have to do a whole lot more than just kiss him, Val." When Victoria saw the glum look on her twin's face she immediately berated herself for her comment. She tried to make ammends. "I'm sorry. Please don't be so pessimistic. He won't be that bad."

"How can you say that? Have you seen some of Papa's friends? Take Lord Kent, for instance. There's a real peach of a man. He can't be an inch over five foot and twice as round. And that disgusting running nose of his. He must go through six handkerchiefs a day. Or what about the Earl of Brighton? Now there's a younger man. What a bag of bones! I'll bet I weigh more than he does. If I ever hugged him, I'd break his sternum. And there is no one so fastidious as Lord Asherby. They say he changes clothing three times a day because he has an aversion to dirt. He drives his laundress to tears because his clothing must be impeccably clean. If I were to marry him, he'd probably inspect my skull for lice every day. No, Vicki, I don't see how this Lord Hawkeston could be any different from the rest. I'm doomed! I just know it!"

Victoria felt tremendously guilty that Valentine was so unhappy. "It's not the end of the world—"

"How would you know? Have you ever met this Lord Justin Hawkeston?"

Victoria shook her head as Valentine looked at Aunt Cherise. Their aunt turned her lovely, though stern, middle-aged face toward the window.

"It's easy for both of you to be smug. It's not *your* life on the brink of disaster!"

"Valentine!" Aunt Cherise whirled back to her niece. "Your dramatics are uncalled for. My brother would never have made a deathbed bargain that you were to marry Lord Hawkeston if he didn't think it was the right thing to do. Milton only had our welfare in mind. Lord Hawkeston has agreed because he was very close to Milton. Lord Hawkeston is very wealthy and can provide for your welfare. Because you are the eldest—"

"By four minutes," Valentine said sullenly.

"Val!" Victoria exclaimed.

"Sorry," Valentine apologized. "It's nobody's fault that I have to marry this old friend of Father's to pull us out of the depths of poverty. Oh, why must we be so poor!"

"Milton lost his ambassadorship here to Venice when the king assigned someone else to the post."

"It was stolen from us!" Valentine said flatly.

"It's the king's choice whom he wants to represent him. Milton's tuberculosis kept him bedridden for nearly a year before he died. He could not serve his office here in Venice from his bed. You know these things, Valentine."

Valentine rested her chin in her hand glumly. "It's just that I had hopes of marrying someone who loved me. Someone I could love the way Victoria loves Andrew. Not some old Ninth Earl of Kingsmore and the owner of a Venetian glass factory. And a rogue to boot!''

"How do you know that?'' Aunt Cherise asked with a gasp.

"I overheard you and Father talking about how Lord Hawkeston was a favorite of the ton.''

Victoria shot her sister an accusing look. "You eavesdropped!''

"What of it?''

"Must you be so outrageous, Val?''

"Must you be so prim, Vicki?'' Valentine argued.

"Girls!'' Aunt Cherise was used to stepping into the middle of forays between her nieces. She knew these skirmishes were never meant to hurt, but only to vent their mutual frustrations. Valentine and Victoria loved each other more than they loved themselves. They were all under pressure these days with Milton's death only three months ago, and the weight of Valentine's forthcoming marriage was pressing on them all.

"I'm sorry, Vicki. I didn't mean to hurt your feelings. I envy you and Andrew so much. He loves you a great deal. I can see it every time he looks in your eyes. Both of you are practically glowing. I just wish I could look forward to having that same kind of love, but fate has different plans for me and I'll just have to get used to it.'' Valentine sighed heavily. Just once, she thought, I wish God could give me a miracle . . . just one night, one magical night so that I could have something to remember the rest of my life. She was asking too much of God, she thought as she looked down at her white satin buatta. She wished she really could hide behind her mask.

Victoria reached out and held her sister's hand comfortingly. Aunt Cherise put her arm around Valentine and let Val rest her head on her shoulder.

"We'll get through this together, girls. We still have each other."

Valentine shot her aunt a glaring look, wondering where Aunt Cherise would be when she would have to walk into her marital bedroom and face the toad. The truth was that from tonight forward, she was alone.

Valentine turned back to the window and stared out at the labyrinthian Venice streets. Beneath Gothic bridges and along the ancient cobblestone streets she saw lovers slipping behind doors to private gardens. She witnessed a young girl dressed completely in white with a white mask playfully slip away from her lover, race across the street and scamper down stone steps to the canal. The girl stepped into a waiting gondola decorated with garlands of greenery and bright flowers. Her lover, dressed in a black cloak and purple mask, chased after her, then took her in his arms as the gondolier pushed his large pole against the stone wall and off they sailed down the canal. Valentine could hear their laughter become mingled with the gay songs and laughter of other couples, people in love on a night meant for love.

As Valentine viewed the ancient architecture, the mysterious, forgotten little gardens and shimmering canals, she could almost feel the sensuality of the city rub off on her. When the carriage came to a stop, Valentine was totally unaware of the passage of time. She'd been lost in a dream world where she had wanted to remain.

The line of carriages bent around the corner in front of the countess's enormous fifteenth-century mansion. It was three stories high, topped with carved marble angels that decorated each of the 28 columns supporting the roof. A stone wall with huge iron gates, which in former times had kept enemies at bay, enclosed the manse. Under the velvet indigo mantle of night, the mansion was a glimmering jewel as candlelight poured from all the windows.

Valentine was in awe. "I've never seen such a beautiful mansion."

"It's a palace, my dear," Cherise corrected her. "It belonged to the countess's family during the Renaissance. They were one of the first merchant princes. Fortunately, their riches have never been diminished."

As they alighted from the carriage with the aid of a footman, Victoria pointed out the colorful mosaics along the loggia, the open gallery.

Valentine, Victoria and Cherise joined in the throng of brightly costumed and bejeweled guests as they entered the magnificently ornate palace. Inside the enormous vestibule were rich mural paintings and marble sculptures by famous Venetian artists.

"We've seen St. Mark's and so many beautiful buildings, but all this seems different somehow," Valentine commented.

"That's because we know the person who owns all this," Victoria replied.

"I can't imagine possessing such wealth."

Aunt Cherise leaned down and whispered, "Try very hard. I've heard that Lord Hawkeston's art collection is far more grand. The countess told me herself that she is not in the same league as Lord Hawkeston."

Valentine's eyes shot to her sister in despair. "He must be even older than I thought!"

Victoria patted her hand as they mounted the thickly carpeted white marble staircase to the second-floor ballroom. "Just keep telling yourself that he won't be."

"What good will that do? Time is running out. I don't have much longer to fool myself. I think the time has come to prepare myself for the worst."

"Perhaps you are right." Victoria's eyes were solemn.

When they stood atop the landing and looked down at the spectacle of the masquerade a half dozen marble steps below them, both girls smiled. Every manner of disguise was represented. They saw harlequins in jewel-toned diamond-paned satin outfits with black masks and floppy hats. They saw Byzantine harem dancers, French Renaissance kings, Oriental empresses, Egyptian pharaohs and Ottoman princes. Everyone wore masks. No one knew who the guests were, and neither did Valentine or Victoria. Unlike most balls, this one offered no announcer, no introductions and no way that anyone could know the identity of any of the masqueraders. All identities would be revealed at midnight, the girls were told by the butler who took their pelisses.

Valentine was quick to notice the butler's lingering gaze on her partly exposed breasts. For a moment she wanted to cover herself. But then she thought better of it. This night was the end of her life. She had wanted to be a bit daring, even to seek adventure. This dress was a symbol of that attitude. If she was going to present a dangerous persona on the outside, she had to begin by believing it on the inside. Valentine pretended not to see her aunt's disapproving glance.

"How wicked of you, Val," Victoria whispered.

"It's the same costume as yours," she whispered back.

"I know. But I think I shoved my . . . self down and you shoved yours up!"

"I did." Valentine giggled.

"How I wish that Andrew could be here to see this," Victoria said as she gazed over the crowd again.

Aunt Cherise smiled and her blue eyes sparkled behind her black, unadorned mask. "The countess has a

17

surprise for you, my dear. Andrew has indeed been invited.''

''But he is not a noble. Not even a merchant prince. He is only a bookkeeper. How did you accomplish that?''

''The countess is a friend, in every sense of the word. I like to think that I have helped her in times past when she needed a friend. Someone to listen. Now, I need her. She is happy to do these small favors for me.''

Victoria hugged her aunt. ''I can never thank you.''

''There's no need for that. Simply have a wonderful, wonderful time.''

Victoria scanned the room. ''How will I know him?''

Valentine couldn't help laughing. ''The man of your dreams and you won't know him? Vicki, dear, you must be slipping.''

''I mean his costume,'' Victoria retorted as she continued to study the guests. Just then, behind a pruned conical-shaped tree she saw a man dressed in a dark suit with a bright emerald green satin cape. He stared at her. Then he smiled.

''It's Andrew! He's wearing my favorite color!'' Victoria tried to be ladylike as she scurried down the marble steps and rushed into Andrew's waiting arms.

Valentine sighed happily. ''At least one of us will know true love.''

Aunt Cherise took Valentine's arm and patted her hand. ''Think happy thoughts and banish those dismal ones. Life is what you make of it, dear. It can be as good or as bad as you desire. Come, let me introduce you to my friend.''

As they walked down the steps, Valentine was aware of many eyes watching her from behind masks. Some of the glances were nearly lecherous as they focused on her low-cut gown. She wondered if the masks were to

blame for their owners' boldness. Valentine did not like
this eerie feeling. She felt as if a strange veil of intrigue
was whirling about her.

They approached an astonishingly beautiful woman
dressed in a black velvet gown encrusted with pearls
around the square neckline and banding the long, wide
cuffs of the sleeves. Valentine knew at once it was a
copy of a Medici gown . . . or the original. On her head
was an elaborate black velvet and gold headdress and
around her neck were the most perfect diamonds and
rubies Valentine had ever seen. The Countess Cioppoli
was over forty years old, but looked ten years younger.
She was a tall woman with silver-blond hair, nearly as
light as Valentine's own. But of all her attributes, it was
the countess's radiant and friendly smile that Valentine
found most appealing.

"How wonderful of you to come," the countess said,
taking Valentine's hand as Valentine rose from a curtsy.
"No need for that now. We are quite informal here,
especially tonight. Your aunt has been my dearest friend.
I feel that you are practically one of the family."

"You are most gracious, Countess," Valentine began,
but the countess waved her comments aside.

"I want you to have fun this evening. And at midnight
I personally will announce your happy news to everyone
after the unmasking." She glanced quickly around the
ballroom. "Though I haven't seen Lord Hawkeston as
yet. I would think that this once he would be punctual.
In the meantime, please meet some of my friends. This
is Mardi Gras. You can be anyone you wish to be. Even
if just for a little while." The countess took Cherise's
arm in hers. "If you don't mind, I would like to steal
your dear aunt away for a chat. We've had so little time
to ourselves, what with your father's passing." She
raised her hand and caressed Valentine's cheek with the

lightest touch. "My condolences to you and your sister during this time of mourning. I liked him very much."

Sadness again filled Valentine's heart. "Thank you. You are very kind."

Suddenly the countess's smile was back and more radiant than before. "Now go meet my friends. Supper has been prepared." She gestured toward a long buffet table. "I'm certain you'll find something there to delight you."

Aunt Cherise nodded to Valentine as the countess took her arm and they moved into the crowd with their heads together, exchanging gossip Valentine knew was not meant for her ears.

"Hmph," Valentine muttered to herself. "No doubt it is me they are discussing."

As Valentine turned toward the sumptuous buffet table, she discovered that the man standing next to her was leering at her breasts. She kept her eyes focused on the roast pheasant and kept moving forward. For the first time, she wondered if she had been wise in her choice of costume. Didn't these men have anything to do at this ball other than to stare at her bosom?

Valentine took a gold plate and began piling it with every manner of food on the table. Turkey, roast pork, beef, boiled potatoes, and two slices of cake. As she picked up a sterling knife and fork, she heard a deep, husky voice from behind her.

"Is that plate for your husband or for you?"

Valentine whirled around and found herself face to chest with the tallest man in the room. She bent her neck back to look into the clearest, bluest eyes she'd ever seen. Startled, she took a step back.

"I was hungry."

"Hungry? Or simply bored?" he asked with so much

sensuality in his tone that Valentine felt as if she'd been touched physically.

He was dressed completely in white satin with a flowing white satin cape about his shoulders. His mask was also white but devoid of any ornamentation. His shirt sported a white lace ruffle down the front and lace on the edge of each cuff. His shoulders were extremely broad and seemed to strain the seams of his closely cut jacket. His knee-length breeches were tapered against his muscular legs covered with white stockings. His shoes were white leather with silver buckles. There was no hat to cover his thick golden hair. Though half his face was hidden, she could still discern his strong jawline, sensual lips and even white teeth. His lips parted in a half smile that was at once charming and wicked. Valentine believed that if she tore off his mask at that moment, she would find that the rest of his features were just as attractive as what was revealed to her now. It was that sense of mystery, the not knowing that intrigued her. She wondered if he was a saint . . . or a sinner.

She remembered that for a few hours she was not Valentine St. James, betrothed of Lord Justin Hawkeston, but simply a girl in costume. A girl ready, even anxious, for adventure and romance. She boldly returned his smile with a seductive smile of her own.

"Bored, now that you ask."

"I thought so," he said and moved a half step closer. His eyes glanced down at her breasts but did not linger there as the other eyes had that night. His gaze climbed slowly back to her face where it locked on her deep brown eyes.

Valentine felt a strange shockwave shoot through her veins when he looked at her. It was if he were some kind of sorcerer and was trying to bewitch her. "I . . . I don't know many people here."

Catherine Lanigan

He took the plate from her hand and handed it to the man behind him. "Now you know me. I'm all you need to know." Possessively, he took her arm and led her away from the buffet table and onto the ballroom floor where the guests were dancing a minuet.

"You're dressed for the part," he said, placing his hand on her waist and leading her in the steps. "Shall I call you Marie?"

"Marie?"

"Antoinette. Isn't that who you are supposed to be?"

"Oh, yes. Of course." Valentine was having difficulty keeping her bearings. She could feel the heat of his hand straight through her gown, her corset and her chemise. She nearly felt as if he were branding her. She tried to be nonchalant as she asked, "What is your name?"

"Baldassare Castiglione," he replied after a moment of thought.

"I never heard of him."

"I wouldn't admit that in public if I were you. His treatise on courtly manners gave expression to the new human ideal that changed social and political Italy forever."

"I see," she said and looked away.

"You don't believe me."

"No. But I will ask the countess. She has an extensive library."

"Ah! An untrusting soul. How very wise of you."

"Do you think so?"

"Yes, I do," he said, placing his face very near hers.

Valentine's thoughts were confused. She wanted him to be nearer still, but at the same time she almost wished he would go away so that she would not have to confront the tumultuous feelings inside her.

As they continued in the dance, Valentine noticed that his fingers seemed to dig more possessively into her

22

waist. When they bowed to each other and came together
with their arms extending over their heads, he never took
his eyes from hers. When the music stopped and the
dancers left the dance floor, he was still staring at her.
Their faces were so close together, she could feel his
breath on her cheek. She had nearly become fixated on
his beautiful mouth and she could not stop wondering
what it would be like to kiss him.

"Have you ever experienced Mardi Gras in the
streets?"

"No. I've never . . ." She decided she would not reveal too much about herself. She didn't want him to
think that she was not a worldly person, nor that this
was her first Mardi Gras. She wanted to be someone else
tonight. "I've only been to private parties. You understand, of course."

He stiffened. "Of course."

It wasn't her imagination, Valentine knew. He visibly
reacted to her statement. She didn't know what she'd
said that displeased him. But something had.

"Have . . . you celebrated carnival in the streets?" she
asked as demurely as she could.

His seductive tones returned. "Many times. Would
you like to come with me?"

"What? Now?"

"Yes, now," he said in a low gruff voice that Valentine thought should be outlawed except for the bedroom. He tugged on her hand. "I'll show you."

Valentine glanced around the room, thinking that
Aunt Cherise would appear any second and rescue her
as she always seemed to do whenever Valentine was
about to do something that might be improper. She
caught sight of Victoria dancing with Andrew. They
were so intent upon each other that Valentine doubted
even an earthquake would distract them.

"Are you certain the countess wouldn't mind? Leaving her party to go to another isn't quite proper, you know."

"Proper? You, Marie, are concerned with what is proper?" He laughed and pulled her against his chest. As he looked into her eyes she thought he would kiss her right there in front of everyone. What surprised her most was that she wanted him to kiss her. She didn't care what kind of scandal she started. She didn't care if Lord Hawkeston himself was watching her. She only wanted to know what it would feel like to be kissed by this handsome and exceedingly sensual man. Valentine could hear her heart slamming against her ribs. With each pounding heartbeat she grew afraid, not so much of him and his mastery over her, but of her need to experience his power.

"You look like the kind of woman who thrives on intrigue."

"I do?" she asked, stunned at her reaction to him. Her hands had turned cold and she could feel beads of perspiration springing out on her forehead. How could she feel like fire and ice all at once? "I mean . . . of course, I do!"

"Come, cara mia," he said with a smooth Italian accent. "My carriage is outside."

They worked their way discreetly through the crowd, slipping past Lucifer, Nefertiti and King Louis XIV and out the door. He hailed his driver, who brought a sleek black lacquered carriage around straightaway.

"Baldassare" lifted Valentine into the carriage, placing both his hands around her waist. She noticed that once she was inside, his hand slipped slightly and nearly cupped her breast. She was not quite certain if it was an intentional move or not. He sat next to her on the velvet cushion rather than across from her. Then he rapped on the ceiling with his cane and the carriage bolted forward.

Night fog blanketed the city with an eerie silvery glow as it whirled around the coachlamps and lights from the villas and houses. Valentine thought that even nature had joined in the masquerade.

''I'll show you things you've never dreamed existed,'' he whispered close to her ear, skimming the edge of her lobe with his lips. Chills tingled down her throat. She felt the bottom of her stomach career down some internal landslide, causing her to feel as if she'd lost control of herself. Valentine could not allow herself to sink under his spell. He was a stranger. If she were truthful with herself she had to admit that it was mainly because he was a stranger that she found herself sitting next to him at this moment. She would never see this man again after tonight. He would vanish from her life, but not from her memories. He would never have to know her true identity nor she know his. There was such sweet safety in this anonymity, she thought as he blazed another ring of kisses around the shell of her ear. She wanted to cry out from the sheer ecstasy of it all, but instead she hid her emotions behind her satin mask. She must not, would not, lose control.

''What manner of things will you show me?'' she asked haughtily, pretending to know more than she did.

''Don't forget, I am Baldassare. I know everything about Venice,'' he replied in an equally arrogant tone.

''I suppose you plan to show me a museum? Or a library? I will have you know I have seen them. I have heard the bell of the Torre Dell' Orologio, the Basilica, and the golden altar, Pala d'Oro. I've seen Titian's paintings and crossed the Bridge of Sighs. I know just as much about Venice as you, sir. Perhaps more.''

He casually placed his arm around her shoulder and stroked the side of her throat. ''I promise you, the places you will go with me and the sights you see, you have never seen before, nor will see them again.''

Valentine's resolve slipped a notch when she moaned aloud. Out of the corner of her eye she saw a wave of satisfaction curve his mouth. She tried to move away from him, but he drew her even closer. She heard a groan of pleasure deep in his throat and she was surprised at her own reaction of triumph.

''First we need some wine, sweet heady wine for milady.''

He rapped on the ceiling again with his cane, signaling the driver to stop. He leaned across her, thrust open the door and alighted from the carriage. Again he placed his hands on her waist and lifted her down. Slowly he put her on the ground, keeping his hands on her waist and his eyes trained on hers. Valentine believed that his every movement, look and touch was calculated and deliberate. He wanted her to want him. It was an exotic notion.

The street was a narrow serpent that twisted below the Rialto Bridge. They stood before a stone edifice with a solid wooden door and iron hinges and knocker. Valentine saw no signs or any windows to indicate this was a public building, but she could hear loud voices within. ''Baldassare'' rapped three times on the door.

A fat woman dressed in a Renaissance court costume opened the door. She neither smiled nor frowned, but admitted them immediately. She whispered to Baldassare and he whispered something back to her. The fat woman moved quickly for one with so much girth. They followed their escort down a narrow hall and into a large room set with crude trestle tables and benches. Huge iron chandeliers hung from the beamed ceiling, illuminating the room with hundreds of candles. In the corner by the enormous stone fireplace stood a trio of mandolin players whose lilting strains were nearly drowned out by the raucous laughter of the patrons.

They were seated in a far corner at a small table covered with a stained white linen cloth. Valentine's companion explained that these tables were reserved for the gentry. They were brought a bottle of Chianti and crude glasses filled with an aperitif.

"Drink," he commanded and lifted his aperitif. He downed his in one gulp.

Valentine sipped the bitter-tasting drink. It was green and tasted of anise. "What is this?"

"Absinthe. It's not good for you."

"Why are we drinking it?"

"Because we shouldn't. It will make your head spin. Now try this Chianti. It is the best."

Valentine did like the wine, though she'd tasted more expensive wines she liked better. She lifted the glass and drank freely while she scanned the room. What she saw was shocking.

In the middle of the room she saw a man dressed in a Greek tunic turn to the woman next to him and kiss her openly in front of the dozen or so people at their table. Then the man unlatched the broach that held the woman's tunic at the shoulder and exposed her large, voluptuous breasts. With no mind to the others in the room, the man bent his head and began kissing the woman's breast. The woman made no move to stop him. Valentine watched as the woman placed her hand on the man's head and pressed him to her breast, entreating him to molest her further. The woman flung her head back, groaned with pleasure and slipped her hand beneath the table. Valentine could not see what the woman was doing to the man, but she heard his moans. Suddenly the couple fell to the floor out of Valentine's sight.

What shocked Valentine most was that no one in the

room paid them any mind. Everyone continued with their drinking and merrymaking without regard to the pair who were most certainly copulating on the floor.

Valentine quickly turned her gaze back to her wineglass. She could feel flames of fire burn in her cheeks. Her hands were shaking with such intensity that she could barely lift her glass to her lips.

"Something wrong?" Baldassare inquired with an innocent air.

"No. Nothing," she replied sharply. Valentine didn't like the heat that raced through her insides. She didn't like the way she was imagining her companion doing the same things to her. She wondered what it would be like to have him touch her breast. She didn't dare let herself think of his lips on her. Suddenly she wanted to flee. "Where else do you plan to take me tonight?"

"Oh, I'm sorry you don't like this place. It is a trifle crude. But this is how the peasants revel."

"Peasants?"

"The working class, rather. You would prefer something more genteel?"

She lifted her eyes to him. "Proper. Yes. I would like a more proper setting."

"Of course." He tossed two coins on the table for payment, rose and took her hand.

Valentine nearly raced out of the building and into the carriage. In less than two minutes they were off again.

"I know just the place for you. It isn't far."

Valentine noticed that this time as they drove, he did not try to touch her, did not whisper in her ear, and in fact, he seemed quite distant. He kept his eyes trained out the window as if looking for something.

Suddenly he rapped the cane on the ceiling and the carriage halted.

This tavern was indeed an improvement. A huge beveled glass window was curtained in lace and the door was fashioned of carved wood with brass hinges. The maitre d' was dressed in formal black attire and black mask. They were ushered to a table draped in fine Belgian linen with a silver candelabra and white lilies as a centerpiece. The champagne was French, the wineglasses were the thinnest of Venetian crystal, and the music was refined and mellow.

"Is this better?" Baldassare leaned over and touched Valentine's hand.

She smiled happily. "Oh, yes. So much better."

He raised his glass and they both drank deeply. Valentine liked the soft glow of candlelight that suffused the room. She had forgotten that she'd had nothing to eat that day and was not aware that the wine had begun to distort her vision. The costumes here were as opulent as those at the ball. The revelers moved from table to table, speaking with friends and embracing each other. It seemed such a happy, proper place.

"Do you see that woman over there dressed as Queen Elizabeth?"

Valentine looked to the far side of the room at the woman who was listening intently to a dark-haired man dressed in Elizabethan garb. "Yes. Do you know her?"

"Him."

"No, not the man, the woman."

"The woman is a man. In fact, most of the women here are men dressed as women." His smile was sardonic as he spoke.

Valentine's mouth gaped open. "How . . . can that be?" Her eyes shot back to the lovely woman. "She is clearly a woman."

"I tell you that she is not. He is a very naughty boy who prefers men to women."

Valentine gulped more champagne to steady herself.

She looked about the room and spied a buxom woman in an extremely revealing French gown. So revealing was the neckline that even at a distance Valentine could see the woman's nipples. They looked as if they'd been roughed. Boldly, she pointed the woman out. "That is a woman."

"Yes. But the man with her is a woman."

Valentine was gasping for breath. She glared at Baldassare. "You brought me here on purpose. You wanted me to see these vile creatures. Why?"

"I told you I would show you things that you would never dream about."

"You were right." She shot to her feet. "Take me back to the ball. I wish to see no more of this."

He was laughing to himself, which served only to infuriate her more. "Very well. Your wish is my command," he said insolently.

Valentine snatched up her reticule as Baldassare signaled the maitre d' and slipped him the coins to pay for the champagne.

Valentine was furious with her escort and didn't care if he knew it. She spun on her heel and stomped toward the door. "I'll find my own way back, thank you," she told him curtly.

"Don't be a child. With so many people in the streets tonight, you could be accosted. I would never forgive myself if anything happened to you."

Her brown eyes had turned jet black with rage. "I doubt that very seriously, sir."

He tried to take her arm, but she snatched it away from him. "Calm down, little one. I brought you here to titillate your fancies. But I see that I have made a mistake. You are not as adventurous as you purported to be. It was I who was led astray, madam."

"How dare you blame me for this!" Valentine started

down the narrow, twisting street unmindful of her direction. At the intersection, a huge band of revelers in common costumes swept her up into their midst. Borne away into the crowd, Valentine lost sight of Baldassare. A young man dressed as a court jester played a flute and another youth played a trumpet. Valentine felt a thick, callused hand on her arm pushing her in front of him. The man's movements were clumsy and he stumbled. Valentine realized that they all must be drunk. A woman pushed into her, nearly causing her to fall herself.

At the next intersection they were joined by another group of merrymakers. Valentine felt as if she were being swept out to sea. Straining on her tiptoes, she searched for her companion but could not find him. Panic filled her.

"Baldassare! Where are you?" she screamed at the top of her lungs.

He appeared out of nowhere, like a white vision that was half man and part of the swirling winter fog. Though she was relieved to see him, she didn't want him to know it.

"Where were you?" she demanded tartly.

"I thought you said you would be safe. I thought you knew the streets."

"I lied," she said flatly.

He grabbed her hand and yanked her away from the burly man who held her arm in a viselike grip.

"Come. We'll travel back to the ball by way of the canal."

They raced through labyrinthian streets and down the steps to the water. Baldassare chose an elaborate gondola draped with purple, gold and green fabric and hundreds of flowers. The driver covered his passengers' legs with a soft woolen blanket. As the gondola swept out into the canal, Valentine leaned back against the seat and let her

31

anger subside. Tendrils of fog twisted around the bridges and skittered down the canal, transforming the scene into a dreamlike fantasy. The lanterns on the gondola flickered like tiny fireflies in the mist.

Baldassare took Valentine's hand in his, lifted it to his lips and kissed her fingers one by one. "Your tension has eased. I'm glad."

Valentine liked the feel of his moist lips against her skin. When he drew her forefinger into his mouth and ran his tongue down one side of it and then the other, she thought she would scream from the forbidden pleasure it gave her. She wanted to withdraw her hand, but she didn't. She should have moved away from him, chided him for taking liberties with her, but she couldn't. Valentine wanted to feel everything she was feeling. She liked this daring and very bold woman she was discovering within herself.

He kissed the palm of her hand. Then he kissed the pulse point of her wrist where the blood was closest to the surface. He lingered there for a long time. She knew he was counting the quickening beats of her heart. He most certainly knew how he was affecting her.

Suddenly his arm was around her shoulder and his face was next to hers. She gazed into his eyes, which seemed to gleam even in the night mist. She raised her hand and started to remove his mask.

"I want to see you. All of you," she breathed.

"All of me?" he returned with that wicked grin she'd seen before.

"Your face, I mean."

"No." He grabbed her hand and placed it on his heart. "Not my face. Know me by my heart, the way that I know you."

He placed his hand over hers and pressed both of their hands to his chest. She could feel the firm muscles in his chest. She could also feel the rapid beating that matched her own. Valentine could barely catch her breath. She felt as if she'd been running and had slammed into a brick wall.

"You see?" he said gently. "I want you as much as you want me. Admit it. You would like me to take you right here. Right now. You would bare yourself to me. You would expose your flesh and give yourself freely. Say it."

"I . . . I . . ." Valentine couldn't think. She was only feeling. Flashes of the night's earlier scenes blazed across her brain. She saw the man again removing the tunic from the woman. She remembered the way his tongue ringed the woman's nipple. She focused on the thought, wondering what it was like to feel a darting tongue on such an erotic part of her body.

"No," she began breathlessly. "I can't."

"Oh, yes, Marie. You are a woman of daring. A woman of romance and adventure."

"I am," she sighed softly. She was hypnotized by his gaze. She was certain now that he was a sorcerer. He wove a powerful spell around her. His every velvet word captivated her willpower. She forgot her resolve. She barely knew who she was. Was she Valentine or Marie?

His hand glided from her wrist up her arm and to her throat. He held his thumb against the base of her neck where he could still feel her pulse beat. "You are mine, Marie. There is only this moment." He cupped his fingers around her neck. They gripped the back of her neck. "Holding you the way I am, do you realize that your entire life is under my control? I could take you. I could kill you. I have mastery over you."

Valentine blinked twice as his words sunk in. She did not twist away in fear. She only glared at him. She did not think before she spoke. She only reacted. "Take your hand away from me. No one has mastery over me. Certainly not you. You are a fool, sir, if you think so.''

His fingers loosened their grip. Then he threw his head back in laughter. ''Ha! You are the one for me, Marie. Nothing frightens you. How I admire your courage. I think I shall reward you.''

Impulsively, he captured her mouth with his lips. They were soft and yet wildly possessive. His movements were assured and well practiced. He was the guide and let her know it. Valentine tried not to participate in the kiss, but found she was willing. All too sweetly willing.

Valentine gave in to the kiss. She kissed him back with all the pure and unbridled passion of her own nature. She had never been kissed before and she wanted to relish every thrilling second of it. Her mind told her she would never feel emotions like this again. This was her night to be herself. She wanted to feel and never think again.

When he separated her lips with his tongue she was eager for its entry. She caressed his tongue with hers. She met him on a beautifully lit plain of desire and waltzed with him willingly. She was a wanton and she found she didn't care.

She felt as if she were whirling in a bright pool of color and excitement. She put her arms around his neck and drew his head closer to her. She plunged herself into the kiss. She entered his mouth and possessed him. She dug her fingers into his thick hair and clung to him as if she were drowning and he were her savior.

Like a branding iron, his hand sought her breast and freed it from her low-cut gown. He gently pressed the bud of her nipple between his forefinger and thumb and rolled it back and forth. Valentine jolted beneath the myriad of shockwaves he was producing in her. He increased the pressure. A sultry moan, which he captured deep in his throat, escaped her lips. Valentine urged her breast into his hand, demanding more pleasure. Tiny pillars of fire raced through her body to the pit of her loins. She began to undulate her hips against his thigh. She felt as if she were a volcano about to explode, but she found no release. Passion and desire clamped their hands around her, and she came to recognize her jailers. She wanted to succumb to them even more.

"My God, I have never met one as you," he breathed hotly into her ear, where he strung a necklace of searing kisses. Again his lips returned to her demanding mouth.

Valentine's hands left his head, skimmed over his mask and explored the regions of his jaw, throat and chest. She did want all of him, she realized. Her hands traveled down the flat plain of his hard stomach. Just as she was about to move farther, a warning bell clanged in her head.

"I must stop," she moaned.

"No, never," he groaned. "You are my wanton . . ." His hand splayed across her full breast. "God in heaven, are you harlot or angel?" He continued to kiss her.

"I must . . . we must stop."

Valentine removed her shaking hands from his belly and pulled away from him. Her eyes bore into his. They were smoky blue pools of desire. She'd never seen such a look in anyone's eyes. She wondered if her desire shone as brightly. "Please release me, sir."

He shook his head. "Never," he said and started to claim her mouth again when the boat stopped abruptly.

Valentine looked up to see the gondolier tie up the boat, then turn toward them.

"Oh, Lord," she said frantically and twisted her body away from the gondolier so that he would not see her exposed breast. She yanked up her gown, shoving her breasts down into the dress as Victoria had done. She knew now that she had made grave errors in many of her choices this evening.

Baldassare said nothing as he aided her from the gondola. They walked up the drive, but rather than entering through the front door he took her around the right side of the palace, down the loggia and through a side door. "No one will see us return," he assured her.

Just as they slipped through the door, he grabbed her arm, spun her around to face him and kissed her quickly. "I must see you again, Marie."

"That is impossible."

"Nothing is impossible." His eyes were downcast as he thought for a moment. "There is something I must do tonight, but I don't want you to become alarmed. It is you that I want. Remember that."

"What is it?"

"I'd rather not say right now. You will know in time. Just know that I am my own master. I do whatever I want, whenever I want, and with whomever I want."

Valentine's eyes filled with confusion. "You are making no sense whatsoever."

"It can't be helped. Please tell me where you are staying so that I may call on you."

"No, Baldassare. I will be leaving Venice soon. I was Marie tonight. That is all you need to know." She smiled and touched his cheek. "Thank you for my dream. I wish it could be otherwise, but it was not meant to be." Quickly she turned away from him, picked up her skirt and scurried down the hall and up the backstairs that led to the ballroom.

Valentine moved from topiary tree to marble pillar to buffet table as easily as a trained spy. Most of the food was gone, so she filled a plate with remains. She had just stuffed a slice of turkey into her mouth, thinking how ravenous lovemaking had made her, when she heard Aunt Cherise's voice.

"There you are, Valentine. I havé been looking everywhere for you."

Valentine crammed a thick piece of bread into her mouth. She turned a wide, innocent gaze on her aunt. "Me?" She chewed quickly. "I've been here stuffing myself all night." She swallowed. "I don't know how you could have missed me."

Aunt Cherise cast a suspicious look upon her niece. "I never did see you on the dance floor."

Valentine shook her head. "How could I dance? I don't know anyone here. Besides, what if Lord Hawkeston should see his beloved bride-to-be dancing with another man? I wouldn't want to be the cause of a duel."

Aunt Cherise's eyes rolled in her head. "Your romantic imagination will be your undoing, Valentine St. James. No one is going to fight a duel over you." She glanced down at Valentine's bosom. "At least not now that you adjusted your gown. A wise decision, my dear," she said with an approving smile.

As Valentine shoved a chunk of pork roast into her mouth to avoid any reply, Victoria and Andrew walked up.

Victoria's cheeks glowed rosy pink from the exuberant dancing and from happiness. "Isn't this the most marvelous party in the whole world?" she gushed as Andrew lifted her hand and kissed it. She turned and gazed into his eyes.

Valentine stuck three juicy red grapes into her mouth. "Marvelous," she mumbled with her cheeks puffed out with food. "I've had a marvelous time."

Aunt Cherise glared at Valentine. "I don't recall that I've ever seen you quite so famished, Val. What's gotten into you?"

Valentine placed her gold plate on a nearby table. She wiped her hands on a white napkin. "I thought they fed all prisoners well before they went to the guillotine."

"Oh, Val," Victoria sighed. "Please don't think that way. I have been asking people about Lord Hawkeston."

"*What* about him?"

"How old he is. What he looks like. And I've found out some things," Victoria said triumphantly.

Valentine's eyes widened. "Well?"

"He's not old. I heard he's only thirty-one."

Valentine frowned. "Thirty-one *is* old. Andrew is only twenty two, after all."

Victoria thrust her hands on her hips in frustration. "Val, he could have been fifty or really old like Papa. This is better than we thought."

"You have a point there. What else did you discover?"

"This is the best part. He's handsome, Val. I mean to tell you that three women told me that he is nearly beautiful." Victoria was so excited with her news that she clapped her hands together. "What do you say to that?"

Valentine watched her sister and realized her exuberance hid something that Vicki didn't want her to know. Her eyes narrowed suspiciously.

Victoria lost her smile. "Why are you looking at me like that?"

"Tell me the rest, Victoria," Valentine demanded.

"There isn't any more," she replied sheepishly, moving next to Andrew for support.

"We're twins. We practically have the same brain. Remember you told me that yourself. I know you. You're hiding something from me. Tell me."

Victoria looked down at the floor. She didn't want to be doing this. She had wanted Valentine to be happy.

This part of her discovery was decidedly not good news. She also knew that she had never and could never keep anything from Valentine. Her sister had a way of picking the truth out of her.

"Very well. Those three women who told me about Lord Hawkeston?"

"Yes?" Valentine felt a clutch of dread inside her.

"They were all his mistresses."

"What?" Valentine gasped.

"Oh, Val. It was shocking. They all knew each other. They were friends. They talked openly among themselves about him. Intimate things. Things I could never, ever repeat."

"Tell me." Valentine leaned closer, needing to hear the details, yet wanting to remain ignorant.

"I'd go to hell for repeating such scandalous things."

"Perhaps you shouldn't. The less I know, the better."

Aunt Cherise placed her hand on Valentine's arm, hoping to reassure her, yet knowing that nothing she could say or do would improve the situation. "Your wisdom is growing daily, my dear."

Valentine glanced at her aunt. "Wisdom, Aunt Cherise? Or stupidity?" She shook her head. "Well, at least I don't have to worry about warts on his mouth." She laughed derisively to herself.

A blast of trumpets nearly sent Valentine out of her dancing slippers. An announcer came to the top of the stairs.

"It is five minutes to midnight. Five minutes to unmasking."

An exuberant cheer went up from the crowd. Then the countess came and stood in the announcer's place. She beamed down at her guests. She was the first to unmask herself. Valentine thought she was even more beautiful than she had been told.

"I have a happy announcement this evening, everyone. The waiters are passing among you with champagne. Please take a glass for a special toast we will all be giving tonight. My dearest friend, Cherise St. James, is here with us this evening. She has been gracious enough to allow me to announce the forthcoming marriage of her niece, Valentine.

"I ask that Valentine come up here to join me. When the trumpets sound midnight, would you all please unmask. At that time Valentine's betrothed will join us here also. Now, take your champagne and please move closer to me," she instructed.

The guests milled about, gossiping about the forthcoming betrothal since few knew Valentine and none knew the identity of her future husband. With glasses in hand, they moved closer to the marble steps as the countess had commanded.

Valentine worked her way through the crowd, and just as she reached the bottom step the trumpets blared. The crowd cheered and one by one the masks came off. People laughed and kissed each other. Valentine kept her mask on as she mounted the third step, then the fourth.

From behind a blue velvet curtain edged in gold fringe appeared a very tall, blond man dressed completely in white. He walked over to the countess and stood next to her.

Valentine nearly stumbled on the step when she saw him. "It cannot be!" she mumbled beneath her breath. At first she was elated, thinking that the dream man that had come to her this night would be hers forever. She looked up into his eyes knowing she would see the same desire that she had kindled there only an hour ago. Valentine was mistaken. The eyes that looked back at her were brimming with ice and contempt. She was nearly knocked down from the intense force of his scorn. What had she done to displease him? Hadn't he told her he wanted to see her again? Hadn't he begged to call on her? What had changed his mind?

Suddenly she knew. Earlier she had been Marie. A faceless woman without morals. A woman he could take advantage of and forget instantly. She blushed crimson when she thought of what she had done. God in heaven! She'd made so many irrevocable, fateful mistakes to-night. He had said all those beautiful things only to keep the illusion alive. They had been dealing with the unreal. Now they were both faced with reality. She was to be his wife. Not because he wanted her, but because he owed her father a favor. She was part of a bargain and worth no more than a pile of material goods.

The countess stretched out her hand to Valentine.

Valentine raised her hand to meet the countess, but she could not take her eyes off the cold, steely blue eyes of the man in front of her.

"Friends, I wish to present to you the future Lord and Lady Hawkeston." The countess raised her glass of champagne. "May they live in happiness and harmony all the days of their lives."

"Hear! Hear!" shouted the crowd.

At that moment, Lord Justin Hawkeston ripped his mask from his face and glared menacingly down at Valentine.

Defiantly she flung her own mask to the ground. "Molester!" she growled softly at him.

"Harlot!" he shot back at her with equal anger.

The cheering of the crowd drowned out their private words, but there were those with eyes who could see. Aunt Cherise clapped her hands together and muttered a prayer. "God help her."

Victoria watched in stunned silence. She leaned against her beloved. "Oh, Andrew. I'm afraid that for every measure of happiness that has been meted out to us, Valentine will have to pay with an equal measure of pain. Never have I seen such hate between two people in my life.''

Valentine glared at Justin. Angry sparks flew between them. Champagne corks popped, the trumpets blared again, and the guests of Countess Cioppoli commented to each other what a handsome pair Lord and Lady Hawkeston made.

Chapter Two

Ash Wednesday brought a messenger from Lord Hawkeston commanding that Valentine, Victoria, Aunt Cherise and Andrew be ready to depart Venice one week hence. They were all to sail on his private ship, the *Spirit,* down the Adriatic Sea, then on to the Mediterranean and up the coasts of Spain and France to London. Lord Hawkeston's driver would call for their trunks at seven in the morning on the day of departure. The messenger did not wait for a reply.

Valentine crumpled the parchment between her angry hands. "How dare he!" she exclaimed to Victoria who sat on the settee next to her in the salon. "Does he expect us all to jump to his every whim?"

"Obviously so. May I point out, Valentine, that we don't have much choice. Besides, we all must return home sometime."

"Ooohhh. What I wouldn't give to be face to face

43

with that beast right this second.''

Victoria grinned playfully. ''And what would you say to the beast?''

''I would counsel him on his manners.''

''I'm certain that would be helpful, dear. To counsel him, I mean.''

Valentine slumped back on the settee. ''Couldn't you show just a little sympathy for my predicament? You almost sound as if you are on his side.''

''Val, I've always been on your side. And I do sympathize. What I don't understand is why you appear to hate him so violently. It's almost as if he'd done something to you already. You only met last night.''

''Done something?'' Valentine stiffened and felt a hot flash of shame singe her cheeks. ''He *has* done something. He is marrying me when he doesn't give a fig about me or you or Aunt Cherise.''

''Leave us out of this.'' Victoria pulled compassionately on Valentine's hand. ''Besides, you've known all this for months. I thought you were preparing yourself for the inevitable. But once you met him last night, I got the strangest feeling that you knew him and he knew you. Of course, that is impossible.''

Valentine nearly choked on her own breath, but managed to remain composed. She knows, she thought to herself. It was an admission that was difficult enough to make to herself, much less to Victoria. ''As you said, Vicki, that's impossible.''

Curiosity gleamed in Victoria's eyes. ''I never saw anyone quit a room as swiftly as you did last night. Why, you were nearly curt with the countess in your goodbyes. That's not like you.''

''I've already sent her a note . . . a very gracious note, to thank her. I simply didn't want to be near that man any more than is necessary.''

"But, Val, you're going to spend the rest of your life with him."

"Precisely. So why start before I must? I have these few days all to myself before we leave. And if he is a proper gentleman, which I doubt, he will not thrust himself upon me sooner than is necessary."

"I don't think you need concern yourself about that! From the look in his eyes, he would just as soon be cast out onto a desert without water as to be with you."

"Thank you, Victoria dear," Valentine snapped.

"I'm not implying that you are wanting. I'm saying that I think Lord Hawkeston must have a bat loose in his belfry. I cannot understand his reaction to you at all."

Valentine looked off through the undraped window and saw a bird sitting in the winter branches of a tree. Flashes of the night before scribbled themselves across her mind. How could she have done all that she did? What had happened to her morals? Why had she gone off with him? And dear God in heaven, why had she allowed him to take such liberties with her? Most disquieting of all was the fact that if she had to do it all over again, she would.

"He's a rogue. Aunt Cherise stated it plainly. Of course he is not going to like me. I will interfere with his comings and goings."

"What comings and goings?"

Valentine released an exasperated sigh. "Mistresses, silly. Honestly, Victoria, must I explain all the ways of the world to you?"

"I yield to your vast experience," Victoria laughed.

Stricken with the vision of herself in the gondola with "Baldassare's" hand on her breast and her tongue caressing his, she blushed. She physically shook her head to banish the image. "You know what I mean."

Mirth flashed in Victoria's grin. "I adore teasing you, Valentine. Especially when the subject is so serious. I suppose it is ill-bred and insensitive of me to do that. Please accept my apology."

"Accepted." Valentine lifted her eyes to her sister and matched her amused smile. "You have a strange way of taking my mind off my problems. You always have. And I'm so very glad for it. Besides, if we were both bemoaning my impending doom—"

"Forthcoming marriage, you mean. Let's not be too dramatic," Victoria interrupted.

"Doom!" Valentine blasted back. "At least allow me a bit of self-pity in my time of woe."

Victoria reached over and gently caressed Valentine's shoulder. Her eyes were filled with sympathy. "You can have all you want. You're entitled to a wagonload. Oh, Val"—Victoria stifled a sob—"if I had fallen in love with a rich man, perhaps you needn't have been sacrificed to this cold and obviously cruel man."

Valentine rubbed her sister's hand, fighting back her own tears. "I thank God for you. I'm afraid I'm going to need your support in the years ahead."

Victoria nodded in agreement. "I'm afraid you're right."

February 13, 1815
Dear Diary,

Lord Justin Hawkeston is an evil, vile, wretched monster. I hate him with every drop of blood in my body and every breath I take. I vow that I will never allow my heart to succumb to him.

Sincerely yours,
Valentine St. James

Valentine watched their trunks being hauled onto Lord Hawkeston's carriage at precisely 7:00 a.m. February 20th. She rammed her precious diary beneath a chemise and a cotton batiste nightgown in her tapestry valise, mumbling blasphemies against Lord Hawkeston and thinking up new curses she could use when she finally came face to face with him.

"Rake. Blackguard, pirate . . . scoundrel. No . . . that's not bad enough. Muck-covered, wart-infested *snake*. Hmmm. That's better. Yes, snake is a most proper and fitting name for my lord."

The rustle of Victoria's petticoats in the hall and the tramping of servant's shoes heralded their departure.

"Hurry, Valentine! We'll be late," Victoria exclaimed as she burst into the room. She was dressed in a black watch plaid traveling dress with a black wool pelisse. A small black hat with a blue feather to match the blue of the plaid sat saucily on her silvery curls. There was a thrill of adventure and excitement in her eyes. There was also the anticipation of her own forthcoming wedding filling her mind, Valentine thought as she stared morosely at her sister.

"I wish I could see this trip in the same light as you do, Victoria."

"We're going home, Val. Home," Victoria commented dreamily. "I'd forgotten how much I missed my friends, Andrew's family."

Valentine's eyes were downcast. "I know. I've missed them, too. But this is where Papa is buried. Venice will always be part of lives . . . forever. So much has happened here. Home will never be the same."

Victoria was undaunted. "I won't have you thinking like that. This is a time of new beginnings. No matter where they may lead us."

"How wise you are, Vicki. And you are absolutely

right. It's time to put away our grief and move ahead,'' she said valiantly.

Victoria scowled.

"Too dramatic? Oh, well. I can't help it.'' Valentine lifted her valise off the bed and started toward the door. A capricious smile sat on her lips. "I'm off to do battle with the snake.''

"Oh, is that how we are to address Lord Hawkeston now?''

"Yes,'' Valentine replied with a firm nod of her head. "Until I think of something more offensive to call him.''

The carriage ride to the docks was uneventful save for the kisses Andrew surreptitiously placed on Victoria's hand despite Aunt Cherise's eagle eyes. Valentine joined in their escapade by involving Aunt Cherise in an amusing lecture on the history of the architecture they passed on the street.

Each time Andrew winked at Valentine she would point out a piazza, bridge or church to Aunt Cherise. Valentine would lean over, stick her head almost completely out the window, and then recite a description of the edifice that usually came from Valentine's imagination and not from any known travelogue.

"I don't recall ever hearing that particular legend about the Rialto Bridge,'' Aunt Cherise said as Valentine encouraged her aunt to lean further out the window.

"It's true, I tell you. I heard it at the countess's ball from one of the guests.''

"Which one?''

"The man dressed like Alexander the Great.''

"Well, no wonder! He is a new acquaintance of the countess and this was his first trip to Venice. She told me so herself.''

Andrew planted three kisses on Victoria's hand. Victoria giggled. Valentine grinned at them both while Aunt

Cherise continued to wistfully peruse the towering stee-
ples and majestic palaces.

The carriage came to a halt at the end of the cobblestone street. They were met by a boatman who ushered
them to the dinghy that would row them out to the *Spirit*.
Valentine refused the man's hand when he offered to
assist her into the boat.

Aunt Cherise's eyebrows wrinkled into a frown and
she shot her niece a glaring look.

Valentine stumbled awkwardly into the dinghy and sat
next to her aunt. "Don't berate me, Aunt Cherise. I
wouldn't put it past Lord Hawkeston to have paid the
man extra to dump me into the sea and have me
drowned."

Aunt Cherise rolled her eyes. "You're exaggerating
again. His Lordship would do nothing of the kind."

"How do you know?"

A wry smile slide onto Aunt Cherise's lips. "Too
many witnesses, my dear."

Valentine broke into laughter as the boat moved away
from the dock.

The *Spirit* was a majestic ship with four masts. Valentine didn't want to be impressed with its fine teak
wood and immense size, but she was. She wanted to
find fault with anything and everything to do with her
future husband, but she had to admit, if only to herself,
that his choice of vessels was superb.

They climbed aboard with the aid of four seamen.
Once on deck they saw that all hands were scurrying
about making ready to set sail. Valentine spied their
three trunks and instructed one of the seamen as to
which trunk belonged to Victoria and Aunt Cherise. Valentine was informed that her sister and aunt would be
sharing a cabin. Andrew was to sleep with the crew, and
she was to have her own cabin.

While the others followed their belongings below decks, Valentine went to the rail and looked out at the city of Venice for perhaps the last time in her life.

A vision of her father's smiling, loving face swam before her eyes. "Papa, I can only pray that you are looking over me. I think I miss you more today than ever. I know you believe that you have chosen wisely for me . . . but, Lord! He is such a monster."

Ensconced in his cabin, Justin Hawkeston was informed by the first mate that his guests had arrived. He did not look up from his maps or logs when he muttered a terse response. The mate left the cabin.

Justin had only to think of the silver-haired Valentine and his hand clenched into a fist and slammed down onto the table. "How could I have let this happen to me?" he demanded angrily of himself. "No man should be saddled with a vixen for a wife." Then he remembered his friend Milton St. James. Of all the men he knew in England, he respected none more highly. Milton had never been rich in the way Justin himself was, but Milton had had integrity. He had been honest and his word had been his bond. Milton had been the kind of man Justin admired. Though most of the Hawkeston men had been either gamblers, lechers or drunks, Justin had spent his life following another path. How the line had lasted this long was a miracle. Somehow God had blessed his father with a truly loving and honorable woman. Had it not been for his mother, Anne, and the years spent under her direction, Justin probably would have become just like his ancestors. Or worse, like his brother, Arnold.

What a boil on the backside of humanity Arnold is, he thought derisively. Twice last year Justin had bailed Arnold out of jail for drunkenness. His gambling debts were the bane of Justin's existence. He'd informed Arnold the night before his departure to Venice that he had instructed all of his solicitors, his bankers and the owners of the gambling halls by written notice that he, Justin, would no longer subsidize Arnold's debts.

The scene had been an ugly one that Justin wanted only to forget.

Arnold's blue eyes had blazed furiously at him.

"I am your brother, damn you to hell. It's your responsibility to see to my welfare. Father went so far as to state exactly that in his will. I'll never forgive you for this, Justin. I'll see to it that you pay for your abandonment of me."

Justin did not alter his stand. "Enough is enough, Arnold. You're my kin, agreed. But if Father were alive and still up to his old tricks, I wouldn't pay *his* debts either."

Arnold came at Justin with his fists raised. He swung at Justin. Justin ducked and let Arnold stumble to the floor.

"You're drunk."

"So what if I am," Arnold growled.

"And pathetic. Now get out of my house."

Justin had been forced to pick Arnold up by the collar and shove him out the door bodily. Arnold had tumbled down the front steps, rolled onto the sidewalk next to the wrought iron gate, and landed at the feet of Lord Willington, who was out for his evening stroll.

The old man tipped his black silk hat to Justin and smiled at him. "I see you're putting out the rubbish, Lord Hawkeston."

Justin laughed and bowed to his neighbor. "I should have done it long ago."

Lord Willington nodded solemnly and continued his

evening constitutional without giving Arnold a second glance.

Justin shook the unpleasant memory from his mind and glanced out the raised hatch above his head. He saw a black trunk being carried below decks and suddenly remembered that Valentine was aboard.

''It seems I've traded one kind of rubbish for another.''

Justin rose from his seat and quit the room.

Chapter Three

Wingless angels were said to walk the earth, according to an old Italian fable. As Justin approached Valentine, her beauty stopped him cold. She reminded him of an ancient tale he'd heard from one of his glassblowers years ago. It was said the angels had come to earth in the days shortly after Christ died. They disguised themselves by taking on human form in order to move freely among the Romans. They could appear and disappear at will and were able to place their thoughts into the minds of the pagans. Thus, they were able to appear to men in dreams. The angels found much sadness in the world and a great deal of work to be accomplished, and unselfishly they elected to remain on earth to help man. One could recognize the angels by their silvery white hair and a white glow that surrounded them.

Standing in the morning sunlight, dressed in a pearl silver traveling gown, Valentine seemed to radiate an ethereal light. She was unaware of his presence as she gazed at the city.

Justin found himself responding to the delicate curves of her face. As he watched, a glistening tear dropped from her long, sooty lashes to her cheek. She was smaller than he remembered. Her shoulders were narrow but held proud and straight. Her small back tapered to a waist so tiny his hands had completely encircled it when he'd assisted her into the carriage the night of the ball. The image of his hands on her body shot through his brain and sent a thunderbolt of desire charging down the network of his veins. All too easily he remembered the pliant velvety breast his hand had caressed. He remembered her nearly savage kisses. He heard again the passionate moan of pleasure she had uttered so givingly and without calculation or restraint.

Even now he wanted to slowly unfasten the back of her gown, hook by hook. He would touch her skin and kiss the length of her back, vertebra by vertebra. He wanted it to be agonizingly slow. He wanted to pull her to his chest, slip his hands from her back to her breasts and revel in their fullness. He would kiss the back of her neck, and then and only then, he would turn her head and capture her lips. God! How he remembered her kisses.

When his lips had first touched hers he'd almost believed she'd never been kissed before, but so quickly had her passion come alive that he'd discounted the impression. It had been that kiss that had confused him. She was at once innocent and a practiced wanton. He'd never kissed a woman quite like Valentine. He wondered how many men it had taken to teach her the captivating artlessness that baffled and intrigued him.

Justin's logic told him to erase these thoughts from his mind, but his body clung to their memory. "Fool,"

he berated himself when he realized he wanted—
needed—to torture himself with her all over again.

Justin prided himself on self-control. He was the master of his fate and had always plotted and planned his
affairs through every phase. If there were to be surprises,
they should be of his invention.

Enmeshed in grief over her father, Valentine was unaware of Lord Hawkeston's approach. She blinked back
a new onslaught of tears and saw a man's long shadow
cover her. It was not necessary to look upon him, or
hear his voice, for Valentine could feel his familiar presence. A curious sense of protection cloaked her, which
was at odds with her emotions. She didn't like anything
about this man, and he didn't like her. They had each
fortified their encampments. She was prepared and ar-
mored.

"Shedding tears over your lost lovers?" he asked
condescendingly.

Valentine's hands drew into tight fists at her sides. It
was all she could do to will them immobile. She shoved
her anger deep inside herself and looked up at him with
a coy smile on her lips. "And a very good day to you,
Sir Snake."

Justin stiffened at the unexpected onslaught. This girl
was going to be a challenge. The game would be an
equal test of wills. The novelty of fencing with a woman
excited him. "How many are there?"

"How many what?" she sniffed.

"Lovers."

She grinned a bit too broadly and her nearly black
eyes crinkled with merriment. He could not tell if she
was telling the truth or not. "That is none of your business."

Her insolence caused his teeth to grind. She'd made
a direct hit and she knew it. Justin was unaccustomed

to an adversary winning the first round. He decided to change the rules.

"You will meet me in my cabin in ten minutes. We have much to discuss," he boomed as if issuing an edict.

Valentine lifted her hand and casually patted her curls. "I should think we do, sir. I am most interested to hear what you have to say for yourself."

"What I have to say?" he growled incredulously. He snatched her hand in his and pulled her closer to him. A ferocious look twisted his face. Anger spewed out of his eyes. "I have to answer to no man . . . and certainly not to any woman—for anything."

Valentine affected a coquettish batting of her eyelids and continued to smile so sweetly he thought her lips would drip honey. "Why, sir, whatever did I do to upset you so greatly? And you are upset. I can see that. Why, you're practically spitting those nasty innuendoes at me. You should see how your nostrils flare at me. Goodness, you truly should put a rein on your temper. It says in the Bible—"

Justin was breathing heavily. "I don't give a damn what the Bible says—"

"That's quite obvious," she interrupted righteously.

Justin gripped her arm even tighter. He didn't like the kind of thoughts that raced across his brain. He wanted to kiss the impudence off her lips. He wanted to feel her succumb to him as she had before. He wanted to feel her heart pounding the way his was at this moment. But she was as calm as the sea on a windless day. Nothing he said had ruffled her. It was he who was losing control, and Justin had never lost control of anything in his life.

"See that you are in my cabin, miss."

Valentine gently tugged on her wrist while keeping her smile intact. "I said I would be there, sir," she purred. "Now please unhand me."

Justin let go of her wrist as if it were a hot poker. He spun on his heel, crossed the deck in less than five strides, and disappeared below deck.

Valentine watched him leave. Once he was out of sight, she stomped her heel against the newly swabbed deck, hit a patch of water and slipped. She landed on her rump. Her skirts shot up over her knees, displaying shapely legs. She immediately righted herself and smoothed her skirts. "Ooohhh! I hate that man! I truly and most earnestly do. Hmph. Lovers. What ever is he talking about? He *has* to know how unpracticed I am. He was the one who seduced me. I am the one who should be outraged. Not him." She struggled to her feet, quickly looking about to see if anyone had witnessed her unladylike fall.

A half dozen crew members hung in the rigging laughing. As she glanced up at them, they instantly turned away and went back to their work. The seaman who was still busily swabbing the deck stifled a giggle and started to come to her aid, but she waved him away.

Another group of men were hoisting the anchor and had seen nothing. Suddenly the ship lurched as wind filled the open sails.

Valentine steadied herself by clinging to the rail. She looked around her at all the activity. Then she smiled playfully to herself. "I've always wanted to know about ships and just exactly how they work. I think now is as good a time as any to further my education. An undertaking such as this should take me . . . all afternoon," she said to herself brightly.

She walked up to a man who was adjusting one of the ropes on the main sail. "My good man," Valentine began with an eager smile, "Lord Hawkeston has ordered me to learn as much as I can about sailing. Would you be so good as to explain to me your work here?"

The dumbfounded seaman scratched his head, shrugged his shoulders, and began his explanation about sails.

Justin waited in his cabin for one hour and fifteen minutes before storming onto the main deck in search of Valentine. He inquired of his first mate and two crew members before finding her standing at the helm with her daintily gloved hands on the wheel and the helmsman behind her. Fortunately for the helmsman and his job, he had not given the wheel over to her. He had his burly hands placed right next to Valentine's own. It was the moonstruck look on his heavily jowled face that set Justin off on a tirade.

"What in the hell is going on here?" Justin demanded.

Valentine smiled as innocently as she knew how. "To what are you referring, sir?"

"You know damn well what I mean. And get your hands off my wheel!" he bellowed.

"Your wheel?" She tilted her face up to the helmsman. "But Mr. Midgeon told me it was his wheel. Didn't you, Midgy?"

Justin's entire body tensed. "Midgy?" He looked from Valentine to his helmsman.

Valentine used the tenderest tones her voice knew so that the words rolled off her tongue like syrup. "That's what I call Mr. Midgeon now. I made it up. It's between us." She gazed back up at the helmsman. "Isn't it, Midgy?"

Justin nearly burst out laughing at her ploy. She was trying to make him jealous, he realized. Many women had made similar efforts in the past, but none had been so transparent as Valentine. For a brief moment, he nearly believed she knew nothing of the ways of the

58

world and the games that men and women play. However, Justin told himself, he knew better.

He folded his arms over his chest nonchalantly. "I was busy with my maps and instructions to my first mate. I had forgotten about our meeting. Come along, Miss St. James." He crooked his finger at her.

Valentine couldn't help the frown that furrowed her brow. Now he was treating her like an errant child. First he accused her of having lovers and now he acted as if he were leading her off to receive a spanking. She wanted to embarrass him in front of his crew. She'd like to see him slip and fall. However, this wasn't the right time. If she planned it well, she would find her revenge and it would be sweet.

Valentine slipped around the wheel, patted Mr. Midgeon's hand in farewell, and stepped down the three wooden stairs that led to the main deck. Justin turned his back on her and led the way to his cabin.

Valentine followed him all the while grumbling to herself. "Blackguard . . . rapist . . . foul-smelling, rancid-breathed lizard . . ." Valentine felt her mood lift considerably with each new curse she invented for Lord Justin Hawkeston.

He stood off to the side as he opened the door to his cabin and graciously waited for her to enter.

"Please," he instructed as he pulled out a chair at the end of the table, "sit here."

When she breezed past him, he noticed the intoxicating scent of her perfume. It was the same one she'd worn the night of the ball. It smelled of exotic oils, roses and jasmine. As it filled his nostrils, he remembered that she liked to wear the majority of her perfume low on her throat and just above the swell of her breasts.

"Thank you, Lord Hawkeston," Valentine said courteously as if he were a waiter.

Her statement jolted him back to reality. Justin took his hands from the back of her chair and placed them in his pockets where they would be unable to reach out and touch her. He was unaware of the beads of perspiration that formed on his upper lip.

"Is it warm in here?" she asked.

"Yes. I think it is." He went to the side of his bunk, where he kept a jug of water next to his bottle of brandy. Absentmindedly he lifted the brandy, first thinking he could use a drink. Quickly he replaced it and took the water. He poured two glasses. "This should help you."

She smiled. "Oh, I didn't mean that I thought it was hot. It seems you are the one who is uncomfortable."

"You deliberately failed to attend our meeting," he accused.

"You said you were busy."

"You didn't know that at the time. I gave you a command!" He slammed his fist on the table.

Valentine jumped and so did the glasses. She refused to let him intimidate her. "I am not one of your crew, sir. I am your intended wife. I don't respond to demands or commands," she said haughtily.

He moved next to her in one stride and bent down. His face was nearly touching hers. "What do you respond to, miss?" he asked in a low, sensual voice.

"I think you already know."

She tried not to lose herself in his crystal blue eyes. She tried not to feel the incredible animal heat of his body. She tried to keep a distance between them, but he was so forceful his gaze pulled her to him like a magnet.

He wanted to kiss her. The thought hit her like a cannon burst. For the first time she realized that it was she who had the power. She could control him. It was a heady, exhilarating piece of knowledge and she wanted to revel in it.

Justin bolted upright and backed away from her. "Damn well, I do know," he said. "And that is why I wanted this meeting. I think it most imperative that we put matters straight between us at the onset."

"What matters?" she asked, suddenly confused by his altered behavior.

"The matter of our marriage."

"Oh, that," she replied with downcast eyes.

"Yes, *that*," he returned coldly. He sat at the far end of the table from her. "We have each made a bargain with your father. I am an honorable man and I want you to know that I intend to keep my promise."

"How good of you, my lord," she said indignantly.

His glare was stern. "I don't like this any more than you do."

"Don't you?"

"I don't." He paused, and then began again more thoughtfully. "I have a small townhouse in London that should be suitable for Victoria and her new husband. It is close to Grosvenor Square, and she will be able to come visit you often since it is not far from my house. She will have servants and also a carriage and driver at her disposal. Should Victoria's husband be so inclined, I have made arrangements with the manager of my importing business to ready a position for him. I cannot at this time offer him a position any higher in the company than head bookkeeper, but if his work is good and he earns advancement, I intend to reward him according to his merit. Your aunt may live with Victoria or she can choose to live in my house, unless she prefers to live alone. Have you any idea which would please her most?"

Valentine was stunned at his generosity. She had wanted to place him in the role of ogre, but he was nothing of the kind. Not until this moment had she realized the extent to which his vow would cost him. Houses, servants, food, horses, clothing, even an obviously better paying position for Andrew. Lord Hawkeston intended to pay for everything. In addition, he was willing to allow Aunt Cherise to live in his very own house. "You are most kind, Lord Hawkeston," she said in awe. "I truly believe you have done far more than my father requested."

"Had our positions been reversed, he would have done the same for me."

Her eyes were level with his as she gazed at him. "He never had your kind of wealth, but you are correct. He would have done the very same."

Justin was touched by her sincerity. Her love for her family was inescapably written across her beautiful face. He wondered what it would be like to have a family with whom he could share feelings and trust. "You are all quite blessed people, you know."

"We've always helped each other. Now you are helping us." She nodded in assent. "We are blessed."

Justin didn't like the way she chipped away at the sturdy barricade around his heart. He cleared his throat at the uncomfortable thought and continued in a more brusque tone. "Now as to the matter of our wedding. I have begun the preparations already. There is nothing that you or your aunt need worry yourselves over. You will go to a dressmaker on Regent Street that comes highly recommended. I know little of such matters, but I am told that the work is good and I will not be made a pauper by their prices in the process. I have also—"

Valentine threw up her palm as she interrupted him. "Am I to understand that I have no choices, no decisions in my very own wedding? Not even my gown?"

Justin was taken aback. "I am paying the bills. I will make the decisions."

"But it's *my* wedding!"

"And I'm paying for it."

"Ho!" she nearly shouted. "Simply because you own me lock, stock and barrel for the rest of my life does not give you the right to dictate even my clothing to me."

Justin ruminated on her comment for a moment. "I have made these arrangements."

"Change them," she said simply.

"Change them? Why should I?"

Valentine realized that pleasing her was not his aim. She had to find another avenue to gain her wishes. "Every woman dreams of her wedding day, sir. And one of the most important parts of that dream is her gown. For one thing, I have specific ideas about what I want to wear. The other consideration is that if this dressmaker is a friend of yours, she might be persuaded by you to reveal the cut and fabric of my gown to you. That wouldn't be proper. And it would be bad luck."

A curious grin bent his mouth. "So which is it that bothers you most? The impropriety or the bad luck?"

Valentine's eyes gleamed merrily. "The bad luck."

"At least you are honest. Very well, you may choose your gown. Now to the date—"

"I want to be married on my birthday," she interrupted.

"I have already chosen the first of May. It cannot be changed," he said defiantly.

"I want to be married on the same day that Victoria marries Andrew. April eighteenth."

"I didn't know you were so anxious to get into my bed," he replied with an amused smirk.

Valentine was coolly adamant. "It's nothing of the kind, I assure you. The thought had not crossed my mind," she lied. "It has always been a special day for me. Since I am being forced to marry you, I wanted to have some happiness on that day."

The blow hit Justin deep inside. He hadn't realized how distasteful this marriage pact was to Valentine until this moment. He found himself wondering if he knew anything about her at all. One moment she was a sentimental girl, the next the dutiful daughter. He'd seen the harlot in a Mardi Gras mask, the scamp at the helm, and now she was a cold negotiator. She knew what she wanted and she didn't give a whit as to how brutal she needed to be in order to reach her goal.

"By all means, you should grab happiness when and where you can. We all do," he responded icily.

"Then I can name the date."

"April eighteenth. As you wish, miss."

Valentine rose from the table. Her face was placid and stern. "I trust we have finished our business?"

"We have," he answered flatly.

"Then I may retire to my cabin?"

"Yes," he said as he rose and opened the door for her. He bowed curtly as she moved quickly past him, keeping as much distance between their bodies as the narrow doorway would allow. Justin then turned back to the table and took out his log. He raised his quill pen and started to write. As he made his entry he found that his cabin was filled with the lingering scent of rose and jasmine.

Valentine sat on the edge of her bed as she rifled through her valise. She found her diary and opened it to a clean page. In the drawer of the bedside table she found ink and a long white feather quill pen.

February 20, 1815
Dear Diary,

After further observation of Lord Hawkeston, I find that though he is generous to my family, he is inordinately unkind to me. I mean to him no more than he means to me . . . a debt that is owed. I find him cold and dispassionate. Fortunately for him, I understand his position, and therefore I feel no emotions about the man whatsoever. I have managed to gain two concessions from him regarding the wedding. I believe I won them justly. If I must marry a man who is incapable of love, I will do so in a manner that would make Papa proud.

Sincerely yours,
Valentine St. James

Valentine blew on the ink until it dried and then she closed the diary. She fell back on the down pillow and shut her eyes. She couldn't tell the diary how difficult it had been to be in the same room with Lord Hawkeston, negotiating her future with him as if she were a crate of wine goblets. She didn't tell her diary how handsome she found him. Nor did she mention that for a fleeting moment she had thought that she wielded a mysterious power over him. And never, never would she write that he exuded such a strong power over her that when she drifted off to sleep that day, she was sure he would invade her dreams.

Chapter Four

Valentine stood on a forty-foot-high cliff near the ancient Sicilian city of Taormina. Sunbeams danced on the deep azure surface of the Mediterranean Sea. In the distance a band of ominous charcoal gray clouds marched across the sky. White-capped waves shattered against the rocks below and shot a sparkling mist skyward where it mingled with the sun and wove a golden aura around Valentine. The winter wind swirled her skirts around her ankles and lifted the ends of her cravat high above her neck. She stood strong against the forces of nature, defying them to move her from her vantage point. To the north she could see Mount Etna spewing narrow tongues of fire and rock into the air. The powerful and deadly volcano had raged at man from the beginning of time. In ancient Greek mythology, it was the burial place of Vulcan, who had been cast into its fiery depths by Zeus. Valentine was awestruck by the timeless beauty and power of nature. She wondered how many others had come to this place and contemplated their futures. Were they as forlorn as she? Perhaps there were other maidens with heavier hearts; ones who chose more desperate means to end their misery. Perhaps some had been pushed to an end not of their choosing, she thought as she peered down at the jagged rocks below. A sense of doom pervaded her thoughts and spun a gloomy cloud over the scene that only moments before had been filled with golden light. What other tales could be told of this beautiful but perilous place?

It had been her idea to make the trek up here. Victoria and Aunt Cherise had complained most of the way, until they came to this breathtaking view. It was stunning in its majesty. Even in winter, the tall conical Italian cypress trees were a bright green as they trooped down the slopes of the hills in perfect military rows. With awed smiles Victoria and Aunt Cherise agreed that the journey was worth the effort.

"Do you think the volcano will erupt?" Valentine asked Aunt Cherise as she gazed at the glowing crimson lava.

"Good heavens, no," Cherise replied, tipping her parasol to shade her eyes.

"How do you know?" Valentine asked.

"Frankly, the thought had crossed my mind earlier when we docked. I asked the first mate, Mr. Henderson, if there was any danger. He assured me that no one would be going ashore if there was a threat to our safety."

Valentine's muddled thoughts suddenly sharpened into focus. Her instincts had always served her well. She was wise enough to pay strict attention when she sensed alarm. Obviously, even Aunt Cherise had doubts about this venture to shore. "Quite wise of you, Aunt Cherise," she said. "I wouldn't put it past Lord Hawkeston to dump us all here and let a volcano do his dirty work for him."

Victoria clucked her tongue. "How can you say that, Valentine? He's been extremely polite to all of us. And I must say that I've never known of anyone quite so generous. His plans and provisions for all of us are far beyond anything Father could have dreamed."

"That is my point, Victoria," Valentine said, pointing her finger righteously in the air. "He's too generous. Too good to be true. Why should he do so much for us? I tried to put his generosity into pounds and numbers, and the final figures on an annual basis were staggering." She folded her arms across her chest. "I don't trust him. He's got some scheme in mind."

Victoria rolled her eyes. "Don't you get tired working over your mind like that?"

"I'm serious. Think about it. It's a simple thing to promise gifts, houses, servants and carriages to us now. We aren't in England yet. There's a lot of sea between here and there. A great many things can happen in that length of time and on board a ship."

"What kind of things?" Victoria inquired.

"Accidents. I could think of a hundred different things that could result in death at sea."

"I've no doubt about that!" Aunt Cherise retorted. "If you were surrounded by the Queen's Royal Guard for protection, *you* could still concoct a method by which Lord Hawkeston would be the cause of your demise."

"I don't trust him," Valentine spat.

"You've made that abundantly clear. I'm afraid it's your imagination that will be your downfall . . . not Lord Hawkeston," Cherise scolded. "From my own observations of Lord Hawkeston I have found him to be polite, kind and generous. I rather like him."

"I agree with you, Aunt Cherise," Victoria piped in.

Valentine threw up her arms in exasperation. "I don't believe this! My own family has turned against me."

"That's not true in the least. We love you. But it seems to us that when it comes to Lord Hawkeston you invent and imagine situations that aren't real. He has done nothing to hurt you. And he certainly has not displayed any kind of behavior that warrants the reactions we are seeing in you. I understand that this match is a loveless one. But it doesn't always have to be that way."

Valentine glared at her sister. "Just what are you saying to me, Vicki, dear?" she said sarcastically.

"It is possible, sister dear," Victoria retorted in like tones, "that you could come to have affection for him if you would let yourself."

"That's absurd and totally out of the question."

"Why?"

"You simply don't know him the way I do. He's a heartless, self-centered and cruel man. I think more highly of myself than to give my . . . feelings to someone as debased as Lord Hawkeston. I don't know what has happened to you both. It's as if he's cast some spell on you, bewitched you so that you will turn against me. He's bribed you both with promises of new houses and expensive finery. What hurts me the most is that you've accepted his 'generosity' so willingly."

Valentine turned her back on them and faced the sea. A wave of shame crashed over her heart. She couldn't tell them the truth. How could she tell them that she had surrendered herself to a faceless, nameless man with no regard to propriety, let alone morals? Sackcloth and ashes were too lenient a punishment for her, she believed. What had happened to her mind that night? "Lord forgive me," she mumbled to herself as she thought of the shame she would bring upon her family if they ever discovered the truth.

Just then, Valentine heard the sound of horses' hooves on the stony trail that led up to the lookout point. Her moment of repose had ended. "I hear my jailer approaching."

"Valentine!" Victoria scolded and then turned to look toward the path they had climbed at Valentine's insistence. She smiled brightly when three horses thundered around the bend below them.

Lord Hawkeston wore a murderous look on his face as he reined his horse to a halt. "I instructed you to remain at the bottom of the cliff. What are you doing up here?" he demanded in angry tones. His eyes shot straight to Valentine as if he knew this expedition was her idea.

"I wanted to see the volcano," she said tartly. "I persuaded the others to join me." Valentine was not afraid to assume responsibility for her actions.

"The view below is quite adequate," he growled as a scowl burrowed deeply into his brow.

"I have judged that it is not."

Justin gave the signal to the two men with him to dismount. "Take these ladies back to the ship," he commanded.

Mr. Henderson, a burly man with flashing green eyes, was the first off his horse and he immediately turned to Aunt Cherise and extended his hand. With a smile, she went to him and thanked him for his assistance as he hoisted her onto his horse. He then mounted the horse, sat behind Aunt Cherise, and turned the animal down the path.

Victoria looked at the other seaman, who was waiting to assist her. "Where is Andrew?" she asked.

Justin kept his eyes riveted on Valentine while he spoke. "Since he is now my manager, I left him in the village to attend to my business matters there. He will join us on the beach.''

Victoria's face filled with pride for Andrew. This outing was meant to be a test for him, and she knew he would prove himself capable and worthy of Lord Hawkeston's trust. She was anxious to learn the details from Andrew. Eagerly she mounted the horse, and with the seaman behind her in the saddle, they followed Mr. Henderson and Aunt Cherise down the rocky path to the stony beach. Just as they turned around the bend, she lifted her arm over her head and waved to her sister.

Valentine never took her eyes from the scowling face of her betrothed, though she caught Victoria's wave out of the corner of her eye.

''Why must you test my patience?'' Justin boomed at her.

''Why must you test mine?'' she blasted right back at him. ''Why do you think that because I am to marry you, I should think and act like one of your crew?''

''You have been charged to my care. Therefore you are my responsibility. Precisely like my crew. Now get on this horse.''

''I'll walk, thank you very much.''

''Perhaps I should let you walk. But time is running short and we must get under way.''

''I'll do as I please,'' she said, taking a step backward as his horse started toward her.

Justin was keenly aware of the unstable rocks beneath their feet. Valentine was dangerously close to the edge of the cliff. Her defiant behavior was placing them both in peril. He was also aware of the high winds that were heading their way. Even now, erratic blasts of wind whipped across his face and stung his eyes. He was aware of the tangle her skirts had become, a factor that could impede her balance. ''Miss St. James! Get on this

71

horse now!'' he shouted as a warning.

"I will not," she retorted as a huge wave crashed against the rocks below and the wind careened around the base of the cliff and rose upward.

Suddenly Justin's horse whinnied as it sensed the oncoming storm and reared back on its hind legs.

With lightning-quick movements, Justin yanked on the reins, spurred the horse forward and galloped to the edge of the cliff. A second blast of wind hit Valentine from the side, causing her to lose her footing. Her right leg buckled, and though she tried to steady herself, the frightening vision of the oncoming horse and angry rider sent her to her knees.

A trickle of fine rock tumbled out from beneath her and cascaded down the cliff. She screamed. Justin cursed.

The horse raced toward her. Valentine lifted her arms to shield her face. A huge rock broke loose under her and fell over the edge. Valentine knew she would be the next to tumble to the jagged rocks.

"Are you trying to kill me?" she screamed as his arm shot out, grabbed her uplifted arm, and roughly pulled her up. She flopped onto the horse's back belly down.

Justin turned the horse around just as a huge boulder broke free under the horse's hind leg and sailed over the cliff's side. It was the boulder upon which Valentine had been standing.

"I'm trying to save your life," he roared angrily.

With the wind knocked out of her, Valentine could not reply. She gasped for breath with every gallop, but she kept bouncing up and down on the horse's back. Breathing was impossible. Hate was not.

"Let . . . me . . . down . . ." she finally croaked as they turned the last bend in the path.

Justin looked down and saw that Valentine had nearly

turned blue. With an amused expression he reined the horse to a halt. He grinned at the comical sight of the tempestuous, stubborn Valentine lying across the withers of his horse. "At least I've found a way to temper your tongue, woman."

Valentine slid off the horse and gulped blessed quantities of air. She filled her nostrils, lungs and abdomen and felt her blood begin to flow. Her color returned and so did her anger. "You brute! You were going to kill me!"

Justin howled at the picture before him. The veins in Valentine's neck were still swollen and blue as she gasped for air. But her cheeks were nearly as crimson as the fire in her black eyes. With each intake of air, her ribs swelled and her breasts strained against the tight-fitting jacket she wore. His laughter faded. Desire replaced amusement and smoldered deep within the pit of his loins. With massive self-control he contained the fire within, for he did not want her to know the extent of her power over him.

Valentine did not understand the alteration in his demeanor. Clearly, he thought her a fool. She detested the fact that he was right. Obviously, she had been too near the edge. But how was she to know that the rocks were precarious? She'd never been here before, but he had. He had told them to remain on the lowest point. Valentine was uncertain now if she hadn't ventured to that tenuous, though breathtaking spot simply to defy him. She had coerced the others on the pretense of viewing the volcano. She realized now that she had placed them in danger, as well as herself. She owed them all an apology for her actions.

As she looked into the darkening blue eyes of Lord Hawkeston, she vowed she would not change her mind about him. She trusted him less now than she ever had.

She didn't know what he wanted of her, or why.

A swarm of menacing gray clouds appeared overhead, and with them renewed gusts of wind across the island. Long tendrils of silvery hair freed themselves from Valentine's chignon as the wind swirled around them. Her ascot flew in her face.

Justin reached down. "Come, little one. We must hurry. The storm will be upon us in no time."

Valentine glanced out to sea and realized that he was right. This time, she would not be foolish. Her sister and aunt were awaiting them in the dinghy. She reached out and took his hand. He pulled her onto the horse. She was as light as a feather, he thought as she sat in the saddle behind him.

"Put your arms around me," he said.

Valentine wriggled back and forth trying to make herself comfortable in her sidesaddle position on a saddle fashioned for an astride position. She yanked on her skirt. "What did you say?"

Justin offered no answer. Instead, he grabbed her arms and placed them around his chest. "Hang on," he said gruffly as he spurred the horse into a gallop.

As they raced down the hill and onto the stony beach, Justin was acutely aware of her body behind his. With each gallop, he could feel her breasts against his back. Sensuous chills coursed through his body. Brilliant memory flashes of her kisses shocked his nerve endings and caused his pulse to race. He could feel her warm breath on the back of his neck. Her fingers dug into his ribs as she steadied herself on the horse. The oncoming storm created a sense of urgency in him and heightened his awareness of the power of nature both without and within him. Never before had his sexual need engulfed him so stealthily or with such intensity. He tried to convince himself that she was simply another responsibility, this slip of a girl. But there was something haunting about her presence that wouldn't fade. He pressed his knees into the horse's flanks to spur him on. The sooner they were on the boat, the better he would be able to regain his control.

They raced onto the beach and rounded the rocks to the cove where the dinghy was docked. The stableboy from the village had arrived to take the horses back to the livery. Mr. Henderson had boarded Victoria and Aunt Cherise, and the seaman sat with his oars uplifted, ready to set out to the ship.

Justin reined the horse to a halt and nearly jumped out of the saddle, so glad was he to put physical distance between himself and Valentine. Valentine did not wait for assistance. She quickly slid off the horse to the ground and rushed to the waiting boat. Mr. Henderson assisted her into the boat, where she settled herself next to Aunt Cherise. Victoria and Andrew exchanged excited whispers about the transaction Justin had made in the village. Valentine pretended to listen to their conversation, but her thoughts were mired in a swirl of emotions about Lord Hawkeston.

She, too, had been aware of the closeness of their bodies on the ride down from the cliff. Her hands still felt the strong chest muscles beneath them and now ached with the absence of his flesh. He'd worn no hat that day, and she realized how long the hair on the back of his head was. The wind had tangled her silver tendrils with his golden blond, making ribbons of light across his black wool jacket. She remembered his straight, proud back and shoulders. His was the kind of frame needed to carry the weight of the world. She knew too that everything about him was hard . . . cold and hard. He had showed her nothing but disdain. Not once had she sensed an easing of his demeanor, a glimpse of sensitivity. He understood nothing about her, nor did he care to search for understanding. He was a man with no feelings, and consequently he could not recognize other people's feelings.

Justin pushed on the prow of the boat until the water was up to his knees, then swung himself on board.

"Make haste, Mr. Henderson. This storm could impede our departure."

"Aye, Captain. Perhaps we should wait 'er out."

Justin shook his head. "It's just a squall. We can use the winds to get us past the coast; then we'll turn up to the north and sail out of it."

Seaspray misted their faces as they rode over the incoming waves. Justin kept his eyes on the storm, mentally assessing the wind velocity and the breadth of the cloud cover. He took up an oar himself in order to make better time. Andrew followed suit, cheerfully pitching in alongside Mr. Henderson.

When they reached the ship, everything was in readiness to set sail. Valentine had never seen such organized commotion aboard a ship. However, she thought to herself, she'd never been in a storm at sea, either.

The anchor was hoisted, the sails unfurled, and the ship moved out of the inlet.

Justin turned to Andrew. "Take the women to their cabins and make certain they are safe. The last thing I need is to find your future sister-in-law taking over my helm again." He glared at Valentine, started to turn around, and then he stopped. "By the way, Andrew. Do you know anything about sailing?"

"A little. I've observed a great deal already. If nothing else, I've a strong back and good constitution," Andrew replied firmly.

"Then come back up here. We could use another hand if it gets rough."

Andrew ushered the three women below decks, where they remained in Victoria and Aunt Cherise's cabin. Just as he was about to close the door, Victoria rushed to him and kissed his cheek.

"Be careful," she whispered.

"Don't worry. It doesn't look all that bad to me."

Victoria closed the door behind him. When she turned around she looked at Valentine sitting in a straight wooden chair with her arms folded tightly across her chest. Obviously, the storm brewing outside was going to be nothing to compare with what was about to explode inside this cabin.

"That lout! Did you hear what he said about me?"

"Yes, I did," Victoria replied. "And I can't say I blame him."

Valentine gaped at her sister. "I beg your pardon!" she said saucily.

"Aunt Cherise and I were watching you from the bottom of the cliff when you nearly plunged to your death. If Lord Hawkeston hadn't been there to save you—"

"Save me? Save *me?* It's because of him and his ill-tempered horse that I nearly did fall over the edge. He came at me so quickly—"

"And good thing he did." Aunt Cherise could hold her tongue no longer. "I don't mean to sound critical, but your escapades have taken a dangerous turn of late. And all of it seems to stem from your aversion to Lord Hawkeston."

Valentine averted her gaze. They knew her too well. She could not risk their discovering the truth about her. "You just don't understand," she said mournfully.

Victoria felt a wave of sympathy wash over her. "I know we don't. But we're trying. Truly we are. It's just that you seem to be making this more difficult on yourself than it is."

"No, Victoria, *he* is the one who is difficult," she sighed heavily as a dark veil of sadness fell over her heart. "That's what you don't understand." When she looked up at her sister and aunt, there were tears of fury in her eyes. She tried to will them away, but to no avail. These were not the kind of tears she wanted her family to see. Immediately, without another word, she turned on her heel and raced out the door to her own cabin.

She slammed the door to her cabin, wishing Lord Hawkeston's backside was on the other side. "Ooohhh, how I'd like to inflict bodily harm on him."

She sat on the edge of the bed and reached beneath the down pillow. She withdrew her diary. With her familiar quill pen in hand, she began to write.

Dear Diary,

   This is the saddest day of my life, because today I have discovered that my family has sided with the enemy. Lord Hawkeston has beguiled them with his money. He is more than a snake, he is evil incarnate. I know now that I must not only fight him, but I must win my family back to me.

   I will never be sure if he meant to save me or to kill me on the cliff today. I will never forget the fury in his eyes. Should anything happen to me on this journey, I hope that Victoria reads this diary and knows that I believe he would stop at nothing to disentangle himself from this cursed vow.

Sincerely yours,
Valentine St. James

Chapter Five

Lord Hawkeston had been wrong and everybody knew it. The cook knew it, the crew knew it, Mr. Henderson knew it, and so did Valentine. The storm raged for two days and three nights. Rather than sailing away from it, they sailed into it. The most seasoned of the crew exclaimed that they had never experienced a storm of this magnitude. Violent winds pummeled the ship for 48 hours before subsiding. Wave after wave rose in fury and assaulted the ship. They lost course and then found it again. Lord Hawkeston relieved the helmsman after the first ten hours, lashed himself to the helm, and remained there for the duration. He wanted his men to see his resolve if not his strength. What he had lacked in judgment, he compensated with courage. When the storm subsided, Lord Hawkeston emerged a hero.

Valentine came out of her cabin the color of green. Pea green. Vomitous green. Never had she been so sick.

Never had she been so bruised and battered. She had two lumps on her head from when the ship pitched to one side and then the other and she struck her head on the hanging lamp. She blackened her eye when her hand jerked off the beam she was clinging to for support and she socked herself just above the right cheekbone. The bruises on her hip and on her lower leg were inflicted by a chair that sailed back and forth across the cabin because she had failed to lash it down before the storm. After two chair attacks, Valentine mustered her courage and set the chair on its wall hooks. Valentine emerged the victor.

Seasickness proved to be the ultimate foe. When it was over she was amazed that she'd been hunched over the chamber pot for only two days. It had seemed an eternity. If any of her internal organs remained intact, it was only by a miracle, she thought as she ventured onto the top deck. The crew members were scurrying about tending to their duties, chattering like magpies about the events of the storm.

One man hoisted a huge bale of rope onto his back. "Did ye see 'im, mate? Aw, 'e looks as if 'e'd been fightin' Lucifer 'himself, 'e does."

"I ain't seen none the likes 'o me lord. 'E's a 'ero. Pure and simple," a second seaman replied as he mopped the deck. " 'Tis been a long time since I seen courage like that on the seas. Blimey, if he ain't a surprise."

"How does 'e know so much?"

A third seaman in a striped shirt and black tam passed by and upon hearing the conversation retorted, "Ain't nothin' to know when one is workin' on guts and instinct. 'E wanted to save us, an' save us 'e did!"

Valentine didn't know what the men were talking about, but it was clear that Lord Hawkeston was not only to be commended, but thanked. The idea of prostrating herself before him sent another wave of nausea barreling through her intestines. On unsteady legs she wobbled to an overturned barrel before she sank into a heap. She felt cold sweat break out on her forehead and neck. Her stomach lurched. She slammed her palm over her mouth as her eyes frantically searched for the quickest route to the ship's edge. Depleted of energy, she found she could barely stand, and so she opted for a crawl over huge hemp ropes that were strewn everywhere. She felt as if she were crawling over tree trunks. Her stomach lurched again.

How can there be anything left? she wondered as she pulled herself up the side and hung over the rail. She gagged. She heaved. Nothing happened. She felt worse than before. Sweat was pouring off her face. She leaned over further as a new wave of nausea overtook her. She gagged again.

Suddenly she felt a huge hand on her back. Even on the edge of death, she would know that touch anywhere. "You have my permission to kill me now, my lord."

"Looks to me like you're doing a very good job all by yourself." His hand slid up her back tenderly and then back down again.

Valentine twisted her face around to look at him. He was staring at her backside, but his expression was pained and incredibly exhausted. Was he trying to comfort her? She pushed herself away from the rail, but the effort sapped the remainder of her energy. She sank to the deck and stared at the weary, pale face in front of her.

"You look terrible," she said, taking in his sea-soaked clothing, his tangled and matted hair and the deep lines of worry still embedded in his face.

"You look awful," he replied, sparing her any sentiment. He, too, felt drained and sat on the deck next to her. "I don't know when I've seen a woman wearing quite that shade of green in her cheeks. And what happened to your eye?" He reached up to touch it.

She languidly pushed his hand away. He let it drop. "Don't touch me. It hurts," she said, wincing when she blinked. "Let's just say I had a rough night or two."

He tried to chuckle but it came out as a moan. "We all did," he said simply.

Valentine nodded and it was then that she noticed his wrists. They were circled with bands of torn flesh and dried blood. On the right wrist, something had cut so deeply she could see a part of the wristbone exposed. "God in heaven, who did this to you?"

"I did."

She looked at him quizzically.

"I had to lash myself to the helm so that I wouldn't be tossed overboard. I sent everyone else below decks."

"By yourself? You steered us through that storm alone?"

"My men are too valuable to lose. I didn't want to jeopardize their lives any further on my account. Besides, there was nothing to do but ride it out. Now the sails must be mended, the riggings re-strung."

"And someone needs to tend to those wounds of yours. I'll get a needle and some salve."

She started to rise when suddenly his hand clamped around her wrist with a force she believed he was incapable of under the circumstances.

"You just go get the cook. He can stitch me up. I'll not have you taking a needle and thread to my flesh."

"How difficult can it be? One uses the same procedure as embroidery, I would think."

Justin rolled his eyes in horror. "I am not some tapestry to stave off your boredom, madam."

Valentine cocked her head to side. "Nursing isn't all that difficult. I've actually done quite a bit of it."

"I don't believe you."

"When Victoria had a fever, I applied cold compresses to her forehead day and night. And once when Aunt Cherise was stricken with a cold, I administered a mustard pack."

"That is hardly medical treatment. And certainly not what I require."

"What's the matter, Lord Hawkeston? Don't you trust me?" she bantered.

"Absolutely not," he retorted. "Go get cook."

Valentine started laughing. She laughed so hard that a new wave of nausea rolled over her. She clutched her abdomen, rose to her feet, and leaned over the rail again. She gagged.

Justin sat below her and yanked on her skirt. She flopped down beside him. "It's the dry heaves. When you find the cook, tell him to give you some paregoric."

Valentine was too exhausted and sick to argue. She nodded and started to crawl away.

"What are you doing?" Justin asked.

"This is the way I came and this is the way I'm leaving," she replied haughtily, knowing she could never stand without needing to find the rail again.

Justin watched Valentine's derriere as it swished and swayed across the deck. Never had he seen a sight quite so tantalizing, and never had he felt as uninterested. Before he had a chance to ruminate over the loss of his libido, his eyes rolled back in his head and he passed out cold.

Valentine returned with needle, thread, salve and bandages. The cook, she found, was in worse condition than she was. She took a large measure of paregoric and followed it with the brandy that the cook assured her did more for the constitution than the medicine did. She did not argue.

Lord Hawkeston was sound asleep when she found him. She ordered two ship's mates to move him to his cabin. She followed them below decks. Because he showed no sign of awakening anytime soon, Valentine took the opportunity to check on Victoria and Aunt Cherise.

When she entered their cabin, she found precisely what she'd expected. Pea green faces. She administered the paregoric and brandy as the cook had instructed and left them to rest.

Back in Lord Hawkeston's cabin, Valentine placed the brandy and paregoric on the table, threaded her needle, and poured fresh water into the ceramic basin. She dipped a clean cloth into the water and wrung it out.

As she looked down at the sleeping Lord Hawkeston she was struck by the softness in his face. Gone were the perpetual angry lines in his forehead, and the rigidity of his jawline had seemed to melt away. Long blond eyelashes cast tiny shadows on his cheeks. A three-day stubble covered his cheeks and neck, but when she grazed the edge of his jaw with her forefinger, she found it was as soft as down. Just as she was about to lift her finger from his face, his lower lip trembled and he rolled his head to the side, cradling his cheek in her hand. She told herself it was a reflexive movement, unconscious, and therefore the tug she felt in her heart was unwarranted.

Suddenly he looked nothing like the hero the crewmen were calling him; nor did he resemble the rogue she'd met in the white mask; least of all did he bear any likeness to the angry and cold Lord Hawkeston to whom she was betrothed. The morning sun filtered through the netting that surrounded the bed and cast delicate patterns on his face. For the first time she saw the child within him, the little boy who could be hurt and wounded.

Valentine knelt by the side of the bed and picked up his arm to inspect the wound. She slid his shirtsleeve above the elbow and held his forearm in the sunlight that streamed into the room through the hatch overhead. The flesh had been torn away, as if peeled off his muscles and tendons by fine hooks. Repulsed by the bleeding wounds, Valentine felt her stomach lurch again. Quickly she replaced his arm gently on the bed and went to the table.

She leaned against the table for support. She spied the bottle of brandy and uncorked it. She held it to her lips and took a small sip. It felt warm as it slid down her throat and filled her insides with courage.

She contemplated the bottle, looked over at her patient, and then back at the bottle again. "I think I need this more than you." This time she gulped the brandy before replacing the cork.

Valentine cleaned the wounds with the wetted cloth before she began. Carefully she smoothed the pieces of flesh over the gashes as if she were fitting pie crusts together. Then she applied a thick smear of salve. After inspecting every area twice, she realized she was finally going to be forced to use the needle.

A huge bilious lump rose in her throat and she thought she was going to be sick again. But her resolve pressed her on. She sank the needle into the first fold of flesh and winced. Lord Hawkeston did not so much as flinch. With careful precision and gentleness, she pulled the thread through the bloody flesh. She took a second stitch, then another and another. With each new piercing of his skin, Valentine waited for the numbness of familiarity to overcome her and ease her task. It never did. With each stitch, she winced, grimaced and chewed on her bottom lip until it nearly bled. It seemed an eternity to finish the first arm. When her task was finished, she found that a film of perspiration had sprung out across her forehead. She wiped it away with her sleeve.

Before she began on the second wrist, she went back to the bottle of brandy and this time took two long gulps of the warming liquid.

She discovered that his right arm was more badly lacerated than the left. In order to see her work more clearly she had to climb over his legs, onto the bed, where she crouched over his arm. The sun had moved enough that now his body lay in shadows. She twisted her torso and his arm into the remaining light. Blood encircled his wrist like a bracelet. She cleaned the wound and followed the same procedure as before. This was the arm where she could nearly see the wrist bone. Working on instinct, she made deep stitches below the flesh, joining muscle to muscle. Dread filled her brain as she worried that perhaps she should wait for the cook to recover. Again, a sixth sense banged in her head, urging her to proceed. She suddenly feared infection. The thought of Lord Hawkeston without a hand or arm was too repulsive an option for her to give it even a moment longer. Chewing on her bottom lip, she continued her work with patience and determination. If he could risk his life to save his crew, herself and her family, she could find enough courage to see this surgery through to the end. Luckily, the bleeding had long stopped. Had she been faced with a severed artery, she would not have had the proper knowledge to proceed. She thanked God and continued to sew and pray.

She tied the end of the thread three times for good measure, salved and bound the wounds in fresh, clean bandages, and then leaned back against the wall, suddenly depleted of all energy.

The combination of lack of sleep, seasickness and brandy caused Valentine's head to swim. She closed her eyes, saw the familiar tiny flickering white lights behind her eyelids, and quickly drifted off to sleep.

Justin awoke to find a woman in his bed. Since it was not the first occurrence of this kind in his life, he was less concerned about the woman than he was with the splitting pain in his head. It took long moments to organize his thoughts. He didn't remember the day, how he got to bed, or how it had come to pass that Valentine was with him. The dull, throbbing pain that rolled methodically up his forearm brought his memory into sharp focus.

He lifted his left arm and inspected the bandages that encircled his wrists. Then he looked down at Valentine.

She was curled in a heap on his right side with her head lying across his lap. Long silvery curls spilled over his thighs, blanketing them with shimmering light. One delicate hand rested on his knee, the other on his abdomen.

Justin was unable to resist the urge to touch her hair and stroke it. It spun around his fingers like silver rings. Her hair was like fine silk, he thought, nearly weightless in the possession of his hand. He pulled his fingers through it, watching the fine silver webs release him as they left their mark only on his memory. Even in his pain and half-conscious state, Justin was keenly aware of how different this woman was from the others he'd known. She was the first woman he'd met who didn't want him. In fact, she was very nearly repulsed by him. She'd certainly let him know that much in more ways than one.

He unraveled the bandage on his right wrist and inspected her handiwork. To his surprise, the stitches were meticulously sewn. The wound would heal with only a fine scar, if any at all. He doubted that the cook could have done as well as Valentine. She'd told him she had no nursing experience, and yet, somehow, her courage and strength had carried her through the ordeal.

What an enigma this woman was, he thought. He wondered, too, if he was willing to explore her mysteries.

Suddenly she stirred, and as she came awake, she moved her face back and forth in his lap as if it were a pillow. Justin was especially aware of the erotic rubbing. He wished it were intentional.

She yawned and moaned sleepily, stretching her arm across his abdomen. Her eyes were still closed and he could tell she was disoriented. Again she rolled her head and he felt himself come alive. Gone was the shooting pain in his wrists, the fatigue, the fever from dehydration, lack of sleep and food. His pain turned to pleasure as currents of fire ignited his loins. He placed his hand on her head and gently pressed her to him. He closed his eyes, and a low sensual groan rumbled deep in his throat.

The sound of his groan penetrated Valentine's sleep-filled mind and jolted her awake. She bolted to an upright position. She blinked and then rubbed the sleep from her eyes with her palm. She focused upon the pained and contorted look on Lord Hawkeston's face. Sympathy filled her voice and heart.

"Sir, is it painful?"

"Oh, you have no idea," he groaned low, feeling the power of his erection.

Valentine lifted her hand and placed it against his feverish forehead. "You're very hot."

"I know," he said as his eyelids lifted slowly.

"Is there anything I can do?" she asked, deeply concerned.

A voluptuous grin slid across his mouth. "There certainly is . . ." He touched her hand and moved it to his abdomen and began to slowly slide it downward. Suddenly he stopped. He looked into her eyes and saw innocence, purity of motive and genuine empathy for his condition. He realized he'd never looked into a woman's eyes and found these qualities.

"Tell me what I can do," she urged him. Valentine did not see the passion smoldering in his eyes. She did not feel the shift in his affections as if the earth had spun on its axis. She was blind to his needs, all of them. She only knew what she was feeling inside her. And her emotions were many. She wanted to tell him how serenely he'd slept. She wanted to kiss his closed eyelids and touch his cheek and brow with tenderness. She wished that their ill words had never passed between them. She wanted to know if there was another Lord Hawkeston living beneath the icy glares she'd come to expect from him. But she was afraid.

Huge deep brown pools blinked at him as she awaited his request. Bewildered by her altruism, he peered at her. "Bring the cook to me."

Valentine was wounded by his request. Obviously he did not trust her. She struggled with her disappointment, refusing to let it show. "Of course," she replied quickly and scrambled over his legs and off the bed. When she stood, she found she was dizzy from both her illness and the tension from the surgery she'd performed. She didn't want him to know of her weakness. She never wanted him to see her vulnerabilities whether they be physical or emotional. She placed her hand on the table for support while pretending to look around the cabin for something.

"Why do you tarry?" he croaked as new blasts of pain shot through his body.

"I thought I should return the salve," she explained, wounded a second time by his impatience with her.

She picked up the salve, the remainder of bandages, the needle and thread, and left the room. Valentine was only halfway down the corridor when anger stepped in to replace her sympathy. Her fists balled and her eyes danced with rage. She stomped rather than walked. New epithets for Lord Hawkeston raced through her brain like a litany. "Yard dog . . . contemptible lizard . . . heinous, bug-eyed *rat*," she mumbled as she approached the galley. She rapped sharply on the cook's door, pretending the surface was Lord Hawkeston's face.

"Come," the cook answered.

Valentine found him a new man. His face was no longer green. Instead, his fat cheeks were rosy again and he was busily stirring a huge pot of stew. Tantalizing aromas of cooking vegetables, freshly sliced oranges and baking bread filled the galley. To her surprise, Valentine found she was ravenously hungry.

"My lord requests your presence," she said, eyeing the stew. She watched as he lifted the spoon, tasted the thick brown gravy, and added more pepper.

"I'll attend to him at once," cook replied as he put the spoon on the wooden board. "I suppose he is as hungry as you appear to be, milady."

Valentine shook her head. "His wounds demand your attention."

"What wounds?"

"You were too ill last night and half unconscious yourself. I came for you, but I realized you were in no condition to attend him. Lord Hawkeston had lashed himself to the helm and—"

"Say no more! God in heaven." His eyes shot about the room.

Valentine held out her hands sheepishly. "You're looking for these?"

"How did you get them?"

"You gave them to me . . . and the brandy."

He chuckled under his breath. "I don't remember it, but at least I was aware enough to do that much. I'm sure he needed the brandy."

"Oh, it wasn't for him." She looked away from his piercing eyes. "The brandy was for me."

The cook roared and patted her on the back. "You have the makings of a great surgeon. I would have done the same myself."

Valentine's eyes opened wide in surprise. "You would?"

"Yes, milady. Now I'm off to inspect your handiwork. Although I have no doubts as to your expertise."

"Lord Hawkeston appears to have enough doubts for both of us."

The cook shook his head as he saw the despair in her eyes. He shrugged his shoulders solemnly and quit the room. He went straight to Lord Hawkeston's cabin and was admitted without ceremony.

"You wished me to see to your wounds, sir?"

Justin shook his head and smiled. "That won't be necessary. It seems that you may need to worry for your employ. I have inspected them myself and found naught to be wanting. I doubt you could have done as well as our Miss St. James."

"I am pleased to hear this."

"I should think so. It was not a pretty sight, nor an easy task. But I have need of nourishment. A great deal of it."

The cook smiled broadly and crossed his fat arms over

his huge stomach. "I have prepared a stew and biscuits."

"Bring them at once. And see to the others. As soon as I have my strength back, I must see to the crew."

"Mr. Henderson has everything well in hand, sir. And it appears that the only casualties are the passengers."

Justin's eyes widened in horror. "Was someone hurt?"

"Only in a manner of speaking. Seasickness, sir."

"That is to be expected. Very well." He waved the cook away. Then he paused. "And cook, not a word of my condition to anyone. I don't want them to know my weakness."

Perplexity knotted cook's brow. "Sir, the men think most highly of your sacrifice. They would understand."

"It's not so much the crew I'm concerned about, but my new family-to-be. Once we are in London, there is much about the Hawkestons they will learn. Our weaknesses are legendary. I don't want to add another to the list. I prefer that none of the St. Jameses know more than is necessary."

"Sir, I think they would understand—"

"Not a word, cook!" Justin snarled at him. He leaned his head back against the wall. "Milton St. James was more courageous than I could ever be. Their expectations are quite high, and deservedly so. It is bad enough that my fiancée has seen me like this. The less said, the better."

"But she will tell them."

"I can only pray that she will keep her mouth closed." And a true miracle it would be if she did, he chuckled to himself as the cook left the room. Justin also knew that heretofore, Valentine had not confided in her sister or aunt about their escapade the night of the ball. If she had, Victoria and Aunt Cherise would not be as accommodating to him as they were. He knew that he would already have experienced their scorn and wrath. As much as Valentine herself was to blame for the incident, he knew they would hold him accountable. In addition, Valentine had not mentioned the specifics of that night to him. It was as if she wanted to forget his kiss. Justin was unsure about her response. Was it that his kisses were so forgettable that they simply didn't matter to her? Or was it that he was one of many lovers and his kisses didn't measure up to the men who had gone before him? Both possibilities nearly drove him insane with anger.

He forced himself to think rationally. It was possible that Valentine would keep silent about sleeping together in his cabin. Her desire to maintain the appearance of propriety was on his side. It might be enough to ensure her silence.

In the galley, Valentine went to the stew, stirred it and tasted it. Her stomach rumbled loudly. If she was this hungry, she knew her family must also be in need of nourishment. She made a large pot of tea and readied a plate of biscuits, put them on a tray, and carried them to Aunt Cherise's cabin.

There was nothing to be done about Lord Hawkeston at the moment. He had made it painfully clear that he did not trust her in the least. He had not shown her one iota of appreciation for tending his wounds. Her earlier assessment of him had obviously been correct. He was heartless. There wasn't a drop of human blood running through his veins. Her father had always told her to trust her first impressions. He'd told her many times that those initial feelings were there for a reason. Father had been right.

Fortunately for Valentine, there was a lot of sea between them and London. Which meant she had blissful weeks in which to take solace before she would be forced into marriage and Lord Hawkeston's bed.

All she could do now was tend to her family. Her own hurt feelings would have to wait.

Chapter Six

Valentine found Victoria and Aunt Cherise so weak from illness and lack of nourishment that she had to feed them herself.

She placed a large plate of stew on the mahogany table in their cabin, and then poured cool water into a huge tin mug.

"Victoria, drink this." Valentine held the cup for her sister.

Victoria barely had the strength to put her hands on the cup. "Val, I can't."

"You can and you must," Valentine urged her. "You have to get your strength back. I need you to help me with Aunt Cherise."

Victoria's eyes felt hot and dry. She lifted her lids slowly and glanced at her beloved aunt.

Aunt Cherise was half asleep and half awake. She looked as if she were a hundred years old. Her white hair was disheveled and her skin pasty. She was covered with perspiration. Cherise had not only lost weight, but she looked as if she were half dead. Valentine was worried about her.

Victoria sipped the water slowly. "I've never felt this wretched in my life, Val."

"I know." Valentine stroked her sister's back while she drank. She remembered the feel of Lord Hawkeston's hand on her back earlier that morning. Somehow, the rhythm of movement had improved her well-being. Valentine realized she had not been sick to her stomach since then.

What kind of magician was he? Valentine didn't like the idea that she could actually learn something from Sir Snake, especially since she held knowledge of all kinds in high esteem. It was important for a person to constantly strive to improve oneself. How many times she remembered her father instructing her and Victoria on the importance of education. Yes, there was some kind of trick here that Lord Hawkeston had used on her. The difference between her skin color and Victoria's was three shades of green. Valentine's hands were pink again. She was able to sit erect whereas Victoria was still slumping over the cup. Valentine's energy was not only up to par, she was as good as new.

Valentine noticed that as she ran her hand up Victoria's back, her sister drank more deeply of the water. Her head lifted. Her eyelids fluttered as if she were just waking up. She smiled. "I feel better, Val."

"Maybe some of this stew will help you." Valentine let Victoria hold the cup while she took the plate of stew from the table.

She dipped the spoon into the stew, deciding to start with a chunk of potato, and screamed.

"*Aaahhh!*" Valentine dropped the plate on the floor.

Victoria's eyes popped open. "Valentine! What is it?"

Valentine threw one hand to her cheek and pointed with her other at the stew that was now splashed on the floor. "Maggots!" Valentine screamed.

Tiny little worms swam in the gravy.

"*Aaaahhhh!*" Victoria screamed as loudly as her sister. She jerked her knees up under her chin and scooted back on the bunk. She didn't want even her toes near the vile food.

Aunt Cherise heard the girls' screams through her lassitude. She was their protector. She must rescue them. She roused herself onto her elbows. Her mouth was dry. It was a struggle to speak. "Valentine . . . was right. He is trying to kill us. . . ." She plopped back down on the bed and fainted dead away.

That was all Valentine needed. She jumped to her feet. "That foul churl! That nefarious . . . sordid . . . ruthless ass!"

"Val!"

Valentine was still cursing when she looked at her sister. "Sorry. Asp."

Victoria only nodded.

"So, mass murder is his game now! My death isn't enough for him. Now he plans to kill my whole family!" She pushed up the ruffled sleeves of her gown. "Well, over my dead body!"

Victoria grimaced at the unintended pun.

Valentine sped out of the cabin with the force of a whirlwind.

Victoria shook her head. Not for one minute did she believe Lord Hawkeston was trying to kill her or her aunt. Victoria liked to believe that somewhere under Justin's crusty, aloof exterior, he had as big a heart as her Andrew.

Andrew thought the world of Justin already. Victoria was coming to like him, too. She wished Valentine could see him the way they did.

She looked down at the worms as they crawled over each other in the stew. She shivered. She didn't know what was happening on this ship, but it was a sure bet that no one could stir up a hornet's nest like her sister. She just hoped it was worth the trouble.

Valentine's fists were balled as she walked into the galley and found no one about. She inspected the flour bin, the sacks of sugar, the salted meats, the glass jars filled with brine. She rooted through the small cupboards and wooden boxes filled with vegetables, fruits and other staples. She carefully checked the cooking utensils. She inspected the insides of the small clay baking ovens.

She could hear laughter coming from the captain's dining room next door. She flung open the door and placed her hands on her hips. She felt invincible with her new evidence of Justin's murderous plot.

Justin sat at the head of the table. To his right was Mr. Henderson, the first mate. To his left was Mr. Midgeon, the helmsman. Rabb, the thirteen-year-old cabin boy who had brought her fresh water during the storm, sat next to Mr. Henderson. The cook stood behind Mr. Henderson lading the stew into plates.

The cook had stopped mid-motion when she barged into the room.

Valentine had no idea she was the first woman ever to set foot in this room and that her act was considered bad luck by the crew.

Everyone at the table gasped at her presence.

Justin glared a warning at her.

She glared right back. She was face to face with her would-be murderer. She wondered if any of the crew had any concept of the magnitude of his villainy. His

. . . Suddenly her thoughts halted. Her eyes flew to the ladle filled with stew that the cook was about to pour into Mr. Henderson's plate. Just over the edge of the ladle, she saw the vile white worms.

Quickly she yanked the spoon out of Rabb's hand and threw it to the floor. She overturned his plate. Then Mr. Henderson's plate went sailing to the floor, followed by Justin's and Mr. Midgeon's.

Justin bolted to his feet. "Have you gone mad?"

"Don't eat that foul filth!" She pointed at the worms and then whirled to point her finger at the cook.

"It's poisoned!"

Justin's eyes rolled back in his head. "It is no such thing."

"Really?" she asked and stomped haughtily over to the cook. She grabbed the ladle out of his hand. She turned up her nose and refused to look at the maggots another time. She shoved the ladle in Justin's face. "Look there! Are those maggots or are they not?"

Justin looked at the tiny squirming white worms. "Thunderation! What the hell is going on here?"

Rabb turned white, threw his hand over his mouth, doubled over and pushed himself away from the table. He raced from the room.

"I'd like to ask you the same thing!" Valentine demanded. "I thought you were trying to murder my family. Now I see that once again I have saved your life."

"Milady, you have never saved my life," Justin reminded her.

"Don't be a stickler for details. I'll grant you this is the first time then. Nevertheless, I have saved you."

Justin eyed the disgusting stew. "I'll give you that." His eyes went to his cook.

"Did you prepare this meal?" Justin demanded.

"Yes, sir." The cook's eyes darted about the room.

There was noplace to run. He was on a ship.

"Well, then, man. What is your explanation of this?"

"I . . . uh . . ." The cook's eyes were filled with terror. It was obvious he could not escape. But if he told them the truth, the captain would hang him from the yardarm.

Valentine looked at the cook's hangdog expression and guessed she knew why he'd done it.

"Ignorance," Valentine said as the cook stuttered and searched for an alibi. "My papa used to tell us that ignorance was more often a killer than any other single motive mankind could dream up." She pointed an accusing finger at the cook. "You, sir, are no cook."

"What?" Justin's eyes went from Valentine to his cook.

The cook dropped his head sheepishly.

Valentine continued, "I know nothing of your business on this ship. Will you attest to that, Lord Hawkeston?"

"Yes." He groaned at her dramatics but let her continue. He was as curious as the others to see where this was leading.

"I have never been on this ship before and I do not know who has been in your employ for years. Nor do I know whom you have recently hired. Correct?"

"Yes. And get on with it."

"This is the cook's first voyage." Her black eyes were damning as she glared at the man. "Not only has he never sailed before, he's never cooked a meal in his life. Isn't that right, cook?"

"She doesn't know what she's talkin' about, Cap'n," the cook said defensively.

"I know exactly what I'm saying. When we went onshore in Sicily, I heard Lord Hawkeston order you to take on food supplies. He gave you a great deal of money to buy these supplies.''

"Sir, I—'' the cook tried to interrupt.

"Lord Hawkeston, I believe that your cook is also a thief. He spent only half the money you gave him and pocketed the rest. Before coming in here, I searched the galley. There are only half the supplies there should be for a voyage of this length and for this size crew. Half the vegetables are rotted and the meats are foul. Frankly, my lord, if we do not stop for supplies soon, there will be nothing to eat in less than two days.''

"She's lying, Cap'n!'' the cook shouted, his fat cheeks aflame.

"I'd say she presents a fairly strong case. All I have to do is walk in that galley and see for myself,'' Justin said.

Valentine walked up to the cook. She was not afraid of this fearsome-looking man with arms the size of hams and a pockmarked face. There was fear in his hazel eyes. He reminded her of a frightened animal. One thing her father had taught her was that desperate people do desperate things. "You didn't really mean to hurt any of us, now did you?'' she asked with compassion in her voice.

"I . . . I didn't.'' He shook his head. "You're right. I'm not a cook. I'm a cabinetmaker. A good cabinetmaker. But I've not been able to find work. I heard that the English would pay fortunes for Italian craftsmanship. I have no family left. My mother and father are long dead. I never married. No woman wants a man who looks like me. I have only these hands that can make beauty out of wood. I had no money for the voyage to England. Then I learned that Lord Hawkeston was hiring on this ship. I know nothing of sailing. The only position I could get was that of the cook. So I lied to Mr. Henderson and I got the job. When I went onshore, I realized

I could buy cheap foods and take the money for myself when I got to England. It was like you said. I was desperate.''

As Valentine listened to his story, her heart filled with sympathy. Unconsciously, she put her hand on his huge forearm.

Justin was impressed. Her theatrics aside, he had to admit she'd done a damn good job with her deductions. And she'd brought out a grown man's confession. However, this was *his* ship and *his* crew. He leveled his gaze at the cook.

''There will be retribution to make,'' he said to the cook.

''I understand,'' the cook replied.

Valentine turned to Justin. ''May I have a word with you, my lord?''

''No.'' Justin sensed she would try to talk him out of having the man put ashore, which was what he intended to do. And he had to find himself a decent cook and fresh supplies. Damn! This mess would cost him another day at sea when he'd already lost two days due to the storm.

Valentine turned back to the cook and whispered, ''What is your name?''

''Alfredo Thomas. My mother was Italian. My father an English merchant.''

She nodded. She turned back to Justin. ''I realize you intend to flog this man—''

''Flog?'' Justin was amazed at the lengths to which her imagination could carry her.

''Flog?'' Alfredo gasped. ''Flog?'' His eyes began to roll back in his head. He looked as if he would faint.

Valentine smiled. ''Ah! I see that you do not intend to flog Alfredo.''

Alfredo's head rocked back and forth on his thick

neck. He tried to steady himself. It was not as bad as he thought.

Valentine continued. "That being the case, Lord Hawkeston, may I suggest indenturing him?"

Justin shook his head. He would never learn to follow her line of reasoning. "For what purpose?"

"This man is a cabinetmaker. Upon the event of our marriage, we will be taking up residence together, will we not?"

"Yes. Yes," Justin said.

"I will require armoires, bureaus, a rocking chair for the children I intend to have one day. I will need cribs, chifforobes. Then there are tables, chairs and any number of sideboards, consoles—"

"I get the point. Who will I use for a cook in the meantime?"

"I'll cook," she said winningly.

Every man in the room broke out into raucous laughter, including Alfredo Thomas. Valentine glared at them. Then she stuck her chin up in the air and swiftly walked past them. They were doubling over with laughter. Mr. Henderson was actually clutching his ribs. Justin had tears running down his cheeks.

Valentine expelled an enormous sigh. "Well, then. I suppose I will just have to make all of you eat your words."

She pushed open the mahogany door to the galley and closed it quietly behind her.

Chapter Seven

Valentine's first foray into a kitchen had been at the age of five. Her father's business had not gone well that year and he'd been forced to fire the house staff. Milton St. James had instructed Aunt Cherise to explain their reduced circumstances to the girls. Because he was a proud man, Milton did not want the neighbors in their fashionable neighborhood to know the truth. Aunt Cherise explained to him that once the staff was let go, word would be out in a wink. And it was.

Milton and Aunt Cherise taught the girls to make do and to keep their heads proudly aloft. He told them all that they would not always be poor. About that, he was correct. The children discovered that their father's income was never to be stable. Some years there was plenty, some years not so plenty. But as long as he was alive, they had enough to eat, clothes on their backs, and plenty of love to keep them warm and hopeful.

Valentine and Victoria assured their father and Aunt Cherise that they would do all they could to pitch in. They cut back on their clothing allowances, learned to live with a bit less coal and wood in the winter, and learned to cook.

Valentine found two chickens that had not yet spoiled. After stoking the underbelly of the stove with wood and lighting the fire, she set a pot of water on to boil. She added salt, cracked pepper and sage leaves. She scoured the galley for the rest of the spices she would need for cooking and was appalled to find none. She supposed that until they landed, it was just as well she did not prepare highly seasoned food, since so many were still recovering from seasickness. She found carrots, onions and potatoes and chopped them up.

When the chicken had cooked through, she deboned the birds, tossed the bones in a second pot, and chopped the meat into tiny bits. Then she skimmed off the fat and residue and threw it away. While the chicken soup cooked she made a fine dough and rolled it out flat between two floured linen cloths. She used a sharp knife to make thin strips of dough, the way she'd seen the pasta makers do in Venice.

She mixed yeast, sugar, salt and oil with flour and placed huge round balls of dough near the stove to rise for the bread they would eat that night.

She sorted the rotten fruits from the good ones. She threw the spoiled vegetables overboard.

While the soup finished cooking, Valentine made a mental list of the supplies she would buy when they reached shore. Later, she would take a page from her diary and write everything down. Then she would double-check the list to make certain she'd missed nothing.

Valentine served her family first.

Victoria was clearly feeling better. She'd bathed herself and dressed in a clean muslin gown when Valentine entered the room. It wasn't until that moment that Valentine realized the room reeked of vomit.

"Victoria, do you think you are well enough to help me clean this room? The linens are putrefied. Aunt Cherise can never get better in these reeking quarters."

"I know what you mean. I opened the window and that has helped some. We'll strip the bed and take the linens to the galley and ask the cook to clean them."

Valentine shook her head. "The cook was fired."

"What? Then who made this soup?"

Valentine shrugged her shoulders and smiled sheepishly.

Victoria looked at the perfectly clear consommé and the precisely sliced vegetables in her bowl. Her eyes flew open in shock. "He's cast you into the kitchens? My God, Val. He's really gone too far this time."

"Now who's being theatrical? I love to cook and you know it. I went there of my own accord."

"Valentine, that was a ridiculous thing to do. You're to become Lady Hawkeston. You can't be cooking and scrubbing pots. I mean, I understood when it was necessary for us to do things like that, but we were children."

"I suppose you'd rather eat maggots and weavils and all the other atrocious things I found in that galley."

"Yech!" Victoria's face twisted into a grimace. "I see your point."

Valentine went to the bed and sat next to Aunt Cherise. She touched her forehead and found it had cooled. She smoothed the wiry strands of gray hair from Aunt Cherise's face. "Please wake up, Aunt Cherise. I have some lovely soup for you."

Aunt Cherise moaned. "My head hurts." She languidly lifted her arm and put it over her eyes. Then, as if it were too much weight for her to bear, she dropped it back to the bed.

"You're dehydrated. You must eat," Valentine urged.

Valentine gathered the pillows from Victoria's bunk and placed them against the wall so that Aunt Cherise could sit up. Valentine spoon-fed her aunt.

Aunt Cherise ate slowly, but with each spoonful her appetite returned. She finished the entire bowl of soup.

"I think you liked it." Valentine smiled at her aunt.

"It needed some rosemary to perk it up."

"I couldn't agree with you more, and when we pull into shore, I shall make that the first of my purchases."

"Shore?" Victoria asked, finishing her soup. "We aren't scheduled to put in to shore."

"Well, we are now!" Valentine said triumphantly. "There's not a bar of sweet soap on this ship, let alone anything to clean linens with." She shook her head. "I just don't know what Justin was thinking of when he prepared this ship for departure."

Aunt Cherise wiped her mouth with the edge of the sheet. "I believe his mind was on other matters, Valentine." She raised her eyebrow accusingly.

Valentine frowned. "Hmmm. Remind me to ignore you the next time we are in a life-and-death storm."

"Valentine! Aunt Cherise has had a very difficult time," Victoria reminded her sister.

"It was my soup that put her back on her feet, and already she's siding with the enemy."

Victoria rolled her eyes. "You are incorrigible!"

Valentine took the dirty dishes. "I have to feed the crew. You help Aunt Cherise, the traitor, get bathed and dressed the best you can. We'll work on these awful linens later."

Valentine left the room not believing she was actually

looking forward to going back to the dingy galley. But she was.

She kneaded the dough a second time. She pulled the dough into long loaves and set it to rise. She went into the captain's dining room and found Alfredo sitting by himself amidst a pile of dirty dishes. He looked positively glum.

"What's the matter, Alfredo?" she asked.

"I suppose I should thank you for getting me the job of cabinetmaker. And I suppose I should thank you for saving me from the cat-o'-nine-tails. And I suppose I should thank you for taking over my duties in the galley, but . . ."

Valentine was smiling to herself as he listed her accomplishments. She hadn't realized she'd done quite so much, but she had. She allowed a glowing sense of self-satisfaction to warm her insides.

She looked at Alfredo. Why wasn't he smiling? "But what?"

"It's unmanly to be exposed by a woman."

Valentine didn't know whether to laugh or to slap him. "You don't regret being caught, then? Only that you were caught by a simpleminded woman?"

"Well, yes."

Valentine put her hands on her hips to keep from throwing things at him. Plates, statues, chairs. Any object would do. The bigger the better. Maybe he'd get some sense knocked into him. She was beginning to think the only intelligent man she'd ever met in her life was her father. Lord, how she missed his wit!

"Alfredo, help me clear these dishes, please. And then would you tell Lord Hawkeston and the others I am serving?"

"Yes, ma'am."

*   *   *

Lord Hawkeston, Mr. Henderson, Mr. Midgeon and Rabb inhaled their soup and called for seconds before Valentine had finished ladling out the first round.

They made no comment as to the taste, the tenderness of the bird or the crispness of the vegetables. She knew they were all half-starved and probably would have eaten Alfredo's maggots by this time.

Valentine went back to the galley and finished making a second and larger pot of vegetable soup for the crew. She wrapped a linen towel around the handle of the pot and handed it to Alfredo, who was to distribute the soup in tin mugs to the men on deck.

When she returned to the dining room to ask if anyone wanted fruit, the room was empty save for Lord Hawkeston.

He looked at her and smiled.

She smiled back, patiently waiting for her accolades. They didn't come.

"I will not have my fiancée cooking in the galley like one of the hired hands," he said, rising and pushing his chair away from him.

Valentine frowned. "Victoria said you might feel this way."

"It's not proper," he said flatly.

"Proper? When has anything between us been proper?" Valentine pushed a long lock of silvery hair away from her face. It fell back over her eye. She glared at him. What a pompous one he was, she thought. Here they had been tossed around the ocean for days, and then served up rotten food, and he was worrying about propriety. She was exhausted trying to figure him out.

"Quite right," he said, clasping his hands behind his back. He glanced at her out of the corner of his eye and then turned his head away. He went to the window and looked out.

He had to keep moving about, he told himself, to keep from taking her in this very room on top of this very table. All the saints in heaven weren't going to be enough to keep him off her. How did she do it? he wondered. She'd been just as sick as everyone else. He'd seen her green complexion earlier that day. Her black eye had turned a dark purple, but the curve of the bruise followed the line of her lid and only seemed to make her eyes look more intense. Her hair streamed down her sweaty neck and chest and clung to her throat like silver streams of light.

She was more breathtakingly beautiful at that moment than she'd been the night of the countess's party.

That night! God! That night! Would he never get the memory of it out of his mind?

He wanted to go to her and hold her in his arms and thank her for saving his wrists from infection. He'd seen gangrene set in before and knew he could have lost a hand. She'd saved himself and his key staff from being the victims of food poisoning, which would have cost him dearly. She'd routed the truth out of Alfredo and rather than allow Alfredo to be put ashore where he would do himself and no one any good, she'd negotiated a bargain that would give him enough furniture to fill a mansion. Two mansions!

And the devil of it was she could cook. Granted, he'd only tasted her soup, but he'd never tasted better in his life. The noodles were so light he thought they would float out of his bowl. If she could do that with odds and ends, what could she do with choice roasts, imported spices, cocoa, smooth butters and fine cheeses?

He hated like hell to give her her due. She was a fiery devil, and if he let out his rein on her, she would take over his ship completely. That he would never stand for. A man had his pride. His dignity. His honor.

"I was only thinking of yourself."

"Me? You were putting my interests before yours? I don't believe it," she said boldly.

"Actually, yours and mine. When we're back in London I wouldn't want word of your 'galley days' to leak to the ton."

"Oh, ho! The ton. I do remember hearing that you are a favorite of the ton. Of course, that was all I heard about you before our engagement was announced. That and the stories . . ." She was about to blast him with the gossip his mistresses had spread about him. Then she thought better of it. She might need that ammunition later.

"What stories?"

"Nothing. It isn't important. What is important is that you think some idle gossip is more significant than our survival here. I should think you would be glad to have me take over for you."

"Frankly, I am." He unclasped his hands and went back to the table. This time he placed his hands on the high back of one of his red velvet upholstered chairs.

Valentine couldn't believe her ears. "You are?"

The effect of her exuberant smile on him was amazing even to himself. He couldn't be certain, but to Justin it seemed that the entire room had lit up. "Yes." He coughed and cleared his throat. Did she have any idea of her radiance? Her eyes were shining at him like black pearls. They were so deep, he thought. He wondered if she consciously used them to cast this spell over him.

"I would like to strike a bargain with you, Valentine."

"What kind of bargain?" she asked, her eyes revealing her suspicion.

"This is not an easy voyage, though it isn't dangerous either." Then he laughed to himself. "I guess we've already proved that any ocean trip is potentially dangerous. At any rate, though I don't like the idea of my fiancée working in the galley, I see no way around it for the time being. Alfredo certainly can't handle the job, but I want you to use him as an assistant. I will not have him idle. I've told him he is to take all his orders from you."

Valentine remembered her earlier conversation with Alfredo. The poor man. It was going to be his fate to learn to eat his condescending words about women. She chuckled to herself.

"I'm amusing you?" He thrust his arms out and looked at the ceiling and then the walls. He looked back at her with a quizzical expression.

"No, my lord. It was something else that amused me. I'm sorry I interrupted your train of thought."

"I've asked the navigator and Mr. Midgeon to take us to the next port of call for supplies."

"I've already started my list," she said happily.

"Very good. If you wouldn't mind, please feel free to make an assessment of whatever else you feel you might need."

"There are some laundry items and beeswax, wicks—"

Justin waved his hand. "Don't overload me with details. Just see to it," he said. "Is that agreeable to you?"

"Yes, my lord."

"Good." He nodded curtly to her. "That's all I have to say. You may leave."

Valentine rose and pushed her chair next to the table. "Justin, I like working with you," she said softly and left the room.

Chapter Eight

They docked in Barcelona. Being an educated woman, Valentine was anxious not only to shop the markets but to investigate the historical sights of the city. She wanted to see the Plaza del Rey and stand in the courtyard surrounded by medieval towers where Christopher Columbus had announced his discovery of the New World. Valentine had always thought that anything Spanish sounded incredibly romantic. Often she'd dreamed of Gypsies and roguish vagabond men who danced around fires to the sound of tambourines and flutes. She wondered what it would be like to be held in the arms of a hot-blooded, romantic Spaniard. He would be huge, she thought, with arms like steel and a chest so expansive she could get lost in it. His hair would be black as night and long, like a stallion's mane. He would have stormy dark eyes that flashed with passion . . . but only for her.

Every time he looked at her, he would hunger for her.

He would write melancholy poems for her and sing midnight seranades for her. He would do anything for her . . . die for her.

He would be everything Lord Justin Hawkeston was not. But for now, Valentine thought morosely, Justin was the one she must deal with.

Because the ship was scheduled to dock at dawn, the noise the crew made topside had awakened Valentine at five o'clock. She heard Rabb knock on Justin's door bringing him fresh water, towels and coffee. Valentine knew she must hurry or Justin would be so busy with the crew she would not get a chance to speak with him until later. Valentine was an organized type of person. She needed Justin's approval of her shopping list and the money to make the purchases.

She quickly sprang from her bed and grabbed her peignoir. It stuck on the rough peg. She yanked it. She realized that in her haste, the top closure ribbon had torn off. She could mend it later, but for now there was no hope for it. She stuck her arms into the peignoir. She started out the door and glanced at her reflection in the small oval mirror on the wall above the chest of drawers. Lord! She looked like a hag with her hair flying all over the place. She knew she should have braided it before she went to bed, but it had been such an exhausting day. She frankly couldn't remember putting on her cotton nightgown, much less crawling into bed.

She heard Rabb leaving Justin's cabin.

"Oh, bother!" she said to her reflection. Her hair would just have to do.

She tapped on Justin's cabin door.

Justin was shaving when he heard the knock. He was wearing his trousers but that was all. "Come."

He glanced toward the door as it slowly opened. "Did you forget something, Rabb?" Justin lifted the straight razor to his face and stopped in mid-motion.

She stood in the doorway with peach-colored dawn light blushing her body. She was dressed in a transparent gown and robe through which he could see her pink nipples. She clutched the thin robe at her neck, making a show of propriety, he guessed. The position of her arm only served to push her breast forward and up over the top of the low-cut nightgown underneath.

The morning light illuminated her silver tendrils, making her look like an angel. Her face was still puffy from sleep, rendering her childlike and vulnerable. But there was nothing innocent about those full pink lips. All too easily he remembered what it was like to kiss those lips and taste her sweet tongue. He recalled the exotic dance she had performed with her tongue in his mouth. He could only dream about what else he would like those sexy lips to do to him. Unconsciously he licked his lips.

He tasted soap.

"Ugh!" He spit it out. He looked back at her.

What was he thinking? She was no angel. She was doing this to him on purpose! Just look at her standing there in that diaphanous gown. All he wanted right now was to lock himself in this room with her, kiss every inch of her tempting body, and bury himself deep inside her . . .

"My lord, I need a word with you," Valentine said, placing her hand against the door jamb. She had never seen a man without clothes on. She had certainly not seen Justin without a shirt, barefoot, and his trousers hanging so perilously low on his hips. Why, another inch and he would reveal himself. She tried not to look at the flat planes of his stomach and lower to his abdomen where a patch of blond hair sprouted. She told herself things such as the tight muscles of his ribcage did not matter. She was not in the least bit interested in the

115

bulging muscles in his arms, shoulders and chest. That chest! Even her outrageous fantasies had not dreamed up a chest so large and well sculpted.

She felt faint. She was definitely going to swoon right in front of Justin. She needed to calm herself. She must not look at his body. She raised her eyes to his.

He was glaring at her with such coldness that she shivered. Had she been standing in the middle of the North Sea she couldn't have been any colder. She could feel chills race down her spine and up her thighs. She shifted her weight, trying to shake off the intense feeling of dislike he emanated.

What was the matter with him? he thought. Why not beckon the harlot in? Why not bed her and be done with it?

Because she is to be your wife. Fool! he scolded himself. "What is it, Valentine?"

Valentine wished he would stop shaving. She wished she didn't have to watch the morning light play against his muscles as they rippled with each movement. She must have been crazy to be dreaming of a roguish Spaniard when Justin was here in the next room. She stood just inside the door, but she could smell the scent of spicy soap even from this distance. She wanted to nuzzle her face in his neck as she'd done on the gondola when he'd been Baldassare.

She moved a step closer. Then another step. She was still more than a yard away, but she stood behind him. God help her, she wanted to kiss him again. She wanted to walk up to him right now and put her arms around him, touch his belly and his . . .

"I . . ." Her mouth went dry. She couldn't speak.

Justin glanced at her reflection in the mirror. She had moved closer to him. He could smell the scent of rose, that scent he'd come to associate with Valentine. Her woman scent was heady.

He nicked himself. "Damnation!" He tossed the razor onto the marble-topped chest. He spun around and glared at her. "Out with it, Miss St. James. I haven't got all day."

Valentine gave him a curious look. "Are you always so grouchy when you awake?"

"No," he retorted quickly. "Yes! Damn! Please say what you have to say and then remove yourself."

Valentine hadn't been prepared for such a mercurial change in his mood. "Didn't you sleep well?"

He ground his teeth. "Valentine . . ."

She stuck her chin up in the air. "Very well. I'm here about the supplies. Here's my list." She had to drop the handhold she had on the neck of her robe to reach in her pocket. Her left breast nearly popped over the top of the nightgown.

Justin groaned. But he kept his eyes on her breast.

"Here," she said, handing it to him.

He quickly looked it over. Actually, he couldn't see anything in front of his eyes except her breast. He handed it back to her. "It all seems in order."

Justin turned around and opened the bureau drawer. He took out a small burlap bag tied with a burgundy cord. "There's more than enough money in there to buy what you need. Bring me back the rest when you finish."

Valentine took the money and smiled. The bag felt quite heavy to her. She knew that with his kind of riches, this was probably nothing to him. She curtsied to him, hoping that his foul mood would pass soon.

Justin had to look at the ceiling when she curtsied. Not only could he see the expanse of her voluptuous breasts but he could see down further to the small rounded abdomen and further to a soft triangle of blond fuzz.

"Valentine!" he boomed angrily. "Please let me finish my shaving. I would appreciate it if you would leave now."

"Certainly, my lord," she said and turned to walk out of the cabin.

"Three, four, five, six . . ." Justin had to count to himself. He was turning into a barbarian before his own eyes.

She reached the door and looked over her shoulder at him. He was furiously angry at her. She didn't know what she'd done, but it must have been something horrific, because he looked as if he would rip the room apart.

Justin looked into Valentine's fearful dark eyes. He stalked to the door. Better she be afraid of him than for him to fall prey to her wiles. He took hold of the door.

She smiled.

He shut the door in her face.

Justin nearly doubled over with the hardest, most painful erection he'd had in his life. God's blood, that woman would drive him insane yet!

Valentine quickly padded her bare feet back to her cabin, shut the door and locked it. She couldn't for the life of her imagine what had caused Justin to act so surly. She, for one, intended to cut a wide path around him today.

The seaside markets were teeming with activity. Alfredo accompanied Valentine, Victoria and Andrew while they shopped. Aunt Cherise was still not feeling well enough to spend the day on shore. However, she did dress and had accepted a luncheon invitation with Mr. Henderson and Justin on board ship. Valentine had prepared a mixture of fruits and fresh bread. Since it was the last of the edible food on board, Valentine thought they had docked at Barcelona none too soon.

"I don't understand why His Lordship did not come with us, today," Victoria said, taking Andrew's arm in hers and raising her parasol to the sun with the other hand.

"Dearest, Lord Hawkeston has a great deal on his mind. There was severe damage to the hull that he intends to have repaired with Mr. Midgeon's help."

"Damage?" Valentine asked. "Why didn't he tell me about it?"

"In only a few short days in his employ, Valentine, I have learned that Lord Hawkeston is a man of many secrets. He is closed-mouthed about a great many things. His business interests are varied and widespread. It is no easy task simply familiarizing myself with the books he's given me so far. And this, I am led to understand, is only a small percent of what awaits me in London."

"I know you'll handle everything brilliantly," Victoria said to Andrew.

Valentine opened her own parasol. "If you ask me, Lord Hawkeston should be pleased to have you, Andrew. You are such an even-tempered man. Which is more than I can say of His Lordship," Valentine said with a frown.

"Whatever do you mean, Valentine?" Victoria asked.

"This morning he nearly bit my head off when I asked him for the money I would need today. Gracious, he was foul!"

Victoria eyed her sister. She knew Valentine well enough to know that she'd done something to set Lord Hawkeston off. There was no mistaking the sparks that flared between the two. How she wished Valentine wouldn't press her luck. "Let's not think about him today, Val. Let's just have a wonderful time in this beautiful place. Hmmm?''

Valentine hated it when Vicki played nursemaid to her. But for the sake of peace, she decided she would let it go.

Valentine had made up her mind to look for a few more things than were on her list. They would be difficult to find, she knew. But it was her belief that if she couldn't find them here in this mysterious and sensual city, she never would.

The market stalls were beautifully decorated with bright winter flowers. Even the fish vendor had buckets of greens and flowers circling his canvas tent. Valentine ordered crates of oranges, lemons, grapes and olives. She bought onions, garlic, tomatoes and squash. She paid handsomely for flour, wheat and barley with which she would make breads and soups. She bought lentils and salted pork, hams and bacon. Eggs were cheap. Brown sugar from the West Indies was outrageous, so she bought only a little. She supplemented the sugar with three gallons of honey.

Victoria was intrigued with the brightly colored materials she found. The cottons were tightly woven and felt like satin, and she marveled to Andrew how exotic it would be to have a gown made of such bright reds, magentas, indigos and purples. Andrew told her she could only wear the dress for him. And when she agreed, he bought the fabric.

Valentine and Alfredo inspected the plucked chickens and roasted geese. They wandered further into the main marketplace where only the locals shopped. Here there seemed bargains galore, Valentine thought.

She found exquisite wrought iron candlebras and huge blown glass hurricane lamps. In the next stall she found beeswax, wicks and candles. She asked the toothless old woman who owned the stall where she would find spices and herbs. She had a difficult time making her wishes known to the woman. Valentine's Italian was nearly flawless and her French was good but her Spanish was only rudimentary.

"Elana!" The old woman pointed to a faded red and white striped tent across the way. "Sí! Elana!" The old woman smiled broadly and nodded her head.

Valentine turned to Alfredo. "I don't want them to deliver the candles to the ship. Instead, would you please gather them now? I don't trust candlemakers. They seem to always switch the unbroken tapers for broken ones or ones with faulty wicks. Do you mind?"

"Lord Hawkeston said that I should stay with you."

"Good heavens! You can see that tent from here. I'll be right there. When you finish, I'll meet you there, if that will satisfy you."

"It does," he said flatly.

Valentine shook her head. Men! What a bother they were, always having to look over one's shoulder. They weren't happy unless they were reading one's very thoughts.

Valentine walked toward the tent the old woman had indicated. She could smell basil, sage, cumin and cinnamon even from a distance. But would Elana have what Valentine was looking for?

Elana was in her early thirties, with streaming hair as black as a raven's wing. Her eyes were brown, but not as dark as Valentine's. Her cheekbones were so high and sharp they looked as if they'd been slashed into her face. Her nose was long and not pretty at all. It was a powerful nose that could sniff out enemies and smell money. Her skin was brown as a berry and smooth as marble. Her lips looked as if they'd been reddened with dye.

Elana was tall and very voluptuous. Her hips were

twice Valentine's and so were her breasts. She wore a low-cut cotton blouse with long sleeves and a muticolored skirt that was sewn in tiers. On her feet she wore gleaming black leather riding boots. In her ears she wore long gold chains studded with garnets and topaz.

Valentine knew in an instant she was looking at a Gypsy woman. She believed that here she would find what she was looking for.

"Elana?"

"Sí?" Elana smiled at Valentine. She made no pretense of the survey she took of Valentine. Elana's dark eyes scoured every inch of Valentine's face. She even went so far as to place Valentine's chin between her thumb and forefinger. She twisted Valentine's face to the sun, turned it to the left and then to the right. "English?"

"Yes!" Valentine replied indignantly.

"Hmmm." Elana dropped Valentine's face. "You come to me. What you want?" Elana asked curtly in broken English.

Valentine looked behind her to make certain Alfredo was still back at the candlemaker's tent. "I want some oils."

"For a man?" Elana smiled a knowing but wicked grin.

"Well, yes. . . . No." Valentine had never been so flustered in her life.

"How you want him? You want his blood to be hot? You need mimosa, cassia, myrtle and myrrh. But I no got."

"You haven't?" Valentine's hopes were dashed. She was terribly anxious to have these oils she'd read about in her father's books. She knew she could never apply them directly to him, no matter how delicious the

thought was, but she intended to slip them to him surreptitiously.

"It's February. Shipments are slow." Elana picked
her teeth with a long fingernail. "You are virgin!" Elana
said the word as if it were a curse. "Those oils are too
much for virgin. You go slow. Warm up slowly. That's
what you need." Elana poked Valentine's chest with her
finger. Then she stuck her finger in the air. "Elana have
what virgin need."

Elana ducked out of sight and then popped back with
a wooden tray of brightly colored vials.

Valentine nearly lost her breath looking at the oils
she'd dreamed about. It was a treasure trove of aphro-
disiacs!

Elana smiled sagaciously. "This angelica." She
pulled out a honey-colored vial. "This ginger. Fenu-
greek. Jasmine. Neroli. Savory. Rose maroc. Ylang-
ylang. Hyssop. Juniper. Peppermint. Rosemary. Sandalwood."

"How much?" Valentine asked.

Elana smiled. "You got gold crown? British?"

"That's outrageous! I'm not going to pay that for one
tiny vial!"

Elana leaned over the table. "You should learn . . .
put a high price on virginity."

Valentine was shocked. "I'll give you the gold
crown."

Elana smiled.

Valentine grinned back. "For all the vials."

Elana's eyes were wide as saucers. She feigned shock.
"You rob me! You Gypsy!"

Valentine knew she had her. "And I want the formula
you would use to make a love potion. And if it doesn't
work I will personally come back here and wring your
neck."

"You no come back here. You never come back to Barcelona. It not your destiny."

Valentine noticed that Elana's eyes had a faraway look. Was she telling her fortune? "What is my destiny?"

Elana seemed to be in a trance. "I see much heartbreak . . . so sad. Your father, he come to me. He say he love you. He tell you he watch over you. He sorry."

Valentine pressed her hand to her cheek. How could Elana know about her father? How could the Gypsy know her heart was broken when he'd died and she'd learned she was to wed Lord Hawkeston? Elana must be a witch. Valentine couldn't wait to hear more.

"I see a man. Big man. I see a hawk over his head."

Valentine gasped. "Hawkeston."

"He hurt you. He try to kill you. There is much danger ahead for you." Elana suddenly stopped. "I no look anymore." She looked down at the vials as if to get her bearings in the real world. "Take all the vials."

"Do you mean it?"

Elana peered into Valentine's eyes. "You will need more than potions to help you."

Valentine did not like negativity of any sort and she especially didn't like it in her fortune teller. "Tell me how to use them."

Instantly Elana was back to business. "What kind of man is he? Sad? Slow to arouse? Depressed? Faraway and distant?"

"Faraway and distant. Definitely. He's like ice."

"Ah!" Elana's eyes were wide with her superior knowledge. "I know that kind. This recipe works good. One drop savory. Four drops ylang-ylang. Four drops ginger. Nine drops clary sage."

Valentine memorized the formula quickly as she heard Alfredo's lumbering footfalls approaching behind her. "Quickly, do you have any other advice?"

Elana placed her hand on top of Valentine's. "No matter, listen to the heart. The heart never lie." Elana winked at her.

Alfredo stood next to Valentine.

Valentine pretended to be finishing an order. "I'll need cinnamon sticks, vanilla bean, if you have it. Basil, sage, rosemary. Those dried bunches over there will do. One of each, I think."

Valentine looked at Alfredo who was loaded down with bundles. "I'm almost finished."

"Yes, milady," he said, trying not to pay attention to the beads of sweat forming on his brow. The mid-morning sun was beginning to beat down. Alfredo had never been able to stand the heat. He would be glad to get back on board and be under way again.

Valentine paid Elana, thanked her and left.

Valentine never saw Elana make the sign of the cross to ward off the evil she'd seen around Valentine.

Chapter Nine

Valentine found Victoria and Andrew kissing near the basket weaver's tent. It wasn't a chaste kiss. It was a long and deeply passionate kiss. Valentine knew she should feign interest in the brightly colored strung beads the dark-skinned young boy was showing her or the intricately designed woven floor mats and rugs the basket weaver's wife was hawking, but she didn't. She blatantly stared at her sister's naked passion for Andrew. And his for her.

It was the first time Valentine had witnessed Andrew being anything more than sweetly enamored of Victoria. Andrew had always seemed sweet and tender toward his fiancée. He was the type who quoted poetry and plucked wildflowers. He'd kissed her hand. He'd stared dreamily into Victoria's eyes. He was young, nowhere near Justin's thirty-plus years. Valentine had wrongly thought Justin to be a man and Andrew a boy.

She realized, as she watched Andrew's mouth slant over Victoria's and his hand roam down the small of her back to cup her buttocks and then press her into him, that Andrew was just as much a man as Justin.

It wasn't just the warm temperature that made Valentine retrieve her fan from her reticule and wave it briskly. All she could do was think of the heat she'd felt that very morning when she'd been with Justin. How easily she remembered his passionate kisses. Saints save her! How she wished she were kissing Justin now.

Alfredo was not the voyeur that Valentine was. He shifted his bundles and walked on to join the crowd gathering in the center of the market square. It was coming on to noon time and word had passed through the shoppers and vendors alike that the Gypsies were about to perform.

Colorful painted wooden wagons pulled into a semi-circle. A juggler tossed three red balls up in the air and kept them spinning aloft. The crowd applauded. Then he added a fourth ball. The crowd applauded again. But when he added the fifth and sixth balls, the crowd gasped in awe. Many in the crowd threw coins to the juggler.

A thin man with streaks of gray in his jet black hair jumped out of the back of one of the wagons carrying three long sticks, each with a wad of cloth on the end. He lit the torches from the lighted lantern that hung on the back of the wagon. He stood in the center of the crowd and proceeded to put the fire in his mouth. When he pulled the stick out of his mouth, the fire had been extinguished.

Valentine lost interest in Andrew and Victoria when she heard the wild applause from the crowd. She turned to watch the fire eater as he performed his magic. She was mesmerized by him as he relit his torches and ate

127

the fire a second time. Then he tossed the lighted torches to the juggler, who threw them in the air and kept them sailing in a circle in front of him.

Valentine turned back to her sister. "Victoria! Are you going to kiss Andrew all day?"

Victoria nearly jumped out of her skin. Andrew bit his lip, he was so startled. Victoria laughed at him and pulled a handkerchief out of her sleeve and dabbed at the drop of blood on his lip.

"Honestly, Valentine, you should be ashamed of yourself for watching," Victoria scolded.

Valentine smiled at them both as they walked toward her. "I admire you for taking full advantage of Aunt Cherise's absence. However, we still have much to do."

Andrew frowned at Valentine. "Do you have any idea how difficult it's been for Victoria and me to be alone?"

Valentine lifted her arms and motioned to the busy stalls around them. "You call this alone?"

Victoria expelled a deep sigh. "He means without being watched by anyone we know. We didn't realize you'd become a peeping Tom."

Andrew nodded. "Your Aunt Cherise is worse than a Spanish duenna. I've never had two seconds alone with Victoria since we announced our engagement. The woman is obsessed with keeping us apart. I would wager she suggested I work for Justin night and day, just to keep me from bedding your sister."

"Andrew!" Victoria looked at him, horrified.

"Well, it's the truth. She thinks I'm out to pounce on you at any opportunity," Andrew said.

"Aren't you?" she asked frankly.

Andrew's grin was characteristically sheepish, yet seductive as he looked at Victoria. "I certainly am!"

Victoria good-naturedly punched his arm. "Andrew! You shouldn't say such things."

"Why not? You're the most beautiful woman in this market." He turned to Valentine. "Which is the same as saying that about you, too, Valentine. Why, there isn't a man in this bazaar who isn't drooling over you. I'm not blind, but you both must be. Justin was wise to send both Alfredo and myself with you. Frankly, I think you should have armed escorts at all times and in all places."

"I hope you're not going to be one of those boorish controlling husbands . . . as Justin will probably be," Valentine said to Andrew.

"My dear sister-in-law to be, Justin *should* keep an eye on you. You have a tendency to attract trouble wherever you go."

"Andrew!" Victoria exclaimed. "I will not have you say such things about my sister," she said in Valentine's defense.

"What ho! I'm only saying what you've thought!"

Victoria glared at him.

Andrew's eyes were steady and resolute as he stared back at her.

Victoria looked at Valentine. She shrugged her shoulders. "Actually, I've said as much to Val myself. Many times."

Valentine frowned at both of them. "A thousand times. Since the day she could speak, if you want to know the truth, and I'm sick of it. Trouble does not seek me out. It's just that . . . I'm misunderstood," she said defensively.

"It's those daydreams you have in your head, Val. You get so wrapped up in them, you forget what reality is. Then when things don't turn out the way you want, you get angry, and *that's* when you get into trouble," Victoria said.

"I'd rather dream than not." Valentine put her hands on her hips for emphasis. "It's easy for you to be critical

129

when you have Andrew who loves you. I've got Sir Snake to look forward to for the rest of my life.''

Victoria wasn't going to let her sister feel sorry for herself. ''I think you do Lord Hawkeston a disservice, Val. I think he could be quite pleasant if you didn't needle him all the time.''

Valentine raised her hand for Victoria to stop. ''I had decided just that myself when he agreed to give me responsibility for the galley. I actually thought we could work together for the benefit of everyone on board. Then he turned on me. He showed his true colors this morning.''

''What did he do?'' Victoria asked.

''Why, he practically tossed me out of his cabin. He was rude and surly.''

Andrew's eyes narrowed suspiciously. ''What did you say to him to upset him, Valentine?''

''I simply gave him my shopping list, which he approved.'' Valentine chose not to tell them she'd spent a good deal of money on erotic oils and herbs. Since she intended to use them on Justin, she didn't think he would mind. It was a gift, she rationalized. He would understand . . . eventually. ''Then he gave me the money for the supplies. When I thanked him, he gave me the oddest look and then demanded I leave his cabin at once.''

Andrew shook his head. ''There's more to it than what you're telling us.''

''No, there isn't,'' Valentine insisted. ''He's a snake, and I hate snakes,'' she said with a good deal of false anger. How could she tell Victoria and Andrew how much she envied them their passion? How could she tell Victoria she wanted Justin as much as Vicki wanted Andrew? The problem was that Justin had no use for her at all. He thought her to be a harlot and not the virgin she was. The way Valentine saw it, she had no choice but to play the role he'd given her. If Justin wanted a whore, she would be the most passionate and aggressive whore he'd ever known. Yes, she told herself, she would fight fire with fire.

Victoria didn't know what to make of Valentine's story. She was used to Valentine's overactive imagination and tendency to exaggerate, but deep down she knew Valentine was hurting. Valentine usually exaggerated when she'd been overlooked or she felt unwanted. Victoria vowed to get the truth out of one or both of them, Valentine and Justin, before this voyage ended. They could not go back to England like the fighting tigers they'd become. "Val, I know it's difficult, but maybe you should try being overly sweet to Justin and see how he responds."

"What?" Valentine wondered if Victoria was reading her thoughts again. She had always supposed that because they were twins they were better able to read each other's minds than other people. It had happened a lot when they were children. Now that they were more mature and their lives were going in different directions, it didn't happen quite so often.

"Lord Hawkeston carries a great deal of responsibility, Valentine, what with his business, the ship and now all of us. He hasn't just become engaged like Andrew, Val, but he's been encumbered with an entire family. We all depend on him now. He must be reeling under the weight of it all. Give him some rope, Val. Be kinder to him."

Valentine nodded. She had to agree with Victoria. Those same thoughts had occurred to her, too. She wondered if it would ever be possible for him to think of her as anything but a burden. She wanted him to think of her as an asset. Not a responsibility. That was why she'd offered to help him as much as she could. She *did* want to be a helpmate to him. She never wanted him to think she was one of those helpless, frivolous women of the ton that she'd heard her father and Aunt Cherise discuss.

"I think you're right, Victoria. I know you are. I'll do just that. I will be kind. In fact, let's pick out something special I could prepare for supper tonight. Maybe even a sweet cake. I would like tonight to be a celebration of our coming through the storm. Lord Hawkeston will be very tired tonight after working on the damage all day. Let's see what we can find."

"That's a wonderful idea, Valentine," Andrew said.

They went to the winemaker's tent and purchased a Madeira port and several bottles of red wine. Valentine found grapes, dark and golden raisins. Though they were more expensive than she wished, she purchased dates, dried apricots and coconuts that came from West Africa. When Valentine had spent nearly all her money and arranged for the last of the supplies to be taken to the ship, she agreed with Victoria that they should try the shish-ke-bobs one of the vendors was grilling.

The smell of cooking garlic, lamb and pork was potent. Valentine's mouth was watering before she put the first tender bite-sized piece of pork in her mouth. She asked the vendor for preparation instructions, but because her Spanish was not good, she decided to watch him prepare the meat.

She noticed that the chunks of meat sat in a bowl of olive oil, basil, garlic and honey. He squeezed a lime over the meat as it grilled over the wood smoke fire. She smiled and thanked him.

They went in search of Alfredo, who was still watching the Gypsies perform.

It was long past noon when the Gypsy dancers burst out of the backs of the covered wagons and whirled about the market square tossing their tambourines into the air and bouncing them off their heels. Most of the women were long past 25 and were beginning to show their age, Valentine thought. Their skins were dark, but the sun had made wrinkles around their eyes. Alfredo explained that many of the Gypsies worked in the vineyards at harvest time and in the orchards. They were entertainers, to be certain, but they were chiefly migrant workers who roamed from farm to farm, harvesting whatever crop was ripe. Because it was winter, just now they were dependent upon the money they made by their performances.

Valentine noticed the Gypsy children who sat on the front of the wagons holding the reins of the horse teams. Several of the children played the flute, harmonica or small drums. They created a slowly building tempo to which the women danced. Valentine thought the children looked thin and their cheeks were hollow. The smallest boy, who sat next to a girl of about ten, looked as if he hadn't eaten in days. Valentine's heart went out to him.

She reached into her reticule and pulled out the last coin. It was a gold crown. Valentine was aware that this much money could feed the vagabond tribe for over a month. She knew Justin approved of charity. He'd certainly been charitable to her own family. Surely, he would not find fault with her for helping the hungry child. Valentine worked her way through the crowd. She went up behind the back of the wagon and tapped the boy on the shoulder. He turned to look at her.

Up close, the boy seemed to be in even worse health than she'd thought. He had sores on his lip and his eyes were dull. Valentine was shocked at his appearance. Why, if she had the money, she would have gone to each of these booths and bought rations for all the children. She felt guilty for buying the fat goose, lamb and

133

pork she intended to prepare for Justin that night. She took the gold coin and pressed it into the boy's hand.

"God bless you," she said in English.

His smile was wan and pained. She could tell the sores hurt him a great deal. He didn't understand what she said, but he did understand the pity in her eyes.

He straightened his shoulders proudly. He looked at the coin. It was British and he had no idea how much it was worth, but it was gold. He bit on the coin. It was real, he judged, and gave her his best smile. "Gracias, senora."

She patted his hand and went back to join Victoria and Andrew, who were standing in the front of the crowd.

The dancing women wore brightly woven scarves over their hair and bright gold earrings. Several of them wore bells on their wrists. As the music built to a crescendo, the women spun around each other like colorful whirling pinwheels. Just as their skirts whipped high above their knees, the music crashed to a stop and the women dropped to the ground in a crouch. They lowered their heads to their knees.

The crowd burst into applause.

Copper coins rained down on the women, but they did not move.

The crowd had been watching the women dance and had not noticed the man who now stood on the roof of the center wooden wagon.

One of the children hit a tambourine.

The man shouted a cry in a Spanish dialect that Valentine had never heard.

All eyes raised to the man.

Valentine gasped. It was as if she'd conjured him up from her dream. He was as tall as Justin. Maybe taller. He wore a red shirt open to the waist. She and everyone else could see a very bronzed, very wide chest. His trousers were so tight she could see every muscle flex in his thighs and his buttocks when he moved from left to right. His arms were raised over his head as he banged his tambourine. His belly was so flat and muscular it looked like a washboard. He wore long black boots, and a purple scarf over the top of his head. The rest of his hair hung in a long unbridled stream to the middle of his back. His skin was tan, his perfect teeth white, and his eyes as black as her own.

Valentine was wide-eyed as she stared at the vision of masculine perfection.

He pranced like a peacock and moved like a panther. He shouted again and the music started. He jumped off the wagon and landed on his feet with perfect ease. He stared at Valentine.

He danced around the Gypsy women. He performed cartwheels and flips. He picked one of the women dancers up and whirled her around his head and then around his body as if she were weightless.

The crowd was mesmerized.

Together with the women, he performed all sorts of acrobatics. He stood one woman on his shoulders and then hoisted a second on top of her. He sat two women on his shoulders and then each of them did a handstand on his outstretched arms. The crowd couldn't clap enough.

When the performance was over, the dancers and the Gypsy man took several bows. He turned to whisper something to one of the women dancers. She, in turn, whispered something to each of the other women dancers.

All Gypsy eyes were on Valentine.

The Gypsy man walked over to Valentine. He reached into his sleeve and pulled out a red rose. Valentine burst into a smile and thanked him.

"How did you do that? There are no roses in February," Valentine asked, but the man did not understand English.

He began speaking to her, thanking her for her generosity to their Gypsy tribe, but Valentine didn't understand a single word.

Valentine was so fascinated by him, she couldn't say a word.

He looked into her eyes and whispered in his own blend of Rumanian and Spanish. "You have Gypsy eyes," he said, pointing to her eyes and then to his own. "These are the eyes that see the heart."

Then he touched her heart. He slipped his other arm around her waist. He kissed her cheek. Then he kissed her other cheek. "Thank you for seeing the heart of my son. May you be blessed with much love in your life."

Lord Justin Hawkeston began to feel his anger simmer before noon when Valentine did not return from shore. The damage to the ship had not been as extensive as he'd thought, and the crew were able to handle the chores without him. Then came the word from shore that because they were a British ship, they were being advised to leave the port as soon as their supplies were delivered. Barcelona was still a controlled French region, and even though the Treaty of Fontainebleau had exiled Napoleon Bonaparte to Elba island, the most recent news was that Napoleon had escaped Elba with a detachment of his guard. Word was that he was expected in Cannes by March first.

Though the British were at peace with the French at present, no one could predict what would happen now that Bonaparte was on the loose. War could break out any second.

Seduced

The crowd was applauding the dance and Valentine's generosity when Justin forced his way through the crowd with Mr. Henderson.

Many of the Spanish-speaking people in the crowd were pleased with the blessing the Gypsy man had given the Englishwoman. Others in the crowd were dead certain these dramatics were all a ploy to catch them off guard while the Gypsy pickpockets stole them blind.

Justin had come to stand next to Victoria and Andrew when he saw Valentine being mauled by an incredibly good-looking dark-haired man.

Valentine was definitely enjoying herself, Justin thought. She seemed to be enthralled by him. Then the man touched Valentine's breast.

A stranger to jealousy, Justin had no idea why his fists clenched and unclenched. He didn't know this man at all. He'd never laid eyes on him in his life, and yet he wanted to pound the living daylights out of him. Already, he knew that sinking his fist into the Gypsy's devastatingly handsome face would bring him pleasure. Justin saw red.

Victoria heard Justin's low, throaty growl before she turned and realized he was standing next to her. "Lord Hawkeston! What are you doing here?" Her eyes flew from him to Valentine.

Her sister was enjoying herself far, far too much. Why, Valentine looked as if she would swoon in the man's arms. And the man had touched her breast! God in heaven! What could Valentine be thinking?

Valentine had not gotten the kind of attention from Justin that Victoria thought she needed, even if Valentine wouldn't admit it. True to her nature, Valentine had unwittingly placed herself in a position where she got what she wanted . . . but at a price.

That price was Lord Hawkeston's anger.

Victoria's stomach squeezed as anxiety clutched her. "Please, Lord Hawkeston. It isn't what you think."

"Oh, no?"

"I know it looks bad." Victoria watched as the man put his arm around Valentine and then . . . Oh, no! He wasn't going to . . . kiss her. Oh, he did! Oh, this was terrible. Justin might get the wrong idea.

Victoria looked at Justin. His eyes had turned vacant and as cold as ice. He looked as if he could kill. Victoria unconsciously stepped away from him. She was afraid of what he would do.

He should leave the harlot alone, he thought. He should let this Gypsy king take her off. Let *him* try to deal with her. If he were smart, he would say good riddance to her.

The Gypsy kissed Valentine's other cheek.

Justin noticed how she leaned back on the man's arm, as if he were the master and she were under his power. She had closed her eyes when he kissed her. Justin couldn't believe it. She hadn't closed her eyes when he'd kissed her. Or had she? He'd closed his. Or had he? All he knew was that he hadn't kissed Valentine in much too long a time. Here he'd been fighting his passions for her and she was out on the streets of Barcelona selling herself to a Gypsy.

Justin was so furious he thought he'd explode. And he did.

"I'm leaving!" he told himself. "I am leaving her here where she belongs," he growled to himself as he took the first step toward his fiancée. "I am leaving . . . just as soon as I . . ." He took another step, then another. He was at Valentine's side in an instant. "Take what is mine!"

He yanked Valentine's arm so forcefully, she flew out

of the Gypsy's arms and nearly bounced off Justin's chest.

"Whaaaaat . . ." Valentine opened her eyes and found herself staring into the face of fury. She knew instantly why Justin was there and why he was angry. If she'd come upon the same scene, she would be, too. But it didn't give him any right to manhandle her. "Justin!"

He glared at her and she thought ice flecks spewed out of his eyes. She'd never seen such anger or hate.

Justin turned to the Gypsy, who was smiling appreciatively at Valentine. He pulled back his fist.

The Gypsy saw the fist and ducked. Justin swung again. The Gypsy ducked again. Then the Gypsy jumped out of the way as Justin started to ram his head into the Gypsy's body. Justin found himself sprawled on the ground and the crowd laughing at him.

"Stop!" Valentine shouted. "He was just thanking me," she tried to explain, but Justin's anger was implacable.

Justin righted himself.

The Gypsy women scrambled through the dirt and cobblestones for the copper coins the crowd had tossed. The children put their instruments away and readied the horses. The women jumped into the backs of the wagons. Some of them took the reins. They shouted private signals to each other. Victoria could tell they had been through this situation before.

The first wagon headed out of the market square toward the north. The second wagon followed. The Gypsy man smiled to the crowd, waved a salute to Justin, and blew a kiss to Valentine before jumping onto the lower marble ledge of the three-tiered fountain at the north end of the square. As the third wagon passed by the fountain, he did a back flip onto its rear running-board. He waved to the crowd as the wagon picked up speed and then disappeared down the narrow city street.

Valentine looked at Justin. He was covered with dirt and wore a black look on his face. She'd never seen such rage.

She wanted to run from him, but she had noplace to go but the ship. It was his ship. She'd have to confront him sooner or later. She might as well get it over with now.

Two could play at this anger game, she thought. After all, she hadn't done anything wrong. He only thought she had. She had made the mistake of opening her heart to a poor child and Justin wanted to make more of it than it was. So what if a devilishly handsome man had kissed her? So what if she didn't fight off his advances? So what if she looked a little too long at his bulging biceps and his handsome dark eyes? She never would have reacted to the Gypsy if Justin hadn't been so cold to her. It wasn't as if she was going to let him really kiss her. Justin was carrying this whole thing too far.

Justin was the one who'd made a fool of himself in front of all these people. He was the one who had started the fistfight. Why, when she reasoned it all out, *she* should be the one doing the scolding and not Justin.

Incensed at his groundless anger toward her, Valentine turned her fury on him. She rammed her fists onto her hips and marched toward him. Her eyes were spewing fire. She was about to explode.

"You take that black look off your face, Lord Justin Hawkeston. You owe me an apology!" she demanded self-righteously.

"I? I owe you? Ha!"

"You most certainly do."

He dusted himself off with forceful slaps to his own body. Hell, he needed to hit something. "And for what do I need to apologize?"

"For jumping to conclusions," she said with her nose high in the air.

"I walk into the town square and I find my fiancée in the arms of a stranger, kissing him and mooning into his eyes as if he were the last man on earth, and I owe you an apology? I'd rather fry in hell."

"He was thanking me," she said tartly.

"For what? For not charging him the full rate?" Justin sent the poisoned barb right to her heart.

God! He could play dirty when he wanted, she thought. Justin still thought she was a prostitute. Nothing she ever did would convince him otherwise. She had been right all along. She was doomed to a life without love.

She was so furious she could not speak. She chose instead to walk away. She turned her back on him.

"Don't you dare!" Justin growled. He went after her and grabbed her arm.

"You're hurting me, Lord Hawkeston." Her eyes were like black flint. "But I suppose that's the point, isn't it?" She yanked her arm out of his.

Victoria had had enough. She went to Valentine and Justin and placed herself between them. She spoke to Justin first. "You're both too angry to speak. Please stop now before one of you says something you'll regret."

Justin tore his angry eyes from Valentine and turned toward Mr. Henderson. "Make sure we have all the supplies. And get these women on board immediately. I want to set sail in one hour. No more."

"Aye-aye, sir," Mr. Henderson said.

Alfredo was speechless. He'd been on the bad side of nearly everyone so far on this trip. He just wanted to get back to the ship. He gathered his bundles and scurried off behind Justin.

Valentine watched Justin's back as he stalked away.

She burst into tears. She turned to Victoria and put her head on her sister's shoulder and found comfort in her arms.

Andrew placed his hand on Valentine's back. "Maybe I can talk with him, Val."

"It's no use. He's hated me since the moment he laid eyes on me."

"Maybe if I just—" Andrew began when Victoria cut him off.

"Andrew, please. Can't you see she's distraught? The damage has been done, I'm afraid." Victoria lifted Valentine's chin. "You must compose yourself, Val. You can't let him see you cry under any circumstances. Then he'll know he's gotten your goat. Be strong now. We'll beat him at his own game."

Valentine wiped her tears with the palms of her hands. "Do you think so?"

"I know so," Victoria said encouragingly. "The vendors must have our parcels ready by now. Let's hurry so we don't upset him any more than necessary."

Valentine and Victoria walked away from Andrew, who was still scratching his head over the scene he'd just witnessed. He might be young and not as worldly as Justin, but he sure never acted that much of a fool. For the life of him, Andrew couldn't understand what was the matter with Justin. Why didn't he simply admit he was in love with Valentine and be done with it?

Chapter Ten

Lord Justin Hawkeston kept his ship to the west of normal sailing routes around Spain due to the changing political climate. He could not take any chances that war had been declared on Britain again without his knowing it. A hundred miles east of Cape Trafalgar, they happened upon another British sailing vessel. As was the custom, they sailed within shouting distance of each other so that Justin could learn the latest events. The captain of the *Ladyship* informed Justin and everyone on board who was listening that Napoleon Bonaparte had landed at Cannes on March first just as he'd planned. He was making his way across the Alps, and every regiment that had been sent by the Bourbon government to stop him had joined forces with Napoleon. The word was that the French people were unhappy with the restoration of the Bourbons and that Louis XVIII was in danger of losing his crown. The people wanted the essential elements of the Revolution reinstated. Napoleon was using this time of unrest to reestablish his stronghold on France. If Napoleon were to once again be proclaimed emperor, he would turn his sights back on Britain and the war at sea would be on.

Lord Hawkeston was sick of war. He had lost friends in both England and on the Continent who had died in battle either supporting or objecting to the "little corporal." Justin was a peacemaker, not a warrior. He liked to think of himself as an architect of the future. He was a builder. He wanted to build his company, increase his coffers, and provide for his future and that of his children and his children's children.

How odd it was to think that his plans for the future would include Valentine. For years, the future to Justin had been a nebulous place in the very far distance. He was so busy working to pay off his father's and his brother's debts and build his own company that he'd never thought about a wife or children. And ever since he'd been rejected by Amanda, he'd scorned the idea of love. He always told himself he would do something about a family the next year. Then the war came and his shipping schedules got delayed or canceled. The demand for glassware fell as everyone focused on war. But as the war dragged on, parties came back into fashion and the demand for his kind of glassware soared once again.

Then he had the problem of getting the beautiful gold-rimmed crystal goblets, wineglasses, champagne flutes and decanters from Venice to England without the shipping vessels being looted. That was when he decided to purchase his own ship.

Justin had abhorred the social scene as much as his father and brother had clung to it. Justin thought balls, parties and weekend outings a waste of time when he needed to concentrate on business. Justin was not a drinker, or a flirt, or a gambler. He was boring company for most of the ton. They knew it and he thought that was just fine. However, he found there were times when he needed the support of the ton for his business. The acquisition of his ship was one of those times.

One of the reasons Justin detested gambling was not only because his father and brother were so bad at it, but because he was so good at it. It was a boring pastime for him. Taking money from people without the satisfaction of working for it posed no challenge to Justin whatsoever.

Justin's thrills came from pitting himself against foreign traders. He liked using his strategies to invest in foreign industries and then watching the companies grow. He owned glass factories in Vienna, Budapest and Krakow. He loved the travel. He loved the excitement of cutting deals and negotiating prices.

Justin had researched the price of a ship and knew he could not afford one. But for his business to survive and make even more money, he knew that sailing his own ship through perilous war-torn waters was cheaper than paying inflated prices to shippers. Justin believed he was being forced to the gaming tables.

Justin talked to Harold Parkington, a renowned gambler who traveled in the best circles in London. Justin's brother, Arnold, had never been invited to play with Harold Parkington, or Lord Bromley, or the Earl of Pemington. These men owned territories that spanned the globe. They were not just born to wealth, but created even greater fortunes with their endowments. They were men of vision, men who knew that great visions can be fulfilled with tenacity and patience. Justin learned to think like them.

These men worked diligently and they played just as hard.

Justin carefully weighed his probabilities of winning against his chances of losing. He came up with mathematical formulas that would dictate his mode of play. Aside from his well-thought-out mathematics, Justin knew how to depend on his keen instincts to tell him when to play and when to leave. In the end, it was his gut and not his head that won in gambling.

A private room was procured on the second floor of the Huntsman's Club on Thursday night, May 12, 1813. Nestled in the heart of London, the club was frequented only by the most wealthy men of the ton. The four gamblers and Justin were joined by the Duke of Atwater and Lord Hensley.

The game they chose was Twenty-one.

After the first hour of play, each man had won his share and the fortunes had not shifted. After the second hour, Justin decided that though he'd won more bets than the others, his winnings had not been substantial enough. After the third hour, the earl declared he'd had too much Scotch and left for the night, promising to return the following week.

It was after two in the morning before Justin and Lord Bromley squared off. Justin had won over one hundred thousand pounds that night. Each of the other men had stated they never wanted to play with him again. Justin told them they wouldn't have to after tonight.

All of the men had assumed that Justin would lose as did his brother, Arnold. They discovered their assumptions to be inaccurate.

Justin bet Lord Bromley all of his winnings against the lord's smallest sailing vessel, the *Spirit,* that the next card Harold turned up for him would be a ten or greater and that Lord Bromley's card would be less than an eight. Justin was showing a six. He had a five facing down. Lord Bromley was showing a ten. He had a three facing down.

Lord Bromley was aghast. "I've never seen anyone bet as recklessly as you, Justin. How can you possibly know what I've got and what I need to beat you? Why, you would have had to memorize every card played since Harold shuffled the deck."

Justin continued to stare at Lord Bromley.

Justin *had* memorized every card. He'd learned that trick many years ago when still in his teens. He glanced at the thin pile of cards still in Harold's hand. He was taking a chance, he knew, but he wouldn't have been out a penny if he lost this round. He'd be at square one. The way he saw it, he had everything to gain. He'd come here for a ship, though none of these men knew that. He'd spent the night working the game to this point. His gut told him to bet. He trusted his instincts.

"What do you say?" Justin asked the older man.

Lord Bromley liked a challenge. Hell, he felt he'd invented the word. Time he taught this young snapper a thing or two. "Bet."

Justin nodded to Harold, who slowly flipped the next card down in front of Lord Bromley.

"A seven!" Harold said.

Lord Bromley turned over his three. "I have twenty points, Justin."

"It seems a secure position, my lord," Justin said.

Harold dabbed at the perspiration on his forehead with a handkerchief. It was at times like this he hated this game. There was no hope for it. On this card rested the entire evening's gamble. There was no way Justin would get the right card, he thought. He quickly peeled off the card and deposited it on top of Justin's showing six.

"Knave of hearts!" Harold exclaimed.

The others slapped Justin on the back. "Good going!"

"I say, well done, boy. Well done!" the Duke of Atwater said.

Lord Bromley simply stared at the card that had cost him his ship. He looked at Justin and shrugged his shoulders. He smiled. "I should know better than to gamble."

Justin shook his hand. "I can say the same myself, sir. I promise you won't find me here again."

Justin had his ship and Lord Bromley had Justin's promise that the lord and his family were welcome aboard anytime. Fortunately for Justin, the men parted amicably.

Justin was proud of the ship, and though it was his, he always felt he owed Lord Bromley a debt. As with all his other possessions, he was meticulous about its upkeep.

Justin had always been careful about his money and his investments. That was why it was not normal for him to wait three days after leaving Barcelona before he asked Valentine to return the remainder of the money he'd given her when she went to shore.

Valentine was furious that Justin had sent for her by way of Rabb as if she were a servant. "What do you mean, Lord Hawkeston wants to see me immediately?"

Rabb wiped his nose on his sleeve. "That's what 'e tole me to tell ye." Rabb sniffed and started to lift his arm again.

Valentine grabbed his arm in mid-motion and stopped him. "For heaven's sake!" She handed him a clean handkerchief. "Please learn to use a handkerchief, Rabb. A gentleman does not use his sleeve."

"I ain't no gentleman," he sniffed.

She glowered at him. "Well, I intend for you to be one someday. Since I'll be Lady Hawkeston for the rest of my life and your mistress as long as you choose to remain in Lord Hawkeston's employ, you will most certainly learn to speak with better diction and to use the handkerchief. Now here. Blow," she commanded him.

Rabb blew his nose. He put the handkerchief in his pocket. "Never had one o' them things before."

"You do now." She smiled at him and rumpled his hair.

Valentine liked Rabb a great deal. He was a good boy and tried his best to please Justin. His loyalty was commendable. Rabb had been orphaned from the age of three and had lived in the streets until Justin had found him when he was nine. He'd been working as a cabin boy for the past three years. The *Spirit* was Rabb's home.

"His Lordship has been locked away in his cabin for nearly three days now, Rabb. You're about the only one of us who has seen him. Why, he didn't even come to the dining room for his meals."

"'E tole me 'e liked the things you cooked."

Rabb's observation didn't tell her much. Justin's mood had been blacker than a sea squall since his encounter with the Gypsy. Valentine had spent hours in the kitchen chopping vegetables with the largest and sharpest knife she could find to vent her frustrations. She could only guess where Justin had put his anger.

Because the weather had been good, the crew easily handled the ship without Justin. Valentine had taken over the galley and the meals were prepared on time and in abundance. There were no complaints from anyone.

There were also few compliments. Except for the raves she received from Victoria, Andrew and Aunt Cherise, few of the crew had said a word.

Valentine did not know that the crew was waiting to observe Lord Hawkeston's reaction to Valentine's behavior with the Gypsy. The crew were not condoning her, nor were they condemning her. They were simply waiting.

She thought their inaction was prudent behavior on their part. Justin was paying their wages, after all.

"'Is Lordship said 'e wants ter see ye now," Rabb insisted.

"Fine. I'll be there in a few minutes." Valentine had no intention of hurrying at Justin's beck and call.

"Pleeze, milady! 'E'll be mad at me if ye don't come straightaway."

Valentine looked into the boy's imploring eyes. "I suppose you're right." She touched his cheek.

She had just rolled out sweet dough between two floured linen cloths. She was making breakfast rolls for the next day. She took off the apron she wore to protect her blue flowered muslin gown. She put the apron on Rabb. "Would you like to help me finish these rolls, Rabb?"

Rabb loved to help out in the kitchen because he could steal some tasty morsels of food when Valentine was not looking. "What do I do?"

"Spread the dough with this sweet butter. Then sprinkle the brown sugar over the butter. Then grate the cinnamon onto the dough. Sprinkle the almonds, raisins and dates over it. When I get back I'll show you the rest."

"This will be easy," he said and started in on his project.

Valentine left the galley, but just as she closed the door, she peeked back at Rabb. He was cramming an entire handful of juicy raisins into his mouth, just as she knew he would. She smiled to herself as she started toward Justin's room.

She lifted her hand and tapped on the door.

"Come," Justin said.

Lord! She hoped he still wasn't in a snit about that Gypsy thing. She'd never seen him so mad. Maybe it was a good thing she'd kept herself so occupied the last three days. She didn't want to be anywhere near the ogre when he was in such a black mood.

Valentine squared her shoulders, took a deep breath, and prepared herself to meet the enemy. She opened the door.

Justin was nearly hidden by stacks of papers, huge record books, journals and maps. He dipped his quill pen into an inkwell and continued to transfer his figures into his log. He had not looked at her.

"You sent for me, Your Lordship?" she asked flatly.

"I did." He did not raise his head but continued working.

A long silence followed. "Is there something I can get you, my lord? Some tea, perhaps?" She was at a loss to know what was so urgent. Maybe Rabb had misconstrued the message. Perhaps Justin had forgotten himself.

He propped his elbow on the table and extended his hand to her. He still had not looked at her. "My purse, please?"

"Sir?" Valentine was confused. "I don't have your—"

Justin nearly leapt out of the chair. "My money, Miss St. James. Where is it?"

She shook her head. She was startled at the venom in his voice. "I . . . I . . . don't know . . ."

"Then let me explain it to you as clearly as I can. I sent you to buy supplies. This stack of bills"—he clamped his hand down on a pile of receipts, many of which she recognized from her trip to the market in Barcelona—"does not add up to the total amount of money I gave you that morning when you left the ship. I am minus two gold crowns. I would like my money back.''

''I don't have it,'' she said flatly.

His eyes narrowed. ''You don't have it?'' He threw his head back and laughed. When he looked at her she noticed his eyes were bloodshot. His hair was uncombed and he hadn't shaved for days. What had happened to him? He glared at her with the eyes of a madman.

Valentine took a step back toward the door.

He continued, ''You who made a banquet out of rotted food? You who saves orange rinds to use in the potpourris you concoct in the kitchen?''

''Rabb told you—'' she interrupted.

''I have spies everywhere, Miss St. James.''

Saints above! She hated when he called her that. What had happened to turn him so violently against her? Could he possibly be this upset over two gold crowns?

As usual, Valentine's own anger gave her courage. Her outrage at his unjust treatment of her caused her to glare at him and take back the step she'd earlier lost in a retreat. She advanced two steps toward him. The game had commenced.

''I don't care if you have a thousand spies, *Your Lordship*. You'll not find what you are looking for.''

''Oh, ho! And I suppose you think you know what I'm looking for.''

She advanced again. ''Yes, I do.''

''What is it?'' he retorted angrily. He stood his ground.

''You're looking for an excuse to hate me.''

''I don't need an excuse. The truth will do just fine. Where is my money?''

Her eyes bored into his. ''I gave it to the Gypsy—''

He was horrified. ''You paid for his kisses?''

It was Valentine's turn to be stunned. "I have never had to pay for a man's attention, Lord Hawkeston. Just because you are being forced by your loyalty to my father to marry me doesn't mean that other men—men better than you—are not attracted to me." Valentine was so angry her fists balled.

"You said you gave it to the Gypsy," he countered, hoping to use her own words to condemn her.

"You didn't let me finish, Lord Hawkeston. You're so anxious to prove to yourself that I am a harlot that you won't even listen to anything that resembles the truth. Truth? Ha! You'd twist the truth!" She took another step forward.

"You've cloistered yourself in these rooms for three days looking for evidence to pass judgment on me. You look like hell, Justin. If I hadn't sent you some decent food every day, you probably would have starved yourself." She poked his chest with her forefinger for emphasis. "The truth of the matter is that I saw a young boy no more than five or six. A Gypsy boy. He and the other children were starving, Justin. I felt guilty buying all these wonderful foods and spices for us. I had some money left over and so I gave the money to the child. The child was the son of the man you saw me with. The man was thanking me for giving them the money. I knew that money could feed nearly all of them for weeks. He wasn't trying to accost me, or ravage me, Justin. He was thanking me. And that was all."

Justin was speechless.

"Because you have chosen to treat me as if I did something terrible and blackened the good and virtuous Hawkeston name, which I am soon to call my own, your crew treats me the same way. Not one of them will speak to me until you do. I have fed them. I have helped them with their aches, pains and colds, and they treat me as if I had the plague. This cannot continue, Justin! I haven't done anything to deserve this treatment.''

Valentine's rage had worked itself into such a frenzy she was afraid she'd smash everything in his cabin if she didn't get out of there quickly.

She continued to look at him with the same icy glare he gave her. As calmly as she could, she turned on her heel, walked out of his cabin, and closed the door behind her.

She went to her cabin and closed the door.

She sat on the bed and slowly opened her balled fists. Maybe she would have felt better if she'd rammed one of them into his belly. Or his face.

She went to the dresser and opened the middle drawer. She took out her diary and opened it to a clean page. She wrote in it with her quill pen.

March 5, 1815
Dear Diary,

Lord Hawkeston has proven to me beyond the shadow of a doubt that he is heartless. He not only now believes me to be a thief, but a whore. He thinks that I paid the Gypsy to make love to me. What a ludicrous thought. And how very unkind of him to believe that I would pay for love.

Justin is worse than a snake.

He has no feelings or compassion for other humans in need. When I explained that I had given his money to the child, he refused to comment. He still didn't believe me.

I fear I am doomed to marry a man who not only does not love or want me, but who I doubt will have any capacity to love our children, either. I fear he will hate any child I bear him.

Even Victoria has commented on the fact that

he has secluded himself away from us and the crew. Aunt Cherise has said that moody men, which Justin most definitely is, are not only poor husbands but the worst fathers because they frighten children with their inconsistent behavior. I am losing hope.

Sincerely yours,
Valentine St. James

P.S. I did not tell Justin how much money I spent for the herbs and spices. He was not in the mood to understand in the least.

Chapter Eleven

"Fool! Fool! Fool!" Justin blasted himself when Valentine left the cabin. He slammed his open palm against his desk. "I've never been the fool! Never, Valentine!" he shouted to the closed door.

Damnation, that woman was driving him to his limits!

What was happening to him of late? He'd never jumped to conclusions in his life. And if he'd ever slipped before and done such a thing, he'd jumped to the right ones. What was there about Valentine that turned a logical-thinking, orderly type of person into an empty-brained lout?

And he was a lout. There was no doubt about that. He'd had to sequester himself in his own quarters for three days just to keep himself from taking out his anger on his crew and anyone else who dared to cross his path. Then there was the matter of Valentine herself. He didn't know whether he wanted to turn her over his knee and spank her, or rip her clothes off and show her that no Gypsy king could possibly make love to her and satisfy her the way he could.

The fact of the matter was that he wanted to do both.

Justin raked his hand through his hair. He rubbed his temples. He was going insane. That's all there was to it, he'd lost his mind.

In all the years that Arnold had gambled away the money that he, Justin, had worked so diligently to earn and save, not once had he ever wanted to raise his fist to him. He'd paid Arnold's bills and been rid of him usually for months. Arnold would promise not to gamble, then he'd break his vows to himself and Justin, begin gambling, and usually win for a few weeks. His winnings would go to his head, and he would bet too much and find himself in trouble again. It was a predictable cycle and it usually took three months.

But it was predictable. Justin could count on Arnold's weakness like rain.

That was nothing like this!

This . . . this tempestuous woman with whom he was about to enter the state of matrimony followed no patterns whatsoever that he could see. Justin knew that all sane individuals were logical. They had patterns of behavior that formed a framework of organization in their lives. Justin was that type of admirable person.

He worked from dawn to dusk or till midnight, depending on the up or down swing of business that quarter. He ate, he slept, and in between times, business permitting, he would see his friends at the Huntsman's Club or attend a dinner or party.

But he never went traipsing into the streets of Venice in search of debauchery the way Valentine had. He'd only known of the places he took her through friends; he didn't frequent such establishments himself. He'd never allowed strangers to kiss him the way Valentine had . . . or at least he didn't make a practice of it, he rationalized.

And for the love of heaven, he'd certainly never given his hard-earned money to a starving Gypsy boy, and then allowed anyone to think he'd thrown himself into the arms of some . . . some Gypsy woman!

He'd never allowed himself to make a fool of himself the way Valentine had.

No, he was a better man than that.

He paced back and forth in the small cabin with his hands clasped behind his back. The problem was that she *had* done that to him and he didn't know what to do about it.

Justin had allowed the crew to think the worst of Valentine. Mr. Henderson had spread the gossip and Justin had done nothing to stop it. The entire crew was sitting on pins and needles waiting for Justin to make a move.

Instead of punishing her, he'd remained in his cabin fuming. Justin was positive that Rabb had duly reported his sour mood to the crew. Justin had barked orders to the boy so much that even he was sick of hearing his tone of voice.

And what good did it do? Valentine had gone about her life as if little had happened. She stayed clear of Justin, and rightly so. Rabb told him she'd taken over most of his duties, all of Alfredo's duties, and was ordering the men to bring their dirty linens to her. According to Rabb, Valentine, Victoria and their aunt not only were cleaning the crew's clothes but the towels and sheeting on board as well.

Valentine set the time of meals, the time the crew were to arise, and the time they were allowed back to their bunks and hammocks to sleep. She had given firm instructions on bathing and shaving. Valentine had told

Rabb that she was appalled at the stench she'd encountered on board. When she realized the smell came solely from the men and their filthy living habits, she believed it was her duty to rectify the problem. For days she had Rabb scurrying about the ship stripping beds and hammocks, bringing her pillows to be cleaned and aired and helping her iron and fold towels.

The men told Rabb they liked settling into a clean-smelling bed at night. Mr. Henderson had told Rabb that Valentine had specially scented the feathers of Mr. Henderson's pillow with patchouli, an herb that reminded him of his travels to Malaya and India. Rabb had told Justin that Valentine had inquired of each man what his favorite scents were and she'd scented their laundry with something to please everyone.

The crew was well aware of Justin's disapproval of Valentine, but she was being so sweet to everyone that they were in a quandary as to whether the woman was devil or angel.

Justin didn't blame them. He'd wondered the same thing himself. He also realized that his own sheets had not been stripped, cleaned and perfumed. Nor had his shirts been washed and ironed since they left Italy. They hung on the peg on the back of his door. Now that he knew what Valentine was up to, he felt slighted by her. It was his guess that she knew he would react this way when he eventually learned of her preference for the crew.

God! She was a wily one!

The crew did not dare provoke her wrath by not abiding by her schedules because they greatly admired her cooking skills. Valentine had won their loyalty through their stomachs.

Justin had been aware of all these events when he had sent for Valentine that morning. He'd had just about enough of her back-stabbing power plays and efforts to win over his crew. She had provoked his anger by kissing the Gypsy.

He had wanted to explain to her with cool logic that no fiancée of his was going to go about the Continent throwing herself at strange men!

Justin rammed his fist into the palm of his hand. By God! He was in a hell of a mess now that she'd explained her actions.

How would it look to his men if he chastised Valentine for giving charity to starving children? He might as well be lighting the torch to Joan of Arc's pyre. They'd hate him.

Somehow, Valentine had managed to turn herself into the saint and he into the sinner.

Blast it! He was going to have to do something he'd never done in his life. He was going to have to apologize.

So she had lied to him, Valentine thought to herself as she opened the new muslin casing Victoria had stitched together. So what if she'd stretched the truth and said the crew was not speaking to her? So what if she'd made their guarded aloofness sound like contempt? She'd needed to bolster her position.

Justin had condemned her before hearing her out. That was the way he worked. Once she did something wrong, he doomed her to paying for that crime for the rest of her life. Would she ever be able to rectify her reckless behavior on Mardi Gras night?

Not with Justin you won't, she told herself.

She inserted the washed, sun-dried and Turkish-rose-scented down into the casing. Valentine inhaled the exotic floral scent and smiled as she finished her task. This pillow was to go to Mr. Smalley. He'd told her he'd traveled throughout the Turkish Empire and always bought this oil for his wife whenever he went to Istanbul or Izmir. Valentine had found that her simple task of cleaning the bed linens, most of which had not been throughly washed for years, had provided her with hours of entertainment.

Each crew member delighted in telling her of his voyages, his exploits and his longings for home and family. She learned that most of the men had been at sea nearly all their lives. They were able men who worked hard for a living. And each of them had a wanderlust that could never be fulfilled by living in any single country.

Valentine had traveled with her father and sister to Venice, Milan and Rome and then back to England, but she'd never seen or even read about some of the exotic places these men had experienced. She marveled at the tales of China and the beautiful slant-eyed, golden-skinned people who had introduced Mr. Osen to sweet-smelling incense, grilled squid and the ivory carvings he kept next to his bunk.

She learned of Buddhism and monks who concentrated so perfectly with their minds they could lift their bodies off the floor and float. She listened as Mr. Jenkins described Arabian horses, harems and dancing girls who performed in costumes that exposed half their flesh, and of Arab wives who wore black clothing that covered their entire bodies except for their eyes.

When Valentine started her project to eliminate the stench on board, she'd only been interested in channeling her nearly uncontrollable anger at Lord Hawkeston into something constructive. Aunt Cherise's idea of embroidering her trousseau was not active enough for Valentine.

Valentine was so furious she thought she could rig the sails singlehandedly. She needed to exhaust herself.

Cooking was a pleasure for her, and though the task took up most of her day, it still wasn't enough to tire her so that she could sleep at night. Since the day she'd first kissed Justin, masquerading as Baldassare, she had not slept an entire night through.

Since Victoria and Aunt Cherise were not only better at sewing and other handwork than she, but enjoyed the tasks too, Valentine volunteered to do the washing. She arranged for an unused stove to be hauled up from the bowels of the ship to the deck. She boiled the linens, which she was certain were full of lice and other crawling things she didn't want anyone to identify, in a combination of salt water and ash. The second boiling was accompanied by a few drops of indigo, the blue of which made white linens appear whiter, and several drops of one of the precious oils she'd bought from the Gypsy woman, Elana.

Valentine was not in the least sorry for the lie she'd told Justin about giving both his crowns to the children. Actually, she'd only told half a lie because Elana had been a Gypsy and maybe she had children. If she did, they would need to eat, wouldn't they?

The oils had proved to be one of the wisest purchases of her life. The men had not only thanked her for scenting their linens, but had given her little tokens of their appreciation both in the fascinating stories they told her and in other ways. They liked her.

After her encounter with Justin this morning, Valentine had a feeling she would need the crew's support.

Valentine sat on a huge roll of hemp rope and scooped the last of the sun-dried down into the casing. Once Victoria sewed the casing shut, the pillow would be ready for Rabb to deliver along with the clean sheets that also smelled of Turkish rose.

"Miss St. James. I would like a word with you," Justin said.

Valentine was so startled by the sound of Justin's voice that she grabbed onto the pillow, hugged it to her, and in the process spewed down and feathers into the air.

A feather hung on her lower lip. "Pppttt." She spit it out.

She glared at him.

He was standing with his back to the sun. She held her hand over her eyes to shade them. Sunrays danced in his blond hair as it blew in the breeze. He held his hands on his narrow hips. He wore very tight cream-colored trousers and a clean white shirt with full sleeves, which was open at the neck. His stance was wide and his black boots were planted firmly on the deck. He'd never looked so handsome, or so powerful. He looked as if he'd just walked out of the sun, a golden god.

Justin had not been topside since they left Barcelona. If his anger had sent him to his quarters then, it must surely be his anger that brought him out now.

She braced herself. "What are you doing here?"

"It's my ship! Or had you forgotten?"

Valentine swallowed the lump of fear in her throat. His mood hadn't changed a bit. She was also aware that Mr. Henderson, who stood just to the port of them, had stopped looking at his map and consulting with the navigator, Mr. Aukland. She heard Mr. Midgeon's intake of breath. She felt she could almost hear the rest of the crew rolling their eyes heavenward, pretending to be uninterested when in fact each one had fine-tuned his hearing.

Nobody was going to miss this fight.

"I hadn't forgotten, Your Lordship," she addressed him primly.

Justin was aware that the entire crew was on guard. He wondered whose side they were on. They were practical men, he thought. They knew he paid their wages. He wondered if she had told them her side of the story. He wondered if they thought him a lout.

No, he thought. He had not mistreated Valentine. He'd simply gone to his cabin and tended to his accounts.

He glared down at her. Or tried to.

She had never looked so tempting as she did just then. As the clumps of down floated around her, he had the impression that she was suspended in the clouds. Like all angels.

She'd obviously been working over the steaming iron pot of boiling linens because beads of sweat and condensed steam rolled down her cheeks and throat. She had turned in the collar of her blouse and exposed a good deal of neck, shoulder and chest. She had pushed her long sleeves above her elbows. Her beautiful hands were red and rough from the scrubbing she'd been giving the clothes on the washboard. Her hair had fallen out of the chignon she wore at the back of her head, and wet silver spirals cascaded over her forehead and cheeks. Her lashes were wet and cast long, spiky shadows on her cheeks.

He wanted her so desperately he thought he would lose his mind. He wanted to reach out to grab her and pull her into his arms. He wanted to ravage those sweet lips and thrust his hand down into her open blouse. He wanted to whisk her away to his chambers and make love to her for the rest of the voyage.

Mr. Henderson coughed.

Justin suddenly remembered the crew. He dropped his arms. He clenched his fists instead. Then he rammed them into his trouser pockets. ''What do you think you

164

are doing, Valentine?'' he asked.

She tore her eyes from him and went to the task of picking the clumps of down off her chest, her lap and the deck around them. She stuffed them back into the pillow.

Lord! How wonderful life had been for three days without Justin around. Paradise did have its boundaries, however, she told herself. ''I've been laundering the down.''

She rammed a fistful of the fluffy stuff into the casing.

''I can see that. But why?''

''Because no one has done it for years. And in case you were not aware, this is expensive down. Eiderdown, to be exact. This isn't that cheap stuff that comes out of China. Nor is it simply Polish or Hungarian down, although those are fine qualities, to be sure. I've heard that since Napoleon's fascination with Russia, it will be years till the English see Siberian down again, but eiderdown is incredibly fine—''

''Valentine, I didn't ask for an education on down. I asked what *you* were doing at these stoves.''

She bolted to her feet and clutched the pillow with her left hand. ''If Your Lordship had paid any attention to the condition of this ship, you would have realized that this place was a pigsty! Filthy linens breed disease, Your Lordship. I'd already discovered that Rabb was catching cold. An influenza on this ship could easily wipe out your crew for days. It could have led to death. Considering the fact that everyone has been underfed lately, that was a real possibility. The only hope for the matter was boiling the linens and bedding.''

''That is commendable of you, Valentine. And I thank you for looking after the well-being of my crew.''

''Boiling kills the lice,'' she continued as if she hadn't heard him, ''of which there is a great deal on this ship.''

He smiled at her.

"What did you say?" she asked.

"I commended you."

"That's what I thought you said," she said softly, smiling at him. Suddenly her natural suspicion of him returned. "Why?"

"Why what?" he asked good-naturedly. He wondered if she knew that her damp blouse was plastered against an equally damp camisole underneath. He could see her nipples. His eyes shot around the deck as he scoured the eyes of his crew. Had they seen her nipples? No doubt they had.

"Why are you commending me?"

He reached out and grabbed her free hand. He jerked her toward him as he took a step back toward the door that led to the deck below. He could not and would not allow his crew to look at Valentine's nipples. If anyone was going to gawk, by God, it would be him.

"I said I wanted to speak with you," he said forcefully as he continued dragging her toward the door.

She tripped on a piece of rope and sailed into his backside.

"Ooomphhhh!" Her cheek slammed against his back. The rope entwined around her ankle and would not free her. As Justin continued walking, Valentine remained stationary, and her face slid down to his lower back and across his rump before she fell to the deck.

Justin turned around. "No more tricks, Valentine." He leaned down and kept his voice to a whisper. "I'm not going to hurt you. I just want to talk to you. There's no need for your theatrics."

"I'm not being dramatic, Lord Hawkeston." She pointed to her ankle. "My foot is caught."

Justin untwisted the rope and freed her. He glanced at Mr. Henderson, who was about to burst into laughter.

"Come," he said as he put his hands under her arm-pits and lifted her. He felt a very full breast in the proc-ess. "Let's go to my cabin."

She wrenched herself out of his grasp. "We'll talk here." She shoved the pillow in his face. "I have work to do."

He leaned his face into hers. "I think you should know that your blouse is so wet that the crew can see your . . . your . . . breasts."

Valentine was mortified. She hoisted the pillow to her breasts and hugged it. A crimson blush went to her cheeks. She didn't dare look at Mr. Henderson or Mr. Midgeon. No wonder they'd all been so nice to her, telling her stories while she boiled the down and stirred the linens! How naive could she be?

She'd been the object of their jokes for days! How would she ever hold up her head again?

"Your cabin will be fine, my lord."

Valentine went to her own cabin and changed clothes. When she looked in the mirror she gasped at her reflec-tion. Saints alive! She'd turned into a washerwoman! She lifted her hand to her sunburned nose and cheeks. Her chest and neck were turning to tan just like the sail-ors'. Her hands were red from the caustic soap and hot water. Her hair was a sight! It would take Aunt Cherise days of messing with the irons to fashion this rat's nest.

How could Justin have stood to look at her? He must have thought her a madwoman, taking on such duties. And to lose her looks in the process was insanity.

Yes, that was what had happened. She'd worked her way into madness. But the truth of the matter was, if she hadn't worked she would have gone crazy from lack of sleep. Any way she looked at it, Justin was behind her downfall.

She stepped out of her wet clothes and put on a clean camisole, scented with rose and jasmine. Then she put on a buttercup yellow day dress which was trimmed with white lace around the rounded bodice, the edge of the elbow-length sleeves, and under the breasts where the Empire waistline was formed.

The dress was several years old. In fact, she'd had it made when she was only fifteen. She realized as she frowned at the snug-fitting bodice that her body had matured quite a bit since then. It was the only fresh gown she had. The others were being laundered or were still packed in her trunks below decks. Though it was ill-fitting, this dress would have to do.

She started for the door when she heard a knock.

"I thought we could talk in the dining room," Justin said, opening the door. He gasped.

Ever since their earlier encounter, he'd thought of nothing but Valentine's breasts. He'd paced his room until he couldn't stand the wait for her any longer. He was about to jump out of his skin. He'd gone to her cabin hoping to catch her in the act of dressing.

He would kiss her, he thought. He would let her take the course of action from there.

He couldn't take his eyes off her breasts. They were nearly popping out of the low-cut yellow dress. He could see her nipples practically popping through the thin cotton. He gaped at her.

Valentine took one look at Justin's startled face and knew he hated the dress. "I'm sorry, my lord, but it's all I have right now. I was laundering the rest of my clothes."

He shook his head. Maybe if he moved his entire head he could take his eyes off her breasts. "It's lovely."

"It's quite ill-fitting. It's old, you see. Over three years old. I was much . . . thinner . . . then."

168

He forced his eyes to her face. God, she was lovely. She'd arranged her hair for him. Not being privy to a ladies' maid, or even the irons to curl her hair, what she'd done with just a brush amazed him. The act of arranging her silver hair in soft cascades that fell well past her shoulders was probably the sweetest thing anyone had done for him in a long, long time.

He realized he was just about as lucky as the Gypsy boy she'd given his money to.

"You . . . look wonderful," he assured her.

He stretched out his hand and helped her over the threshold.

Suddenly he was acting as if she were made of fine porcelain. Valentine didn't know what he was up to, but it was something. From what she'd observed of Lord Hawkeston, he had a purpose to every move he made.

She followed him down the passageway to the dining room. He opened the door and stood back while she entered. He smiled at her as she went inside.

Passing so closely to him she could smell his cologne. She smiled to herself. He hadn't been wearing any earlier that day. He was trying to win her sympathies. She wondered why.

"Valentine, I'm going to do something I've never done before."

"And that is?"

"Apologize. To you. I'm going to apologize to you," he said firmly and proudly. He kept his hands clasped behind his back so they wouldn't betray him and suddenly attach themselves to her breasts.

Valentine smiled but remained silent.

"You didn't hear me?" he asked. After all, this was a monumental occasion in his life. He'd never done this before. Shouldn't she be responding to his magnanimity?

"Yes, I heard you."

"And?"

She bristled as she watched him preen just a bit too much. "You haven't done it yet."

He hated it when she took him down a notch. But she was right. "I'm sorry, Valentine, for thinking so ill of you."

She smiled. Now she was preening. "And?"

"And what?" he snapped.

She supposed that since he'd never done this before, he was not well versed in apologies. Once he'd made as many mistakes in life as she had, he'd get used to it. "You don't think I enticed that handsome Gypsy to kiss me anymore now, do you?"

"No," he barked. "You think he was handsome?"

Her eyes widened. If Justin didn't think the man was handsome it took some of the thrill out of her victory. "He was practically the most handsome man I've ever seen. In fact, he could easily be a dream-come-true type of man."

"No woman in her right mind would dream about a savage-looking man like that!"

"I did," she confessed.

Justin's eyes flew open. She was toying with him. He wouldn't let her get away with it. "As I said—"

Valentine cut him off. "Let's not worry about who is and who isn't in my dreams. You're sorry. Very good. I accept your apology."

"Thank you."

"You're welcome," she said softly.

Justin felt better now that he was back in control of the situation. "There is another matter I wanted to discuss with you."

"What is that?"

"I want you to stop this foolishness about the laundry."

"Foolishness?" Of all the things she'd done in her life, Valentine was proud of her work with linens. She remembered learning about soaps, lyes, blueing, starching with rice, and the proper temperatures for ironing from the French maid, Gisette, her father had employed during the good times, before the wars and before the money had run out.

Valentine had never been afraid of hard work. She had never shunned a duty or task that her father or Aunt Cherise had given her. She had been taught by them both that honest work was a gift from God. She'd been taught to put all her concentration in her work and do the very best she could at any task.

Valentine had learned from Gisette not only to care for fine embroidered and hand-drawn linens, but to love them. Gisette taught her how to appreciate the beautiful fabrics that adorned their tables, beds and baths. She loved looking at a stack of snowy white French linen towels, all perfectly pressed and tied with white ribbons resting on shelves of the armoires in their house. Valentine had first learned about the making of sachets and blending potpourris from Gisette. She and Victoria had made linen sachets from scraps of fabric when they were small girls. Every drawer, every closet, chifforobe and armoire in the St. John house smelled of lilac, lavender, rose, jasmine or honeysuckle according to the season of the year. Valentine had always blended scents to dip their sheets and pillowcases into. She remembered the praise her father had lavished upon her for her work. During the days when they'd been impoverished, he told her that someday he would hire a maid again like Gisette to help her with the household chores. But her father had died before making good on his promise.

"Lord Hawkeston," Valentine addressed him formally. "I take it that you pride yourself on the work you do."

"I do."

"And that you are quite successful with it."

"I make a living, yes," he said modestly. "But what does this have to do with the laundry?"

She held up her hand. "Just as you are proud of your work, I am proud of mine. The laundry is not 'foolishness' to me. It was a necessary task that needed to be undertaken, which we have already discussed. However, what you fail to realize is that I enjoy this work."

"Impossible!"

"It's not. I don't think you've yet understood that our little family has not lived your kind of life for many years. All these gifts you intend to give my sister and aunt are wonderful, but not necessary. My father and my aunt have resorted to lies and trickery to make everyone think we had money. Papa was insistent that Victoria and I wed into titles and wealth. He knew that was the only way we could be provided for. The money he had to spend on ball gowns, hired carriages, parties and more clothes could have been spent on procuring himself a better doctor."

"Valentine, you can't blame yourself for your father's death."

"I blame no one. I'm just trying to make you understand. We are not children of privilege, Justin. We work just as you've had to work. I'm proud of what I do. I'm proud that I know things about cleaning and fabrics that other people don't. I'm proud that I have been able to rid this ship of lice, and possibly the cause of influenza, which might have led to serious illness. I'm proud that when your crew goes to sleep at night, each man has a reminder of home or a faraway place he's been where he smelled the perfumed oil I use in my rinse water. I'm proud of what I do, Justin. Don't diminish me by diminishing my work.''

She didn't lift her chin when she walked to the door. She didn't have to.

Chapter Twelve

"I suppose I owe you another apology," Justin said as Valentine reached for the door.

"Two in one day, my lord?"

"Two in less than an hour," he said solemnly. "I'm truly sorry. I had no idea. I want you to know that I felt terrible when I heard about how hard you were working. My men think I've driven you to become my slave. And that's not the case at all. In fact, quite the opposite is true."

He took her hands in his. "These are a lady's hands. I don't want to see them rubbed raw from scrubbing linens. I think it is admirable that you do this work. I do. But Valentine, you are to be my wife. Think how it looks to the men to see you working on a lower status than they."

"Now you are being impossible."

"No, I'm not. It's not good for morale."

She scowled at him. "I think morale is just fine on this ship, my lord."

"All right. It's fine. I'm the one whose morale is low right now. I know these men. When we get to London, they will tell everyone about what you did for them. The word will spread and every member of the ton will be laughing at you."

"At me?"

"At me, then. At us." His exasperation was growing. "This is precisely the kind of thing your father did not want for you. He wanted you to be a lady, Valentine. He wanted you and your sister to ride in fine carriages and wear beautiful clothes. He wanted the best for you. I would think any father would want that for his child."

"You do?"

"Of course, I do. I know I would want to hamstring any man who forced my daughter to work the way you've been working. It just isn't done, Valentine."

Valentine listened to his plea. If she hadn't detected sincerity and earnestness in his voice she would have retaliated. She realized that Justin was trying to do what was best for them all. But then, so was she. "Except for your cabin, the most taxing part of my work is finished. In order for you to procure either a cook or laundress for the duration of this trip we would have to put ashore. I understand from Mr. Henderson that to find qualified people, the search could take days. Since we are now off the coast of France and Napoleon has retaken Paris, that is out of the question."

Justin nodded. "Not unless we want to be blown to bits."

"Therefore, myself, my sister and aunt are the only members of the crew who are qualified."

"What are you suggesting?" he asked.

"That you go to the crew and explain to them what

I've just said. If we stop the gossip before it becomes a problem, your dignity will be saved, the boat will run efficiently, and the ton will not have my name to bandy about this season.''

He stared at her. "That . . . makes perfect sense." He smiled. "I'm impressed."

She glowered at him. Justin had the uncanny ability of tossing her emotions into the air one moment and then trampling on them the next. "You've never had a woman make sense to you, my lord? Or is it just me?"

"I didn't mean it the way it sounded," he said, trying to defend himself.

"Just how did you intend it to sound?" Valentine felt her anger twist free inside her.

He threw his hands up in the air. "Go ahead! Get mad at me! Nothing I say or do is right with you anyway. I was trying to compliment you."

"You call that a compliment?"

"It was the best I could do." He turned away from her and instantly left the room.

Valentine stared at the closed door. "Your best isn't good enough," she said aloud, but there was no one to hear her.

Supper was served in the dining room with Justin being attended by Mr. Henderson, Mr. Midgeon, Aunt Cherise, Victoria and Andrew.

Valentine had chosen not to swallow her pride but to ram it down Justin's throat.

She prepared a feast.

Rabb assisted Valentine in the galley.

"Fold the napkins like so," Valentine instructed Rabb. "The Hawkeston monogram should be on the outside bottom left corner."

After folding the napkins, Rabb assembled the water

goblets and wineglasses. Valentine chose the white china plates with the gold Hawkeston coat of arms in the center. She showed Rabb how to set a proper table, placing the napkin under the forks to the left of each plate.

"When Lord Hawkeston puts to sea on his next voyage, Rabb, I want him to know that you could handle all the preparations for a formal dinner. If he entertains a dignitary or an important business client, I want him to know that you can handle the situation."

"I never thought of my work like that," Rabb said with awe in his eyes.

"There is no job on this earth too lowly for us to perform, Rabb. Sometimes it is only our perception of roles that must be altered. Do you understand?"

"Not at all."

"All these years you've thought of yourself as just a cabin boy. You didn't realize until today how important your job can be at times. You thought too little of yourself. Now you see yourself through new eyes. Now you can see the future and that the day will come when your skills and talents may be the one thing that tips a business negotiation in Lord Hawkeston's favor. Your efforts make an impact."

Rabb smiled at her. "I like to think of myself like that."

"You're a very important person on this ship, Rabb. You have just as much right to claim the success of this voyage as anyone else. Everyone must work together to make this ship sail. And that includes you."

"I understand perfectly now," he said happily. As he finished folding the napkins Rabb whistled softly to himself, unaware of his newfound sense of importance.

Throughout the rest of the afternoon, Rabb helped Valentine to prepare the meal and decorate the dining room.

At eight o'clock he lit the candles on the table and not the oil lamp hanging from the ceiling. Valentine had explained that people digested their food better when the meal was eaten by soft light rather than in the smoke and glare of a whale oil lamp.

Rabb placed a clean pressed linen towel over his arm as he served the meal according to Valentine's instruction.

Rabb carried warm plates filled with baked fish topped with a pureed tomato, garlic, olive oil and basil sauce. Valentine had told Rabb to serve from the left and to clear the dishes from the right. Or was it serve from the right and clear from the left?

He served from the right.

Next, he brought in warm caraway bread and blackberry preserves. This was followed by bowls of steaming vegetables, fruit compote and hot coffee.

Lord Hawkeston was the first to declare the meal not only delicious but the best fish he'd ever tasted.

Valentine and Rabb joined the dinner party once the food was placed on the table.

"Truly, Miss St. James, the meal is splendid," Justin repeated for her benefit.

She smiled sweetly and nodded in his direction, but she did not lift her eyes from her plate, nor give him the satisfaction of a reply.

Justin chewed the delicate fish and watched her. She was deliberately ignoring him. She wanted him to suffer for the slights and barbs he'd administered. Hell! He'd apologized, but in the end it hadn't been worth it. He was still right where he had been with her. Which was nowhere.

"I've never tasted fish prepared like this, Valentine," Aunt Cherise put in when she realized that Valentine was not speaking to His Lordship. She glanced sidelong at Lord Hawkeston. Land of Goshen! His blue eyes could get stormy black when he looked at her niece.

Aunt Cherise had never married, but she had been in love. She knew firsthand that love took many twists and turns and had several odd edges to it. Unfortunately for Valentine and Lord Hawkeston, their feelings for each other were getting bogged down in pride, willfulness and misconceptions.

Those same sins had plagued her at a young age. She knew what it was to be torn between love and pride.

It was her guess that Valentine and Lord Hawkeston were falling in love. The sparks that flew between them would put fireworks to shame. Ordinarily, Aunt Cherise chose not to involve herself in the twins' personal affairs. She wanted them to make their own decisions and live their own lives. But something had gone astray for Valentine in these first weeks aboard ship.

Aunt Cherise had heard the story about the Gypsy king from Victoria and Andrew. She knew about Valentine's charity, and she also knew that Valentine had a way of walking into trouble with blinders on. If there was a remote chance of danger, Valentine seemed to sniff it out.

Aunt Cherise was convinced that Valentine wasn't totally without guile in her escapade with the Gypsy. Cherise believed that Valentine was trying to make Justin jealous, even if the thought was unconscious. Aunt Cherise believed it was time she had a talk with her niece before Valentine created a situation from which she could never extricate herself.

Valentine lapped up the compliments like a cat. When she served an almond cake drenched in apricot sauce, she almost preened under their accolades.

''Marvelous!'' Andrew hailed as he tasted the dessert.

Catherine Lanigan

"I don't remember this recipe at all, but it's wonderful," Victoria said.

Justin closed his eyes and savored every bite. "Incredible."

"Is it going to be this delicious every night?" Mr. Midgeon asked timidly.

They finished their dessert and coffee, and one by one the men excused themselves in order to get back to their posts. Victoria and Andrew promised to help Rabb with the dishes after they took a moonlight stroll around the deck.

With his newfound pride in his work, Rabb would not hear of it. He had learned how to properly stack the gold dishes with fine pieces of muslin inserted between the plates. The crystal was to be carefully wrapped in tissue and then placed in a special cupboard. He wanted to polish the silver himself. He wanted to make certain that tomorrow night was just as special as tonight.

Once the dishes were cleared, only Valentine and Aunt Cherise were left in the dining room.

"You're in love with him, aren't you, Valentine?" Cherise asked, taking her niece's hand.

"Good heavens! Whatever gave you that idea?"

"You're not acting like yourself."

"In what way?" Valentine's eyes held a quizzical look.

"Well, that's not altogether true. You are yourself, but you're not. You and mischief have always been playmates. But what I sense now is that your pride has gotten out of hand."

"Really?" Valentine didn't like the stern and probing tone of Aunt Cherise's words.

"Sit with me a moment, Valentine." Cherise pulled out a chair and sat opposite her niece. "I know that you and Victoria think I'm a meddling old fool half the time and that you could have much more fun without me tagging along—''

''Aunt Cherise, we love you. We don't think anything of the sort.''

''Don't lie quite so blatantly, Valentine.''

Valentine hung her head.

''I feel I've been lax in my duties as chaperone on this trip. But I've also mellowed over the years. Victoria and Andrew should be allowed some moments to themselves in which to plan their future and make their dreams. That's why I stay in my cabin so much. Thanks to you, they are able to make those dreams come true together.''

''I am happy about that.''

''I want to tell you something I've never shared with either of you girls, Valentine. I've never told you this story because I was too ashamed.''

''You? Ashamed?'' Valentine couldn't believe her ears. Aunt Cherise had never made an improper move or said an improper word in her life. She conducted herself according to the strictest rules and guides. She was horrified when Victoria or herself strayed from those guidelines. Valentine had often thought her own bad behavior was a direct result of Aunt Cherise's very strict rules. Valentine had simply wanted the challenge of breaking those rules.

''Yes. Ashamed.'' Aunt Cherise paused for a long moment. She folded her hands tightly in her lap and then looked up. ''When I was young, not much younger than you are now, I fell in love with a young man.''

Valentine didn't mean to gasp. But she did.

A tiny smile sat briefly on Aunt Cherise's lips before fading away. A sadness appeared in her eyes. ''His name was Bartholomew. He was titled and wealthy. We were very much in love. He wanted to marry me. In our joy we had not realized that others did not think our love was quite so grand. His family had other plans for Bartholomew. His father, the Earl of Havenshire, had planned for Bartholomew to marry Lady Estelle Princegate. She was older than he by five years, and he didn't like her, much less love her.

"As I've told you girls before, my parents wanted me to marry a Scottish earl. Well, I put up such a ruckus about it that my parents were forced to drop the idea.

"Bartholomew and I planned to run away to France together. That was long before all this Napoleon business and long after the French Revolution. We thought we would stay away from the cities and live in the country, perhaps in the South of France. We dreamed of owning a vineyard and living among the beautiful fruit orchards I'd visited in my fifteenth year when your father and I were young. We made all sorts of plans. I dreamed a million dreams staring at the stars at night.

"At the time we lived in Oxfordshire, near Oxford, and a close friend of our family's, Mr. Morton, came to visit my parents one day. As he was recounting the gossip from London, he informed us that Bartholomew and Lady Estelle had married. I tried not to let my shock show. I asked Mr. Morton if he'd seen Bartholomew and he said no. He told us that Bartholomew and his new wife had chosen not to honeymoon since they wanted to enjoy the season in London. They were the toast of all the dinners and parties.

"I told Mr. Morton that I had heard earlier that Bartholomew was being forced to marry Lady Estelle.

"He was shocked at my story and asked where I'd heard it. I told him I'd heard it from Bartholomew's sister, Jane.

"Mr. Morton couldn't understand why Jane would lie about such a thing when Bartholomew and Lady Estelle had been courting for over a year. That was the same year he'd said he loved me. Clearly, he said, Bartholomew was 'entranced' with his new bride. I'll never forget how Mr. Morton used the word 'entranced.' ''

Valentine reached out to her beloved aunt. ''How horrible to be betrayed like that. Poor Aunt Cherise.''

Cherise shook her head. ''No, that isn't all the story.''

She wiped a lone tear from her eye and continued. ''I was devastated. I remember giving an excuse to go to my room. I cried all night. And the next and the next. I cried for a year. When we went to London I always found an excuse to break away from my family and take a carriage ride past the house where Bartholomew lived with Lady Estelle. I always hoped I would meet him someday. I wanted to ask him why he'd chosen to betray me.''

''I would never have lowered myself!'' Valentine rushed to Aunt Cherise's defense.

''Oh, I had those days, too, when I cursed his name. Days when I would walk around Oxford asking God to put me a million miles from England. A million miles from my memories of Bartholomew's kisses. The touch of his hand.''

Valentine's sympathy for her aunt swelled. She could nearly feel her heart breaking.

''I never allowed another man to come within spitting distance of me, Valentine. I never let my heart melt long enough to find love with someone else. I blessed the day when your father married and then when you girls were born. I told myself you were my babies. I told myself God had saved me from a disastrous marriage so that I could be a mother to you. I pretended it didn't matter to me that Milton shuttled us back and forth across the continent. I told myself the days of lack and want were short-lived, and of course, now they are. I told myself I didn't need a man in my bed like other, weaker women. I had too much pride to be weak and sentimental like other women.

"Then one day, when I was thirty-one and long past marriageable age, I was in London shopping for clothes for you girls when I ran into Bartholomew."

Valentine's hands flew to her mouth as she gasped, "You saw him?"

"Yes. It was on King's Road. I was coming out of a shop and literally bumped right into him. He gasped and sputtered and asked me how I was. He held my hand and told me I looked beautiful. He told me that not a day passed without his thinking of me and sending me loving thoughts.

"I, of course, broke into tears. I lambasted him for lying to me and telling me that he had no feelings for Lady Estelle when all along he'd played me for a fool. I told him about Mr. Morton's visit and that I'd learned the truth from him.

"Bartholomew's hands shook and he started to cry. He told me there was no truth to what Mr. Morton had said. His mother had discovered one of his letters to me in which he'd made plans for us to run away to France. His father forced him to marry Lady Estelle.

"And then he told me the most shocking thing of all, Valentine."

"What was that?"

"He told me that Mr. Morton had been Estelle's lover! He said that Estelle's family had forced her to marry Bartholomew. Mr. Morton had been forbidden to see Estelle ever again. When Mr. Morton saw me at my family's house, he was on his way to Scotland. Bartholomew said that Mr. Morton was so embittered he wanted me to suffer as much as he, and that was why he told me that Bartholomew had married Estelle.

184

"But Bartholomew told me that he had not yet married at the time of Mr. Morton's visit to my family's home. Mr. Morton had lied. The marriage did not take place for another month. Had I gone to Bartholomew right away, we might be married today."

Valentine was crying silent tears for her aunt, for Bartholomew, Lady Estelle and even the bitter Mr. Morton. They had all loved and lost . . . tragically.

Aunt Cherise pressed Valentine's hands to her cheek. "Don't let pride keep you from happiness, Valentine. Find a way to get to know Lord Hawkeston. There are sparks between you two. I've seen them. Let them be sparks of love and joy. Don't let anger rule your heart. It isn't easy to grow old alone."

"Oh, Aunt Cherise." Valentine hugged her. "I never knew. Victoria never knew. I wish you'd told us this a long time ago."

"Why? I don't want your pity. I want your love. But now that you and Victoria are making lives for yourselves, my role is becoming small. Quite small, indeed."

"Small?" Valentine queried. "How can you possibly think such a thing when quite the opposite is true. I will be marrying Justin and having babies. Victoria and Andrew want no less than six children. So you cannot possibly think that your place in our lives will be diminishing."

Aunt Cherise's eyes were wide as saucers. "Six? I have heard nothing of this. That will be a family!"

"It certainly will, and we expect you to be there for every joyous moment of it."

Aunt Cherise smiled. "I will be, dear. I will." She rose and started to leave the dining room. "Valentine, promise me you will think about what I said."

"I will think very long and very hard on every word," she replied.

Valentine watched her aunt leave.

Valentine had never heard such a sad story in her life. And to think it had happened to her very own aunt. Why was it that life's lessons had to be so hard?

Wisdom was what Aunt Cherise was trying to show Valentine.

Valentine promised herself that she would become wise.

Chapter Thirteen

Gypsy tricks were a last resort, Valentine thought, but she was desperate. In a large tin pot she melted several clumps of beeswax. With a mortar and pestle she ground four leaves of sage. She had hidden her secret vials of potent oils in a low pantry cupboard underneath burlap sacks of turnips and carrots. She took off the protective cheesecloth that she'd wrapped around the small crate. The vials glittered in the morning sunlight and cast a rainbow of color on the galley walls.

"Why, they're almost magical," she said to herself as she pulled out the four vials she would need.

She'd used many of the scents to perfume the linens, pillows and bedding. But these four that the Gypsy had told her would alter Justin's attitude toward her had not yet been uncorked.

As the beeswax melted she added the magic formula of nine drops of clary sage, one drop of savory, two drops of ginger and four drops of ylang-ylang. She prepared the wick and stood it in the center of a short cylinder mold. Then she poured the beeswax into the mold.

She had to admit the aroma was enticing. All she could hope was that the Gypsy was right and that this fragrance would make Justin feel less faraway and distant.

Earlier that morning she had laundered Justin's bed linens and ironed three of his shirts. She'd added sandalwood to his sheets since she knew that for a man sandalwood acted like a sedative. To the rinse water for his shirts she added five drops each of orange and rosemary just because she liked the clean fragrance.

As she worked with the different scents, she observed her own reactions to each and wrote them down in her journal. If she blended jonquil, sandalwood and bergamot, her anxieties seemed to disappear. When she mixed lemon, coriander and nutmeg, her tension and mild headaches vanished.

She also noted, in the interest of science and her experiments, that the source of her anxiety, tension and headaches was Lord Hawkeston.

She frowned when she realized that if she was going to be married to him for the rest of her life, she would be mixing scented formulas for a long time.

Victoria walked into the galley just as Valentine was testing the hardening beeswax.

"My! It smells wonderful in here, Val. What is it?"

Valentine shut the galley door behind her sister. She didn't want anyone to overhear them. "I'm making candles."

Victoria's eye caught the array of brightly colored vials. She instantly knew her sister was up to something. "Is that what you've been using to scent the linens?"

"Yes."

188

"My God, Val! What do you have here?" Victoria passed her hand over the treasure trove of corked vials.

"Just about everything you can imagine," Valentine said proudly.

Victoria's eyes were appreciative as she lifted a vial filled with a deep purple liquid. "This is heaven!" She inhaled the scent of patchouli. "It smells sinfully exotic."

Valentine feigned innocence. "Really? The Gypsy told me it was erotic."

"Val!" Victoria gasped and quickly corked the vial and put it back in the crate. She couldn't stop staring at it. She picked it up again and uncorked it. She drew in a deep breath of the pungent, spicy aroma. "It is utterly divine."

"Not too much, Vicki." Valentine took the vial from her sister. "I don't want you swooning."

"Honestly, Valentine. I'm not that faint-hearted."

"I'm just teasing. But I am glad to see this adventurous side of you. Does Andrew know this about you?" Valentine laughed.

Victoria smiled broadly. "He will soon enough." She gleefully rubbed her hands together. "This *is* exciting, Valentine. I can see why you've practically locked yourself away in here. What fun!"

She looked at the candle Valentine had made. "And this?"

"It's a special gift for Lord Hawkeston. When he lights the candle, the scent will fill the room. The Gypsy told me it would make him less faraway and distant."

Victoria's face screwed up into a puzzled look. "What in heaven's name are you talking about? Justin isn't faraway and distant."

"He most certainly is," Valentine said.

Victoria shook her head. "If anyone is distant, it's you."

"Vicki, sit down. You've lost your mind." She put her hands on her sister's shoulders and pushed her into a chair.

Victoria was having none of it. "Sometimes I think you are so brave, Val. And then other times I wonder how we could possibly be related, much less twins."

"Your comments are always appreciated, Victoria," Valentine said sarcastically.

"You are so addle-headed! You're the one who pushes Justin away every chance you get. He compliments you on the meal you've made and you ignore him. He has ordered his men to give you full reign on his ship. He lets you come and go and do as you please any time of day or night. Even I know about your sleeplessness and your strolls on deck at midnight."

"Oh, ho! That's like the pot calling the kettle black! And who is trying to hide behind the dinghy and steal kisses? I've seen you and Andrew sneaking around the ship . . . and in the daylight, too. You should be ashamed."

"Oh, hush!" Victoria wished she wasn't quite so prone to blushing. She didn't feel guilty for kissing Andrew. She just wished the time would pass more quickly so they could be married. "We're not talking about me. We're discussing your situation."

"You mean *you* were discussing my situation," Valentine countered.

Victoria tossed her a frustrated look and continued, "Justin has a faraway look in his eyes all right. When he looks at you, he looks as if he wants to take you far away with him. I should know. I've seen that very same look in Andrew's eyes and I've asked him what it meant. That's what he told me."

Valentine was astonished at Victoria's comment. "Vicki, you're not just saying that to make me feel better?"

"No. I thought you were aware of it. I thought *that* was the problem between you. And all the time you felt Justin was being distant." Victoria shook her head. "I thought you were supposed to be the worldly one."

Valentine folded her arms across her chest. "I am more worldly, and don't forget it." Valentine instantly remembered that her only worldly encounter had been with Justin the night of the ball. But she couldn't tell Victoria her secret. It was best she drop her haughty attitude. She changed the subject. "Help me with these candles, Vicki," she said, going back to the safety of the stove.

"All right."

Victoria held the wicks in place while Valentine poured the melted beeswax into the molds.

"It's too bad they aren't as pretty as they smell," Victoria said. "I'd love to decorate them somehow."

"Victoria, this is not an embroidery project," Valentine said, taking the cooled candles out of the molds. Then she prepared a set of wicks for hand-dipped tapers. She thought she would scent these tapers in bois de rose, one of her favorites.

Victoria began rummaging through the galley. She found parchment paper, a marble rolling pin, and bits of savory leaves, bay leaves, long thin blue silver pieces of sage, dried rose petals, and dark purple sprigs of lavender. On a flat wooden board that Valentine used to knead bread, Victoria laid a piece of parchment and then artfully arranged the dried flowers into a pattern that looked like a spring meadow.

"I want to try something, Val. Would you bring that melted wax over here?"

Valentine was curious as to what her sister was doing,

191

but Victoria was not willing to explain. She instructed Valentine to pour the wax over the flowers. The first attempts were disastrous. The dried flowers floated everywhere. With the tines of a fork, Victoria corrected the placement of the flowers. Quickly, before the wax cooled, she placed a second piece of parchment over the flowers and then rolled the paper, wax and flowers around the rolling pin so that it formed a cylinder.

Next, Victoria put her cylinder of wax and flowers into the oiled candle mold and removed the paper. Victoria held the wick in place while Valentine filled the mold with hot beeswax.

When the wax cooled, Victoria pulled out her creation.

"It's beautiful," Valentine said.

Victoria was quite pleased. "Beautiful to look at. Beautiful to smell."

Valentine agreed with Victoria that a house filled with their wonderful candles would be paradise. While Victoria attended to the flower arrangements for the candles, Valentine experimented with the oils.

They worked all afternoon creating an array of candles.

Valentine personally went to Justin's cabin with his linens, shirts and candle. She carefully placed his shirts in a drawer and inserted tiny sachets filled with dried orange peel, ginger and cardamon. She made the bed with the perfumed sheets. Between the pillow and the linen pillowcase she slipped a small sachet filled with sandalwood and rose petals.

She smoothed the sheets with her hands, making certain the linens were tightly tucked. She'd never been so meticulous about making a bed. She realized she wanted to please Justin.

She'd given extra care to his shirts, hoping he would

lip. "I know I should have. I kept thinking this voyage would last forever. Now we are only a few days from London and every old bag and crone in the ton is going to comment on my working hands. What'll I do?"

"Is it my imagination," Aunt Cherise began with an accusatory glint in her eye, "or did I not say those precise words to you less than a week ago?"

Valentine hung her head sheepishly. "You did."

"Then why all of a sudden have you chosen to listen to them?"

"Couldn't you just tell me what to do?"

"I'll grant you it's a provocative question. Your answer will tell me quite a lot about what's going on in that reckless head of yours."

Valentine was cornered. "I . . . I don't want Lord Hawkeston to have any reason to . . . to . . ." Valentine's eyes darted around the room. She didn't want her aunt to know about her feelings for Justin. She had wanted to keep them a secret. She'd walked into this one, all right.

"To what, Valentine?" Aunt Cherise knew if she didn't press her niece, she'd never get an answer.

"You're the one who told Victoria and me how those people talk. How they exaggerate things. I wouldn't want them to think that Justin had been forced to marry a laborer."

"But you are proud of your work, Valentine. You've said as much many times," Aunt Cherise egged her on.

"Yes, I am. However, people like that just don't understand people like us . . . me. They won't understand about our impoverishment. They will try to convince Justin that I'm common, though we do have noble blood."

"Thin as it is. Yes, we do. Your grandfather was a landed lord in Oxfordshire. You have just as much right

201

at court as any of the others. However, it takes a great deal of money these days to keep up appearances.''

"So you've said many times."

Aunt Cherise eyed her niece suspiciously. "I don't believe you are at all concerned about what the ton thinks, Valentine.''

"No?" Valentine said innocently.

"I think your concern about your hands is because you want Lord Hawkeston to be proud of you. Proud of your ability to be a good wife, and that would entail your being accepted by his social circle. Isn't that a bit more accurate, Valentine?"

"Yes." Valentine folded onto the chair. "I'd never thought about all these things until I realized today that we are so very close to home.''

"You thought you were going back to the life we used to lead, didn't you?"

"It was childish of me, but I did." Valentine sighed.

Aunt Cherise put her arms around Valentine's shoulders. "There now, it will be all right. The ton will grow to love you. The men will think you are beautiful, and with all of Lord Hawkeston's money to outfit you, there won't be another woman in London as striking as you, my child.''

"Oh, I wish that were so," Valentine responded glumly.

"Have you forgotten the appreciative glances you got the night of the ball at the countess's palace?" Cherise reminded her.

"Ugh! I'm mortified when I think about it. Aunt Cherise, those gentlemen were staring at me because I was practically falling out of my bodice! And I only did that because I was angry. I wanted to shock everyone.''

"And you did."

"I thought my life was over. I thought my future husband was going to be an old toad!''

Aunt Cherise started laughing. She grabbed her sides and laughed some more.

Valentine frowned. ''It's not funny!''

''I'm sorry, Val. I forget sometimes how very naive you are. And how active your imagination can be. Didn't you hear me when I said I'd heard from the ton years ago that Lord Hawkeston was a rogue?''

''Yes . . .''

''Well, how could he have that many women if he were ugly? Of course, he would be handsome as the devil. And he is.''

Valentine pouted her lips and folded her arms across her chest defensively. ''Is this conversation supposed to make me feel better about my future husband? And just what does that mean, 'many' women? I want to know. I certainly do not want to appear naive any longer, Aunt Cherise.''

''It was just a manner of speaking, Valentine. I didn't mean anything specific by it.''

''Who told you that Justin was a rogue, anyway? Was it more than one source?''

Aunt Cherise had to pause and think. ''Come to think of it, I don't remember there being any more than one person. Lady Sarah Whitecastle. Yes, that was it. She was an incredible gossip. I've never met anyone like her. Everyone in those circles is notorious for spreading rumors, but she is incorrigible. She seems to know when a couple is having difficulties before they do. She knows who is pregnant before the husbands are told. She knows not only personal but financial information about everyone who attends court. She can recite most everyone's blood lines back as far as Henry VIII. She knows who is inheriting what and how much. I've often heard it commented that Lady Sarah Whitecastle has a catalogue

in which she keeps rumors . . . in alphabetical order!''
Aunt Cherise laughed.

Valentine lost her sense of humor. ''What a despicable person! I can't believe you associated with her!''

''It's rather difficult not to. If you intend to accompany your husband to a single party in London at any time in your life, I promise you will meet Lady Sarah Whitecastle.''

''It sounds to me as if she has no life of her own. She must be terribly bored and lonely to involve herself so much in everyone else's life.''

Aunt Cherise smiled proudly at Valentine. ''You are such a contradiction, Valentine. At one moment so sheltered and naive, and the next . . . There are times, my child, when you amaze me with your wisdom.''

''I do?'' Valentine was puzzled.

''Yes,'' Aunt Cherise put out her hands to her niece. ''Let me take a look at those hands.''

Valentine was glad she'd finished preparing the evening meal before she let Aunt Cherise and Victoria perform their remedy on her hands.

Cherise made a salve of rosewater, glycerin, aloe and witch hazel. She smeared Valentine's hands with the concoction before heating a pot of beeswax.

''What is that for?'' Valentine asked as she watched the wax gain in temperature.

Victoria checked the consistency of the wax. ''It's not ready yet, Aunt Cherise.''

Cherise looked at Valentine. ''Now, don't be afraid, Valentine. It won't hurt. I'm going to put the wax over the salve and then you will put on these cotton gloves. Then Victoria and I will wrap your hands in very hot steaming towels to drive the salve and the healing properties of the wax into your hands. When the towels cool, we will put a second set of hot towels on your hands. After the third set you will go to bed but keep the gloves on all night.''

Valentine's eyes were huge with disbelief. ''Who devised this torture?'' She started to stand.

Aunt Cherise pushed her back into the chair. ''Believe it or not, it's a miracle cure. Your hands will be nearly as good as new by morning.''

''It's worth it, Val,'' Victoria said as she dipped a wooden paddle into the wax and let the wax stream off the end.

Valentine was horrified as she looked at the wax. ''Must you gloat so, Vicki?''

''Ready!'' Victoria pronounced and moved the pot of hot wax to the kneading board where Valentine's fingers were splayed.

Aunt Cherise did not let a single drop of wax fall on Valentine's hands that she had not tested for proper temperature with her own delicate fingers first. Valentine was surprised that the procedure was not only painless, but soothing.

Valentine felt ridiculous with the giant swabbing of steaming towels around her hands, but Aunt Cherise assured her the results far outweighed the unattractiveness of her present condition.

Suddenly Valentine gasped. ''My beautiful supper!''

''Don't worry about a thing. I'll help Rabb serve,'' Victoria offered. ''Right now, we need to get you to your cabin.''

''We must hurry, Vicki. I don't want Jus . . . anyone to see me like this.''

''I'll come to your cabin after we've finished supper and feed you myself,'' Victoria promised.

''Thank you,'' Valentine said, rushing to the door of the galley. Reflexively she reached for the door handle.

Her padded hands were useless. She turned to Victoria. "I want you to know right now, I hate this."

"I understand, Val. Truly, I do."

Victoria checked the passageway to make certain no one was about and whisked Valentine to her room and shut the door. She helped Valentine into her nightgown and then pulled back the covers. She lit the lamp, as the sun had nearly finished setting. She handed Valentine a book to read.

"How do you expect me to turn the pages?" Valentine asked with a glum look.

"I don't know. Use your chin. Don't read. Stare at the wall instead."

Valentine waved her away. "I'll manage."

Victoria kissed her on the forehead. "For what it's worth, I think you are very brave, Val."

"You do?"

"Yes. And I'll be back in no time with something to eat."

Victoria let herself out of the room and went back to the galley to help with the last-minute preparations for the evening meal.

Valentine had prepared a lamb roast, rice, steamed green beans with shallots, bread, wine and cherry tarts for dinner. As was now their custom, everyone extolled Valentine's prowess in the kitchen.

Justin had been busy all afternoon making out his invoices to his clients who would be receiving their shipments of his fine Venetian glassware. He'd had a very difficult time concentrating on work when all he wanted to do was go back to Valentine and continue kissing her for the rest of the day and the night.

He waited patiently for her appearance at the supper table.

Victoria sat next to Andrew as usual and then bowed her head for the prayer.

"Where is Valentine?" Justin asked quickly. "We can't start without her."

"She's indisposed," Aunt Cherise explained. "She won't be joining us for dinner."

Justin watched Victoria give Aunt Cherise a quelling look. The two women were keeping a secret from him. But what could it be?

Had Valentine told them about his kiss that day? Had she been so upset with him that she'd found it necessary to take to her bed? He'd held himself back. Maybe he shouldn't have. Was she disappointed? Was she angry? Knowing Valentine, he had to consider that possibility. There was no doubt about it, something was wrong.

Valentine was a hardy young woman. She'd fared better in the storm than any of the others. She'd stitched and bound his wounds and done such an expert job of it that his wrists were marred only by narrow scabs. She'd taken on the job of cook and scullery maid. She'd tended his crew and undertaken the monumental task of cleaning the bedding and linens aboard ship. Valentine was no shrinking violet.

Justin eyed the women suspiciously as he cut into the lamb. Something was afoot. And they didn't want him to know about it.

Justin pretended that Valentine's absence did not bother him. Nothing could have been further from the truth. This was the first meal aboard ship that he had not truly enjoyed. The tarts were wonderful, but he would rather have been free to go to Valentine's cabin and uncover this mystery.

Mr. Henderson asked for Justin's help immediately following dinner.

Justin declined. He had to seek out Valentine.

Mr. Henderson insisted, and finally Justin agreed.

After Justin and Mr. Henderson left the dining room, Victoria prepared a plate for Valentine. She instructed Rabb to clean the dishes and then to set the table for breakfast the following morning.

"You can trust me, Miss Victoria. I know exactly what to do," he said, proudly puffing out his chest.

Victoria thanked him and went directly to Valentine's room.

Valentine was famished and ate ravenously. Victoria couldn't cut the lamb fast enough.

"Did Lord Hawkeston ask about me?" Valentine inquired.

"Yes, he did. Aunt Cherise told him you were indisposed."

"What?" Valentine opened her mouth and Victoria stuffed a piece of lamb into it.

"He seemed concerned about you . . ."

Valentine tried to talk with her mouth full of food, but it was no use. "He'll think I'm sick." Victoria scooped up a spoonful of fluffy rice.

"You are sick. In a manner of speaking."

Valentine had her mouth stuffed so full her cheeks were bulging. She wanted to berate her sister for letting Justin think something serious might be wrong with her.

Just then there was a knock on the cabin door.

"It must be Rabb. I told him to bring you some hot tea."

Valentine continued chewing as she nodded to her sister.

"Come in, Rabb," Victoria said as she lifted another spoonful of rice to Valentine's mouth.

"It's not Rabb," Justin said, scowling at Victoria and Valentine.

"Oh no," Valentine said and quickly swallowed.

"Lord Hawkeston . . . what are you doing here?" Frantically she tried to bury her hands under the sheets, but Victoria was sitting on the bed and she couldn't lift the covers. Then she realized she had not worn a peignoir. She knew he would be able to see her nipples through her gown. She tried to cover her breasts, but her bound hands flopped about the bed like porpoises jumping out of the sea. She looked down at her grotesque hands. She was mortified.

She had wanted to be beautiful for him. She had failed miserably.

"What am I doing here? What are *you* doing? And what has happened to your hands, Valentine?" He rushed to the bed.

"It's . . . nothing."

Justin turned to Victoria. "Maybe you would like to explain this to me."

Victoria stood instantly. "I think I'd better go see about the tea." She put the plate of food on the table and rushed out of the room.

"Coward!" Valentine shouted after her sister as she closed the cabin door.

Justin sat on the edge of the bed. He lifted her hands. "When you bound my wounds, nothing this severe was called for." His eyes were earnest and filled with compassion. "Did you cut them while cooking? It's all right, Valentine. You can tell me anything." He braced himself for the worst.

Valentine started laughing. She couldn't quit. Her face screwed up and hysterical tears streamed down her cheeks. She shook her head from side to side. Her ribs hurt and her back tensed, she laughed so hard.

"Valentine . . ." He clutched at her forearms. She'd lost her mind.

"Jus . . . Justin. It's nothing dire. I promise. I wanted

to have a lady's hands again. And mine had become so rough and gruesome-looking that Victoria and Aunt Cherise made a salve and bandaged my hands for me. I have to leave the bandages on till morning. They tell me this is a miracle cure.''

He looked down at the monstrous-sized bindings. ''And Victoria was feeding you because you couldn't do it yourself.''

''Yes, that's right.''

''I missed you at dinner.''

Her eyes softened. The last of her mirth skipped away. ''I missed being there.''

''I'll miss your cooking when we get to London,'' he said.

''I won't be cooking?''

''No. I have cooks for that.''

''Oh,'' she said and nodded sadly. She would miss the ritual of food preparation. ''What will I be doing in London, Justin? If I'm not cooking, I mean.''

He was staring at her breasts. He knew he shouldn't be, but he couldn't take his eyes away.

''I hadn't planned on your visit this evening, my lord,'' she said primly, hoping to distract him from her breasts. ''If I'd have known, I would have worn a peignoir.''

Justin jerked his head up and looked at her. He had to stop thinking about sex. ''You . . . look just fine.'' He got up from the edge of the bed.

''You're leaving?'' She was surprised at how disappointed she felt. She would have liked him to stay, but under the circumstances, she knew he was right to go.

''There's a great deal of work to do.'' He hesitated. What was he thinking of? He could finish his journal entries tomorrow. There was plenty of time for work. If he had half a brain he'd stay here and finish what he'd started earlier that day.

She did look rather ridiculous bound up as she was, but delectably ridiculous. He liked the way she laughed at herself and was so quick to put his mind at ease when she realized he was worried about her. She didn't play games with him. She didn't whine or carry on the way some women did to elicit sympathy. Valentine laughed at herself and brought him into the fun. He liked that about her.

"I think you should get some rest, Valentine. You've worked very hard on this voyage. Harder than I have." He leaned over and kissed her forehead. He let his lips linger on her smooth brow. She smelled like roses and jasmine. It was all he could do to restrain himself from nuzzling her neck.

Valentine closed her eyes when he kissed her forehead. She could smell the orange and sage she'd rinsed into his shirt. She wondered what he would say if she asked him to spend the night with her. She wondered if he would think she was bold, or would he understand that she simply wanted to be with him?

What a scandal it would be if Justin did sleep with her. Even if they remained chaste in the morning, no one would believe them. Both of them would suffer the loss of credibility.

They were less than 72 hours from docking, and already Valentine could feel the stranglehold of the ton.

Naively, she had hoped their life would not change when they were back home. But as Justin left her room that night, Valentine knew that for them nothing would ever be the same.

Chapter Fifteen

Like the pigeons that flocked to St. Paul's Cathedral, the ladies of the ton covered the granite steps to Lord Hawkeston's London townhouse by the dozens. Fat-breasted with white feathers in their hats, they peeped through the leaded glass door. They ruffled their ruffles and inspected each other's attire, casting mental votes as to whose plumage was most beautiful. Their heads bobbed up and down as they jockeyed for lead position. They chirped amongst themselves, creating useless cackles with little melody. Their round eyes surveyed the grounds, the porch and the butler's attire and manners, looking for faults. They placed their cards on the butler's silver tray like droppings.

"They're here!" Valentine shrieked as she peeped out the window. "I had no idea there would be so many of them. And all at once!"

Aunt Cherise grabbed Valentine's arm. "Come away

from that window. You mustn't let them know you are in the least bit interested in them.''

Valentine dropped the curtain and did as she was told.

Victoria finished wrapping a long royal blue ribbon around her silver curls. "But we *are* interested."

Aunt Cherise picked a piece of lint off the sleeve of her black day dress. "I've thought this through a great deal. This morning will be critical to our futures. They have doubtless heard stories about Valentine's betrothal. They've formed their opinions already. That display downstairs only proves my point. They want more grist for the rumor mill.''

"They do, do they?" Valentine's eyebrows knitted. "I'd like to show them—"

Aunt Cherise grabbed Valentine's shoulders. Her eyes were stern. "If ever you use the few good manners you've managed to assimilate in all your years with me, today is the day, Valentine St. James. No outbursts. No tricks. No teasing or toying with them.''

"But I—"

Aunt Cherise shook her for emphasis. "I mean it. These people are Lord Hawkeston's life's-blood. He depends on their trade to sustain his business. You have no idea how connected to the Continent these people are. They have relatives and friends around the world. One false move by you and we'll all pay dearly for it.''

"I was going to say I will do nothing to embarrass you or Lord Hawkeston.''

Aunt Cherise dropped her hands. "Oh. Well. Then, very good.'' She recovered herself.

"Please don't worry about us, Aunt Cherise," Victoria said, coming to stand next to Valentine. "We'll be perfect.''

They smiled at their aunt.

At times like this, when they were dressed identically

down to their hair ribbons and earbobs, even Aunt Cherise couldn't tell them apart. They wore royal blue velvet day dresses with black braided trim, black velvet buttons and black epaulettes on their military-style pelisses. Last year the military style was all the rage in London, but since Napoleon's recent victory in Paris, Aunt Cherise wasn't certain if the dresses were correct or not.

However, Aunt Cherise had rehearsed her response if the girls were brought up short on the matter. Because of Milton's death, she and the girls were in official mourning. Since their departure from Venice was so soon after the funeral, there had not been enough time to have mourning dresses made. Because the weddings were set for April, they were already breaking the convention that a year must pass before a wedding could take place. Aunt Cherise had discussed this matter with Countess Cioppoli and Lord Hawkeston.

The countess had advised Aunt Cherise to talk the girls into waiting. Victoria had waited two years already for her wedding to take place. Aunt Cherise was afraid if they didn't move hastily, Victoria had just enough fire in her to elope. No, the wedding dates could not be changed.

Lord Hawkeston believed his clout with the ton would override any disapproval. Aunt Cherise pointed out to Lord Hawkeston that he was setting himself up for censure. She warned him that people would think Valentine was already pregnant.

''Let them think anything they want. When they discover she is not carrying, they will drop the matter,'' he'd told Aunt Cherise.

Cherise worried. She worried that the girls would say the wrong thing or do the wrong thing. But that was nothing compared to Lord Hawkeston's headstrong will. It was no wonder he and Valentine clashed. They were two peas in a pod, she thought.

Cherise smoothed the folds of her black bombazine mourning dress. She hoped the fact that she wore the correct attire would be enough to satisfy the gossips.

The butler knocked on the door and delivered the calling cards. Aunt Cherise took the cards, and as soon as the butler left, she rifled through them so quickly that Valentine couldn't see how she'd read any of them.

"Saints in heaven!" Aunt Cherise's eyes were wide as saucers.

"What is it?" Valentine rushed to her side and peered over her shoulder at the snowy white engraved card. She swallowed hard. "Is that her card?"

"I'm afraid it is."

"Who?" Victoria asked, sensing their fear.

"Lady Sarah Whitecastle." Valentine said the dreaded name aloud.

"I was afraid this might happen." Aunt Cherise put the card at the back of the pile and finished looking at the rest of the names. "There is no one else of consequence in the bunch. Not a member of the royal family among them, which is good."

"That's good?"

"Yes. It gives me time to prepare you girls. And it tells me that we aren't as noteworthy as I'd thought. Most of these women are busybodies. The only one who can inflict any damage is Lady Sarah."

Valentine patted her aunt on the shoulder. "She'll like us, Aunt Cherise. It'll be just fine."

Aunt Cherise put the cards on the burled wood secretary. "We might as well get on with it." She led the way down the hall to the staircase. Valentine and Victoria walked side by side, their heads held high, backs straight, chins slightly aloof the way Aunt Cherise had taught them.

When they reached the first landing, Valentine gasped.

She had not been prepared for so many of them. The butler stood at the door still taking cards. They filled the salon and the vestibule. The upstairs maids had been enlisted to bring chairs from the dining room to place in the salon. The downstairs maid, the serving maid and the head housekeeper, Mrs. Finch, carried huge silver trays filled with delicate porcelain teacups and saucers. Three silver teapots had been emptied and refilled. The cook's assistant, Miss Reading, served petit fours, tea sandwiches and scones from a gold tray lined with a lace cloth.

Valentine wondered if someone had sent out invitations to the entire city. The only other time in her life she'd seen so many people at a gathering was at the ball at the Countess Cioppoli's. However, the countess had lived in a palace.

Lord Hawkeston's London house seemed large to Valentine with its 35-foot-long salon with two fireplaces and 12-foot ceilings, the dining room that could seat 24 guests, the cozy book-lined library, and the immense kitchen below stairs. There were four bedrooms upstairs and a fifth was being converted into a bathing chamber. The green and white marbled vestibule was nearly as large as the salon in the St. Jameses' old London house. When Valentine had walked into the house last night and seen the four-tiered Venetian crystal chandelier in the vestibule, she realized for the first time how far removed her world had been from that of Lord Hawkeston.

As she cast her eyes over the sea of impeccably dressed matrons, Valentine realized her fears had solid ground. This was one of those times she was very glad of Aunt Cherise's presence.

Aunt Cherise was a marvel to watch as she gracefully

greeted the horde of women waiting at the bottom of the stairs for room to be made for them in the salon. She remembered each of their names from days long ago when she was a girl and from the few times she'd accompanied Milton to court.

She smiled at them all and made them feel welcome. She inquired about their children and their brothers, aunts and cousins. They offered their condolences on Milton's death. Some were sincerely given, some were not. Aunt Cherise thanked them all and made certain each had something to eat and tea to drink.

Valentine marveled at her aunt's memory and ability to say just the right thing to each person. Except for the Countess Cioppoli's ball, Valentine had never had occasion to see her aunt in a social arena. Even then, Valentine had paid little attention during the short time she'd stayed at the ball. Valentine was amazed and delighted as she watched Aunt Cherise glide through the crowd, her head proudly held high as if she were one of them. If she'd been an actress on the Drury Lane stage, Aunt Cherise couldn't have offered a more perfect performance.

Just then, Aunt Cherise gave them their cue. "My dears, come meet Lady Sarah Whitecastle."

Victoria smiled sweetly.

Valentine felt her lower lip quiver when she faked her smile.

They walked up to a fat, white-haired woman of about 60 who sat on a needlepoint Louis XVI chair with a plate piled high with sweets. Aunt Cherise made the formal introductions.

"How do you do?" Valentine offered her hand to Lady Sarah.

Lady Sarah's faded blue eyes flitted from Valentine to Victoria. "Very well, my dear." She looked at Aunt

Cherise. "How ever do you tell who is who?"

"I've raised them since they were three, yet even I have difficulty sometimes," Aunt Cherise said.

Lady Sarah passed her thumb over the top of Valentine's hand. "Have you been in an accident, dear?"

"Pardon me?" Valentine asked.

"Your hand, dear. It's been damaged."

Lord, this woman could spot a cracked cuticle from a hundred yards away. Valentine's hands had never looked more beautiful. Aunt Cherise's remedy had worked wonderfully. Valentine had submitted herself to the torture two more nights before she was personally satisfied that her hands were as good as new. Except for one minuscule chapped spot on the second knuckle of her right hand, no one would have ever known her hands had been damaged. No one except Lady Sarah.

Valentine smiled sweetly. "Thank you for asking. I did have a difficult time at sea, I'm afraid. Did you hear that we were caught in a storm for two days?"

"No!" Lady Sarah breathed false astonishment.

"Yes. Lord Hawkeston bravely lashed himself to the wheel and brought us through the storm almost single-handedly. Why, if it weren't for his courage, his—"

Aunt Cherise cut her off before she'd made Lord Hawkeston out to be Ulysses. "We came through no worse for the wear," Aunt Cherise said flatly and threw Valentine a warning glance.

Lady Sarah didn't miss a single flutter of an eyelash. She'd gone fishing and her prey had jumped to the bait.

Just then the maids entered the room with more chairs. At last the guests were seated. To a woman, they all deferred to Lady Sarah.

Valentine's eyes scanned the room. This was the core of the rumor mill in London, she thought. Valentine wished she'd paid more attention to Aunt Cherise's instructions over the past years. But she hadn't. She'd thought her own thoughts and done just about anything she wanted.

Valentine and Victoria sat on either side of Aunt Cherise with their hands folded daintily in their laps. When the tea was passed, Valentine took a lace-edged napkin first, and because her hands were shaking so much, she declined the honey and lemon she loved.

Victoria took sugar and milk with her tea as always and a petit four. Valentine wished she could have felt as calm.

"I notice that your girls are not in mourning as you are, Cherise." Lady Sarah tossed the first gauntlet.

The women in the room cooed deeply in their throats, approving Lady Sarah's comment. En masse their eyes went from Lady Sarah to Cherise.

"As you know, my brother, Milton St. James, Ambassador to the King himself, died in Venice. The girls and I agreed to accommodate Milton's last wishes and we buried him there. Milton so dearly loved Italy, and the Countess Cioppoli arranged for a burial plot. She also announced Valentine's engagement at her palace. Since Lord Hawkeston's ship was due to leave Italy so quickly, I did not have enough time to arrange for a dressmaker for the girls. And so, now that we are back in London, I will rely upon you, dear Lady Sarah, to guide the girls as to their proper attire this spring and summer. As you can see"—she waved her hand over Valentine's beautiful dress—"we have been on the Continent too long."

Lady Sarah patted a fat white curl at the side of her ear. "The military style is passé, my dear. But, of course, you couldn't have known this. I would be most happy to help the girls. You will no doubt want them to wear violet and white this summer since they are still in mourning."

"Of course," Aunt Cherise agreed. "I hadn't considered anything else."

Violet? Did she mean lavender or that deep rich purple like the Gypsy man wore? Valentine knew she looked like a sick dog in lavender. She surreptitiously glanced at Aunt Cherise's tightly pressed lips. It *was* lavender! She and Vicki looked awful in that color. And white wasn't much better. With their pale hair and white skin they would look like albinos in white dresses. There had to be a way out of this, Valentine thought.

"Now, as to the matter of this wedding, Cherise," Lady Sarah began.

How did they know things so fast? Valentine felt as if her whole life were being swept into this woman's hands, and she didn't like it one bit.

"There are two weddings, Lady Sarah," Aunt Cherise corrected her.

"Yes."

It was evident to Valentine that these people didn't give a fig about Victoria. She was off the hook. Which meant that Valentine would be scrutinized twice as much.

"I want you to know that I have already informed Lord Hawkeston of the impropriety of rushing this wedding," Aunt Cherise said before an outright accusation was made. She'd watched Valentine use this tactic many times and it always seemed to work.

"You have?" Lady Sarah said, cocking one eyebrow.

"Indeed I have. He is well aware that decorum demands a year of mourning. However, if you understood how close Lord Hawkeston was to Milton and how much respect those two men had for each other, you would know why Lord Hawkeston wishes to carry out Milton's dying wish."

"And was that dying wish to offer his daughter in matrimony to Lord Hawkeston?" Lady Sarah asked viciously.

Valentine wanted to slap the woman.

Aunt Cherise quickly slipped her hand into Valentine's. "Is that what you've heard?"

"Yes."

"Then your source is wrong. My brother asked that Valentine not spend even a day, an hour, of her precious life grieving over his death. He wanted her to be happy. He wanted both his daughters to move on with their lives. To become loving wives and mothers . . . eventually, of course."

Cherise could tell that Lady Sarah was not convinced. Going out on a limb was Valentine's method of dealing with crises, not hers. Cherise braced herself as she hung off the end of the branch. "Valentine and Lord Hawkeston are very much in love. Why, you should have seen how he doted on her during our passage. I think it is just wonderful they have each other, and I'm very happy for them."

Valentine couldn't believe her ears. In her entire life she'd never known Aunt Cherise to tell a lie. She was amazed at how calmly and sincerely her aunt delivered the fabrication.

Lady Sarah tilted her chin up and cocked her head slightly.

Valentine could tell from the twitch in Lady Sarah's left eye that the woman didn't believe a word. Valentine prepared for a side attack.

"My source could not possibly be wrong, Cherise." Lady Sarah folded her arms under her ample bosom.

"I beg to differ on that point." Cherise fought for her foothold.

A Cheshire-cat grin spread across Lady Sarah's face.

"Even when my source is Lord Hawkeston himself?"

Valentine swallowed her gasp, squeezed Aunt Cherise's hand, and addressed the tyrant. "May I inquire, Lady Sarah, how Lord Hawkeston informed you of this? Did he send you a letter? Did he visit you in person somehow between the time my father passed on and the time of our arrival last night? Since he left this morning after breakfast with Lord Paxton on business, I doubt it would have been today."

Aunt Cherise dug her nails into Valentine's hand hoping to make her stop. Valentine only squeezed her hand back gently.

"Touché, my child," Lady Sarah said appreciatively. "You have no idea how much I admire gumption and quick thinking."

The flock of pigeons gasped simultaneously, their rounded breasts filled with air.

"Thank you," Valentine said. "But you haven't answered my question."

The beady eyes of the women quickly moved back to their leader.

"Nor do I intend to."

The pigeons exhaled together. Their breasts fell.

Lady Sarah rose. The pigeons rose with her.

The maids circled about the room with silver trays upon which the women placed their teacups, saucers and silver spoons.

If Aunt Cherise was mortified, she didn't show it. She rose, as did Valentine and Victoria. "Thank you for coming to visit today. I have enjoyed this opportunity to get acquainted with you again, Lady Sarah." Then Cherise nodded to the rest of the women. "Ladies all. Thank you for visiting with us. We greatly look forward to the next time we share your delightful company."

They waddled and padded and tiptoed out of the house.

The butler closed the door quietly.

Valentine threw her hands to her cheeks and dramatically flopped into a chair. ''I've ruined us! We'll never be able to go out in public again!''

Victoria put her hands on her hips. ''Lord Hawkeston is going to murder you for sure this time! Maybe he should have pushed you off that cliff!''

''How can you say such a thing to me? No, don't answer that.''

Suddenly Valentine realized that Aunt Cherise was not taking part in the conversation. She was still looking out the window as the last of the women exited through the wrought iron gate. And she was smiling.

Valentine looked at Victoria and motioned her head toward Aunt Cherise. ''Aunt Cherise, are you all right? I know you must be mortified.''

Aunt Cherise didn't answer.

''Are you in shock?'' Valentine asked. ''I could certainly understand it if you were.''

Victoria took her aunt's hands in her own. ''They're warm.'' She passed her hand in front of Aunt Cherise's eyes.

Aunt Cherise waved her hand away. ''I'm perfectly fine, girls.''

''I'm sorry, Aunt Cherise. I just couldn't help it. I don't mind if people talk about the truth, but when they insinuate things they're only guessing at, that is when I take exception. She was just searching for gossip. She doesn't really know how Justin and I feel about each other. Still, I'm sorry I defied her.''

Aunt Cherise smiled broadly. ''Well, I'm not.''

Victoria's eyes popped wide open. ''What?''

"You were absolutely correct, Valentine, and I support you."

"You do?"

"That old cow has had a comeuppance coming to her for years. It was interesting. I watched the faces of the other women, many of whom I've known since I was a girl. They weren't siding with Lady Sarah as much as I'd thought they would. Oh, I'll grant you that you were wrong in pushing Lady Sarah into a corner where you left her no way out. But it was a necessary move. I think there were several in that group who had wanted to do the same thing for a long time. However, only time will tell. Still, Lady Sarah is extremely powerful, and more were on her side than not."

"You mean this could be the beginning of her downfall?" Valentine asked.

"Let's just call it a changing of the guard."

"Is that good?" Valentine inquired.

"As long as you aren't put in the middle of it, we should fare well." Aunt Cherise patted Valentine's hand and started to leave the room.

Valentine stopped her. "Aunt Cherise, do you think I will be in the middle?"

Aunt Cherise frowned. "Unfortunately, Lady Sarah has chosen to make your forced marriage the target of gossip this season. You're not only in the middle, you're the bull's-eye. There will be no half measures, if I know Lady Sarah."

"Couldn't we go to the country for a while? Maybe another trip to Italy?" Victoria suggested her favorite escape routes.

"Absolutely not," Valentine said. "We shall fight till we can fight no longer."

Both Valentine and Victoria looked at Aunt Cherise for her final word. She nodded her head. "I agree with Valentine. We have no choice but to fight."

Chapter Sixteen

Valentine knew without a doubt that her father would have hated this gown. He never would have wanted his daughters dressed in mourning. He would have wanted them to wear his favorite color . . . red. Anything but this, she thought as she looked down at the folds of silk. The only spot of color was a pale lavender ribbon that ran beneath her breasts with streamers that flowed nearly to her knees.

If it weren't for the last stages of sunburn on her nose and cheeks, she would have little color at all. She frowned at herself in the cheval mirror. Her black eyes sparkled back at her. She looked like a snowman with black bits of coal for eyes. In her estimation, she'd never looked worse in her life.

Her hair was piled into an elaborate arrangement of long curls at the back of her head. Kathleen, the maid, had twisted the rest of her hair into small silver Grecian ringlets around her face. Valentine wrapped an amethyst-colored ribbon around her forehead three times as was the fashion. Victoria was wearing a lavender ribbon in her hair and had already told her sister that if anyone at Lady Purdey's dinner party objected, Valentine must simply explain that without the different hair ribbons no one would be able to tell them apart. Valentine felt she was still within the limits of mourning etiquette.

Victoria's line of defense against the ton was to conduct herself in letter-perfect fashion. Valentine chafed at the very thought of someone ruling her life. She merely promised herself that when she strayed from their rules, she would make certain she didn't get caught.

Valentine was expecting Justin, so when a knock came at the door, she called, "Come in, my lord."

Justin was dressed in formal attire. His shirt was snowy white, which enhanced his tan face and hands. The black wool of his coat and trousers made him look formidable and powerful. But his blue eyes looked tired, and though he smiled at her, she knew he was disappointed.

In the week since their return, Justin had not had more than a few hours' sleep each night. He never went to bed before one or two in the morning and he left at dawn each day. Nothing had gone right for him.

The overland shipping company he'd always used to transport his glassware to Edinborough, Oxford, Southampton and Bradford had gone out of business. It took him two days to find another company that was reliable. The house he'd planned to lease for Andrew and Victoria had been sold and he'd been forced to find another. There were no decent apartments available for Aunt Cherise. Everyone seemed to be sitting tight on their property due to the turmoil over Napoleon's resurrection. Until things were settled in France, the political

226

situation in Britain was precarious. Justin knew that in a few months everyone would tire of talking about Napoleon and go back to business as usual. However, Justin wanted his life settled down by summer's beginning. He was a man used to having schedules. He liked his life to be orderly.

Justin's life on this night was anything but orderly. He still needed to go back to his office and finish his correspondence. His country estate needed tending, and his foreman had quit while he was in Italy. If he didn't hire someone promptly, spring planting would be left to the cottagers and undoubtedly mishandled. Justin depended on the money from the estate to keep it running and to pay some of the bills in town. Justin juggled many bills to keep his creditors happy. If he could keep up this balancing act for just two more years, he would finally have enough money put back to feel secure. He was almost there, but one false move, one card out of place, and his own little empire would tumble.

"You hate the dress, too," Valentine said.

"The dress?" Justin hadn't paid any attention to it at all. His mind was overflowing with important matters. Then he looked at her.

The room glowed with the light from the cranberry lamps on either side of the bed and the scented candles Valentine had made on the ship and which she'd placed on the mantel. A soft diffused light seemed to surround her and catch in her silver hair, making her look like a moon goddess. Her eyes danced with happy lights and seemed to pull him into them.

He walked slowly toward her, unable to see anything but the mesmerizing glow in her eyes. Her lips were pink and pouting. She was disappointed about something, but he didn't know what it was. He could still detect a faint trace of sunburn on the tip of her nose.

It reminded him of their days at sea and the kisses he'd stolen from her. He thought of the way she'd taken over his ship and helped everyone who needed helping. The men still talked about her and asked him to mention their names to her when he saw her. They not only liked her, they had each fallen a bit in love with her.

Along with her disappointment, he detected anxiety. It was to be expected. This was their first formal dinner out since coming to London. None of them had found the time to visit friends since their arrival. There had been too much to do. Valentine and Victoria had spent a portion of each day at the dressmaker's, milliner's and bootmaker's. He'd learned of the strict guidelines they were to follow due to their father's mourning. Never having had any sisters, or a mother to remember, Justin had not paid any attention to these rules. Offhandedly, he wondered what difference it made to the dead what color dress a woman wore.

"The dress is beautiful," he said.

"It's white." She shrugged her shoulders. "It's all I'm allowed." Her lips screwed into a sullen frown.

He lifted her chin with his forefinger and thumb. "I think you look beautiful in white." God, he would never get used to the magnetic effect those eyes had on him. He felt he was being swept into a whirlpool of emotion. If he'd had his way, they would call off the dinner and he'd stay home and wrap his body around and inside his Valentine.

Justin could stand it no more. He kissed her lips. He took his time at first, letting his lips caress her mouth, tasting her sweetness. He wasn't prepared for the silky feel of her bare arms as they slid around his neck. He could smell rose and jasmine. She sank her fingertips into his hair and then pulled his head toward her.

She ravaged him. She demanded hungry kisses. She

forced his lips apart with her tongue and dueled with his tongue.

Justin sucked in his breath. My God, she was a passionate one, he thought. She leaned her body against his. Her breasts touched him, and this time he did not hesitate to indulge himself.

He held her throat just below the white velvet ribbon and cameo she wore. Then he let the palm of his hand slide down the column to the top of her chest. Her dress was low-cut and her chest was bare. He slipped his hand inside her bodice and caressed her breast. It filled his hand and he could feel the nipple harden. How many times he'd thought of touching her this intimately. How very many times he'd longed to feel her response. He wondered if she had any idea the joy it brought him to know that her body thrilled to his touch.

Valentine placed her hand over his. But rather than force him to withdraw, she pressed on his hand, craving more. He obliged her by massaging her breast with his long fingers.

She moaned a sound that he'd come to know was Valentine's signal of surrender. She'd come to the brink of the abyss. She could not turn back now. If he'd wanted, he could force her to the floor and take her right here. Right now.

"Are you ready to leave, my lord?" Aunt Cherise said quite loudly and with perfect enunciation.

Justin felt as if he'd been floating in a cloud and something had just pulled him back to earth. "Yes," he croaked over a lump of sexual need. He cleared his throat. "Yes. Quite ready." He put out his arm to his fiancée. "Shall we?"

Valentine took his arm as they walked out of the room.

How did he do that? Valentine asked herself. One

minute he was boldly ravishing her and the next minute he looked as if nothing had happened. She felt that every muscle in her body was quivering. Why, it was all she could do to stand. She'd been whirling among the stars, headed for another world when suddenly he'd stopped. She'd never even heard Aunt Cherise, but there she was standing in the doorway shooting her niece a quelling look.

Valentine didn't know what had come over her. She hadn't planned to be so aggressive, but when she'd looked in his blue eyes, she realized how much she'd missed him these past days. She had barely said two words to him. He was seldom home, and were it not for explicit instructions he'd left with Mrs. Finch, Valentine wouldn't have been certain that he hadn't left the city.

Mrs. Finch had turned out to be a wealth of information for Valentine, although it was clear that the woman's first loyalty was to Lord Hawkeston. Mrs. Finch had been in his employ for over ten years. She ran his home and traveled with him to the country house whenever it was necessary.

Mrs. Finch told Valentine that the house in town was run properly, but the country house was another matter. She blamed the problem on the laziness of the cottagers. They spent their days fighting amongst themselves instead of tending to crops or their duties at the manor house. She told Valentine that she'd never met more insolent people. They acted as if they were too good for the work.

Justin had told Valentine that since they'd recently returned from such a long voyage, he planned for them to take their honeymoon in the country. Valentine was overjoyed with the idea. She could relax in the country. There was no one from the ton in the country.

* * *

Seduced

The carriage was a sleek black lacquered beauty. It had silver velvet seats, silver velvet walls and Venetian crystal wall sconces filled with pink English roses. The team of black horses was equally as beautiful and were dressed in gray and silver livery. The driver wore black and the footman wore gray velvet.

Valentine sat next to Justin. Andrew sat between Victoria and Aunt Cherise opposite them.

"Lord Hawkeston, you look fatigued," Cherise observed. "Would you consider making a short evening of it tonight?"

"Thank you for your concern. However, I have no intention of ruining the evening for anyone."

"You won't be ruining a thing!" Valentine and Victoria pounced on the excuse for shortening this dreaded dinner.

Justin looked at Valentine. Then at Victoria.

Valentine shrugged her shoulders. "Twins think alike."

Victoria nodded frantically, trying to cover their mistake. "We do it all the time. You'll get used to it. Won't he, Andrew?"

"Huh?"

Victoria jabbed him in the ribs.

"You'll never get used to it," he laughed.

Justin laughed with him. He put his back to the corner so he could watch both Valentine and Victoria's reactions. "I've been around long enough to know that you two are hiding something from me. What is it?"

"Nothing," Valentine said quickly.

"We're just . . . thinking of your health." Victoria smiled sweetly.

Justin expelled a deep sigh. "Valentine can lie fairly well, Victoria. You do a very poor job. Now tell me."

Victoria hung her head. Valentine rushed to their de-

231

fense. "We heard at the milliner's shop today that Lady Sarah Whitecastle is going to be at the dinner tonight."

"What of it?" he asked.

"She came to visit us that first morning when we arrived in London. Aunt Cherise told us she was a terrible gossip and even Mrs. Finch confirmed that fact."

He nodded for her to continue.

"Well, we . . . I mean I did not make a very good impression on her."

"And what makes you think that, Valentine?" His voice became stern.

Valentine knew she was treading on thin ice. Obviously, this woman and her influence were even more important to Justin than Valentine thought. However, there was nothing she could do to save herself now. She had to tell him the truth. "When she stated that you had told her you were being forced to marry me, I called her on it. I knew it was impossible for you to have spoken with her. We left Italy so quickly and then we were at sea. There was no time. When I pressed her, she refused to answer me."

"I don't see why she did that—"

Valentine interrupted. "Neither did we."

"Especially since I did write her that I was bringing back a fiancée."

"*What?*" The three women gasped.

"Did it ever occur to you, my lord, that having my private affairs bandied about town would upset me? Did you ever consider my feelings?"

Justin's eyes were cold. His voice was aloof. "Frankly, no."

"You never thought about the untenable position this would put me in?"

"No. I didn't."

A lot of things had surprised Valentine about Lord

Hawkeston, but this selfishness on his part was a shock. She had been coming to think more highly of him, but apparently she'd been wrong to give him so much credit. She would never have been so indiscreet as to divulge personal information like this to anyone. Perhaps Justin was closer to Lady Sarah than she'd thought. These people were strangers to herself, but not to him. She reminded herself to tread carefully in this unfamiliar territory.

''I cannot believe you were only in London a day and managed to upset my friend. Well,'' he said, taking his black gloves off and then putting them back on again, ''I suppose I will have to apologize to her myself.'' Justin couldn't believe it. Until he met Valentine, he'd never apologized to anyone about anything. Not even about Arnold. Then he'd had to apologize to Valentine. Now he was apologizing for her. God, this was not going to be easy.

Valentine watched when he took off his gloves. He'd balled his fists. Lord! He wanted to hit something. Well, she did, too.

Valentine folded her arms angrily over her chest. And to think I let him kiss me . . . touch me! And what's worse, I was beginning to care about him. It's a good thing I discovered his flaw now. I could have lost my heart.

Justin looked at her. She could be angry all she wanted. He was just as angry. He thought it ridiculous for Valentine to be upset with him because he'd written to a friend about his forthcoming marriage. The ton was going to learn the truth when he arrived back in London. Hell, almost all of them would be invited to the wedding. He couldn't understand what was making Valentine so upset. He had more important things on his mind tonight than Valentine's misbehavior, like the problems at his country estate.

The cottagers were practically in revolt, refusing to carry on with the spring planting. Lord Paxton, Justin's neighbor to the west of his estate, had come to town and consulted with him all morning about the matter. Justin supposed there was no help for it; a long trip to the country estate was inevitable. He wondered how Valentine would take to that news. She would probably put up a ruckus about that, too.

Women! What a bother they were, he thought morosely.

Valentine was boiling mad at Justin and at herself. How could she have made such a mess of things? There was no doubting the fact that for Justin appearances were paramount. Even though she thought Lady Sarah was a toad, he did not. She had wrongly perceived Justin as a man who thought for himself and acted according to his inner beliefs. She had been wrong. Justin was no different from any of the ton when it came to acting a part, pretending to love a life filled with falsehoods.

Valentine wondered how she would be able to bear living such a life.

Chapter Seventeen

Lord and Lady Purdey's mansion was decorated in the French style of forty years ago when they'd first married. Everything was pale blue, gold, gold and more gold. Valentine had never seen such opulence. Rococo mirrors studded every available wall. There was hardly any art, quite unlike Justin's house, just chandeliers and mirrors. Justin told her that his factories had made nearly every mirror Lord and Lady Purdey owned. They were exceptionally good clients.

Because Valentine, Victoria and Aunt Cherise were in mourning, they were not allowed to dance or attend large balls and functions. However, small, intimate dinners and teas held in the homes of close friends and relatives were acceptable. Since Lord and Lady Purdey knew they were in mourning, Valentine expected a gathering of no more than twelve that night.

When the butler announced them in the salon, Valentine realized there were over three dozen people in attendance.

Lord and Lady Purdey were in their seventies, both quite spry and in control of all their faculties. They bantered good-naturedly with each other. Lady Purdey made a fuss over His Lordship, touching his hand and kissing his cheek whenever he said something clever. Valentine liked them instantly and wondered what kind of magic they had that had kept them in love all these years.

Lady Purdey took it upon herself to introduce Valentine, Victoria, Andrew and Aunt Cherise to her guests. She was a gracious hostess and with each introduction she remembered something personal about her guest that she relayed with good humor to Valentine. By the time the butler announced dinner, Valentine knew she'd found her first friend in London, and suddenly the prospect of living in town was not nearly so frightening.

As the guests lined up for dinner, Valentine took the opportunity to fall back and seek out Lady Sarah Whitecastle, who had been the last guest to arrive. Valentine knew she couldn't eat a bite until she'd spoken to the woman.

"Lady Sarah, I owe you an apology. Lord Hawkeston informed me that he did indeed write you about his promise to my father. My actions were uncalled for and I'm sorry. It was just that . . . I didn't want anyone to know that he was marrying me for reasons of honor and duty."

Lady Sarah tipped her head in a slight nod. When she looked at Valentine, her smile was thin and malicious. "Lord Hawkeston wrote me that he was bringing his fiancée home. He said nothing of the fact that he was being forced to marry you by a promise to your dying father. I deduced that much myself. Everyone knows that though your father was a favorite of the Prince Regent, it did him little good. Milton never had a farthing. However, Lord Hawkeston not only liked your father, he practically revered him. None of us could understand it. Then there was the fact that Lord Hawkeston had been seen with London's most beautiful and wealthy ladies. More importantly, titled women. I knew there had to be a reason why he would pick you to marry. Thank you for telling me.''

Then she grabbed Valentine's forearm. Her fingers squeezed into Valentine's soft flesh. ''You can apologize all you want, Miss St. James, but no one insults me in front of all my friends and gets away with it.''

Just then Henry St. Claire walked up. He was a tall man with broad shoulders and a trim torso. His black hair was slicked back with pomade. His dark mustache jerked upward when his full lips parted over startlingly white teeth. He would have been handsome except for the lust in his eyes. He was one of those men who leered at a woman's breasts when he talked to her. Henry St. Claire was mesmerized by Valentine's rounded bustline.

Had Valentine not been standing with Lady Sarah she would have said something witty, clever and damning to St. Claire. But one wrong move and Lady Sarah would make her life even more miserable.

''Lady Sarah,'' he said, taking the old woman's gloved hand and kissing it. Still he kept his eyes on Valentine's breasts.

''Henry.'' Lady Sarah preened.

Valentine felt her stomach lurch. Any minute now and the man would start drooling.

Lady Sarah pretended to be friends with Valentine. ''You don't know Valentine St. James, do you, Henry?''

''No.'' He reached out for Valentine's hand. ''But I would be most honored.

While Lady Sarah droned out the formal introductions, Valentine had the feeling that Henry was not only undressing her in his mind, but was doing lewd, unthinkable things to her. The second his lips touched her gloved hand, she snatched it back. "How do you do?"

Henry St. Claire smiled at her. His upper lip stuck to his teeth. "Are you here by yourself?"

"My fiance is waiting for me," she said, backing away. "He's waiting over there. You might know him." She took another step toward Justin. "Lord Hawkeston."

"Ah, yes. Justin. Best wishes, my dear, on your engagement. I'm certain Justin will invite me to the wedding. I'm looking forward to kissing the bride."

Valentine knew she was going to retch. She turned around and kept her eyes on Justin, who was carrying on an animated conversation with Andrew and Aunt Cherise. Only Victoria seemed to be aware of her predicament.

"Val!" Victoria walked demurely up to her and quickly took her elbow. "You look as if you're about to faint."

"I'm going to be sick." Valentine held her stomach.

"You can't! Not here. Not now," Victoria warned her urgently. "Everyone in this room is watching you and Justin."

"It's worse than we thought."

"How?" Victoria tried to smile as if nothing were wrong.

"The old witch has decided to hunt foxes. And I'm the fox. She intends to ruin me."

"Valentine, this is no time for dramatics. Justin is really serious about all this."

"So am I. She tricked me, Vicki. Justin told her he was bringing his fiancée home with him. He never said he was being forced to marry me."

Victoria's eyes flew open in shock. "We're . . ."

"Doomed," Valentine whispered along with her sister.

Dinner was served in a mammoth dining room with two long tables, each with 24 chairs. The tables were so long they required eight silver candelabra. An enormous chandelier hung in the center of the room. Justin explained to Valentine that it had taken his factory over nine months to make the four-tiered, 52-branch chandelier and a week to pack it for shipment. It took a crew of 16 men to mount it. Justin declared it his masterpiece. Valentine agreed.

Valentine sat across the table from Justin. She could only see half his face with the silver epergne blocking her view. Every now and then she would catch him watching her. She couldn't tell if he was pleased with her or angry at her. He was wearing that social mask she'd seen on so many people's faces that night. Their eyes were vacant and they laughed too loudly at jokes that weren't funny. They feigned indifference over social and political issues when they should have shown outrage. They were upset over trivialities when they should have cared less. It was a topsy-turvy world that Valentine was sure she'd never learn to like.

The only good thing she could say about the evening was that the food was incredible. Her favorite was the Scottish salmon. It was smoky, pink and almost sweet. The roast beef was tender, moist and brimming with juices. There were a half dozen kinds of vegetables, three kinds of potatoes and three choices for dessert. Four servers dressed in French court costumes of white and gold satin did nothing all night but pour wine. On her second glass of red wine, Valentine realized how easily she became intoxicated. She declined more wine.

Catherine Lanigan

Blessedly, Valentine and Justin were seated close to the head of the table near Lord and Lady Purdey. Lady Sarah and her escort, Henry St. Claire, were seated near the head of the second table. Lady Sarah had her back to Valentine, and there were enough candles and flowers between them that Valentine was not subjected to Henry St. Claire's leering eyes.

Justin couldn't believe he could be so angry with Valentine and at the same time be incredibly entranced. He would have had to be blind not to notice that every male eye in the room glanced her way. Even the women were not immune to Valentine's beauty. They engaged her in conversation and sought out her opinion on operas, her sentiment on Coleridge's revision of *Osorio*, which was produced as *Remorse* at Drury Lane Theatre. He was amazed at Valentine's insight into the poet, playwright and essayist's life.

"How is it that you know so much about him?" Lord Paxton asked.

"When he went to Italy nine years ago, we were there with father on a visit to the Countess Cioppoli. He was a friend of hers. He was quite ill at the time, as I remember, and I thought he was very sad."

"My dear," Lady Manewood said, "you were only a child. What could you know about his troubles?"

"Quite right," Sir Chilton agreed. "The man was so addicted to cocaine, he hadn't a clear thought in his head. All those problems with his wife and the breakup with his mistress, Sarah Hutchinson, would have been enough to do me in, I can tell you that."

Valentine listened to the way they dissected her favorite poet's private life. She knew little of these facts, if they were the truth, and she wondered if any of them would have had the courage to use their talents the way Coleridge did. What were they giving back to the world

240

except criticism, cruelty and petty jealousy?

Valentine remembered a sad and lonely man who, despite his torments, spent long hours putting his thoughts down on paper and then courageously offering them to the world. He experienced endured pain and heartache so that others could see their own inner souls.

Valentine looked from one self-righteous face to the next. Suddenly she saw her entire life tumbling down a dark tunnel lined with the faces of the ton. They were laughing at her, grimacing and condemning her. She wanted to be free of them and she knew she never would.

Justin raised his wine to his lips and observed Valentine's reaction to the conversation around her. He watched as disdain, then disgust and finally fear were revealed in her eyes. She struggled to keep a smile on her face, but he knew how to read the deepest recesses of her eyes.

Valentine did not fit in this world. She never had and she never would. Naive as she was about protocol and his business connections, he could see that she was uncannily discerning. He watched as she tried to defend her poet friend. The eminent Lord Ranly was condescending toward Valentine. Lady Manewood and Sir Chilton continued with their loquacious litany of Coleridge's faults. Justin knew for a fact that neither of them had ever met the poet, while Valentine had obviously spent hours with him.

Valentine struggled to defend herself against the barrage of veiled insults.

"A child's perceptions, my dear, are not always accurate."

"How could you expect to understand an addict? Would you even know one now?"

The attacks became more direct.

"I'm afraid I never had the pleasure of meeting your father. Exactly where in London did you live?"

"Have you been to court? Have you met the Prince Regent?"

Valentine's eyes came to rest on Justin. He was watching her just as they did. She no longer felt she could go to him for support. He was one of them. She felt terribly alone.

Victoria, Andrew and Aunt Cherise were engaged in a conversation with Lord Paxton, who sat to Valentine's right. They were discussing the beauty of the Cotswolds where Lord Hawkeston's and Lord Paxton's country estates bordered each other.

Victoria turned her head to look at her twin. She knew instantly what Valentine was thinking. "Uh, oh," she whispered to herself. When Valentine felt fear, she always attacked. Victoria sensed this was one of those times.

The waiters were pouring the dessert port. The dinner was almost over. And none too soon, Victoria thought.

Valentine pasted a valiant smile on her face. Sparks of determination crackled in her eyes. "I have met the Prince Regent . . . and he has met me."

Sir Chilton's laugh was clipped.

Hearing the laughter, Lord Paxton tipped his head toward Valentine. He was a man of about 45, subdued in his dress and demeanor. Valentine liked his kindly warm brown eyes and the streaks of gray at his temples. Justin had told her that Lord Paxton had been a widower for six years now. He was a handsome man, and Valentine wondered why he hadn't remarried.

"Well done," Lord Paxton whispered to Valentine.

Valentine's eyes glowed at him. She'd found a champion.

"How did you find the Prince Regent, Miss St.

242

James?'' Sir Chilton baited her.

"To be honest, I don't know His Highness well enough to sit in judgment of him. My father taught Victoria and me to be especially careful of the words we use about others. He told us that to malign another's character was foolhardy and destructive.''

Justin gulped his port to steady himself. Hadn't he given Valentine the directive not to antagonize these people? She was deliberately defying him. She would keep this up all night if he didn't do something to stop her. "Lady Manewood, my fiancée is in the process of ordering her trousseau. Obviously, I know nothing of these things. I was wondering if you would be so kind as to provide me with some direction.''

"Of course, Lord Hawkeston. I would be most delighted,'' Lady Manewood replied happily. "Of course, you would have no way of knowing that the most delightful young designer has come to our attention and she's not far from Mayfair.'' She turned to Valentine. "You will simply adore her, my dear. Her name is Sabrina Grenville. Such a romantic name, don't you think?''

"Yes, very appropriate for a trousseau designer.'' Valentine glanced back at Justin and saw the storm clouds brewing in his eyes. He was angry with her again. Well, he could just stay that way for all she cared.

Just then Lord Purdey invited the guests to assemble in the ballroom for a music recital.

While Justin offered his arm to Valentine, she noticed that Lord Purdey took his wife's arm and then together they escorted Lady Sarah up the wide blue-carpeted marble staircase to the third-floor ballroom. Valentine overheard Lord Purdey thanking Lady Sarah for overseeing his second table of guests. They laughed easily together as only old and dear friends do. Lady Sarah whispered

243

a great deal to Lord and Lady Purdey as they took their places in the front row of gilded, royal blue velvet-upholstered chairs.

Twice Lady Purdey glanced over her shoulder in Valentine's direction.

Valentine knew they were discussing her behavior and the circumstances of her marriage. By tomorrow morning everyone in town would know the truth about her. They would pity Lord Hawkeston. They would exalt him for taking on the burden of a penniless, untitled wife and her entire family.

There was only one thing Valentine could do. She would pretend their opinions did not matter to her.

Lady Sarah Whitecastle sat sedately next to her hosts as she listened to the boring repertoire of music being played by the equally boring musicians. For the life of her she couldn't understand why one had to travel to Vienna or Italy to hear music played the way it was meant to be played. Englishmen simply didn't have the passion for music, she thought. Music was to be interpreted by the soul, not the brain.

Lady Sarah knew a great deal about music. When she was young she'd played the violin herself. She remembered what it was like to direct one's heartfelt thoughts and feelings into the strings of an instrument and then to hear those chords and notes match the vibrations of one's soul. She felt a fondness for composers and true musicians, but these amateurs were giving her a sick headache.

She'd always thought Lady Purdey was tone deaf, and tonight's selection of musicians proved it again. Rebecca Purdey would never ask Lady Sarah's opinion on music, she knew. It was one of those lines they never crossed.

Ever since their girlhood days, Rebecca liked to hold

it over Sarah that she had never married. Though Sarah despised Rebecca for that attitude, she was wise enough to keep her opinion to herself. Rebecca had married well, and Lord Purdey's influence in London was tremendous. Sarah had decided at a young age to keep Rebecca's friendship no matter how many times she had to bite her tongue. Rebecca relied upon Sarah for all the latest gossip. That gossip was often used to further Lord Purdey's position at court. In turn, Rebecca made certain Sarah was invited to every social function in town and in the country. When Rebecca's friends were making out their invitation lists, Rebecca always reminded them to include Lady Sarah. For years, an escort was provided for Sarah. As she matured, the escorts were men twenty years her junior who used the invitation to meet other young people of their own age. In the past years, the ton had accepted the fact that Lady Sarah would arrive alone and leave alone.

Lady Sarah had learned to appreciate her independence. It had not always been so. Once, she had loved passionately, but now the idea of answering to a man for her every thought and action was absurd.

She saw that same kind of independence in Valentine St. James and she didn't like it. There wasn't room in London for the two of them. Valentine was impertinent, daring and too smart for her own good. Luckily, she was not as smart as Lady Sarah. Valentine had played right into her hand this evening. She supposed she had Lord Hawkeston to thank for the apology she'd received from Valentine.

That fact alone told her a great deal about Lord Hawkeston himself and his relationship with his fiancée. He was just as fearful of Lady Sarah's notorious tongue as the rest of London. Unwittingly, Lord Hawkeston had put himself on her side in her battle against Valentine. She had him right where she wanted him.

Lord Justin Hawkeston sat next to his fiancée listening to the music in a room where he'd always felt comfortable and with a group of people he'd thought to be his friends. However, something had changed this evening, and he wasn't quite certain what it was.

He had never seen such blatant baiting of an individual as he had this evening. What had gotten into Sir Chilton and Lady Manewood? They'd never acted this superciliously toward him, yet he got the distinct impression that they and others were out to entrap Valentine. He didn't know why, but he was determined to find out.

Though he was still angry with Valentine for her actions toward Lady Sarah, he found his heart going out to her. True to her nature, she'd retaliated before a second blow was landed.

He admired that quality in her. She didn't whine or sulk. She was willing to back up her beliefs with a ''devil take all'' attitude. True, that same penchant caused him much anguish, but now that it was directed toward someone else, he could see that she fought only when necessary. Few women were like Valentine, he thought.

He reached over and took her hand. He lifted it to his lips and kissed it.

Valentine smiled at him. She needed his support right now and he was giving it. For a long moment they gazed into each other's eyes.

Not an eye in the house was focused on the musicians. Everyone was watching Lord Justin Hawkeston as he lovingly kissed his fiancée's hand. He appeared to be a man in love. She appeared to be infatuated with him.

The observers surmised that Lady Sarah had been

mistaken about the circumstances surrounding Lord Hawkeston's marriage. Lady Sarah would have to be dressed down for her inaccuracies, they whispered to one another. Lady Sarah must be taught a lesson.

Chapter Eighteen

On the south side of Oxford Street in a red brick and gray slate building, Valentine found the wedding gown of her dreams. Though Lady Manewood had clearly not approved of Valentine or her place in the aristocratic world, her choice of dress designer was nothing short of superb.

Sabrina Grenville was the designer and the proprietor of the business. She was a dark-haired, green-eyed woman in her early thirties whose striking looks were more handsome than beautiful. She was tall and thin and wore her clothes with panache. She spoke in clipped, fast sentences and always seemed to know Valentine's response before Valentine did. Fabrics and patterns seemed to whirl around her like the wind. She ordered her seamstresses about with military efficiency, yet they all seemed to cater to her every need.

"This blush-colored silk is exquisite, Miss St. James.

I want you to consider using it for the underskirt and then . . ." She grabbed a bolt of hand-embroidered organza and let the bolt roll across the pink Aubusson carpet. The fabric fluttered in the air like clouds. "I would choose this for the overskirt."

Valentine stood on the wood riser surrounded by three cheval mirrors in which to view the creation being designed on her body. The organza puddled at her feet. "It's magnificent."

"It's Belgian." Sabrina turned to her seamstress. "Aimee. Quickly, now."

Aimee was a Frenchwoman about 50 years old who wore her wiry gray hair in a knot on the top of her head into which she'd stuck pins, needles, a skewer holding buttons, a button hook and other assorted utensils she might need throughout the day. Aimee picked up the blush silk and began pinning it to the muslin dress "pattern" that Valentine wore.

"Giselle, *maintenant!*" Sabrina said to the young black-haired girl who assisted Aimee. Giselle lifted the organza up to Valentine's waist where she could see the effect with the blush silk beneath.

"The silk blush rosettes will encircle the Empire waist," Sabrina said as Valentine nodded at her own reflection in the mirror. "The organza will be gathered from the bodice up to mid throat in transparent but even gathers. A flounce under the chin, another circle of tiny, very tiny rosettes at the neck, each with moss green velvet leaves, then moss green velvet ribbons flowing down the back from the neck and onto the train which will be edged in the larger silk rosettes with moss green velvet leaves. The sleeves will be made of silk with organza overlay. Then, I think a flounce at the cuff and another circle of rosettes around the wrist."

Valentine stared at her reflection in the mirror and

knew the gown would be beautiful. Because her coloring was delicate, she had told Sabrina that a totally white gown would never do. She needed some contrast to her silver hair, yet it had to be socially acceptable as a mourning color. This blush was the color of a pale dawn at first light before the sun had broken the horizon. It gave her skin a warm glow and made her eyes seem even deeper and more intense. She intended to order this color in other clothes she would need for her trousseau.

"What if the sleeves were made only of organza, so that the arm would show?"

Sabrina smiled. "Very French. Cosmopolitan." She shook her head. "It will never do in London."

"Really?" Valentine grinned mischievously.

Aunt Cherise and Victoria had been sitting on a divan next to the draped window sipping tea. Victoria clanged her cup onto the saucer a bit too loudly.

Aunt Cherise frowned. "I think Miss Grenville's taste in these matters should be the last word."

Valentine's eyebrow lifted as she cocked her head to the side. "What if the silk on the bodice were just an inch or two lower?"

"Val . . ." Victoria could see rebellion written all over her twin's face. "Must you upset Lord Hawkeston with everything you do?"

Valentine turned to face her sister. "I'm not trying to upset him. I'm simply making myself happy. I won the right to choose my own dress in our negotiations. I want a gown that will keep London talking for a long time. It is not my intention to upset anyone."

Sabrina smiled. "I know what you want."

"You do?" Valentine asked.

"You want every man to envy your husband when you walk down the aisle. You want every woman to wish she were as beautiful as you. You want the groom to remember precisely why he is marrying you, and you want him to remember you in this dress every night for the rest of his life," she said proudly.

"You mean every *day* of his life," Victoria corrected her.

"No," Valentine replied. "She means every night. And so do I."

Victoria giggled. "If you lower that bodice by two inches, Val, he'll lust after you!"

Valentine's smile was broad. She turned to Sabrina. "Make it two and a half."

For her veil, Valentine chose a blush silk chiffon embroidered with huge English cabbage roses on the outer edge. To secure the veil to the head she would wear a band of rosettes to match those of her gown. Her shoes were made of the softest kid leather to which Sabrina would attach silk rosettes. She would carry blush-colored English roses and English ivy.

Victoria's gown was made in a similar fashion, but without the low-cut bodice and transparent sleeves. She chose a lavender pink underskirt with an organza overlay of hand-embroidered violets. Beneath the bodice Sabrina and her seamstresses would attach a row of velvet violets with moss green leaves. The silk chiffon veil would be edged in hand-embroidered violets. Two clusters of velvet violets just above each ear would secure the veiling. Her shoes were to be made of the same kid leather as Valentine's with velvet violets attached at the toes.

Aunt Cherise helped the twins select day dresses, pelisses, evening capes, two evening gowns each, suitable for the opera, ballet and private dinners. Next spring, once they were no longer in mourning, their ball gowns would be more elaborate and colorful.

Because Lord Hawkeston had informed the women they would be traveling to his country estate within the next week, he requested that both women be fitted for riding clothes, boots and country attire.

Valentine selected a wool blackwatch plaid for a day dress. "Since we won't be entertaining anyone from town, I think it's silly to waste good money on colors we will never use again."

"I agree with Valentine, Aunt Cherise. These velvets for our riding habits are quite expensive." Victoria lifted a deep rich royal blue. "I would love to have this made up for myself."

"And I prefer the emerald green velvet, with black trim and braid," Valentine said.

"There is merit to what you're saying," Aunt Cherise conceded. "These clothes are going to cost His Lordship a fortune."

"I'll explain to him how judicious we've been about his money, and he will understand. These velvets and wools will last for years if our designs are conservative."

Sabrina clucked her tongue. "You are a different breed. Most ladies can't wait to spend their husbands' money."

Valentine stepped off the riser. "Lord Hawkeston is a generous man. I'm certain he would give me anything I asked. However, I intend to be a good client for you over the years, Sabrina. You'll be moving to the fashionable west side of Bond Street soon enough."

"I didn't mean to imply . . . I only meant that—" Sabrina stumbled over her apology.

"You're wise always to think of your business first. I admire your talent and ability to run a business. I like you, Sabrina."

"Thank you, my lady," Sabrina said.

"You should know that I'm not a favorite of the ton. There are some people who would like to see me put down. Some even who wish I would disappear. But I won't. Because you are making these clothes for me, there are some who might ban your shop. Maybe they would suggest to other friends they also shop elsewhere. I think you should know this before you agree to take my business."

Sabrina held the yards of silk and organza in her arms and stared at Valentine. "I don't think I've ever met anyone quite like you, Miss St. James. Certainly none of the ladies of the ton who frequent my shop would be willing to divulge such information about themselves. And none would give a fig about the consequences to me. I have to be honest with you, losing their business would be the end of my shop, the jobs for my girls and my dreams for the future."

Valentine gazed longingly at the rose-embroidered chiffon and her fingers caressed the blush silk. She saw her vision of herself in the gown Sabrina would create for her begin to fade. "London isn't the only city in the world."

Sabrina caught her breath. "No, it isn't!"

Valentine's head jerked up and she gazed into Sabrina's green eyes. "You'll make the gowns?"

"Right, I will. I started this business when everyone in my family told me it was a harebrained idea. I continued on with my ideas for designs that no other dressmaker in London would dare because they haven't got a creative drop of blood in their bodies. I'll be damned if I'll let some old gossips try to run me out!" Sabrina grinned.

"That's the spirit!" Valentine expelled a heavy sigh of relief.

Sabrina made a thorough list of everything that Valentine and Victoria would need. She requested Aimee to take measurements of Aunt Cherise. Valentine ordered a dress for Aunt Cherise to wear at the wedding and two more day dresses for the country. She, too, was to have a riding habit. Though Aunt Cherise protested she had no need of a riding habit, there was a particular mushroom-colored velvet she liked. Valentine ordered the mushroom velvet.

Sabrina gave the women directions to a milliner's on South Audley Street and then to 89 Jermyn Street where they would find Floris, a lovely old perfume shop.

At the milliner's Valentine chose a tall traditional riding hat for herself and Victoria. Aunt Cherise wanted hers with a taller crown and a brown grosgrain ribbon band. Valentine told the hat maker, Harold Berry, that she would have fabric sent over from Sabrina Grenville's shop. Mr. Berry had many dealings with Sabrina's customers and he assured her that his work would equal Sabrina's perfection.

Valentine and Victoria had a grand time trying on bonnets and hats of all sorts, from soft chiffon concoctions to the black and white hats the court ladies and royal families would wear to the Ascot races.

Valentine was in a giddy mood when they left the shop. Spring was approaching early that year and it was a sunny day. The mid-afternoon sun was directly in Valentine's eyes when she heard Henry St. Claire's voice.

"Good afternoon, Miss St. James." He tipped his hat to her.

She held her hand to shade her eyes. He was smiling at her and then quickly turned to Victoria.

"And a good day to you, Miss St. James. And you, Miss St. James," he said to Aunt Cherise.

"Nice to see you again, Mr. St. Claire," Valentine said coolly. She hadn't liked the man in the least when they'd met at dinner two nights ago. She needed to keep up her guard.

"Isn't this a lovely day? So seldom do we have nice weather in March here in London. But then I suppose you know all about that, being from London."

"Yes," Valentine said tersely.

"You must forgive me. It's just that you and your sister are so strikingly beautiful that we . . . I'm not used to seeing such loveliness." His words fell over his lips in charming succession. "Gads! You must forgive me, but I have the most difficult time telling who is who. Please do forgive me, but you are Lord Hawkeston's fiancée, am I right?"

Gone was the lust Valentine had seen at the Purdeys' dinner party. He was laughing at himself and there was nothing but amusement in his eyes as he looked from Valentine to Victoria. He was not as bold as before and did not reach out for Valentine's hand. Rather, he kept his distance from them and did not crowd them on the sidewalk. When passersby walked past them, he stepped closer to the building and away from Valentine rather than pressing himself toward her. She couldn't help wondering if he, too, had a twin.

"I am Valentine, yes," she said with a more friendly tone.

"Oh, thank heaven! I wasn't sure, you know." He rested his gloved hands one over another on a silver-topped cane.

"This is my sister, Victoria, and my aunt, Cherise."

He tipped his hat again and smiled at them. Valentine searched that smile for any sign of insincerity and found none. Henry St. Claire was either an enigma or she'd simply misjudged him due to the fact that she'd met him in the company of so many other insincere people. Valentine decided that her emotions toward Lady Sarah had clouded her entire evening. Henry St. Claire probably meant no more by his appreciative glances than any other man at the dinner that night. She intended to reevaluate her assessment of him.

"I must tell Lord Hawkeston that he is remiss in allowing you lovely ladies to go about town unescorted," Henry said.

Aunt Cherise was smiling at Henry. She liked the idea that he thought her young enough to need an escort. After playing the role of chaperone for so long, it was a delight to hear such charming words. "Lord Hawkeston is a very busy man, we've come to realize. The girls and I had a great deal of shopping to do for the weddings and we all felt his time was much too valuable to be spent with us all day."

"I understand completely," Henry said, smiling widely at Aunt Cherise. "However, the streets of London can be dangerous even in the daylight. If you ever need my services"—he tilted his head jauntily—"I would be most delighted to escort all of you . . . even to go shopping. Please do not hesitate to call upon me." He handed his card to Aunt Cherise. There was no mistaking this time who had caught his eye.

Henry tipped his hat to each of them. "Good day, ladies," he said and walked on.

Valentine watched him walk away, still baffled at the man's altered behavior. She turned back to Victoria and Aunt Cherise, who were reading his card.

"Why, Aunt Cherise, if I didn't know better, I'd say you were blushing."

"Why, so I am!"

Victoria looked at her sister. "Isn't he the man you met at the Purdeys' dinner?"

"The same."

"He didn't seem vile to me at all. I thought him quite charming and very attractive." She handed the card to

Valentine. "If I didn't know better, Val, I'd say you were exaggerating again."

Valentine scowled at Victoria. "Do you know how sick I am of hearing you say that?"

"Do you know how sick I am of saying it?" Victoria countered.

"Now, girls, we can't stand on the street arguing over inconsequentials. We have a great deal to accomplish today. Come along," Aunt Cherise scolded. It was days like this that made her wonder if her identical charges would ever grow up.

Jermyn Street was between Regent Street and St. James Street. Because it was such a beautiful day, the women chose to walk. As the day began to wane, Valentine noticed more and more children coming out to beg. It was unusual to see so many beggars in this part of the city since the shopkeepers worked diligently to keep them away from their premises. Valentine stopped to purchase a bouquet of violets for Victoria from a little flower girl. She gave the girl double their cost.

A boy no more than four years old was selling sacks of roasted chestnuts. She gave him twice their cost, as well, and patted him on the shoulder when she left.

A boy of about ten was selling brightly polished apples. She bought a half dozen of them and gave him triple their price.

"If you keep this up, Valentine, you will have no money left for your oils," Victoria said.

"Quite right, Valentine. Lord Hawkeston is going to require an accounting of the money you've spent. What are you going to tell him when he sees you have none left and nothing to show for it?" Aunt Cherise asked.

"I will inform His Lordship that I know what it is like not to have enough money to feed oneself. I'll tell him that I admire these children for their industriousness.

They aren't sitting on a corner holding out a cup. They are working for their half-pennies and shillings. God only knows how many more of them are at home. Or even if they have a home. It's the least I can do.''

Victoria walked next to Valentine and put her hand on her sister's arm. ''I support you in your sentiments, my dear sister. I just hope your fiancé does.''

''Me, too,'' Valentine laughed.

Because of the weather, the streets were bustling that day. Valentine recognized a face here and there from the evening at the Purdeys and several matrons from their visit to her home with Lady Sarah. Aunt Cherise remembered their names and smiled and nodded. She coached the twins on putting the proper names with the proper faces.

''Going into the stationery shop is Lady Albemarle and her friend, the Marquessa de Aquilla. I like both of them for they are honest and sincere women. They accompanied Lady Sarah, but I noticed that neither of them will support Lady Sarah if she is lying. They could turn out to be allies of yours, my dear. Smile sweetly and nod your head,'' Aunt Cherise said as she waved to the two women and they waved back.

Valentine picked up the scent of the perfume shop a block away. ''Oh, we're almost there!''

The shop offered a sparkling array of imported Venetian perfume atomizers and mouth-blown glass bottles with delicate hand-polished crystal stoppers. From the beamed ceiling hung dried bouquets of every flower imaginable in England and from the Continent. Glass jars and bottles held colored sea salts for the bath guaranteed to cure everything from head colds to a broken heart. Valentine didn't doubt the claims for a minute.

''Where will I find your oils?'' Valentine asked the red-haired shopgirl who was assisting her.

"They are kept under the counter where the sunlight will not destroy their heady properties." The girl went to the counter and pulled out a black-velvet-lined tray. "These are our light florals." She took out a second tray. "The darker-colored purples, blues and greens are heavier florals with some tree scents already blended into them, such as pine and English moss." She pulled out a tray filled with amber, smoky topaz, red, orange, fuchsia and cinnabar colors. "These are the spices, musk and pungent wood scents."

They looked like jewels glittering in a night sky. Now that Valentine had experimented on her own, she knew that the vials she'd bought from the Gypsy were only a smattering of what was available. She couldn't wait to start creating her own fragrances again. She chose the more difficult-to-find spices and musk scents first. She still had quite a few florals, which were easier to come by. She wanted to mix some truly exotic scents. She wondered what Justin would think of this musk blended with vanilla, perhaps.

"I'll need some inexpensive glass bottles to store them in. All I see are the more decorative atomizers."

"We have exactly what milady requests," the shop-girl said. "Look on the upper two shelves on the wall by the window."

"Thank you," Valentine said as she walked past Aunt Cherise, who was inspecting a pink crystal perfume bottle with a twisted spiral stopper.

"Isn't this beautiful, Valentine? It reminds me of Tuscany." She sighed and put the stopper back in the bottle.

Valentine found the shelf with the inexpensive glass bottles. They were exactly what she would need. She hoped they had several dozen, because she knew that once she started experimenting, she always found it difficult to stop.

259

"I'll need one bottle that's a little more masculine-looking," she said to herself. Then she spied a rounded bottle with a silver-covered cork. She wanted to blend a special bath oil for Justin which she would give to him as a gift on their wedding night. "This is perfect."

She started to turn away from the window when she noticed a middle-aged man out on the street who was gazing inside the perfume shop. He didn't notice Valentine at all, but seemed to be staring at someone. Valentine followed the direction his eyes took.

He was watching Aunt Cherise.

At first Valentine thought she'd been mistaken. But as Aunt Cherise walked across the shop to join Victoria, who was looking at a gilded wire shoe filled with rosebud potpourri, his eyes followed Aunt Cherise's every movement. Sure enough, when Aunt Cherise walked to another counter containing perfumed sachets, the man's eyes followed her again.

Valentine wondered if he knew Aunt Cherise. But that couldn't be, or he would come inside and greet her.

Just then the shopgirl came up to Valentine with a log book and quill pen to take her order.

Valentine quietly purchased the pink crystal perfume bottle for Aunt Cherise and the gilded wire shoe for Victoria since they favored those items. Then she ordered three dozen bottles for her experiments, the round bottle for Justin, and the rest of the oils she would need. She gave the girl the address for delivery and told her to send the bill to Lord Hawkeston.

The girl went to the back of the shop and returned with a complete receipt for her order, which Valentine would show to Lord Hawkeston that evening.

Valentine inquired about a candlemaker and discovered there was one located close by. Valentine had every intention of filling Lord Hawkeston's home with the same scented candles she had made on the ship.

When they left the store, Valentine remembered the man who had been watching Aunt Cherise, but now he was gone.

"The girl told me the candlemaker's shop is only a half block away," Valentine said to Victoria and Aunt Cherise.

"How much more shopping do we have, Valentine?" Victoria pressed her hand to her stomach. "I'm absolutely famished."

Valentine laughed. "I'm sorry, Vicki. I'm usually the one with the appetite and I've lost all track of time. After this stop, we'll go home. Come to think of it, I'm hungry myself."

Valentine turned to Aunt Cherise to inquire of her well-being, and over her aunt's shoulder she saw the man who had been looking in the window. "That's odd."

"What is, dear?" Aunt Cherise asked.

"That man has been watching you," Valentine said. "What man?"

"The man down the block, standing under the china shop sign. The one with the tall black hat, the gray suit and the black waistcoat—"

"God in heaven! It can't be!"

"What?" Valentine and Victoria exclaimed simultaneously.

Aunt Cherise said not another word. She started walking toward the man as if in a daze. She was completely unaware of anyone else on the street.

The man started walking toward her. He wore a tentative smile on his lips.

His eyes were deep blue, the color of the Mediterranean, Valentine thought. It was evident from the gleam of happiness in his eyes that he'd known Aunt Cherise quite well.

"Bartholomew," Valentine whispered aloud.

"Who is Bartholomew?" Victoria asked.

Valentine took her sister's arm and turned away from the intimate though public reunion. "Come with me to the candlemaker's shop and I'll tell you all about him."

"We're just going to leave Aunt Cherise on the street with that man?" Victoria's curiosity demanded that she stay and watch.

Valentine kept pulling on Victoria's arm until they were inside the candlemaker's shop.

Aunt Cherise stopped herself only inches from throwing herself into Bartholomew's arms. She sensed he would gladly welcome her embrace. But they were on the streets in London. People would talk. People would not understand how her heart was bursting.

It was as if she were seventeen again. She felt all the same feelings for him that she once had . . . and more. All the years she'd frozen her heart and her emotions to the pain and loss she'd felt suddenly fell away. She felt every nerve in her body come alive again. She heard a robin sing nearby. She heard the clip clop of horses' hooves on the cobblestone streets. She heard a group of children laughing at each other as they played. Suddenly the sun was brighter, the sky was bluer and the air was clean and fresh.

She was catapulted back to a day when she still dreamed of being a wife and a mother. There was no thought of Valentine or Victoria, or her brother's death, which had left her lonely for male companionship. Milton had been that contemporary with whom she'd discussed adult affairs, and not till this moment did she realize how much she missed him.

Some deep inner sense told her that Milton was there,

around her, guiding her to her destiny. Opening a new window now that an old window had been closed.

"Bartholomew," she said to him for the first time in twelve years.

His eyes were gleaming brightly with tears. "Cherise, my God, you're as beautiful as the last time I saw you." Unabashedly he grasped both her hands and pulled them to his lips. He kissed them over and over. He held them to his cheek. "I thought I would never see you again."

"I . . . I didn't dare dream . . ."

He chuckled to himself. "And to believe that I would see you on the street today. I must confess I followed you from the milliner's shop, which was next to my barber's, all the way to the perfume shop. At first I was uncertain. I had to be sure it really was you." He kissed her hands again. "I've looked for you in hundreds of crowds. In thousands of faces, but I'd heard you'd gone to Milan. Then another time I heard you were in Venice."

"I was . . ." A sob of regret for days wasted strangled her throat. "Milton died in Venice, Bartholomew."

He nodded his head and released her hands. "I'd heard that. I tried to find you, but they told me at your old address you had moved away permanently."

Suddenly, Cherise realized what he was saying, but she was puzzled. "Why were you seeking me out, Bartholomew?"

"It's been nearly eighteen months now since . . ."

"Since what?" Aunt Cherise sensed an ominous tone to his voice. Something was not right.

"Estelle is gone, Cherise. It was her heart. It just stopped working."

Aunt Cherise couldn't help thinking it was an appropriate ending for a person who had never used her heart a single day in her life.

"I . . ." She paused as she peered deeply into Bartholomew's blue eyes. He was heavier than when they were young, his face had deep lines around his eyes, and there were silver flecks of gray at his temples, but his eyes were as young and filled with love for her as they had ever been. He was still a handsome man, and she knew that till the day she died she would always love him. "I will never lie to you, Bartholomew. So I'm not going to tell you that I'm grieved over her passing. Because I'm not. She was a hateful woman who never gave the love you deserve. You are a wonderful man and . . ." She had to stop herself. The tears in her eyes were threatening to betray her. She wanted to tell him everything, but she knew she shouldn't. There were many years in between. They had changed. Hadn't they?

"You needn't pretend with me, Cherise. We both know what she did. I was caught in a terrible trap. I had no way of releasing myself. For years I confess I prayed for my own death. I saw no other way out. When Estelle died I began searching for you at once. I know it was wrong of me, but I was rejoicing that she was dead. All I've thought about was you . . . finding you . . . asking you . . ."

"Asking me what, Bartholomew?"

"If . . . if there was any chance you might still feel the same way about me that I feel about you."

Cherise could hardly believe her ears. This was all her dreams come true. She smiled at him and touched his weathered cheek. He closed his eyes when she touched him. Suddenly there were no more tears in her eyes; they had fallen to her cheeks. "Yes, Bartholomew, there is a chance."

Chapter Nineteen

Valentine and Victoria were laughing and badgering their dear aunt for details about the incredible meeting that had taken place that afternoon with Bartholomew Lupass, Earl of Havenshire. The girls bounded up the steps with their giggling aunt who was acting more like her eighteen-year-old nieces than a forty-two-year-old spinster. The butler opened the door as Valentine backed into the foyer, their laughter and merriment filling the house.

"Where the blazes have you been? I want an explanation, Valentine!"

Valentine whirled around and faced Lord Hawkeston's icy glare. He was dressed in tan breeches, a black waistcoat and a snowy white linen shirt. His black riding boots were muddy. His blond hair was still slicked around the edges with perspiration.

Valentine guessed he'd been riding his horse . . . hard.

It didn't take her long to realize he had been out looking for her.

Valentine smiled softly at Justin. He was still glaring at her. "Why are you looking at me that way, Lord Hawkeston?" She pointed to Victoria. "That's Valentine." She smiled at her twin and winked. "I guess sometimes you get us mixed up."

Victoria glared at her sister, but she went along with the charade. "We had a million and one things to do. You have no idea how many details there are to attend to for the wedding."

"Weddings," Aunt Cherise chimed in, emphasizing the plural. Once the die was cast, there was no choice but to go along with the ploy. "Your Lordship, it was all my fault. I met an old friend today. Someone I haven't seen in over a decade and we got to talking. Well, I had no idea how late it was getting. I'm truly sorry. I can see that our absence has caused you a great deal of concern."

He ran his hand through his hair and shook his head. "It is dangerous for you ladies to be out by yourselves after nightfall. Then when I came home and discovered you'd sent the carriage back here and told the driver you would hire a hack, I was outraged." He turned to Victoria thinking she was Valentine. "I specifically told you that I would not need the carriage today and that I wanted him to take you from shop to shop."

"It was such a nice day, we decided to walk," Valentine blurted out.

Justin's eyes scrutinized her face. "Did you now?"

"Oh, yes," Victoria said. "You know that Victoria and I love to walk."

Justin observed both twins with an eagle eye. He was certain they were playing a trick on him, but hell's fire, he couldn't be sure.

Just then they heard a voice from the salon. "Is this family squabble finished or is there still time to toss myself into the arena?"

An incredibly dashing-looking young man, a few years younger than Justin and two inches shorter, appeared in the doorway holding a glass of brandy. He leaned jauntily against the door jamb and smiled charmingly at them. His lips were full and parted over brilliant white straight teeth. His blue eyes danced with mirth and there was a blush of color to his cheeks. He had none of Justin's tan golden skin and sun-flecked hair, and he also had none of Justin's icy glare.

Justin introduced his brother. "This is Arnold. My younger brother," he said.

"Younger, more handsome and more charming brother," Arnold said good-naturedly, taking Victoria's hand and thinking she was Valentine. He lifted her hand. "By God, Justin, you've done better than win the national treasure with this bride. How in God's name did you get so lucky?"

Victoria blushed crimson from her forehead to the base of her throat.

Justin instantly realized which twin was which. He took two steps toward Valentine and leaned his face down to meet hers. "Have a little confession to make to me, do you?"

"Why, whatever are you talking about, Lord Hawkeston?" Valentine said, trying to keep up the charade.

He peered into her eyes. He was right. No one had that flash of fire mixed with cool black like his Valentine did. "You don't blush the way your sister does."

Victoria gasped and held both hands to her mouth. "Uh, oh."

Valentine's gaze didn't waver. She was totally prepared to call his bluff. She could tell he was furious, and the fact that she had played her trick on him in his brother's presence didn't help her cause in the least. For an instant she saw a break in his icy stare. She realized he was being harsh with her because he had an audience. She'd found the chink in his armor.

"Well, now that we're all home safe and sound, I think we should show Lord Hawkeston's brother that we know how to be good hostesses. Have you rung for tea, my lord?"

"Hardly," he said.

"Valentine," Valentine addressed her sister, "perhaps you should do that."

"Delighted," Victoria said.

Arnold produced a crooked arm for Victoria to take. "I don't care which one you are, I will be most happy to escort you to the salon." He looked at Aunt Cherise. "Please join us so that we may all get better acquainted."

They left the foyer, their shoes tapping lightly on the marble.

"Valentine," Justin said tersely.

"Victoria," she replied demurely, refusing to give up the charade.

"There's one way I can find out who you are," he said with a warning in his voice.

"Really?" she quipped cockily.

Justin grabbed her arm and pulled her against him. "Yes," he breathed and kissed her ravenously.

It had been much too long since he'd held her in his arms and devoured that sweet mouth. He'd come home early this afternoon hoping to find her, wanting to talk with her, walk with her in the gardens and simply spend time with her. When she hadn't returned in the afternoon, at first he was furious with her for keeping him waiting. As the sun began to set, he became worried. A ride up Regent Street, down Oxford, up Bond Street and down St. James had made him nearly crazy. He didn't want to think that Valentine had become that important to him, but she had. He almost thanked her for putting him through this charade, because it had given him an excuse to kiss her.

God, she was a more luscious fruit than he remembered. He thought he would lose his senses altogether as she nestled into his arms and pressed her body next to his. Her fingers in the hair at the nape of his neck sent a wave of intoxicating chills down his back.

He plunged his tongue into her mouth and coaxed her to respond to him. He heard her moan. He felt himself falling, tumbling into sensual oblivion. He was surrounded by the taste, the smell and the feel of Valentine. He knew he was panting like an animal in heat, but he couldn't help it. If he had his way, he'd make love to her right here on the floor. The servants be damned.

She moaned. She breathed his name. "Justin . . ." She thought their hours apart were a foolish waste of time when she could be kissing him as she was now. She could feel his heart slamming against his ribcage with a force to challenge Big Ben. A tingling started deep in her belly that caused her to rub herself against him. She wanted to feel his hand on her breast, the way he'd cupped it when they were on the ship. She wanted to know what it was like to feel him inside her. She wanted to spend an entire night in bed with him exploring all the fascinating parts of his body and mind. She wanted to know if he wanted her as much as she wanted him.

She didn't let him take a breath. She didn't let him leave her arms. She didn't let his tongue end the duel of love. She kissed him back, ravaging him the way he'd devoured her. Her nails dug into his flesh at the base of his neck. She could feel his erection against her abdomen. He wanted her.

"It's weeks until our wedding, Valentine," Justin breathed finally.

"We can wait," she said halfheartedly.

Justin wasn't sure if she was serious or not. How could she act so detached when he was on fire? There were times, and this was one of them, when he wondered if she wasn't a harlot after all. He'd never met a woman with sexual tricks and skills like Valentine. He'd never felt such passion for a woman. He'd never paced the floor in his bedroom at night, restless, needing sleep and unable to shut his eyes for thinking about her. He'd never cared a whit whether a woman was early, late or punctual, yet this afternoon he'd practically torn London apart searching for her when she'd been only a few hours late.

Something was the matter with him lately and the only thing he could attribute it to was Valentine. She was a witch and had cast a spell on him.

The only problem was that Justin didn't believe in witches or spells.

"You are a vixen and a scamp," he said finally. "Don't you feel any remorse for lying to me?"

"No, my lord," she said mirthfully.

"None?"

"I didn't exactly lie, because in a way I am Victoria and she is me. We are twins. We are the same."

"Oh, ho! How would you like it if I bedded your sister instead of you?"

"Before or after the wedding?" Valentine challenged him.

Justin expelled a frustrated breath. "You ought to be punished."

"Quit treating me like a child, Justin. Just because you are so old——"

"So old?" Justin's temper was flaring. "You are a child, Valentine. And a brat. I think the only way you are ever going to abide by my rules is for you to suffer the consequences."

Valentine didn't like the hard glint in Justin's eyes. He could get quite testy, she knew. Perhaps she had pressed him to his limit. She was just having fun, though the merriment was at his expense. She needed to teach him not to take everything she said or did so seriously. She smiled winningly at him.

"We have a guest in the parlor and I must change for dinner. We have a great deal to discuss about the wedding and this trip to the country." She stood on her tiptoes, placed a light hand against his hard chest, and pressed her swollen, just-kissed lips to his cheek. "I'll do anything you say, Justin. Anything. Only please don't be so cross with me. I was looking forward to spending time with you alone this evening."

She walked away from him and went into the salon before he could answer.

How did she do that? How could she turn all his emotions upside down again? He felt like the village idiot watching her glide into the salon. She wanted to spend time with him. He'd wanted to spend the afternoon with her. That was why he'd been angry with her. She would be the end of any man's sanity.

Arnold stood at the mantel after lighting a fire to take the evening chill off the room. Aunt Cherise lit an array of candles on the mantel and an oil lamp in the corner. The room glowed with warmth and light.

The cook had been preparing dinner, and the smells soon wafted up the stairs and into the dining room and salon. The clink of fine silver sounded as the servants set the table for the evening meal.

"Come in, Valentine," Arnold said, motioning with his arm for her to join Aunt Cherise on the settee. "I was being instructed as to who each twin really is. I can see that Justin is satisfied as to your proper identity." Arnold's laughing blue eyes settled on Valentine's kiss-swollen lips.

"He knows," she said with a wink.

"I suppose you've told them what a terrible person I am, Justin," Arnold said as Justin came into the room.

Justin glared at his brother. Then he went to a marble-topped console where the butler had placed a decanter of sherry and five glasses.

At that moment Andrew came home from working at Justin's offices. He handed his hat and gloves to the butler and walked into the salon.

Andrew greeted everyone, shook hands with Arnold, and kissed Victoria's cheek. He sat on a needlepoint chair next to Victoria where he could hold her hand.

Justin poured the sherry and served the women. He handed Andrew a brandy and poured one for himself.

Arnold continued his conversation about himself. "Justin won't tell you about me. He's a gentleman. Most people in town think I'm anything but a gentleman."

"How can you say such things about yourself, Arnold?" Valentine asked.

"Because they are true."

"Oh, bother," she retorted. "I think you make these stories up just to make your reputation seem larger than life."

Arnold bowed to her and flashed her a mischievous grin. "Do you, now? Well, I thank you for your vote of confidence."

Justin cleared his throat. "Arnold, why don't you redeem yourself and come to work for me? Andrew is doing a splendid job.''

Andrew raised his glass to Justin. "Thank you."

Arnold's eyes lost their merriment. "And deprive you of the opportunity for chastisement? Who would you blame for your troubles then, Justin?"

"I don't blame you."

"That's not what I hear," Arnold said coldly, looking into his empty brandy glass.

Valentine didn't like the way the conversation was turning. She knew that Justin had difficulties with his brother, but she had been prepared to like Arnold. Indeed, he seemed intelligent and charming. She could only guess there was more underlying their conflict than met the eye. She knew Justin was tired of paying Arnold's gambling debts. That was enough to evoke Justin's scorn, she believed. But was there something else?

"Don't believe what you hear, Arnold. Especially in London."

"They're *your* friends, dear brother."

Justin nearly slammed his sherry glass on the console.

Valentine jumped. Aunt Cherise's head jerked. Victoria's mouth rounded into a silent "Uh, oh."

"My friends don't talk about me. And if they do, they'll wish they hadn't." He looked at the clock on the bombe chest. "Tarnation! It's nearly eight o'clock. What time is dinner served around here anyway?"

Justin stalked out of the room in search of the housekeeper.

Arnold snickered to himself. "There's something about me that boy doesn't like."

"Do you always try to upset him?" Valentine asked unabashedly.

"Every chance I get." Arnold smiled charmingly. "His life would be cruelly boring without me."

"I wouldn't place any wagers on that, Arnold." Valentine rose. "Will you be joining us for dinner or do you have some other pressing engagement?"

"Justin believes my company gives him indigestion. No, I'm afraid I won't be staying for dinner, but I appreciate the invitation all the same." He smiled at her. He walked over to her and took her hand. "I like you, Valentine. You're the kind of woman who will keep Justin on his toes. I'm very happy for both of you. He's a good man, my brother."

The last of Valentine's misgivings about Arnold shattered into dust. "Thank you, Arnold. Your blessing means a lot to me."

"Thank you, Miss St. James. It pleases me that my opinion means something to someone."

He bid his adieux to Aunt Cherise and Victoria. Valentine walked him to the door of the salon. "I am very happy to meet you, Arnold. I'm truly pleased to become a member of the family."

Arnold kissed her cheek and let the butler see him out.

After dinner Justin requested that Valentine meet him in the salon. Everyone else had gone to bed and the servants had finished their duties in the kitchen. The butler brought a tray holding brandy for Justin and a cup of tea for Valentine. The temperature outside had dropped abruptly. Justin closed the doors to the salon to keep the evening chill from invading the room. He placed three logs on the fire and poked and prodded them until the flames blazed brightly, lighting the whole room.

Valentine had changed to an evening dress of black moire. Ordinarily Justin disdained the mourning clothes Aunt Cherise had chosen for the girls, but this dress was cut low with long sleeves and tiny white pearl buttons up the wrist to the elbow and white buttons down the back. She wore a black velvet ribbon around her white throat with a cameo locket dangling just above the swell of her breasts. A cascade of silver curls fell down her neck. The warmth of the fire burnished an apricot glow on her cheeks.

"You said there were details about the wedding you wished to discuss with me?"

"Yes," he said, wishing she didn't look quite so beautiful, quite so entrancing. "I spoke with the vicar of St. Paul's Cathedral."

Valentine's eyebrows knitted into a frown. "It's frightfully large. Do we need such a big church?"

"It's a double wedding, Valentine. I have many friends who expect to be invited. My secretary is now addressing the invitations and they will be distributed throughout town next week. April eighteenth isn't that far away, as you know."

"I know," she said ruefully and looked down at her hands.

Justin continued, "I have arranged for a wedding breakfast to be served here and in the gardens. I've ordered tents to be erected in the back lawns, and the cook has begun devising a proper menu. It will be the usual fare, eggs, kidney pie, sausages, ham, potatoes, breads and whatever else she wants. I'll see to the wines myself."

"It seems you've handled everything."

"Everything except the flowers. I noticed that you and Victoria seem to take a special interest in them. I liked that candle you made for me . . ."

Her eyes widened. "You did?"

"I burn it in my room every night." He smiled, thinking of how she'd felt in his arms earlier that evening.

275

He had to keep his mind on the business at hand. "At any rate, I would appreciate it if you and your sister would take care of the necessary details. You know what you want and what would look right. Just let me know how much it will cost."

"I just remembered." She reached for her reticule and withdrew the receipts from the afternoon's shopping. He was always so careful about his bookkeeping and records, she'd made a point to bring them to him this evening. She handed them over. "I ordered our gowns from Sabrina Grenville, just as I told you. I thought it wise not to purchase many dresses for myself and Victoria until next spring when we will no longer be in mourning."

Justin riffled through the stack of receipts. "I see nothing out of order here . . ." He stopped.

She winced. She braced for the onslaught.

"You spent twenty-five pounds at the perfumery?"

She raced to explain. "My lord—"

"Stop right there, Valentine. Any time you start an explanation with 'my lord,' I know I'm being hood-winked. Out with it. No embellishments, please," he said sternly.

"I wanted to perform more of my experiments," she began, looking up at him, eyes wide and trusting. "Must I truly tell you everything?"

"Everything, Valentine. And I especially want to know all the details about these experiments of yours."

"You're very sure about this?"

"Very," he said gruffly and folded his arms across his chest.

Valentine sucked in a deep breath. She wasn't sure if she should tell him about the Gypsy woman, especially since the reference would bring up the very sore subject of their last argument. But how could she explain everything if she didn't tell him about Elana? "That candle you love so much that I made for you?"

He nodded for her to continue.

"Well, I think I did a fine job with it and I wanted to try other scents. I would like to blend my own perfumes and make something special for you and something special for myself. I have come upon some knowledge that informs me that particular scents have certain effects on individuals."

"Such as?" His curiosity was definitely piqued.

"Well." Her eyes flitted about the room. She didn't want him to know all her secrets, but he had a way of getting information out of her. She lowered her head and glanced up at him from beneath her lashes. Lord! He looked as if he'd wait all night if he had to. "I mixed several scents and put them in that candle I gave you."

"And what effect was it supposed to have on me, Valentine?"

"At the time, if you will remember, you were quite put out with me, angry even, rather like you are now, and the candle was supposed to quiet your anger. Make you more amenable to me." She looked at him and knew she wasn't convincing him.

"You were faraway and distant from me. I thought it would make you want me."

"Want you?" Justin's eyes grew large. "You think I didn't want you?"

"I was being thrust upon you . . ."

She looked up at him and for the first time he realized why he'd been confused about his bride. She wasn't a harlot. A harlot could not possibly be so naive. She was a child. A woman child. And an angel all at once. She had wanted to please him and had gone so far as to concoct a scented candle that would magically alter his thinking. He supposed she believed in fairies and elves, too.

Never in his life was he touched quite as she touched him. All this time she had been innocent of the lurid thoughts he'd been having about her. It was his guess she was a virgin. There was only one way to find out.

Kissing Valentine was a delicious pastime. Tonight she'd never looked lovelier. He thought it amazing how she seemed to grow in beauty every day before his very eyes.

He went to sit next to her on the settee. He put his hand to her cheek. With his forefinger he traced the edge of her jaw. She shivered.

He smiled. Tonight he would have all of Valentine he wanted.

He kissed her tenderly at first, cradling her head in his hand. He intended to orchestrate every moment of his lovemaking.

Her lips were luscious and sweet as ripe cherries, he thought as he slanted his mouth over hers. He ringed her parted lips with his tongue, taunting her, teasing her. As his tongue plunged into her mouth, he leaned his body against hers, pushing her down onto the settee.

Her head rested upon a soft down-filled velvet pillow. Her arms were around his neck pulling his head toward her. She lapped up his kisses like a cat.

His arms were beneath her back, where his hands carefully unbuttoned each button one by one.

He kissed her mouth, her cheeks, and blazed a trail of hot kisses down her throat to the base of her neck where he could feel her pulse beat.

''I don't want you to think you were thrust upon me, Valentine.''

He slid his hand to her shoulder and pushed her sleeve down to her elbow. He gazed at the rounded swell of her breast in the firelight. With his forefinger he traced the upper swell of her breast. He let his finger move lower and lower until he found her nipple.

She shivered again. "But you have to marry me . . ."

"Oh, yes I most certainly do . . ." He covered her mouth with a passionate kiss, pulled her bodice down to reveal both her breasts to him.

He raised his head and looked at her. "By God, you are a temptress, my Valentine." And then he moved his head down to her breast.

Valentine sucked in a rush of air. As her lungs filled she arched her back and thrust her breast further into his mouth. He massaged one breast with his right hand and licked the end of the tight bud of her other breast.

Valentine thought she would go out of her mind with the sensations he was stirring inside her. She squeezed her eyes shut and saw a shower of bright lights as a wave of electricity shot through her body, down to her abdomen and to the center of her womanhood.

Justin raised his head and kissed her mouth while still caressing her breast and toying with her nipple. "I'm going to touch you, Valentine. Touch you as you've never been touched before."

He slid his hand down over her abdomen and lifted her skirts. He slid his hand under her pantalettes and to the soft triangle of hair between her legs.

"Spread your legs for me, Valentine. Let me touch you."

She started to shake her head and demand that he stop. But she was curious. She wanted to know what it was like to feel his touch. She opened her legs.

She felt a wetness between her thighs. His fingers were light as they opened the petals of her flower. He stroked her bud with light feather-like touches that tickled at first and then suddenly sent flashes of shock waves through her body.

Her back arched.

He watched her respond to him. He smiled as she moaned loudly and then swallowed an almost animal-like growl.

"Justin . . ." She breathed his name in between sharp, short pants. She opened her legs even wider. She pushed herself into his touch. It was not enough. It would never be enough.

He flicked his tongue over the taut bud of her nipple and sent chills down her back, across her buttocks and down the backs of her thighs.

"Your juices are flowing for me, Valentine. You want me, tell me you do."

She thought the sensations he was creating in her would send her right off the settee. She was floating somewhere above the room, beyond space and time. She could barely remember her name. All she knew was that she was nearly at the point of satiation. "Please . . ." was all she could breathe.

He stroked her bud and pressed a point in the middle where she seemed the most sensitive.

Her back arched again.

He pressed the spot again. His fingers were wet with her moistness and he knew now he would learn the truth. He easily slid his finger inside her. She was hot and wet and he could feel her walls pulsing around his finger. He found her maidenhead intact.

Justin buried his head between her breasts. He stroked her with slick, fast movements that caused her to stop breathing. At precisely the moment of her release he covered her mouth with a deep, probing kiss.

He swallowed her climatic scream.

"Oh, my God, Justin . . ." she cried out. "Justin . . ."

her arms circled his neck as she came back to earth.

Back to him.

"Justin." She said his name with love. Her eyes were filled with a soft light when she opened them. He'd never seen anything as endearing as the look in Valentine's eyes when she gazed at him. At that moment he was her hero. He could do no wrong in her eyes. He felt invincible. And for the first time in his life, he wanted to be all these things for a woman. He'd never cared about anyone before; he'd always been too busy, too tired or too worried about his estates and his business.

He'd known women who wanted him for his title, for his body, for the things he could give them, but they'd never wanted his love. They'd never wanted Justin.

A long time ago, Justin had given up looking for someone who loved him for himself. That kind of love was a luxury for poets. It was something Shelley and Keats wrote of, but was not to be experienced by an ordinary mortal living under the burden of a title like Lord Justin Hawkeston. For years he thought he'd been wise to turn off his heart and pretend that emotions did not exist in real life.

Because he felt this way, he'd had no qualms about promising Milton St. James to wed his daughter. One woman was the same as another, he'd told himself. She couldn't have been any better or any worse than any of the women he'd known all his life. As long as she didn't gamble, he assumed they would get along.

Justin had planned to marry the St. James girl, set her up in London or the country, whichever she preferred, and then he could go about his business with even greater ease since the matrons of London would no longer see him as a matrimonial prize. He had told himself that a wife would simplify matters.

Then he'd thought Valentine was a harlot. What

ghastly days those had been. She'd nearly driven him mad with wanting and wonder.

Now he knew the truth. Her passions came to her naturally. He also realized that he had feelings for Valentine. Those feelings complicated his life. He wanted to spend long, lazy hours with her and not with his duties or his business. Suddenly she took top priority in his life. As he held her, he thought how delicious it would be to spend every night doing just this and more to his sensitive, sensual Valentine. She was untouched, unspoiled, and he looked forward to teaching her how to pleasure him.

He kissed her again. "You are my Valentine, aren't you?"

She gazed deeply into his blue eyes and wondered why there were tears welling at the corners. She thought she'd made him happy. "I am yours, Justin," she said to reassure him. She hoped it was what he wanted to hear.

He pulled her against his chest and held her. "My Valentine. Always."

Chapter Twenty

On the third floor of a Greek Revival mansion on the far west side of London Arnold Hawkeston waited for his lover. The room was frightfully expensive, but Arnold didn't worry about that kind of thing anymore. He had a new lease on life. He was in love.

Arnold had arranged for this room with the owner of the mansion, Madame Waterhouse. Madame Waterhouse's octogenarian husband had willed her the property, and upon his death five years ago, she took ownership. Always an enterprising woman, Madame Waterhouse renovated the ground-floor rooms to accommodate gaming tables, billiards and a roulette wheel. The second floor was occupied by her "ladies," who were said to provide any kind of sexual favors for a price. Because Madame Waterhouse was a woman of refined tastes, her "ladies" were expensive.

Madame Waterhouse prided herself on appeasing

even the most exotic sexual tastes. Her women came from all corners of the globe. Her Balinese girl not only performed ancient dances in the nude, but was considered an expert in delivering the proper balance of pain and pleasure. A black voodoo priestess from Jamaica excelled in bestiality. The Japanese geisha was innocent, young and still a virgin, but a seductress with her tongue and lips.

Each of her women raised the act of sex to its highest art form. It cost a small fortune to walk in the front door, but every man who exited claimed it was worth it.

As a favor to certain members of the ton, Madame Waterhouse allowed her third-floor bedroom and sitting room to be used for private assignations. When a particular young lady of the ton had fallen in love with a married man and neither of them could afford to be seen in public, Madame Waterhouse provided seclusion and, best of all, a very tight lip.

Madame Waterhouse knew more about the mores and amours of the ton than their most rapacious gossips. She didn't believe in society's rules or the laws of the Bible. She believed there was no such thing as right or wrong between two consenting adults. She felt it was her mission in life to provide games of chance to those who believed they could beat the house odds, and to give shelter and her blessing to lovers when society was bent on condemnation.

Madame Waterhouse liked to believe she was Cupid. The goddess of love. The angel of Eros. She had hired an Italian painter to cover the walls and ceiling of her third-floor quarters with frescoes in which lovers engaged in every form of erotica. Nothing was left to the imagination in these frescoes.

Arnold blessed the day he learned about Madame Waterhouse's establishment. Back then, he'd had no real

284

money other than the allowance he received monthly from the executor of his father's estate, which was a pittance because his father had gambled away nearly every farthing he had. Justin had taken over some broken-down warehouses and glass factories in Italy which his father had won in a card game back in 1795. The old man had let the businesses lie dormant until Justin asked for them in repayment for paying off gambling debts both his father and Arnold had incurred.

Justin had turned the blasted factories into a thriving business. That was another reason Arnold hated Justin. Everything Justin touched turned to gold.

Certainly Justin worked hard for his money, but so what? He'd inherited the title, hadn't he? He got the country estate and the cottagers' income, didn't he? What else did the bastard want? He was first-born. He was supposed to be responsible.

Arnold had known all his life that he would be nothing. He was not the first-born. He was second and last of the Hawkestons. Nobody expected anything of him, and he didn't either. It was his job to live off the ton, spend his brother's money, and have a good time until he died.

Hell's fire! There were many days when he wished he were dead. Most days he wished this whole rotten business of life would just end. There was no purpose for him on this earth. None. Without a title or an estate, life for an Englishman was worthless.

Arnold had just about given up on life when the heavens had smiled on him. He'd fallen in love. God! He almost felt like a schoolboy again. He felt young and clean and new again. Life was wonderful after all!

Arnold poked the fire and watched the flames lick a large oak log. He felt himself become erect. He pressed his palm against his penis. God! Their last encounter had been so incredible, he'd never dreamed love could be like this.

He had to restrain himself. He had to wait.

He turned and went to the mahogany piecrust table draped with an Irish linen damask cloth. A brass bucket was filled with small chips of ice and two bottles of French champagne. The ice, he knew, was not so much to chill the wine as for lovemaking.

The thought of those ice pellets on nipples . . .

Just then the key in the lock turned. The door opened partially.

Arnold nearly jumped out of his skin, his anticipation was so great. "My love." He rushed across the room and into a warm embrace.

Lips clung to lips. Tongues clashed and thrust. Passion met passion, and the heat from their bodies filled the room.

Clothes were ripped and peeled from their bodies. Breathing quickened and then came in short gasps.

Arnold thought he would never get enough.

"My love, I waited and waited. What took you so long?" he asked as his erection grew hard. He needed release.

"I had other matters to attend to," Henry St. Claire answered and then spied the champagne. "How thoughtful of you, sweets." He took Arnold's hand and walked over to the cloth-draped table. "Pour me some."

The amber glow from the fire swept across Henry's massive physique. His wide shoulders, enormous barrel chest and muscular arms made Arnold shiver with excitement as he popped the champagne cork.

Arnold got hard just looking at Henry. He poured the the wine and handed a glass to Henry.

Henry sipped the expensive wine and grinned mischievously at Arnold. He wrapped a huge hand around

Arnold's penis. "Come sit by the fire, sweets, while I tell you my plan."

Arnold thought he would go crazy if he didn't get release soon, but if Henry wanted to talk, they would talk.

Henry sat in a huge overstuffed chair. Arnold sat on the floor at his feet on a down-filled cushion edged in gold fringe and tassels.

"First of all, tell me what you discovered when you went to your brother's house tonight," Henry said.

"Justin is planning to leave London for the country estate. He's heard about the cottagers' refusal to plant. He thinks he can stop the revolt."

Henry burst into laughter. "What an ass! Does he really?"

Arnold nodded excitely. "I do love it when things go according to plan."

"So do I, sweets. You're certain that Crompton will not tattle? He's not going to come back on us and tell your brother we put him up to everything?"

"No. No. *No!* A hundred times no! Crompton was well paid to incite those stupid cottagers. He's got them thinking that they'll go to hell for planting a single seed on Hawkeston land. Don't forget I let Justin think he was the one who hired Crompton as overseer and manager. Crompton went to Justin two years ago for the job. He'd had problems with the cottagers long before you and I devised this plan to use their malcontent to our advantage."

"Very well, then. And did you meet Miss St. James?"

"Valentine? I did. What a twit. She's so young! I can't imagine what Justin was thinking of when he proposed to her. If he did indeed propose. Do you suppose it's true that he's marrying her because of some promise to her father?"

"So I hear," Henry drawled and drank more champagne.

"Well, I never did get the truth out of him on that matter," Arnold said.

"Well, it doesn't matter. What does matter is that all of London thinks he's being forced into this marriage. I've met the woman and I think she'll be an easy target. While they are out of town this week, I'll pour a little grist in the rumor mill. I will find a way to get Valentine off by herself and then I'll make my move."

"What if she doesn't cooperate?"

"Oh, she will, all right. There will be so many rumors about Justin and his past loves and lusts, she'll have to find a shoulder to cry on."

"And you'll be that shoulder."

"Precisely." Henry smiled.

"But what if she isn't as weak as we think? What if she doesn't want to kill herself over him? What'll we do?"

Henry's smile was sardonic and powerful. "We'll just have to help her, won't we, sweets?"

"Such a wicked plan." Arnold giggled to himself.

"Then we merely set our sights on getting rid of your brother. By the time they get back from the country, it won't be so difficult to trap both of them."

"Oh, Henry, this is so delicious."

"Genius, you fop. It's true genius," Henry corrected him sternly.

Arnold nodded his head. "More champagne, darling?"

Henry shook his head. "Did you ask Madame for some oil?"

"Oh, yes! And I can't wait to rub it all over you." Arnold scampered off to the bedroom to retrieve the aphrodisiac oil.

Henry watched the fire. Damn, but he'd done a lot of things for money. Lord Hawkeston's fortune was sizable and growing every day. He wanted that money ... needed that money.

He'd almost given up their scheme when he heard the news that Justin was returning with a fiancée. Before Justin had set sail for Italy last fall, Henry had already put his plan into motion. They had originally planned to have Justin ''accidentally killed'' in a cottagers' revolt, which they were orchestrating.

The presence of Valentine made the plan more complicated, but not impossible.

Arnold was a fool if he thought Henry was going to stay with him. Henry not only intended to leave England, but he intended to take Arnold's half of the money with him. Adding a third murder to his list would be like taking candy from a baby.

Chapter Twenty-one

Built of golden Cotswold limestone and tinted with gray lichen, the Hawkeston country manor house looked like a sun-washed kingdom of dreams. Two stories high, the house dominated the village in the valley below. The house was surrounded by oaks, wide grass terraces, hedges and avenues of lime and horse chestnuts. Behind the house the gardens, filled with roses, violets, daisies, impatiens, bluebells and lilacs, sloped up to the Cotswolds where the valleys of Severn and Avon could be seen. The hills of Alderton, Dixton, Dumbleton and Oxenton loomed over the valleys, and in the very far distance were the Black Mountains of Wales.

For the second time in her life, Valentine fell in love.

"It's lovely, Justin. Absolutely wonderful," she said as the carriage pulled to a stop on the gravel-covered drive in front of the house.

The air was clean and fresh as the first spring breezes

wafted through the budding treetops. The grass had poked green tips through the earth and yellow daffodils danced merrily around the perimeter of the huge limestone house.

Valentine grabbed Justin's arm. "Is this truly yours?"

He delighted in her awe. He kissed her forehead. "And soon to be yours."

"Oh, Justin. I hope I never have to go back to London. This is paradise." She squeezed his arm.

Andrew preceded Aunt Cherise and Victoria as they stepped out of the carriage, and they, too, were taken with the spectacular beauty of Hawkeston Manor.

The huge wooden doors opened and an elderly man servant walked into the sunshine. He did not wear the formal attire of Justin's butler in town, but was dressed in brown breeches and a white shirt whose long sleeves he had rolled up to his elbows. An apron was wrapped around his narrow waist. His white hair was thin and his face deeply lined, but his posture was erect and open. He was smiling at Justin with deep affection in his eyes.

"Lord Hawkeston." His voice creaked like an old wooden floor when too much weight is brought to bear upon it.

Justin turned away from the coach where he was helping Valentine to descend and looked at the old man. He opened his arms and walked toward him. "William!"

They embraced. Justin was much taller and twice the thin old man's size, but Valentine could tell that William was fit and in good health.

"Did ye come down 'ere to straighten out this mess, me boy?" William asked.

"That I did, William. But I'm relying on you to tell me what the devil is happening."

William began trotting off into the house with Justin at his side. "The devil is right, me boy. There's not one

291

of 'em whose mind is set in their brain straight, if you know what I mean. They've gotten into their pea-sized heads that yer not dealin' fair with 'em. An' everybody knows that t'isn't so.''

"How did all this start?"

"Like I said in me letter, t'was that Crompton. What a bad lot that one was. I'm fairly glad to see him gone.''

"Do you have any idea where he was headed?"

William shook his head. "He left in the middle of the night. Took some of the family silver, I might add. I didn't want to tell ye that bad news until ye got here. If I were younger, I would've lit after him meself, I would have.'' William placed his hand on the small of his back. "But lately, I've been feelin' a bit poorly.''

"William, I don't expect you to head up a posse and go chasing over the Cotswolds on horseback. You did just fine. I'll speak with the farmers and cottagers in the morning. In fact, before I leave I intend to speak with every family who lives on Hawkeston land,'' Justin assured him as they entered the house.

That evening before dinner as they all sat in matching green-velvet-upholstered Chippendale wing chairs around the fireplace in the Great Hall, Justin explained that the Hawkeston estate encompassed 4,999 acres of prime farming land. There were 57 houses, all of which Justin owned and leased. There were five major farms that he leased and one farm he worked himself. The remaining 1,400 acres were forest. Most of the farms grew barley, wheat and grass. Every farm grew its own vegetables and fruits and had its own cows, horses, pigs, goats and some sheep. There were five villages on the estate, and he leased out all the buildings in the villages.

"So you can see that for me to deal with a cottager uprising of any sort is no small matter.''

"Lord Hawkeston, is there anything we can do to help?" Aunt Cherise inquired.

"Prayer is always appreciated," he said as William entered the Great Hall and announced dinner.

Justin took Valentine's arm and led her into the dining room. It was an enormous banquet-sized room with three fireplaces, four iron chandeliers dating from the Tudor period when the house was built, and a table that could easily seat forty. The chairs were Tudor style with high backs, dark wood and burgundy velvet seats.

Their places had been set at one end of the table nearest the roaring fire.

Justin sat at the head with Valentine and Aunt Cherise to his right and Victoria and Andrew on the left. As William served the soup, Valentine noticed that the table runners looked stained and not well pressed. The silverware had not been polished and there was a good deal of tarnish on her fork and spoon. Justin's precious Venetian crystal was clean and spotless, but the teacups had stains in the bottoms.

Valentine made a note to speak with the housekeeper in the morning about the condition of the tableware.

The bread on the pewter tray was not fresh and the marmalade was runny. Valentine further noticed that the apples in the epergne were bruised and brown. Something was very wrong.

William ladled huge portions of a vegetable and beef soup into soup mugs. Valentine took one sip of the soup and nearly dropped her spoon. She whisked her napkin to her mouth. She put her other hand on Aunt Cherise's forearm to halt her.

"Don't eat the soup," Valentine said and rose from her chair.

"What's the matter with it?" Justin asked.

She placed her napkin on the table. "It's bad."

293

Victoria's eyes were round. "You mean like the stew on the ship?"

"Very nearly." She looked at Justin. "Which way is the kitchen?"

He stood up. "Follow me."

They walked across the stone floor and to the hall that led to the kitchen.

Mrs. Foley, the cook, was standing at a huge wooden table with a meat cleaver in her hand. She was whacking away at a mutton leg. She was a short, rotund woman with rosy red cheeks, dull brown hair and deep-set hazel eyes. She gasped when Justin and Valentine entered her sanctuary.

"Lord Hawkeston!" Her small eyes widened.

"I want to know if you're trying to poison me, or if it's just an oversight that you suddenly can't tell rotted food from fresh."

"I . . . I don't know what yer meanin', Yer Lord-ship." Her eyes slid over to the scullery maid, Jeanne, who was scrubbing out a black pot.

Jeanne ducked her young head and kept at her work.

Justin looked around the kitchen. "Where is every-body, Mrs. Foley?"

Mrs. Foley was so upset at this impromptu visit and the nature of the interrogation, she was speechless. Her cheeks turned a bloody red. She fidgeted with her fat fingers, folding them over themselves as if they were bread dough.

Valentine could tell that Justin was furious. "Miss Carlyle who made our breads and pastries, where has she got to? And what of Mrs. Bard who put up the pre-serves and jellies and canned the vegetables at harvest? And where the devil is Mr. Small? The tableware in the dining room looks as if it hasn't been cleaned or pol-ished since my last visit."

"It . . . it hasn't, my lord," Mrs. Foley finally answered with great trepidation.

"Why the hell not?"

Jeanne dropped her black pot. She was young and defiant. "They all took off. Jus' like we were 'bout ter do."

"Speak fer yerself!" Mrs. Foley snapped at the girl. She turned back to Justin. "I wasn't goin' nowhere, my lord."

Justin thrust his hands on his hips. "If you want to leave, Jeanne, please do so."

Suddenly Jeanne lost her resolve. She sat back on the floor and took up her work with the pot. "It's jest that we can't go on with these low wages yer payin', Yer Lordship."

"Jeanne!" Mrs. Foley cautioned the girl.

"What is she talking about, Mrs. Foley?"

Mrs. Foley expelled a resigned sigh. "Everybody's gone, my lord. We don't even have day maids for the upstairs bedrooms. Jeanne and I have made all the beds up ourselves. We tried to take the linens to the village and have them laundered in order to be ready fer Yer Lordship and the rest"—she nodded at Valentine—"but no one would take them. We did the best we could. There was no more money left to buy food—"

"No money?" Justin scratched his head. "I sent Crompton money every month in addition to what he was to have collected in rents."

"He never gave us any money to run the house. He said there was none left over and that the rents weren't paying. Mr. McMichael, down in the valley, he told me he paid his rent, but Mr. Crompton said he didn't."

Valentine turned to Justin. "This does look bad. Mr. Crompton was stealing from you."

Mrs. Foley and Jeanne nodded.

"I'd deduced the same myself when I heard about all

295

this uprising business. I've brought plenty of money to go to market in the morning, Mrs. Foley. And I will pay your wages and then some, Jeanne. However, there's nothing else I can do about the situation tonight.'' He looked at Valentine. ''By God, I'm starving.''

Valentine glanced around the kitchen. She unbuttoned the wrist buttons of her sleeves and rolled them up as far as they would go. ''Justin, dinner will be delayed slightly this evening. Would you tell the others to have another cup of tea? Mrs. Foley and I have some work to do.''

''Valentine . . . I don't know about this,'' Justin said.

''Never mind, my lord. This is an emergency just like the one we encountered on the ship. I'll handle everything. Now, please, tell the others.''

Justin shrugged his shoulders and left Valentine to rectify the situation.

She took the mutton leg Mrs. Foley was holding. She inspected the meat and found it to be safe. She put a pot on the stove to boil. Then she chopped several onions into fine pieces and seared them with a bit of garlic and fat in the bottom of a pot. She added water to the mutton leg and seasoned the soup with pepper and salt.

Valentine ordered Jeanne to bring her all the apples she could find. With Mrs. Foley's help, Valentine and Jeanne cut away the bruises and retrieved enough of the apples to make a baked bread and apple sweet pudding.

Valentine found a large hunk of white cheese that was not moldy, flour and sugar to make biscuits, and a glass jar filled with oats they would use to make hot cereal for breakfast in the morning.

The dinner was sparse, according to Justin, who had his appetite prepared for a large country feast. ''However, it tastes wonderful,'' he complimented Valentine.

''I've assembled the ingredients for breakfast so you won't go hungry for long, my lord,'' Valentine said.

Chapter Twenty-two

Valentine and Victoria happily set about setting Hawkeston Manor to rights. Each room was polished with lemon oil to a mirror shine. The bedding and linens were scented with rose, freesia and peach scents. Valentine made special scented candles for the bedrooms, sitting rooms and newly renovated bathing rooms adjacent to each bedroom. Mrs. Foley cleaned every crystal and silver vase in the house, and Victoria filled them all with fresh spring flowers and long sprigs of budding forsythia, apple blossoms and quince.

Victoria enlisted Andrew's help in organizing the greenhouse. The gardener had quit shortly before the Christmas season. Therefore, none of the spring seedlings had been started and many vines, plants and flowers desperately needed repotting.

Valentine teased her sister that she volunteered for the greenhouse job so that she could have time alone with

Andrew without interruption. Victoria giggled and told Valentine her assumptions were absolutely correct.

Valentine loved gardening as much as Victoria. She couldn't wait to spend long hours in the greenhouse herself planting herbs, exotic flowers and cross-breeding roses that she'd read about in the Horticulture Society's pamphlets. With every dawn, Valentine found something else to love about Hawkeston Manor. She wished she would never have to leave.

Valentine was in the kitchen instructing Mrs. Foley how to properly make Greek baklava when there was a knock at the kitchen door. Valentine's hands were covered in sticky honey. Mrs. Foley went to the door.

Mrs. Foley introduced Carrie Ainseley, Tabatha DeWitt and Sally Pudd. Sally was the spokeswoman for the group.

"It has come to our attention, my lady, that 'e might be needin' our services. We know that yer staff has been long gone and tho' we ain't got no idea where they got to, the lot of us is strong and quick t' learn. We was hearin' that His Lordship would pay fer our hours."

Valentine nodded. "That's true." She smiled. "Mrs. Foley could use some help in the kitchen, and there's no one to help me but my sister and aunt with the rest of the house." Valentine's eyes went from face to face. She could tell they were eager for work and all seemed bright-eyed and pleasant in their attitudes.

"We're fast learners, my lady. Jes' show us one time, an' we can do the work."

"There's laundry—" Valentine began.

"That's fer me," Sally spoke up. "I got six men ta home and ever'body in the valley says their britches is the finest clean."

"That's wonderful, Sally. I do have some special things I do that I would like to teach you. And I

298

wouldn't be surprised if you taught me a great deal, too.''

Carrie was the next to speak. "I'm very good at floors and carpets. Me ma told me I was good at it 'cuz I always was lookin' down. I can spot a clod o' clay from twenty feet. 'Tis a lot of floors in this old house, my lady. You can't expect ta do them by yerself! If needs be, I'll have me daughter, Prissy, he'p. She's twelve. A real good worker.''

Tabatha was the last to speak. "I'm odd, I love windows. I walk by this old house month after month and year after year, admiring the windows. If His Lordship still has the iron scaffolding in the barn that I seen a few years back and he puts together some new wooden platforms, I'd be more than happy to clean the windows.''

Valentine gasped. "You would climb three stories high?''

Tabatha's thin lips spread in a grin. "Oh, yes, my lady! I been climbing rooftops since I was five. I like the feelin' that I'm on top of the world lookin' down on everybody and everthin'. It's an adventure.'' Tabatha looked at Valentine as if she were unbalanced not to think the way she did.

Valentine had never been so pleased. They were exactly the kind of women she wanted on her staff. They each had a talent for one thing, and more importantly, they knew what that talent was. They were proud of their work, and Valentine was proud to work with them.

"You are all an answer to my prayers. I'm expecting guests for the weekend. When could you start?'' she asked.

Sally looked at Tabatha who winked at Carrie. "Today,'' they said in unison.

* * *

Valentine and Mrs. Foley wasted no time showing each woman where to find cleaning tools, brooms, mops, pails, soap, rags, ammonia, polish and lye. Within an hour the Hawkeston manor house was buzzing with activity.

Justin walked out of the stable with two horses he'd saddled. As he brought them around to the front of the house he noticed a strange woman sweeping the front stone steps. "Who are you?"

"I'm Carrie Ainseley, Your Lordship. Your new housemaid." She curtsied quickly and went instantly back to work. She swept while she talked. "I want to thank you fer doin' fer the farmers what ye did. None of us knew ye were takin' it in the hind end same as we." Then she put her hand over her mouth when she realized what she'd said. "Pardon me, Yer Lordship."

Justin laughed. "Yes, Carrie. I most certainly did take it in the hind end." He tied up the horses at the hitching post. "Thank you for coming to our rescue, Carrie."

"We're jes' helpin' each other, my lord." she nodded and continued sweeping.

Justin found Valentine wiping her hands on a white apron as she stepped back to admire a painting. He put his arms around her waist and laughed when she jumped.

"Oh, Justin, you nearly scared the wits out of me."

He nuzzled his face in the crook of her neck while she looked at the painting. "You like it?"

"Yes, I do. Who is it?"

"My grandmother. She was beautiful, wasn't she?"

Valentine looked at the heart-shaped face of the blond girl who couldn't have been more than sixteen. Her courtly clothes, tiny corseted waist and elaborate wig seemed to dwarf her tiny frame. "She looks dreadfully uncomfortable."

Justin laughed. "I've always thought the same thing."

"I was instructing Tabatha on how to care for the oil paintings, dust them, polish the frames and such and I realized there are more paintings here than in your house in town. I remember the Countess Cioppoli telling Aunt Cherise that your art collection was not only extensive, but quite valuable."

"I suppose that's true, but I never thought of the paintings that way. They've been in the family for hundreds of years, and to me they're old friends. The countess has family portraits that are similar. I think what she was referring to was my very private collection."

"What?"

"Come with me. I have a room in the east wing I would like you to see." He took her hand and walked her down the hall. He took a key from his vest pocket and unlocked the door.

The windows were covered with heavy damask draperies that hadn't been cleaned in decades. Though the room was dark, there wasn't a stick of furniture anywhere. There wasn't room.

As Justin pulled back the draperies and let sunlight fill the room, Valentine could see nearly four dozen easels with unframed oils sitting on the floor. The walls were crowded with landscapes, still lifes, portraits, children at play, dogs, cats and horses. Their range was everything from dark Dutch masters in the Rembrandt style to the newest romantic school that was currently the rage in poetry, literature and art.

"Where did they come from?"

"Everywhere. Italy, France, Poland, Moscow, Spain, Germany, Ireland, Scotland. Whenever I travel, I look for new artists. I buy what I like. Most of them cost very little; a couple I bought for the price of a meal. I didn't care. I love art. All kinds of art. I wanted them. I wanted to support the artists who took the time to put their visions on canvas.''

Valentine's eyes were filled with awe as she slowly went from painting to painting. She took her time to inspect each one. ''I know nothing about art. I'm afraid my eye is untrained. But, Justin, I can't find one I don't like. I think all these people are talented.''

''So do I.''

''I've never heard of any of these names.''

''They may never become famous. Fame is not a sign of talent but of luck. I do hope for their sakes that they all become well known.''

Valentine's eyes narrowed with curiosity. ''The countess thought your collection was wisely acquired . . . if these people aren't famous . . .''

Justin's smile was discreet. ''Time will tell, Valentine. Now come, I have a surprise for you.''

''I love surprises.''

He walked with her out of the house to where he'd hitched the horses. Valentine noticed instantly that one horse was saddled with a ladies' side saddle.

Justin took the reins of the mare. ''Valentine, meet Stargazer.''

Valentine put her hand on the horse's muzzle. She was a magnificent horse, chestnut brown with white markings and a black mane and tail. ''She's beautiful, Justin. Elegant and every inch a lady.'' Valentine hugged the brown-eyed horse.

''She's yours.''

''Justin! You don't mean it?''

''I do.''

''You realize that if you give me this horse, I could ride away from you at any time and never come back?''

''I know I'm taking a great risk,'' he teased back. Then his smile faded. His eyes were serious. ''If you don't want to be with me, Valentine, I want you to have your freedom. I give you this promise today. I will abide by my promise to your father to provide financially for you, Victoria and Aunt Cherise, regardless if you marry me.''

''Do you know what you're saying?''

''Yes. I'm taking the chance that you want to stay with me.'' He swallowed hard. ''The horse is yours.''

Valentine threw her arms around Justin's neck and kissed his cheek. He pulled her to him and closed his eyes. He wondered why it was he wanted her hugs so much. There was nothing sexual about his feelings at that moment. He wanted to make her happy. He wanted her to always feel free to hold him. When he thought about it, he realized he'd been held very little in his thirty years. He wondered if other men felt that way.

He untied her apron and hung it on the hitching post. ''I'll give you a leg up.''

''Right now? I'm not dressed for riding.'' She touched her hair which fell in long silver cascades down her back. ''I need to bind up my hair. The wind will snarl it.''

''Bother the snarls! Be adventurous, Valentine. I'll brush it for you myself if I have to.'' He boosted her into the saddle and then mounted his own horse.

''Come on! I want you to see the land you will be sharing with me,'' Justin shouted as they trotted down the gravel drive and over the lawn.

They rode over the softly rolling hills and into the open unplowed fields, where they picked up speed.

It had been years since Valentine had been on horseback, but the feel of the horse came back to her in no time. Stargazer was a gentle horse who had been expertly trained, for she took her commands easily. Valentine inhaled the fresh spring air and watched enormous fluffy clouds march across the azure sky.

As they galloped over hills and skimmed the edge of the thick forest, Valentine saw rows of apple trees with fat buds ready to pop open. There were peach trees, pear trees, red bud trees and waxy-leafed magnolias. White and pink dogwoods spread their spindly limbs under huge, still-bare oak trees.

Valentine slowed Stargazer and then she stopped. Justin looked over his shoulder thinking that Valentine was right behind him and discovered she had paused at a group of budding trees near the apple orchard. He turned his horse around and rode up next to her.

"What's the matter?" he asked.

"Everything is perfect," she said and reached out her hand to him. She couldn't decide which was more beautiful, nature awakening to spring or the love beginning to dawn in Justin's eyes.

"I love you, Justin," she said softly. She was surprised at how easily and naturally the words flowed out of her mouth. Perhaps that was because they were heartfelt.

Justin was taken aback. He'd wanted to hear her say that she loved him, but he'd told himself it was too much to expect. He was speechless. He squeezed her hand. "I'd give you the moon if you asked me, Valentine."

She chuckled. "What would I do with a silly old moon?" She gazed at the apple orchard. "By the eighteenth those trees will be in full blossom." She turned back to him. "I know you want our wedding to be elegant and attended by all the ton. But if I could have anything in the world, I would want my wedding to take place in that apple orchard."

"Done, my princess!" he shouted, hoping the sound of his voice would bounce off the clouds.

Valentine gasped. "But you said you ordered tents for the garden—"

"I'll cancel them! I cannot believe how much alike we are, Valentine, and we didn't know it. I have always loved the country, and when I was a small boy I used to go to the apple orchards in spring and sit under the trees and let the blossoms fall on my face. I even dreamed of a princess coming to me there."

"And what did the princess do, Justin?" she teased.

Sincerity sparkled in his eyes. "She held me."

"That's all?"

"Uh, huh. That's all."

Valentine smiled widely. "Then I shall do the very same. I shall hold you under the apple blossoms!" She dropped his hand, took the reins and spurred her horse. "If you can catch me!" she said playfully as she rode toward the apple trees.

Justin caught Valentine, dismounted and laid his coat on the soft ground. Valentine pretended it didn't matter to her that Justin had not told her he loved her. She told herself she was content that he wanted to give her a wedding that suited only her.

He laid his head on her lap while he planned a more restricted guest list. Gone were the kind of people Valentine didn't like and instead were left the people she thought she would befriend for years to come.

They sat for hours under the apple trees planning the kind of wedding they'd both always dreamed about.

Chapter Twenty-three

Collin McMichael was a hot-tempered, red-headed, blue-eyed Irishman whose ego was bigger than the British Isles and whose mouth was bigger still. Collin was forty years old with ruddy skin lined from years of working in the out-of-doors. He loved the earth and watching plants and crops grow. He was an honest man who believed in giving an honest day's hard labor for his pay. He worked the same farm as his father and grandfather before him. He knew every cottager, peasant, villager, woman and child on the Hawkeston estate. Despite his boasting of his personal relationship with Lord Hawkeston, whether he knew it or not, Collin McMichael had power.

Lord Hawkeston took Andrew with him to meet an assembly of villagers at the Severn Tavern.

Although spring had arrived early to the Cotswolds, there was a chill in the air that morning and the tavern keeper had started a blazing fire in the limestone fire-place. The trestle tables were filled with familiar faces when Justin opened the old wooden door.

Men and women had come from almost every farm on the estate to state their grievances. Justin saw Mrs. Bard with her fat arms crossed in front of her defiantly. Mr. Small was whittling a stick near the fireplace, and Justin wondered idly if he were making a spear with which to stab him.

Andrew scanned the sea of rebellious expressions and whispered to Justin, "I feel as if I've just been led to the gallows."

"So do I," Justin replied.

Collin McMichael was the tallest and biggest man in the room. His broad shoulders were nearly as wide as Justin's, and they stood eye to eye. They were both handsome men with intelligent eyes, and each of them believed he was right and the other was wrong.

Justin extended his hand first. "Collin."

"Your Lordship." Collin shook Justin's hand and then quickly pulled away.

"I have something I wish to say," Justin began.

"We don't want no fancy words, my lord. We've heard plenty from your man Crompton. He told us how you feel about us. About the welfare of your estate. We just wanted to see your face when we told you we're not plantin' for you this year or any other year. We're leavin'."

"Leaving?" Justin was shocked. "Everyone?"

"Most of us, aye," Collin continued. "Some of 'em are stayin'. Small over there for one. The Leyniers in Malvern, the whole clan o' them is stayin'. But you won't get no crop out of 'em. They're planning to sell their own goods in the next county. There's some new markets opening up. Even some shippers willin' to take

307

our grains to bigger markets on the coast and sell to other countries. And as long as Napoleon keeps his war a-goin', there's always a market for grain,'' Collin explained and turned to the crowd for their approval. He grinned broadly at Justin.

The villagers mumbled among themselves and nodded their heads at Collin.

''You intend to use my land to sell my grain to outsiders and keep the money yourselves?''

''The ones who're stayin', that's what they intend.''

''That's robbery!'' Justin said, outraged.

''That's fair after what you've done to us this past year.''

The villagers grumbled loudly. A few shouted obscenities at Justin.

Andrew noticed a raised fist. One man spit on the floor. Another snarled at Andrew as he reached in his pocket for a knife.

The crowd had grown dangerous. Justin had to do something quick. ''Please, listen to me, all of you! If you wish to leave my land, I will not stop you. If you wish to stay, I will pay you all your missed back wages and I will pay you to plant this year before the harvest.''

The growling rolled to a rumbling hush. They began to listen.

Justin gave Andrew a signal. Andrew yanked a heavy cloth bag from underneath his coat. He held it high for everyone to see.

Justin jumped onto a bench so that everyone could see him.

''I have brought money to pay you today. I have had to borrow some of this money from a lender. I am not the rich man many of you think I am. I have had to work very hard to save my estate from my father's debtors. I am *not* my father. I am *not* my brother. I am Justin

308

Hawkeston. I am a fair man. I ask that you treat me as such.''

The murmurs subsided and there was silence.

''Mr. Crompton was a thief. He not only stole the money I gave him to pay you, but he took the rents he collected from you. Without you good people, I have no estate. If you leave, then I will leave. We have to work together or we have nothing.''

Justin turned to Collin. ''I am asking for your help. These people respect you. I respect you. It won't be easy just to get us even with what we were before Crompton cheated us, but we can do it. Will you be my overseer?''

Collin McMichael was stunned. He'd come to the tavern today to put the English Lord Hawkeston down and to bury him if necessary. He'd never considered a compromise. He had planned to leave the estate and go back to Ireland.

Collin had built a fine home for himself, his wife and three daughters. He'd been proud to have the most fertile of the farms. He'd been proud to own the finest racing horses in the Cotswolds. Every lord and earl in the area came to him wanting to breed their mares with his stallion, Prince Valïant, who'd won every local race since his second birthday. Lord Hawkeston himself had bred four mares with Collin's prize-winning thoroughbred. But he'd been willing to give up his good life and go back to the poverty he'd known as a child on the rocky, infertile family plot of soil in Ireland rather than be cheated by a man he'd trusted for over ten years.

Like the other villagers and cottagers, Collin was hurt and angry over having trusted Lord Hawkeston. They all felt duped.

In the past two years, Lord Hawkeston had spent most of his time oversees or in London and precious little of it with them at Hawkeston Manor. They felt slighted and unnappreciated.

Collin looked at Justin. "When Crompton announced he was your man of affairs and the new overseer, we were all suspicious. He didn't know as much about the land as he should. We ignored that for a while. Then after he took our rent payments, you came down here last harvest before you went to Italy and you said we hadn't paid. And we had. Then he didn't pay us. You were never here. We thought you were giving him those orders."

"Nothing could be further from the truth. He was a thief. Pure and simple." Justin looked at Collin. "Will you help me?"

Collin looked at the faces in the crowd. Angus McGillivray. Tristan Holden. Henry Throckton. James Keeling. They were all looking at Collin. One by one they nodded their heads.

"I'm willin' if ye are, Collin," said Tristan Holden.

"That goes fer me, too," Angus McGillivray replied.

"You're the only bastard I'd work for, Collin," Henry Throckton laughed.

The danger dissipated. The tension eased. Justin shook hands with Collin and he smiled for the first time in days.

As Justin and Andrew rode chestnut-colored thoroughbreds over the Cotswold hills back to the manor house, Andrew's curiosity over the events he'd heard about that day grew. When they stopped to water the horses in a particularly peaceful brook lined with lichen, moss and spring wildflowers, Andrew turned to Justin.

"How was it that such a despicable person as Crompton came to be in your employ, Justin? You've been so careful, overly cautious really, in giving me different responsibilities, testing my abilities each day before giving me more work. How did you miss what this man was up to?''

''God knows I've asked myself that question a hundred times. I think I had mistakenly believed that the only path out of my financial problems was through the glass factories. I had put all my available cash into them. I had to make them grow. In order to get the glass here and distribute it, I felt it necessary to see to the shipments myself. I'd heard so many tales of sea captains wrecking their ships for the loot, of shipments being sold to the French for black market prices, of thievery at the dock, that I didn't trust anyone. I was so focused on that part of my business that I neglected the little bit of income I received from the farms.''

Andrew shook his head. ''Even before Crompton, the farms were not bringing you a large income?''

Justin shook his head. ''Very little.''

''Then something is terribly wrong. I have a few hunches. Would you mind if I looked into the matter for you?''

''Not at all.'' Justin remounted his steed. ''I'm curious. The land was being planted to capacity. The farmers all worked hard. Where do you think I've gone off the track?''

''I'll have to study your books, but my guess is that you've got too many farmers planting the same kind of crop or similar crops, which would drive the price down when they go to market. Perhaps if we rotated their crops, or planted a wider variety of crops, you would make more money.''

''That is a very good point, Andrew.''

''Thank you, sir. I was also thinking that it would be wise to investigate exports to the Continent and to America. It shouldn't take much to discover what raw

311

products they need and then ship them. Rather than using your ship only for the glassware, we could use your own ship to sail the grains and food crops from the farms to America.''

Justin smiled appreciatively at Andrew. "Good thinking, my man. Very good thinking."

The day had turned out better than he dared to hope, Justin thought. He not only had quashed the potential uprising of his cottagers, but he'd enlisted their efforts to make the Hawkeston estate the most profitable in the Cotswolds.

Andrew's ideas all had merit. And that had been a surprise to him. Justin couldn't stop thinking how odd it was that fate chose to give him a brother who was forever a thorn in his side and who would never lift a finger to help him, and through marriage he would soon be related to Andrew, a brother-in-law who had been more of a help to him than any blood relative. He supposed there was no way to second-guess destiny, but it did give him cause to wonder.

Justin challenged Andrew to a race as they spurred their horses into a full gallop across the hills back toward Hawkeston Manor.

Valentine, Aunt Cherise and Mrs. Foley went to the open-air farmers' market just after sunrise shortly after Justin and Andrew left for their meeting. The farmers came to the market for only an hour or two until all their produce was sold. For the best selections, Valentine wanted to be early.

Victoria and Jeanne began stripping beds and washing linens while the other women were at the market. They washed out the sheets and rinsed them in perfumed water just the way Valentine had on the ship. Victoria showed Jeanne how to treat different food stains with varying degrees of hot and cold water, salt, lemon and buttermilk. In the laundry house a long wooden trestle table was covered with a soft cotton pad covered in muslin. A half dozen irons were heated on a wooden stove. Victoria showed Jeanne how to starch the sheets with rice starch and then how to press them perfectly.

There were *draps de maîtres,* seamless linen sheets of incredibly fine quality from France, which were used in Justin's room. The pillowcases, duvet covers and hand towels were hand-embroidered linen or cambric with either the Hawkeston coat of arms in white on white or with an "H" in gold thread on white linen from Reims. The rest of the 96 sheets were made of flax and linen, resulting from an oversupply of flax in this part of the country. There were 60 sheets of lesser quality for the servants' bedding.

Victoria made a complete inventory of every sheet, body towel, pillowcase, churching sheet, duvet cover, bedspread, bed curtain, tablecloth, napkin, table runner and hand towel. She marked each one how it was to be cleaned, the stains removed, and how she wanted it starched and pressed. Different fragrances of perfumes were assigned to different linens depending upon who was to use the towel or the occupant of the bedroom sleeping on the sheets.

Jeanne was fascinated with Victoria's instructions about each fabric.

"I'd much rather work with these beautiful things than scrub pots in the kitchen."

"I quite agree with you. Embroidery and all facets of sewing have been my favorites since I was a small girl."

"I like putting the sheets in the perfumed water," Jeanne said, dipping a soft pink linen sheet into a tub of jasmine-scented water. She inhaled the fragrance with a broad smile on her face. "I can't think of a more wonderful way to spend the day than tendin' these sheets and towels.''

Victoria smiled at the young girl. "Perhaps we need to change your assignments, Jeanne."

"Do ye think that's possible?"

Victoria nodded firmly. "I will speak to my sister about it today. We both believe every person has a special talent for something in this world. Perhaps yours is fabric, just as mine is.''

Jeanne smiled proudly at Victoria as she grabbed another dirty sheet and began rubbing out the rust spots and body oils that were embedded in the linen.

By the time Valentine and Aunt Cherise returned at noon, Victoria had completely organized the linens throughout the manor house.

That afternoon, William cleaned boots and shoes. Valentine organized the foodstuffs in the pantry while Mrs. Foley and Jeanne prepared the evening meal. Victoria washed and pressed lace-edged white linen table runners for the evening meal.

Valentine had just entered the butler's pantry from an outside door when she overheard Mrs. Foley and Jeanne talking.

"She doesn't act like no lady to me," Jeanne said.

"She isn't Lady Hawkeston yet," Mrs. Foley said. "I'll wait ter see if it really happens."

"You think His Lordship won't marry her?" Jeanne asked.

"I have my doubts. She certainly is like none o' the others he's brought 'round."

"That's fer sure. None 'o the likes o' them would even come to the kitchens, much less work in 'em," Jeanne snorted.

"Lord Hawkeston seemed to like the fact that this one was willin' to pitch in," Mrs. Foley said. "The others acted more like ladies . . . wantin' to stay in bed all day with His Lordship . . .''

Valentine dropped a china plate in the butler's pantry, she was so shocked at what she was hearing. Just how many "others" were there? Maybe Aunt Cherise had indeed heard correctly about Justin being a "rogue." And he'd brought his mistresses to the country where he could carry on with them in bed all day!

Too easily she remembered Justin's sweet lovemaking the night before they'd left London. He'd brought her to a fever pitch in no time. And like the harlot he always accused her of being, she'd given in to him. She'd let him do things to her that she knew must be sinful. They were too erotic and pleasurable to be moral.

She knew he was much too practiced. He must have had dozens, no, hundreds, of women before her! Look how old he was, for heaven's sake! A man with a sensual appetite like his would seek indulgence every chance he got.

How foolish and naive she'd been to think she was special!

And now she had Mrs. Foley's testimony as truth.

Valentine rushed from the pantry and took the back staircase up to the second floor and her bedroom at the end of the south hall.

She was too upset and angry to cry. She wished she could cry like other women. Cry, get it out and over with and go on. But no. Her emotions boiled within her like a slow-burning forest fire. She dug through her valise and found her old journal. There were still a few empty pages left. Then she withdrew a brand-new journal she'd bought in London at the stationery shop. If she didn't have enough space, she would begin her new journal.

Dear Diary,

I have come to Hawkeston Manor in the Cotswolds, and just when I thought I had found not only paradise in England at this beautiful country estate, not to mention heaven in Justin's arms . . . oh, the pleasures he has shown me are unmentionable . . . I discovered that this manor house and those pleasures are ones that Justin has shown to many other women.

I fear that Aunt Cherise was right. Justin is a rogue. He is the seducer I saw in Baldassare. How many times have I told myself that first impressions are seldom wrong?

How many times must I chide myself for giving people the benefit of the doubt only to discover they were deceiving me?

My first impressions are never wrong. I cannot trust Justin. I must caution myself at all times not to lose my heart to him. I must still marry him. However, I don't have to give him my heart.

Once a snake, always a snake. Lord Hawkeston has proven the truth of that statement for me.

Sincerely,
Valentine St. James

She blew on the ink and when it dried she put the journal in the bottom of her valise where no one would find it.

Back in the kitchen Mrs. Foley heard the crash of china in the butler's pantry. "What was that?"

"Someone's in the butler's pantry," Jeanne said with a tense hush. "William?" she called.

Mrs. Foley joined her. "William?"

When there was no answer, Mrs. Foley went to the pantry to investigate. "There's no one about," she said to Jeanne, who followed sheepishly behind her.

Jeanne sniffed the air. "Roses. I smell roses."

"It was Miss St. James. She was in here. But why would she run off without sayin' a word?" Then her hand flew to her fat cheek. "Saints in heaven! You don't think she misinterpreted what I said?"

Jeanne shrugged her thin shoulders. "I dunno. What were ye sayin'?"

Mrs. Foley squatted and picked up the pieces of fine porcelain. "That the other ladies were wantin' to stay abed with His Lordship all day."

"But His Lordship never did like a one of 'em fine falutin' ladies," Jeanne corrected. "He was always off ter seein' about the farms and such."

"That's what I was about to say when I heard the crash."

"Oh, dear."

Mrs. Foley shrugged her shoulders. "I'm probably makin' more of it than it is. If she's to marry His Lordship, she knows he thinks of nothin' but business."

Jeanne smiled and snorted her horse laugh. "Aye. Better she has learned to work beside him."

Mrs. Foley laughed as they left the pantry and went back to their duties. "Otherwise she would never see him at all."

Jeanne laughed along with Mrs. Foley at the odd kind of woman Lord Hawkeston had to find to complement the odd kind of man that he was.

Valentine could hardly wait to confront Justin, but she knew her audience with him would have to wait until after dinner that evening. She knew if she didn't keep herself busy every second, she would be a bundle of nerves by then. She tried not to look at the clock. And failed. The more she tried to ignore the hands of the clock, the more she looked.

The only answer was to leave the house. She picked several dozen yellow daffodils that grew in profusion around the manor house and filled one of the crystal vases from the Hawkeston glass factory in Venice. She put the vase on the dining room table. She filled a second silver-fluted vase and put it on the console in the vestibule.

She wondered if Justin's "other ladies" ever did anything like the things she did for him.

"Of course not, you ninny!" she chided herself. "They were too busy in bed all day!"

Valentine's mind would not settle for envisioning Justin in bed with only one woman, she saw three. A blonde, an auburn-haired beauty and a dark-haired Gypsy. She imagined him doing to all of them the things he'd done to her and more. And with each embellishment she put on the image, the more irate she became.

By mid-afternoon, she was so furious her hands were shaking and she could barely arrange flowers anymore. She knew she was not good company for anyone. Her only salvation was to channel her anger into positive duties.

She would make the candles they needed. She filled her candle molds with hot wax and the unusual scents she blended with the oils she'd bought in London. As the sun set, the tapers were cooled and ready for use. Valentine put three ivory-colored tapers in a silver candelabra and placed it on the dining room table.

She put another half dozen tapers in the candlesticks in the Great Hall and in the library and lit them.

While William ignited fires in the dining room, library and Great Hall, Valentine went to her room to change for dinner. She flung her dresses on the bed, disliking

them all. She wanted something tempting, seductive and
. . . red. But all she had were these mourning dresses in
black, white and lavender.

"Bother!" She groaned and stepped into the lavender
silk Empire-waisted gown that Sabrina had finished the
day they left London. Beneath the bodice were three
ribbons in pink lavender, lilac and deep violet. There
were extra ribbons for her hair. The sleeves were long
and demure, but the bodice was more low-cut than Valentine had ever dared.

She turned to gaze at herself in the mirror. "How
bold!" Her eyes narrowed when she thought of Justin
languishing all day in bed with his mistresses. She must
remember to ask him about the three mistresses he had
in Italy! How many did he have in France, for that matter? She assessed herself again. The dress wasn't bold
at all, come to think of it. It was just right.

At nightfall when Justin and Andrew rode up to Hawkeston Manor nearly every window in every room
glowed with welcoming golden light.

Justin handed his riding crop, gloves and hat to William. Andrew followed suit.

Justin saw one of Valentine's pretty flowered and good-
smelling candles sitting on a brass tray on the marble console. The flame was reflected in the eight-foot-high
Venetian mirror. Then he sniffed the aroma of cooking.
"What is that I smell, William?"

William beamed. "Beef Wellington, Your Lordship.
Boiled potatoes, carrots, turnips. 'Tis a feast for certain,
sir."

Justin smiled and looked at Andrew. "It's been a long
time since Hawkeston Manor has been so inviting."

"I have a bath awaiting you in your room, my lord."

"William, you're too old to be preparing a bath for

me. Tomorrow I'll see to getting you extra help.''

"Oh, no, my lord. I didn't prepare the bath. Nor yours, sir,'' William said, turning to Andrew. "The Misses St. James boiled the water and Jeanne took it upstairs.''

"Very well, then, William,'' Justin patted him on the back.

"Dinner will be in forty minutes, my lord.''

Justin and Andrew bathed, changed clothes and met the women in the Great Hall forty minutes later. Valentine was the last to enter the room.

Justin had just lifted a brandy to his lips. He nearly choked to death when she smiled at him.

"My lord,'' she said sweetly. Ooohhh, but she wanted to throttle his neck.

"Did you forget something, Valentine?'' he asked, the brandy burning a path down his throat.

"Like what, my lord?'' she cooed.

"The rest of your dress!'' He put his glass of brandy on the table.

Victoria winced. "Uh, oh.''

Aunt Cherise was about to side with Justin when he whisked Valentine out of the Great Hall by the elbow and walked her to the library. He pushed her into the room and shut the doors loudly behind him.

He turned to her. "Are you out of your mind? I can practically see your . . . your . . .''

"My what?''

"Navel!'' he boomed.

"I didn't have time for an alteration before I left London. I had to take the dress as is,'' she said, defiantly sticking her chin in the air.

Suddenly he began grinning as he walked toward her. Perhaps she'd done this to entice him. After all, they hadn't had any real time together since their last night in London when he'd given her a taste of what it would be like to lie with him. She'd been alone all day. She'd had a great deal of time on her hands. Perhaps she'd thought about making love with him again.

God knew *he* certainly had thought of it.

Valentine thrust one hand on her well-curved hip and shoved another hand up to halt his advance. "Don't come near me, you lecherous, molesting . . . *snake!*"

"Valentine!" He stopped dead in his tracks. "I don't understand." How could he have misread her pleasure the other night? She had told him she was his, hadn't she? What had changed her attitude toward him so greatly?

"You don't understand? *You* don't understand?" She was so angry she could hardly see him. "When we were in London . . . and in the apple orchard . . . you acted like I was . . . was special to you. Well, I'll never be that foolish again! You can look all you want, Sir Snake, but you can't touch me. Never again!" She growled at him. "Never!"

"You aren't making any sense. Maybe you need to go to bed."

"Bed? Oh! And I suppose you want to stay with me!"

"If it's necessary until you calm down," he said.

"And I suppose you might have another 'friend' join us."

"What the devil are you talking about, Valentine?" He shoved his hands on his hips and glared at her.

"I'm talking about you staying in bed all day with your ladies."

"What ladies?"

"Your mistresses," she said flatly, sticking her chin in the air and proud that she was standing up to him. She almost enjoyed throwing the truth in his face.

He shook his head. "I don't have any mistresses."

"Liar. Victoria met three of them in Venice alone. They were at the ball. Friends of the countess."

Suddenly it hit him. "Judas priest, but you exaggerate things!"

"I most certainly have not. She and two others told Victoria all manner of things you did with them. Why, Vicki said they blatantly compared notes. I . . . I've never heard such things. It was shocking, really."

He started laughing. Tears came to his eyes. He laughed so hard he held his ribs. "That was Maria Pambretti, and the other two were her friends Sophia and Tia. They aren't my mistresses. I wouldn't go to bed with any of them even on a bet."

"What? Well, why not?"

"They are married to three heads of Venice's most important families. They are my very best customers. That would be like biting the hand that feeds me. This is a joke they play because they always want me to meet someone and get married. They were being amusing."

Valentine retreated. She was almost beginning to feel foolish. Almost. "What about what Mrs. Foley said?"

"I don't know. What did she say?"

"She and Jeanne were saying that you used to come to the manor house and stay in bed with your 'ladies' all day!"

"I've never remained in bed past eight o'clock in the morning in my life! You of all people must know that I'm an early riser. I detest laziness. And I have never bedded a woman in this house in my life. At least not that I can remember. I come to the country to get away from my city life . . . city people, and that includes empty-headed women of the ton," he bellowed angrily.

Valentine's eyebrows knitted in confusion. "Then why did she say that?"

"I don't know." He glared at her. "Why don't we ask her?"

As she shook her head, her silver curls bounced in the candlelight.

Justin grabbed her hand and started out of the library. "I'm putting an end to this kind of thinking right now. There are plenty of things I *am* guilty of. Lord knows I've been no angel, but three women . . ." he looked at her.

Valentine's eyes were wide as saucers.

He stopped. "You thought that I was in bed with three women at one time?"

She nodded. "You're very good at what you do. I thought . . ."

Justin was so angry, so astonished and so touched at her naiveté, he chuckled. He touched her cheek. "Valentine, your imagination is going to be the ruin of us all."

He led the way into the kitchen. Mrs. Foley was slicing roast beef.

"My lord, is something the matter?"

"Just a little misunderstanding. Miss St. James heard you and Jeanne talking today about a delicate matter, but one which concerned her a great deal."

"Yes, my lord?"

"Did you say to Jeanne that I have made it a practice to lie abed all day with my mistress?"

"Your ladies," Valentine corrected.

Mrs. Foley's fat cheeks turned beet red. She put the knife down. "I'm sorry, Yer Lordship, truly. Me and Jeanne was talkin' and we did hear Miss St. James in the pantry. Dropped a china plate, she did. I didn't know then what it was all about. But I do now." Mrs. Foley looked over to Valentine. "Ye didn't stay long enough to hear the rest of the conversation. I was tellin' Jeanne

323

that the other ladies Yer Lordship brought to the manor house would never lend a hand the way Miss St. James, here, does. They would lie about in bed, with Yer Lordship leavin' at first light to tend the duties of the estate.'' Mrs. Foley shook her head. ''We was fearin' ye might not understand. I'm glad we had this talkin'.''

''Me too,'' Valentine said sheepishly.

Justin thanked Mrs. Foley and took Valentine back to the library.

''Now, I think you owe me an apology, Valentine,'' he said, taking her hand and pulling her toward him.

Valentine kept her distance. ''It was an honest mistake, as you can see now,'' she said flatly.

''Now, will you go and change your dress?''

She smiled coquettishly at him. ''Of course not.'' She went to the door.

''But I'll go crazy looking at you in that dress all during dinner,'' he replied.

She smiled triumphantly. ''That imagination of yours is going to be the ruin of us, Justin.''

Valentine slipped through the open door and joined the others for dinner.

Chapter Twenty-four

Lady Amanda Hartford stood on the riser in Sabrina Grenville's dress shop and admired herself in the mirror. The Empire-style gown was of emerald green silk with an overlay of sheer silk chiffon with hand-painted gold leaves and hand-embroidered gold stars and crescent moons around the hem. Her chestnut hair hung in thick cascades down her back. Her emerald eyes gleamed with self-appreciation.

Sabrina handed Amanda a half-dozen emerald green velvet and gold silk twisted cords which she would use to tie up her curls. The kid dancing slippers had been gilded.

"I think this dress will do nicely, Sabrina."

"I'm so pleased that you like it." Sabrina breathed a sigh of relief. It had taken four pattern designs, thirteen fabric selections and then rejections and eight fittings to please the bitch, Sabrina thought to herself. "When you asked me to create a gown to showcase the Hartford Emeralds, I doubted I was up to the challenge.''

Amanda's full lips parted charmingly over perfect white teeth. Her aristocratic fine bone structure, round English eyes and white skin were the epitome of English beauty. Amanda had been hailed as London's most beautiful woman since her sixteenth birthday. Now, ten years later, she was even more breathtaking. She liked the fact that even women stopped to stare at her. She always offered them one of her beautiful smiles because she felt it her duty to acknowledge their adoration. Amanda had always believed that apart from the fact that her beauty bought her the style of life she craved, what point was there in being beautiful if one did not have admirers?

Amanda looked down at the inventive and creative Sabrina. She wondered if Sabrina knew how lucky she was to be blessed with the talent, intelligence and courage with which she ran her business. How interesting it was to Amanda that despite all Sabrina's gifts, she was still on her knees at Amanda's feet. Amanda smiled at herself in the mirror. Beauty, then, surpassed all the other gifts of the gods.

''The Hartford Emeralds are magnificent, aren't they, Sabrina?'' Amanda asked, checking the wide-scooped, low-cut neckline of the dress. She would need all this expanse of skin for the canary diamond and emerald necklace and earbobs her late husband had willed to her. Indeed, she had married the old bag of bones for them— and the palatial house in town, the manor house in Sussex, the stable of steeplechase horses, and the castle in Germany on the Rhine that Lord Hartford's first wife had brought to their marriage in 1750. Amanda was 26 years old and felt as if she nearly owned the world, but for her, it wasn't enough. She wanted more.

"I can understand why you had both your liverymen accompany you to my shop with them. If I hadn't seen them, I would never have known how to make this dress. I've never seen anything like them."

"After all the changes we went through, I knew you just didn't understand their opulence. Seeing was believing, wasn't it, Sabrina?"

"Yes, my lady."

Once she tied her hair up, Amanda turned to her companion sitting in a bergère and casting critical gazes at the gown.

"What's the matter, Lady Sarah? Don't you like it?"

"It's too French," Sarah said in her usual clipped manner.

Amanda smiled. "Heavens! Do you think I worry about politics at a time like this? Napoleon be damned! He's not going to ruin my fun."

Lady Sarah smiled. "You're beautiful when you're petulant, Amanda."

"I'm beautiful no matter what, Lady Sarah."

Sabrina nearly choked on her pins. She kept busy with the hem. This was going to be a most interesting conversation.

Amanda gazed at her reflection. "You have no idea how wonderful it is for me to finally have a pretty gown again. Mourning is a ridiculous ritual meant to keep women looking frumpy . . . and from taking a new lover once a husband has passed away."

Lady Sarah harrumphed. "How can you possibly complain? You spent nearly your entire mourning period in Austria and Germany. I would wager you never wore black at all."

Amanda grinned mischievously at her reflection. "Only in bed."

"I didn't think there would be a lack of lovers."

Amanda cocked her head over her shoulder and glared at Lady Sarah. "You breathe one word of that in town and I'll—"

"You'll what?" Lady Sarah challenged.

Amanda glanced down at Sabrina who was still pinning the chiffon. Her carefree attitude was replaced with glacial resolve. Her emerald eyes blazed at Lady Sarah. "I'll make you wish you didn't have a tongue. And I can do it, too."

Lady Sarah swallowed. Her lined face showed not a trace of fear except for the nearly imperceptible tic in her left eye. "I'm not interested in your amours."

"The hell you say," Amanda snapped.

"Only one of them," Lady Sarah corrected herself.

Lady Sarah motioned with her head to Sabrina. Amanda took the signal.

"Sabrina, I heard that you designed Miss St. James's trousseau and wedding gown, is that true?"

"Yes, my lady," Sabrina answered. She sat back on her knees and eyed the hem, making a pretense of being occupied with the dress. She didn't want to answer any questions. She wanted all the business from Lord Hawkeston over the years to come, and yet Lady Amanda spent more money in a week than most ladies of the ton spent in a lifetime. Sabrina couldn't afford to lose Lady Amanda's business.

"What did you think of her?" Amanda looked at her reflection and placed a delicate hand on the alabaster column of her throat.

There was no hope for it. Sabrina was caught. God, how she hated people like Lady Sarah and Lady Amanda who kept London and everyone in it at their beck and call. "She was young," Sabrina said, stating the obvious and the one thing Lady Sarah could do nothing about.

"Eighteen, I understand. A child," said Lady Amanda.

"Hmmm, yes," said Lady Sarah.

"Did you think she was beautiful?" Amanda asked.

"I thought she was beautiful, although it's too bad she's in mourning. Her hair is silver-colored and she needs strong colors like this to bring out her beauty."

"That's too bad," Amanda said, preening. "Have you heard much about her, Sabrina?"

Sabrina cast her eyes toward Lady Sarah. "No more than anyone else."

"Oh? So you know that Lord Hawkeston is only marrying her out of his noble sense of duty toward her father?"

"I've heard that, yes." Sabrina didn't like the way these two women watched each other and herself with eagle eyes. This wasn't idle chatter. They were on a hunt. And she was the fox. Sabrina didn't like being put in the middle of other people's affairs. She was a dress designer and that was all. The fact that she knew more about the lives of the ton than Lady Sarah did probably made the old bag jealous. Perhaps it was time to elevate her own status for a change.

"What else have you heard, Sabrina?" Amanda asked.

"I hear a great deal, my lady, but I've always believed that hearsay isn't worth an ounce of truth." Sabrina's eyes stared at Amanda knowingly. "That ounce of truth may be worth a great deal to you."

"It could."

"I know what most people in London know: that you and Lord Hawkeston were practically engaged ten years ago. From what Lady Sarah has said in this shop, he was very much in love with you but he had no money. Lord Hartford's wealth was no match for a penniless lord. You chose Lord Hartford. Obviously, that was the right choice for you, because now Lord Hartford is dead and you are wealthy and still young.''

Amanda smiled charmingly at Sabrina. ''And that's all you know?''

''Yes, my lady.''

''Good. Would you excuse us for a moment, Sabrina?''

''Certainly, my lady.'' Sabrina rose and left the room.

Lady Sarah smiled enigmatically. ''You see? Nothing to worry about. I never breathed a word that you were pregnant with Justin's child, nor that you aborted it.''

''I never wanted any brats. Pregnancy is hard on a woman's body and destroys beauty. To know that, all I ever had to do was look at my poor mother who had fourteen pregnancies and lost every one but me. And for what? Because her husband was an egotistical bastard. Fortunately for me, Lord Hartford was impotent. God! He could hardly get out of bed after our wedding trip around Cape Horn and to India, much less make love.''

''I'll never understand you, Amanda. Why India?''

''I wanted to see the world. All of it. Lord Hartford had the money to buy me the world if I wanted it. Justin was a working-class lord. I thought it would take him a lifetime to get out of debt.''

''It took him ten years. In a few more years, he'll be as solvent as any of the rest of us.''

''I didn't want to wait that long.''

''So you've said,'' Lady Sarah agreed.

''Well, then. Your scheme is set in motion, I assume,'' Amanda said.

Lady Sarah nodded. ''From what I can see, Valentine St. James is an empty-headed young girl. She easily fell into my trap before. She'll fall for this one, too. You'll get Justin back and I'll get even with that little brat for embarrassing me in front of my friends.''

Amanda cringed when she saw the maliciousness in Lady Sarah's eyes. If she weren't being blackmailed by Lady Sarah herself, she wouldn't think to take tea with the woman. As it was, Lady Sarah knew too much about her past. After spending the past seven years of her married life traveling around the world, Amanda was ready to settle down to the small-town life in London. She'd taken enough lovers in enough different countries to last a lifetime.

There was little excitement in life left for her. It would be a real coup for her to come back to London, marry Justin, the only man for whom she'd ever felt any emotion, and win these people back. To do all this, she needed Lady Sarah.

As long as Sarah kept her mouth shut, Amanda's position was secure. This time, Amanda was on equal footing with Lady Sarah. They needed each other.

Valentine's first social engagement once they returned to London from the country was a small dinner party at Lady Wilton's home on Park Lane. As they rode to the Grosvenor area, Justin explained to Valentine that Lady Wilton, now in her sixties, was the daughter of the fifteenth Earl of Pembroke and the sister of the sixth Marquess of Anglesey. She was a dear friend who had watched over him during his youth, and he'd always liked her a great deal.

The house was only ten years old and Justin had supplied many of the mirrors, chandeliers, sconces, crystal candelabras and glassware in the mansion. The Greek Revival exterior was in keeping with the trend of the times in London, but the interior was avant-garde even for lovers of Regency and Empire designs.

Justin explained that Lady Wilton had made numerous

trips to Egypt while her husband was alive and they'd purchased many artifacts during their stays in Cairo and Alexandria. The interior of the house was floored in sand-colored marble veined in black and gold. Matching marble pillars surrounded the circular two-story vestibule. The salon, dining room, library and conservatory were separated from the vestibule by sheer chiffon curtains rather than heavy doors.

The furniture was Egyptian in motif. There were long divans with circular pillows at each end. Low-slung, cross-legged benches were made of ebony-lacquered wood and leather seats. Stacks of enormous cushions surrounded low marble-topped tables where guests were expected to sit on the floor.

Smoking by both men and women was encouraged, and Lady Wilton kept humidors filled with Turkish tobacco, pipes, cigars, and thin rolled cigars for the women. Conversation at Lady Wilton's parties was always lively and controversial because she assembled her guests according to intelligence, wit and broad-minded thinking rather than social status or title.

Lady Wilton liked to think of herself as a woman of the world.

The butler was black and dressed in a blue and gold satin Moroccan costume. He wore a turban on his head and a fringed satin sash at his waist. He was a massively built man who efficiently took coats, hats and gloves and ushered the guests into the salon for a cup of Egyptian tea before dinner was served.

The salon was huge, nearly 40 feet long and 18 feet wide with windows and French doors overlooking elegant gardens with numerous fountains and pools. There were five or six groups of a half dozen or so people sitting on fat cushions on the floor and conversing.

The butler announced Lord Hawkeston and Miss St.

James in precise, studied English. Lady Wilton rose from the white silk divan she was sitting on and greeted them.

"I was so glad to receive the message that you were back in town, my boy." Lady Wilton kissed Justin's cheek.

"I wouldn't miss one of your dinners for the world," he said, noticing that her hand tremors had increased since the last time they'd met. Her head quivered and she seemed to have difficulty keeping it aloft on her shoulders. Justin sadly realized he wouldn't have many more years of Lady Wilton in his life.

"And this is your bride-to-be?" Lady Wilton's voice creaked with age and ill health.

"Yes. This is my Valentine."

"How do you do?" Valentine greeted her hostess.

Lady Wilton's colorless eyes smiled at Valentine. "Justin has been like a son to me, my dear. You must promise me that when I'm gone you will take very good care of him." Her hands shook as she held Valentine's hand.

"That is a promise I will gladly make," Valentine said with a sympathetic smile.

Justin put his arm around Lady Wilton's thin, stooped shoulders. "Don't talk like that. You're not going anywhere for a very long time."

Lady Wilton smiled at him. "You've been gone from town too long, Justin." She motioned with her head to the back of the room. She lifted her trembling hand and pointed to someone emerging from the shadows.

"What?" Justin's eyes flew open. "Oh, my God. It can't be!"

"But it is, my boy," Lady Wilton said.

Justin dropped his arm from Lady Wilton's shoulders. He felt as if he were in a trance.

333

Amanda stepped from the shadow and into the light. She glided across the marble floor toward him. She was a radiant vision and more beautiful than he remembered. The candlelight caught in her shimmering auburn curls. Her emerald eyes flashed at him and her smile nearly made his knees buckle. He whispered her name reverently, "Amanda."

Valentine's senses went on alert. She felt as if she'd slipped a million miles from Justin's world in a matter of seconds. He hadn't moved a step but he'd never been farther away from her. A hush fell over the room. Time stood still. Valentine's eyes followed Justin's as he watched the incredibly beautiful woman walk toward them.

Valentine realized that every person in the salon was watching Amanda. Valentine was watching Justin's reaction.

He was holding his breath. A smile curved his lips. There was longing in his eyes.

Valentine turned to Lady Wilton and whispered to her. "Who is she?"

"Lady Amanda Hartford."

Valentine felt as if she hadn't a single organ left inside her. Panic had rendered her a shell. She could hardly talk, but she had to know. "She and Justin . . . ?"

"Were only children when they were in love, my dear." Lady Wilton patted Valentine's hand. "It was a long time ago."

Valentine took one look at Justin's face and knew that for him it was no longer ago than this morning. He was back there in time with Amanda. Loving her. Being with her.

Amanda looked like a princess of fire and ice, spring and winter, glittering in front of Valentine in canary diamonds, emeralds and the most exquisite gown Valentine had ever seen.

Amanda was taller than Valentine by a half a foot at least. She was perfectly formed like one of the great masters' marble statues she'd seen in Rome, and her voice was sweet and melodious like spring water trickling down a smooth-stoned brook. She even smelled exotic, Valentine thought, as she detected the blend of Indian patchouli and jasmine. Valentine couldn't help but stare at her and wonder what it was like to have one's physicality formed by the gods.

Valentine's jealousy crept out of a heavily latched trunk in the deepest recesses of her mind. It spun through a narrow labyrinth in her brain, forcing itself to the surface. It curled itself in a coil in the corners of her eyes, ready to strike like a cobra if attacked.

"Amanda," Justin said her name as she reached out her hand to him.

"Justin. How very lovely to see you after all these years. Lady Wilton wasn't sure if you were going to be here. I'd heard you had trouble at your estate. Something about the cottagers?" Her voice lilted and purred as it left her lips.

Valentine wondered how these people knew so much about each other all the time. Their communication system had to be the most efficient on earth.

"Nothing I couldn't straighten out."

Because Valentine's attention was so focused on the auburn-haired goddess standing in front of her, she didn't realize that several others had come up to greet them as well.

"You look lovely tonight, Miss St. James," Henry St. Claire said.

It took Valentine's mind a moment to react to the compliment. "Why, thank you, Henry," she said.

"Do I understand that your presence is no longer required at your estate, Lord Hawkeston?" Henry asked.

"Not for the moment, Henry." Justin replied, but everyone could see he only had eyes for Amanda.

Valentine's jealousy struck. "Perhaps you would introduce me, Justin," Valentine had to remind him.

"Of course!" Justin recovered himself. "Lady Amanda Hartford please meet my fiancée, Miss Valentine St. James."

Amanda's smile was dazzling when she looked down at Valentine. "I've heard a great deal about you, Miss St. James," Amanda said. "A great deal." Her emerald eyes flashed.

Valentine sucked in her breath. She felt as if she were looking into the eyes of a devil. She felt a rush of chills careen down her spine. The hairs on the back of her head stood on end. She did not offer her hand to Amanda for fear she would be marred in some unmentionable way.

"Amanda has traveled all over the world, Valentine. She's been places the rest of us can only read about," Justin said.

Valentine hadn't taken her eyes off Amanda. "Really? Perhaps she'll tell us about her trips after we come back from our honeymoon, Justin." Valentine slipped her arm through Justin's left arm. "By the way, where are we going on our honeymoon?"

Justin looked at her. "I hadn't given it much thought."

Amanda didn't waste a second. "Well, in that case"—she blatantly took Justin's hand—"you'll be interested in the story I was just telling Lady Sarah about the Malabar Coast of India."

Amanda whisked a very willing Justin away to the far table where Lady Sarah was smiling at him.

Valentine knew that if she followed him she would look like like a child tagging along after him. She couldn't scream in anger. She couldn't cry. Everyone in the room was waiting for her reaction. She tried to smile, but her lips only trembled.

"Have you ever seen Lady Wilton's gardens, Valentine? They are quite something to behold," Henry St. Claire said as he came to her rescue.

"I don't believe I have, Henry," Valentine replied coolly and took the arm he offered her.

The guests seated on the floor looked at her as if they were disappointed. They shrugged their shoulders and went back to their conversations.

Henry walked Valentine out to the garden, where she sat on a stone bench next to six-foot-high stone urns filled with young Italian cypress trees and trailing ivy vines.

"Here." Henry handed her his handkerchief.

"I'm not crying."

"I know. Pretend it's Amanda's face. You can shred it to pieces with your fingernails." He laughed lightly, took out a cigar and lit it. He propped his booted foot against the edge of the stone bench.

"Am I that transparent?"

"You would have been in about ten seconds if I hadn't gotten you out of there."

"Thank you," she said and looked toward the windows near where she knew Justin was standing with Amanda. However, all the windows were draped with chiffon and she could only make out shadows as they moved back and forth.

"You don't know, do you?" Henry asked, blowing smoke upward toward the moon.

"About them? No." She fidgeted with the handkerchief. "But you do."

337

"Yes. Are you sure you want to know? Sometimes it's better to remain ignorant."

"I've never found that to be true," she said haughtily.

Henry grinned enigmatically. "That's because you are young. The young think knowledge is wisdom. It isn't. But"—he shrugged his shoulders—"who am I to keep it from you? He was in love with her. Incredibly in love with her. Who wouldn't be? Have you ever seen anyone more beautiful?"

"No," she gulped.

"I'm sorry, that wasn't well put. You are a beautiful woman, Valentine. That's not what I'm saying."

"But I'm not Amanda." She shook her head.

"He was only twenty. What would he know? She was sixteen. Younger than you. They couldn't keep their hands off each other. They lived underneath each other's skin. That's an old Russian proverb I heard once about lovers who are fated by destiny to be together lifetime after lifetime. Never mind, I'm trying to make this easier for you and I'm not. I suppose there is no way around it."

Henry sat on the stone bench next to Valentine. He could see teardrops glistening like morning dew on her eyelashes. He looked at the moon. "Amanda is spoiled. She wanted houses and carriages, gowns and jewels. Justin couldn't buy them for her. So she refused to marry him. She married Lord Hartford. I couldn't stand the man. There was gossip that he preferred young boys. But it was only a rumor," he said, waving his hand negatively in the air. "Lord Hartford bought her everything she wanted. He took her around the world three or four times. Now the old man has passed on and she's back here in London."

"And she wants Justin," Valentine said.

"You're wiser than I'd thought."

Valentine's tears streamed down her cheeks.

Henry tossed his cigar on the brick terrace and crushed it with his boot. He put his arms around Valentine and patted her back the way Aunt Cherise did when she was ill or feeling sad. He said silly, inane things that were meant to make one cheer up.

"There, there," Henry said. He started to move his hand down to the buttons on the back of her dress. Three would do the trick, he thought. Bare her breasts, draw attention to her, and her reputation would be ruined. As he'd said before, it was like taking candy from a baby.

"Valentine? Valentine!" Justin's voice slashed through the night air.

She felt Justin's hand clamp down on her shoulder. She nearly flew off the stone bench and in a flash she was standing next to Justin.

"Nice seeing you again, Henry." Justin grabbed Valentine's arm and quickly escorted her into the house.

The guests had all gone into dinner. Justin took Valentine to the vestibule where the butler was waiting with their cloaks and gloves.

"We're leaving? We just got here," Valentine said.

"I've already thanked Lady Wilton for the evening," Justin said gruffly as he let the butler help him with his cape.

Valentine's jealousy and anger collided. She untied her cloak and let it fall on the floor. "Well, I haven't had my supper, Lord Hawkeston!" She went stomping off toward the dining room, where the guests were being served the first course.

"Valentine, don't try my patience!" He went after her.

She spun around to face him. "What about *my* patience, Lord Hawkeston?"

Neither of them noticed, but the delicate clink of silverware against fine china ceased as the guests strained to hear the argument between Lord Hawkeston and Miss St. James in the vestibule.

"I think it's time I took you home before you go traipsing off to the gardens with all of Lady Wilton's male guests."

"Me? And just when were you going to stop drooling over Lady Hartford?"

"I was doing nothing of the sort."

"How long before you told me about her, Justin? Before the wedding or after?"

Valentine was so furious she couldn't eat anything if she tried.

The butler had just retrieved her cloak from the marble floor when Valentine snatched it out of his hand. She marched angrily toward the front door. The butler was one step ahead of her and opened it for her.

Their carriage was waiting outside the house.

Valentine climbed into the coach and slammed the door. Justin opened the door.

Valentine yanked it shut again. "You're not riding with me. Go back to your . . . *lover!*" she screamed at him and hid her face in her hands. She knew that if she looked at him she'd want to kill him.

"Fine!" he yelled back at her.

When Valentine dropped her hands from her face, Justin was gone. She leaned back on the velvet-upholstered seat and slammed her fist into the cushion. How stupid could she be? She had just given him carte blanche to indulge himself with Amanda. Her greatest fear was that Justin was only marrying her because of his promise. Now those fears had been substantiated.

Justin was in love with Amanda, and Valentine realized that she was deeply, deeply in love with Justin.

Chapter Twenty-five

Justin rode home seated next to his driver Mr. Weems. Justin knew that Valentine had no idea he was sitting in the driver's perch. While Valentine cried inside the carriage, Justin used the time to consider his next move with his fiancée. One thing he knew was that when Valentine was angry, she was impossible to deal with. He and Valentine had already given the gossips enough fodder for the year. The story of their argument would no doubt be all over town by morning.

The odd thing was that he really didn't give a damn about the gossips anymore. What he cared about was the fact that Valentine thought he was interested in resuming his affair with Amanda and that Valentine had turned to Henry St. Claire for consolation.

Stunned as Justin had been by Amanda's presence, it hadn't taken five minutes for him to realize what her game was. Amanda wanted him.

Justin had taken one look into her emerald eyes and realized they were harder than the expensive stones she wore around her neck. Nothing about Amanda had changed in ten years.

Amanda had been fortune hunting from the first day he'd met her. God, he'd been young and stupid then. He remembered riding in her father's carriage and stealing kisses from her in broad daylight. She'd let him kiss her, too, and a whole lot more. Amanda had wanted to explore the world of sex just as eagerly as she'd wanted to travel the globe. She'd made every advance on Justin, and he'd quickly learned to let her do the tutoring. She'd told him she had watched her father with his mistress one night at their country estate. With her mother sleeping in the opposite wing of the house, she'd watched her father perform all sorts of acts with his mistress. She told Justin she knew that a man and woman could have sex for hours and never stop.

Justin had thought she was kidding. Then she proved she was right.

For months Amanda met Justin every chance she could find. They went for horseback rides through the parks and stole kisses under bridges, behind trees and in the gardens of Justin's house. She showed him how to make love to her with his fingers, lips and tongue. She built him to a fever pitch so that when they finally planned to actually have sex, Justin was so excited he could barely think. Amanda made all the arrangements. It was in a cottager's house on her father's estate. Justin had been hard for days just thinking about seeing Amanda totally naked, not to mention committing the act with her.

Amanda nude was a breathtaking experience. Unfortunately, that was about all he could say for the rest of it. Justin had never been so let down in his life as he was after they'd made love.

Somehow, Justin had believed that the union between a man and a woman should be an almost mystical experience, like going to heaven. With Amanda, the anticipation, the months of building up his expectations, had been all there was to their relationship.

Not once in all their times together had Amanda ever told him she loved him. He told her that he loved her all the time. He bought her flowers. He sent her poems he copied out of books. He had been certain that when he finally made love to her she would tell him he was wonderful, that he'd made her feel nearly divine. And he knew she would say she loved him.

But she didn't.

Amanda had shoved him off her after he climaxed. He was breathing so heavily he hyperventilated. "Get off me, Justin, you're heavy."

"Did I hurt you?" He remembered that she'd cried out.

"Yes, you hurt me." She struggled to get up. Angrily she grabbed her clothes. She stumbled to the rickety table. She looked around. "God, can you believe people actually live like this?"

"What?" Justin couldn't believe his ears. Where were the loving words he was supposed to be hearing?

She rifled through the cupboard drawers. "Would you look at these linens? There's not one of them that isn't moth-eaten. God! I hate this." She dipped a cloth into the washbasin and began cleaning herself.

Justin watched as she wiped away all evidence of their lovemaking. She acted as if nothing had happened. She'd just lost her virginity and it was nothing to her.

Then he realized that he'd lost his virginity . . . in more ways than one.

Catherine Lanigan

"I'm never going to live like these people do, Justin. Never. I'm going to have so much money someday that I can go anywhere I want and have anything I want."

"You . . . are?" He wondered where he fit into her dreams.

"That's right," she said as she shoved her arms into her dress. "I'm not going to wait around for my inheritance like some of my friends. You wouldn't believe it, Justin, but some of my friends actually believe that romantic nonsense they read by some of those new poets. They think they're going to fall in love with some Prince Charming and he's going to have lots of money and their lives will be perfect."

She pulled her stockings up to her thighs and secured them with lace garters. "I'm a realist, Justin. I know it's going to take a lot of money to make me happy."

That was it! he thought. She was only worried about the money. He scrambled over to her and knelt at her feet. "I'm going to be very rich someday, Amanda. Very rich. And very powerful."

She touched his cheek. "And just how are you going to do that, pray tell, when all of London knows your father squanders every shilling your family has ever owned? Justin, by your maturation next year there won't be anything left. My father says your father nearly lost the manor house in the Cotswolds last week."

"That's not true!" Justin lied.

"There's no way you can stop him, Justin."

"Oh, yes, there is!" Justin said defensively.

"Prove it to me," she challenged.

And Justin had done just that. He'd gone to the family solicitor, and since Justin was about to reach his maturation, the attorney took it upon himself to help him. By the time Justin had taken over the management of the country estate and the glassworks factory, Lord James Hawkeston fell from his horse and died instantly of a broken neck.

Justin and Amanda made love another half dozen times, but each time she became more detached from him. She began to attend more balls, dinners and parties. She declined his invitations. Then her forthcoming marriage to Lord Hartford was announced, and before he'd had a chance to see her again, she vanished from town.

He heard she wanted a sumptuous wedding on the Continent with dignitaries and royalty in attendance. Lord Hartford gave her the wedding she wanted. Over the years Justin heard stories about her travels from clients or friends. But she never wrote. She never looked back.

There were many in the ton who accused Justin of building his fortunes because he'd lost Amanda to a man with more money. He always denied such allegations.

It wasn't until that very night, seeing Amanda again, that he realized he'd done exactly as he'd been accused. He'd worked himself day and night, building his estate, amassing money so that one day if she ever came back he would be ready to face her.

Tonight she had appeared like magic.

But everything was different now. He was promised to Valentine.

Justin knew he wouldn't trade one second in Valentine's loving arms for a hundred lifetimes with Amanda. His only problem was convincing Valentine of that.

When the carriage stopped at his house, Justin instructed Mr. Weems not to let Valentine know that he'd hitched a ride on his very own coach.

Because it was late and the butler was in bed, Mr. Weems got down from his perch and opened the carriage door for Valentine. He walked her to the house and made certain that she was safe inside.

Justin climbed down from the perch and bid Mr. Weems good night. Once he saw the lamp in Valentine's room being lit, he let himself into the house.

Valentine was so exhausted from her emotional trials that evening she nearly fell asleep while undressing. She could barely see, her eyes were so swollen from crying.

She slipped a cotton nightgown over her head and lifted the comforter. She loved the smell of her rose-scented sheets. She was glad the housekeeper had remembered to launder them the way she and Victoria had shown her.

She turned her head into the down pillow and felt a new rush of tears. She pulled her knees to her chest and hugged them.

A vision of Justin lying with the beautiful Amanda on sheets as fine as these filled her mind's eye. "Except her sheets are probably scented with patchouli and jasmine," she sobbed.

Valentine willed the vision away, but it persisted. She remembered the way Justin had touched her and how she had responded with so little inhibition . . . so little pride. She'd abandoned herself to him, and now he was sleeping with Amanda.

Valentine slid her diary out from under the feather bed. She opened the drawer in the table next to her bed and found her quill pen and ink. She discovered that there was no room in her old diary. She slid the diary back to its hiding place under the bed and put the ink and pen away.

It was just as well she didn't commit her dire thoughts

to paper. Valentine could think of no greater fool on earth than herself. It was one thing to know that one's fiancé was with another woman. It was quite another to be desperately in love with that man.

This time, Valentine knew she was doomed.

Chapter Twenty-six

Justin sat at his walnut desk in his office trying to concentrate on the order he'd received that morning from Lord and Lady Purdey for a half dozen crystal chandeliers. Lord Purdey had designed a new wing of bedrooms to be added to their London house. Justin knew he would have to travel to Venice himself to see to their manufacture and shipment.

Business had been more than good since his return. Orders were pouring in. If this kept up he would have to buy another ship.

He should have been joyful; instead, he'd never been quite so depressed. He rose and went to the window. The problem was Valentine.

He'd knocked on her door last night, but she never answered. He assumed she was sleeping. Even though he'd taken an early breakfast that morning, she didn't join him. When they'd been in the country, she had come downstairs in her dressing gown and joined him at least for tea or coffee. This morning he hadn't heard the first sound from her room.

She was avoiding him. He could feel it.

He looked back to his desk. He wasn't doing any good here. Maybe he should just go home and . . .

Just then the door to his office opened. He smelled her before she entered the room. The exotic scent of jasmine and patchouli announced Amanda's presence.

She practically flew into his arms.

"Justin, dear, whatever happened to you last night? One minute you were by my side and the next I heard you arguing with Clementine—"

"Valentine," he corrected her.

"Yes, well, and then you both were gone." She sidled up to him, put her arms around his neck, and nuzzled his throat. "God, you feel so good, Justin." She kissed his neck.

There was a rap on the door and Andrew walked in. He was holding a sheaf of papers and looking at them and not at Justin as he entered the room. "I wondered if you'd seen these . . ." Andrew looked up and found the most beautiful woman he'd ever seen kissing his future brother-in-law.

Justin's eyes flew open. With both hands he literally pried Amanda off of him and turned her toward Andrew. "Amanda, I would like you to meet my future brother-in-law, Andrew Brittmore. Andrew, this is Lady Amanda Hartford."

"How do you do, Lady Hartford."

"Very well, thank you."

Andrew looked at Justin. "I'll come back later," he said, embarrassed at finding Justin and Amanda together.

"No, Andrew. I'd like you to stay."

Amanda was incensed. "Justin, I specifically came here to talk to you."

"No, you didn't, Amanda," he replied. "You came here to seduce me."

Andrew sucked in his breath, but he remained silent.

"Damn you, Justin! You are about the most infuriating man I've ever met!" She looked over at Andrew to see if she'd put enough indignation in her tone of speech and was satisfied that she had. Justin, on the other hand, was another matter.

"Anything you have to say to me can be said in front of Andrew. I trust him implicitly with all my business."

Amanda flung her burgundy velvet and gold-fringed reticule on Justin's desk and then crossed her arms over her chest. "Do you men always stick together like this?"

"When it's necessary," Justin replied flatly.

"Well, I must have more power over you than I thought if you feel you need a witness."

Justin leaned over and picked up Amanda's purse and handed it to her. He started pushing her gently toward the door. "Where you are concerned, Amanda, no man is safe. I wanted Andrew to see just how you operate, so that he doesn't get taken in by your wiles." He looked at Andrew. "I was not so fortunate as you, Andrew. I didn't have anyone around when I was young to tell me about women like Amanda."

Justin had nearly gotten her to the door.

"No?" Andrew replied, not knowing what to make of the scene he was watching.

"No. I would be a much wiser man today if I'd known about . . ." Justin opened the door very wide to aid Amanda in her departure.

"About what?" Andrew asked.

"Trollops."

350

"Justin Hawkeston, you vile creature! I can't believe you could say such a cruel thing about me!"

His blue eyes twinkled as he looked at her. He put his hand on the door latch. "You have me all wrong, Amanda, I wasn't being cruel in the least. Considering what I know about you, I was being kind."

"Justin—" she sputtered.

"This is fair warning, Amanda. Do not come back to this office, do not go to my home. I can't stop you from frequenting the same public places where I will be, but do not ever think in any way that you are welcome in my arms. Because you are not." He closed the door in her face.

Andrew's jaw dropped as his eyes moved from the closed door to Justin's face.

Justin pointed toward the door. "That was a close call. Thank you for saving me."

"I didn't know women were made that beautiful," Andrew said, still amazed that Justin had thrown the woman out.

"They're not. It's a trick. You should see what she looks like on the inside."

Andrew scratched his head. "Does she have anything to do with what Victoria and Valentine were talking about this morning?"

Justin folded into his chair. "Probably." He wiped his hand over his face. God, he felt weary. Then it hit him. "What exactly were they talking about?"

"Valentine said you created a scene at Lady Wilton's last night."

"I created? I did? Oh! I suppose she didn't tell you I found her in the garden in the arms of another man!"

"Good Lord! You didn't!"

"I most certainly did. Henry St. Claire. What a slimy one that man is. He makes my skin crawl."

351

"Valentine seems to think him rather . . . comforting."

"Is that what she told you?"

"Told her sister, actually. I couldn't make any sense of it at all. All that going on about you leaving with this magnificent creature. Of course, now I realize Valentine was telling the truth." Andrew looked back at the closed door.

"Valentine wouldn't know the truth if it bit her in the leg."

"Justin, how do you know this Amanda? Is it as Valentine said? Is she your mistress?"

Justin threw up his arms. "No! She will never be my mistress. When I was young, very young and too stupid to know better, I was infatuated with Amanda. I suppose I wore some ogling expression all the time, much like you are right now, Andrew."

Andrew righted himself and squared his shoulders. "This isn't any of my business, Justin, but I think you have a real problem with Valentine. She is convinced you are about to take up with Amanda again . . . even before the wedding."

"Well, she'll realize in time that nothing of the sort is happening at all."

"I hope she waits that long," Andrew said.

"What are you talking about?"

"You know Valentine. I can never believe half of what she says. She's always so overly dramatic. But this morning when I could see she'd been crying all night, I realized she's really in love with you, Justin. I thought this woman was a figment of her imagination. Now I see that Amanda is very much a real person. Maybe Valentine wasn't being overly dramatic at all when she said she was going to run away."

Justin was on his feet in an instant. "Run away?"

352

Andrew nodded. "Yes. She said Henry was going to help her."

"Hell's fire and damnation!" Justin grabbed his coat and rammed his fists into the sleeves. "Come on, Andrew! I want a witness." Justin pulled Andrew's sleeve.

"What for?"

"I want to make sure that when I wring Valentine's neck, it stays wrung!"

Valentine peered at her swollen face in the gilt-framed mirror in the foyer. "Oh, Henry, I'm such a mess. You don't want to come calling on me today."

"Hush now, sweets. Let's go into the salon and talk about this." He put his hand on her shoulder as she led the way into the salon.

"You're such a good friend, Henry."

Henry looked back over his shoulder. There was no one in the foyer. The butler must have gone off to attend to his other duties, Henry thought. Henry closed the doors behind him. "By the way, where is your sister and your dear, lovely aunt?"

"Victoria had another fitting for her wedding gown today. My appointment is tomorrow. Sabrina Grenville said she couldn't take us both today. Aunt Cherise is meeting Bartholomew . . . Oh, you don't know about that. Maybe I shouldn't tell you until Aunt Cherise gives her permission."

"You can trust me. I won't tell a soul."

Valentine shook her head. "It's not important."

"Never mind, then. I don't want anything to upset you any further today."

"It's so funny that you're here," Valentine said, still fighting waves of sobs. Justin had not come home last night, she knew. She didn't remember falling asleep at all. She'd waited to hear a carriage pull up, but no hired cabs had come to their house all night. She had to admit that somewhere during the night she had fallen asleep, because Victoria had come in to wake her for breakfast before Andrew had left for the office that morning. To her knowledge, there had been no sign of Justin. If the servants knew anything they weren't talking. At least not to her.

"Funny?" he asked.

"I was a little upset at breakfast this morning. I told my sister I was going to run away."

"After what happened to you last night, I can understand that. Unfortunately, Lady Sarah has already told just about everyone in town. I asked her this morning before I came here why she just didn't print it in *The Tattler*.

"Oh, Henry!" Valentine bawled, and new tears sprang into her eyes.

"I was only joking!"

"I've never been so miserable in my life."

He put his arms around her. He scooted closer to her on the settee.

Valentine couldn't see, hear or feel anything but the vision of Justin making love to Amanda.

Henry deftly moved his hand down her back and one by one he unbuttoned the buttons of her dress. "There, there now," he said.

Just the thought of raping her made him hard. Henry hadn't had a woman in several years. He wondered if he'd like it. Henry wasn't particularly interested in women as a gender, but there was the added incentive that he would be raping a virgin. That made the challenge sweeter. And then, too, there was all that money. That thought made him even harder.

* * *

Justin and Andrew arrived at the house to find Henry St. Claire's coach waiting in the street.

"That bastard has a lot of nerve," Justin mumbled to himself as he got out of his carriage.

"Good Lord! She's really going to run away," Andrew exclaimed.

"Oh, no, she's not!" Justin stormed up the walk. He took the granite steps two at a time.

He opened the door before the butler entered the foyer.

"Where's Valentine?" he asked the butler.

"In the salon with Mr. St. Claire," the butler replied.

Valentine's eyes were closed and her head was face down on Henry's shoulder as she thought about Justin and how he'd deceived her. Why hadn't he told her about Amanda before? He couldn't have simply forgotten someone that beautiful and commanding. He had been hiding the truth from Valentine because he didn't want her to know what he was planning to do with Amanda. Yes, that was what he must have been planning, she told herself.

Valentine felt a new wave of sobs coming on. She sucked in her breath to quash the cries. She choked.

Then she realized she couldn't breathe. Her eyes flew open.

Henry's hand was around her throat choking her. He was ripping her gown off.

She heard the tear of silk as he exposed her breasts.

God! What was happening?

Henry's eyes had turned to beads of glittering red stone. His face was dark and angry, but she didn't know why.

She tried to scream, but no sounds came out of her

mouth. Her eyes were filled with terror. She could feel him lifting up her skirts.

She beat on his chest with her fists, but he grabbed both her hands and yanked them over her head.

"Bitch! Don't fight me!"

She tried to yell out his name, but her voice was only a croak. While he held her hands, she kicked at him with her legs. She got in a good whack with her left foot.

"Owwww! Damn you!"

Valentine sucked in a lungful of air and began shouting, squirming, kicking and biting at his arms.

Henry cursed her again and again, but he couldn't get as good a hold on her as he'd had.

She broke one arm free and socked him on the side of his face.

"Damn you, bitch!" Henry yelled and pulled back his hand to hit her.

"Ju-u-stin!" She screamed when she heard the doors bang open.

Justin was on Henry in two strides. He grabbed Valentine's assailant by his upraised hand and yanked him off his fiancée. He balled his fist and delivered a strong left cross to Henry's jaw. Henry went reeling backwards.

Valentine scrambled off the settee and pulled her bodice up to cover herself. Andrew quickly took off his coat and put it around Valentine's shoulders. Andrew pulled her away from potential danger as Henry went running headlong into Justin's midsection.

Justin doubled over. He ducked quickly and just missed Henry's right hook punch. Justin rammed his fist into Henry's stomach and landed another punch to Henry's jaw. This time Henry stayed down.

Justin was out of breath when he went toward Valentine. She opened her arms and walked toward him. He gathered her into his arms. "He—"

"No, Justin," she said. "You were in time."

Henry rose to his feet. He spit a mouthful of blood onto the Persian rug. "You bloody coward! All you filthy Hawkestons are nothing but a bunch of cowards!"

"You bastard! You think I will allow you to rape my fiancée?"

"Pistols at dawn tomorrow. At the base of Vauxhall Bridge next to the Thames." Henry didn't wait for an answer as he spun on his heel and was out of the house in seconds.

Valentine was aghast. "Justin, you can't do this! Promise me you won't fight him. Please, promise me!" Valentine was hysterical. She grabbed Justin's lapels and clung to him. She put her face on his chest and sobbed.

"Andrew, ask the cook for a sedative for Valentine."

"Maybe I should send for the doctor."

"Yes, that would be wise."

As Andrew left, Justin lifted Valentine into his arms and carried her upstairs to her bedroom. She was still crying as he laid her on the bed.

"Justin, what is happening to us?"

"Valentine, I don't know what Henry was doing. You're certain he didn't . . . touch you?"

"Of course he touched me, Justin! He was trying to hurt me! But he didn't molest me. I didn't let him get that far."

"I'm proud of the way you fought him. You were very brave."

"I didn't have a choice," she said firmly.

Justin thought for a moment as he rubbed her forearm. "I have to ask you, Valentine. Did you send for him?"

"No! He said he was concerned about me because of my argument with you last night. And so he stopped by. Besides, why would I send for him?" She was still shaking and could barely get her breath between the damnable sobs that persisted in creeping up her throat.

"Andrew told me you were planning to run away with Henry."

Valentine winced when she thought of her conversation that morning with Andrew and Victoria at breakfast. She'd said a lot of things in anger. A lot of stupid things. She vowed right then to curb her tongue. She realized that other people would suffer from her imaginings than just herself. "I didn't mean it. I was thinking thousands of awful thoughts ever since last night when you didn't come home."

"Didn't come . . ." He lifted her chin with his forefinger. "Valentine, I was here all night. I slept in the library."

"But how could you have? I listened for a carriage all night," she sniffed.

He sat on the bed next to her and folded her into his arms. "I rode with Mr. Weems, the driver. You can ask him."

"You were here all night?"

He wiped her tears with his fingers. He could see that her eyes were bloodshot and swollen from crying. "You've been crying for a long time, Valentine."

"I thought you were with her . . ." Suddenly she sniffed his lapel and then his neck. There was no mistaking the patchouli and jasmine. "You were with her! I can smell her perfume on you now!" She tried to beat at him with her fists, but she was too exhausted. All she could do was cry. She pulled away from him and buried her face in a pillow.

Justin leaned over and stroked her arm. "Amanda came to my office today, Valentine. She was up to her old tricks again. You were right to worry about her. She was after me, all right. I kept Andrew in the office as a witness the entire time."

He slipped his hand into her tear-dampened silver curls. "I don't want Amanda in any fashion. I don't want to have a conversation with her, or share a meal with her, and I certainly don't want to make love to her."

"You don't?"

"No, Valentine. I want you. I want to talk with you and work alongside you. I want to share my life with you. I love you, Valentine."

Valentine had cried so much her ears had nearly stopped up. She knew he couldn't have really said what she thought he said.

She rolled over and faced him. "What did you say?"

He was smiling at her. He touched her cheek. "I said I love you, Valentine. I don't know when I realized it, but I fell in love with you on Mardi Gras night in Venice. And I fell in love with you the night of the storm. And the morning after that when I saw that you had mended my wounds. I loved you for taking care of my crew and me so unselfishly. You never asked for anything for yourself, except the right to choose the designer for your wedding gown. I found that amazing, Valentine. And then when you turned my country estate into a real home, I knew I'd found paradise. All I could think of every night was you lying in the next room and how much I wanted to go to you and make love to you.

"I wanted to show you all the pleasures of love that I could, because you'd given me so much. You never asked me for jewels or paintings or expensive gowns. You never asked me for anything. But you gave me everything.

"That night before we left for the country when I showed you a glimpse of what lovemaking was about . . . you gave me your heart that night, didn't you, Valentine?"

359

"Yes," she answered meekly, awestruck at his revelation to her. He loved her. She hoped she wasn't exaggerating this time.

Valentine started crying all over again. Her eyes were so swollen she could barely see Justin. Her nose was running, her ears were filled with fluid, she was a wreck, and she'd never been happier in her life.

"Oh, Justin, I love you, too."

Chapter Twenty-seven

Victoria and Aunt Cherise came home late that afternoon from shopping and visiting friends to find the Hawkeston household in an uproar after the assault on Valentine.

Justin had ordered the butler not to let anyone in the house who wasn't family. All doors and windows were to be bolted and locked. He ordered the cook to prepare dinner early, canceled all his meetings, and told Andrew that if anything important happened at the office, Andrew was to come back to the house straightaway and Justin would deal with matters from home.

Justin sent for the doctor, who examined Valentine and found her to be in shock, but otherwise she was not physically hurt other than bruises around her wrists and one at the base of her throat. The doctor gave Valentine a sedative and suggested she soak in a hot bath.

Justin immediately ordered the bath, which sent the

upstairs maids scurrying up the stairs with kettles of steaming hot water.

When Andrew explained to Victoria and Aunt Cherise that Henry St. Claire had nearly raped Valentine and then had the audacity to challenge Justin to a duel, Victoria went racing up the stairs to see Valentine, while Aunt Cherise shrieked and nearly fainted in Andrew's arms.

"Valentine?" Victoria tapped lightly on the partially opened door.

The room was a beehive of activity. The downstairs maid had just delivered fresh towels and a clean bathing robe. The two upstairs maids were in the bathing chamber filling the copper tub with hot water. Justin was sitting on the bed holding Valentine's hand.

Victoria went to the bed, took one look at Valentine's nearly swollen eyes and the bruise on her neck, and screamed, "My God! What kind of monster is that man? Did he hit you in the eyes?"

Valentine laughed and began crying all over again. "No, he only choked me."

Justin put his arm around Valentine and folded her to his chest again. "Your sister has been crying since last night, it seems."

Victoria scowled at Justin. "No thanks to you." Victoria went to the other side of the bed and knelt down. She stroked Valentine's back while continuing to glare at Justin. "Is there anything I can do?"

Justin sighed heavily. "You can quit looking at me as if I were the one who accosted your sister. And for your information, I did not sleep with Amanda last night."

Victoria's mouth dropped open. She quickly snapped it shut. "Oh."

Valentine turned to look at Victoria. "He rode home

on the top of the coach with Mr. Weems. He slept in the library. That's why the staff didn't say anything about his bed being slept in. They probably thought he was out all night, too.''

"Good Lord! My staff thinks this, too?'' Justin rolled his eyes.

"I'm afraid so.'' Victoria shrugged her shoulders.

"I'm glad you're here, Victoria. You can help Valentine take a bath. The doctor gave her a sedative and said that a warm bath would help ease the shock.'' Justin kissed Valentine's forehead. "I'll come back later.''

Justin left the room.

Victoria helped Valentine out of bed and into the bathing chamber. Valentine was still holding her ripped gown to her breasts. Her hand hadn't moved since the brutal attack and now she felt as if her arm would have to be pried away from her breasts.

Valentine felt stiff and aching in every joint in her body.

Victoria poured a good measure of rose-scented oil into the bathwater while Valentine stepped out of her dress and into the water.

Victoria took a big sponge and dipped it into the water. "This bruise on your neck is going to be rather large, Val,'' she said as tears sprang to her eyes. "My God, it must have been horrible for you.''

"It's as if it happened to somebody else, Vicki. His face turned dark and I remember his eyes looking red. It was awful. But the truly terrible part is that Justin plans to go ahead with the duel in the morning. There's just got to be a way to stop him.''

"How?''

"Maybe Andrew could talk to him.''

"That's a good idea, Val. I'll speak with Andrew. Maybe if Aunt Cherise and I talk to Justin . . .''

"Would you?" Valentine looked at Victoria, who was nodding her head. "Yes, if everyone told Justin how archaic the whole idea of dueling is . . ." Suddenly Valentine stopped.

"What's the matter?"

Valentine's eyes narrowed and suspicion arched her brow. "Something is very strange about all this. I know that Henry seemed attracted to me that first time I met him at Lord and Lady Purdeys', but after that he was completely different. He just doesn't impress me as the kind of man who would resort to rape."

"Really? How many rapists have you associated with over the years, Val?"

Valentine clucked her tongue. "He doesn't impress me as being that angry or desperate. He's a funny duck, I'll grant you that, but something doesn't fit."

"Like what?"

"I don't know. That's what doesn't fit."

"I think you're exaggerating again."

"I am not!" Valentine slapped the water in frustration and succeeded in splashing her sister's face. "Sorry."

Victoria dried her face on a towel. It had been rinsed in jasmine-scented water. The scent reminded her of Amanda. Victoria couldn't believe all that Valentine had been through in the past few days. It didn't seem fair that Valentine, the one who was always giving, forever managed to get hurt in the process.

Valentine yawned.

Victoria reached for a large towel and put it over Valentine's shoulders. "Time to get you to bed. That sedative seems to be taking effect."

"I know. And I wanted to join everyone for dinner tonight, too. Justin told me he'd ordered the cook to make roast goose."

"Your favorite." Victoria helped Valentine into a

fresh nightgown. She tied the wrist ribbons, trying not to wince when she saw the bruises. She walked with Valentine to the bed. "I'll tell you what. I'll go downstairs right now and have the cook prepare a tray for you."

"That would be lovely. And some hot tea, too," Valentine said, starting to close her eyes.

Victoria kissed Valentine on the cheek and left the room.

Valentine was asleep before Victoria hit the bottom stair.

Justin met Victoria on his way up the stairs. "How is she?"

"Hungry. I was just getting her a tray."

"That's a good sign. I'll watch her till you return."

Justin crept into the room and found Valentine sound asleep. He sat on the bed next to her and propped his back against the mahogany headboard. He stroked her shoulder tenderly as she slept. He tried to get comfortable, but something was poking him in the hip.

He got off the bed and checked the feather bed. He found a book slid between the feather bed and the mattress. "How odd."

He opened the book to see what Valentine had been reading and discovered it was a journal of some sort. Then he saw his name.

He turned toward the lamplight. The repulsive adjectives preceding his name caused him to slam the book shut.

He didn't want to read anymore. He slid the book back under the feather bed. He looked down at the woman he loved. The woman he was going to marry, if he lived that long.

Tomorrow morning he was going to fire a pistol at a man who had tried to rape Valentine. And that man was going to fire a pistol at him. Someone was going to die tomorrow.

Justin slipped his hand under the feather bed and pulled out the diary again. He had just started out of the room when Victoria walked in with a dinner tray.

Justin hid the diary behind his back. "Shhhh!" he said with his finger to his lips. "She won't be needing that dinner after all."

Victoria nodded, turned and tiptoed out of the room and returned the tray to the kitchen.

Justin went downstairs to his library, poured himself a deep brandy, and began reading Valentine's innermost thoughts about him.

An hour later when the butler announced dinner, Justin had just finished the diary. He downed his brandy and poured a second drink.

How could he have misread Valentine so much? She had told him that she loved him that day under the apple trees. She had told him today she loved him. And yet, all these things she'd written about him made him out to be no better than the son of Satan.

It was occasions like this that caused people to warn against reading another person's diary. He guessed he'd invoked his own demons with this one.

He would have been better off not knowing. But now he did.

He wondered how she could act so sweetly toward him and sound so sincere about her feelings for him, when she really wanted him to disappear off the face of the earth.

Justin thought he would never understand women. They were consummate actresses, every one. He would never be able to tell a woman he loved her and all the while be cursing her name.

Ordinarily, a situation like this with Valentine would

have infuriated him. It was odd that this time he wasn't angry. He was hurt.

He was guilty of all the things she accused him of. He *had* been insensitive. He had treated her like chattel when he'd first encountered her. He *had* thought she was a harlot. In his mind he'd accused her of every depravity he knew. He'd been so insensitive that he'd not believed her until he discovered for himself that she was a virgin.

He leaned his elbows on his knees and put his face in his hands. "No wonder she hates me," he said to himself.

Just then the butler knocked on the door to the library.

"Come," Justin replied listlessly.

Arnold burst into the room. "Tell me it isn't true!"

Justin took one look at his brother's apprehensive face and knew what he was referring to. "It's true."

"Are you out of your mind? Henry St. Claire is one of the best shots in London! I've heard he can hit the right eye of a running turkey hen at fifty paces. He's won the Kent Court shooting competition two years in a row! Blast and be damned, Justin!"

"Well, what the hell was I supposed to do? Let him get away with raping my bride-to-be?"

Arnold stopped suddenly. "Is that what happened?"

"Yes." Justin looked at him. "You look surprised. What did you hear about it?"

"Hell! It's all over town that you called Henry out because of last night at Lady Wilton's party. Everyone in town heard you arguing with Valentine. They're saying you'll kill her next."

"Are they now?" Justin asked pensively.

"Justin, what the blazes is going on?" Arnold demanded.

"I'm not really sure," he replied, thinking that something was amiss in this whole thing but he was damned if he knew what it was. Leave it to the ton to get the truth mixed up with lies every time. "Henry called me out. Not that I wouldn't have done it, mind you. Andrew and I came bursting into the salon to find Henry on top of Valentine, her dress torn to shreds. She's got bruises. He tried to choke her. If we'd have been another minute, he might have succeeded in killing her."

"My God . . ." Arnold dropped into a chair.

"So when Henry called me out, I didn't refuse it."

"But he's a crackerjack shot, Justin!"

Justin rose, poured himself another brandy and one for his brother. He handed Arnold the drink. "I like to think I'm pretty good myself."

"I'll be your second, Justin."

Justin shook his head. "You don't have to do that."

"I want to. I'll be there with you every step of the way. That bastard isn't going to get away with molesting my future sister-in-law." Arnold took a big gulp of the brandy. He was dying to ask the one question he knew he shouldn't, but damn it, he *had* to know. "Did . . . did Henry . . . hurt her?"

"No, thank God. I got here in time."

"Thank heavens for you," Arnold replied. He would throttle Henry himself if Henry even thought about sticking himself in a woman. Any woman. God, the thought was revolting.

"You're going to use Father's pistols, aren't you?" Arnold changed the subject.

"I suppose so."

Arnold rose and went to the false bookcase and pressed the spring lever.

"What are you doing?" Justin asked. "I don't want to see those things now. Tomorrow morning will be soon enough."

"I'm just checking them." Arnold waved away his brother's objections.

Arnold opened the trap door in the wall and pulled out the carved oak case that held their father's dueling pistols. The guns hadn't been fired in years, Arnold knew, since Justin never particularly cared for guns. Arnold remembered playing with the pistols when he was a young boy. He prided himself on being able to completely take every piece of the gun apart and reassemble it in less than two minutes.

The barrels were made of high-quality nickel. The grips were made of polished burled walnut. Each man would only have one shot. Arnold had to make certain that the single shot counted. Otherwise his well-devised plan would fail. Arnold did not intend to fail.

He took the box and put it on Justin's desk. He closed the trap door and then slid the bookcase back into position.

"I'll clean them for you," Arnold offered.

Justin shook his head as he finished the brandy. "I'll do it myself."

"But, Justin. I know these pistols backwards and forwards. I've cleaned them a thousand times over the years."

"Really? So have I."

Arnold felt his hands turn clammy. "You hate guns. When did you ever take a gun apart?" He forced a laugh. He wondered if Justin noticed that his voice cracked and the timbre of his laugh was an octave too high.

"You forget that I've been sailing the high seas for over five years now, little brother. We've been at war, which has caused shipping and sailing to be quite unsafe. Don't you remember I told you I had to protect my shipments?"

"I thought you were talking about insurance."

Justin picked up one of the magnificently made expensive pistols. "Guns are insurance."

Arnold shoved his trembling hands into his pockets. "That's good you know so much about guns, Justin."

Justin put the gun back in the velvet-lined box. "I hope it's enough."

"So do I, Justin."

Justin stuck out his hand. "Thanks for offering to be my second."

Arnold shook his hand. "What did you expect? I'm your brother."

"Yes. That you are," Justin replied as he slapped his other hand on Arnold's shoulder. "I can expect you in the morning?"

"I'll be here before five."

"Good, then we can ride together in my carriage."

Justin walked his brother to the library door and summoned the butler. "Mr. Hawkeston is leaving," Justin said.

After Arnold left the house, Justin instructed the butler not to allow any more visitors into the house that night. Then he went to the dining room and joined Victoria, Andrew and Aunt Cherise for dinner.

Chapter Twenty-eight

Valentine saw two pistols aimed at each other. They fired. There was blood everywhere. Justin's blood. She screamed as she watched him fall to the ground.

The sound of her own scream woke Valentine with a start. She felt as if she'd just fallen from a high building. Her head seemed filled with gravel. She could barely remember where she was or what day it was. She propped herself up on her elbows and moaned. Even the bed felt different to her somehow. Maybe she wasn't in her own bed.

The draperies at the window were still drawn, which kept the room dark as night. She went to the window and pulled them back. The sun had not yet risen. She lit the lamp on the table by the window and focused her eyes on the clock that sat on the white marble fireplace mantel.

"Five o'clock." She yawned, stretched her arms, and

felt the pull of the ribbons around her sore wrists.

Suddenly the events of the previous day came back to her in a rush. Then she remembered the dream. Justin! He was going to die in a duel with Henry!

Then she heard the sound of horses' hooves on the street.

Justin had already called for his carriage. That meant he was up and readying himself to go. Valentine stumbled on the edge of the carpet in her haste to don her robe. She quickly put her arms through the sleeves as she opened the door to her room.

She could hear Justin's voice and that of another man. At first she thought it was Andrew's voice, but then she recognized it as that of Arnold.

She hurried to the stairs.

Justin turned away from his brother, went to his desk, and pulled out a Last Will and Testament that he'd written last night. It was a codicil to his previous will providing for Valentine and her family. He wrote Andrew Brittmore's name on the envelope. He sealed the envelope with wax and rang for the butler.

Arnold was behind the false bookcase retrieving the pistols. "Are you sure you don't want me to clean these guns for you?" Arnold asked, coming out from behind the bookcase.

Justin was standing at his desk with his boot propped up on the edge of the desk. He straightened the leg of his trousers and put his foot back down on the floor as he answered his brother. "I did it myself last night."

The butler knocked on the door and entered the library. Justin handed him the envelope. "Take this up to Mr. Brittmore and tell him we're ready to leave."

Arnold's eyes grew wide. "What's he coming for?" Arnold asked a bit too demandingly.

Justin's eyes narrowed suspiciously. He turned away from Arnold and studied a sheaf of papers dealing with his business. "In case I die, Arnold, there are several orders that I want him to see to."

Arnold shook his head. "How can you think of glassware at a time like this?"

Justin did not look up from the papers as he replied, "If I live, business will proceed as usual. These orders are important."

And a lot of good they do me, Arnold thought. You won't part with a farthing for my benefit. Arnold smiled sardonically to himself as he pretended to be sighting the gun, but actually tampered with the firing mechanism. All that is over now, dear brother, he thought. Upon your death, I shall inherit the entire Hawkeston estate and your damned glass factory!

Arnold looked down the barrel of the gun his father had used to kill the Earl of Westham when he found he'd been cheated in a card game. These were fine guns. Ones that had proven their worth. But today, only one of them would fire.

Arnold didn't like the fact that Andrew Brittmore had become so important to Justin lately. This turn of events was another reminder to Arnold that what he was doing was for the preservation of the Hawkeston name. Such as it was. At least Arnold wouldn't water down the family ties by befriending a raft of commoners as Justin had. Arnold's friends were still the highest-ranking members of the ton. He hadn't dirtied his hands with common labor the way Justin had.

He shook his head. Lord! What his father would think of Justin's behavior made his blood curdle.

The butler came back to the door and announced that the carriage was ready. Andrew came to the library door shortly thereafter.

Arnold shook hands solemnly with Andrew. "You look as if you hadn't slept a wink last night."

Andrew's eyes quickly glanced at Justin.

Justin shook his head slightly.

"I slept as well as could be expected under the circumstances. I've never attended a duel before," Andrew said.

"Well, I have," Arnold answered.

"You?" Justin was surprised.

"When Father killed that cheat Richard, the Earl of Westham. It was an incredible morning. Much like today, with the fog curling around the ground and the smoking pistols. God! I will never forget how pleased I was that Father counted on me being there with him at that time."

Justin shook his head. "That's because no one else in town would side with the bastard!"

Arnold's eyes flew open. "How can you speak of the dead like that, Justin?"

"Father murdered a man in cold blood and you think he's a hero. Father was the cheat, Arnold. The Earl of Westham was a fine and decent man. He left a wife and three children who had to go on without him. I, for one, will never forgive Father for that."

"You weren't even there!" Arnold screamed, and his hands shook. He felt his blood ignite and his body want to explode when Justin talked about their father like this. That was another reason Justin deserved to die. He continually persisted in destroying his father's memory. Arnold couldn't stand it much longer.

Justin could see the wild look come into Arnold's eyes. He'd seen it once or twice before, when they were children, but ever since his father's death, Justin had had as little to do with Arnold as possible. Not because Justin had turned his back on his brother, but because Arnold insisted on leading his own life. He wanted his own friends. Arnold lived at night and Justin was an early riser. Justin was usually getting up and going to work when Arnold was coming home. There had been no way they could live together, and so, a month after their father's death, Arnold had moved to an elegant townhouse Justin bought for him.

Many were the times Justin thought he'd indulged his brother too much. Perhaps if he'd forced him to become involved in the business, maybe he would have realized how much work and concentration it took to provide the money he so easily gambled away.

He wondered what kind of sickness it was that drove Arnold to put himself on the brink of financial ruin time after time. After dozens of times of paying Arnold's debts, the only conclusion Justin could make was that Arnold enjoyed riding the edge of destruction. Somehow it gave him the thrills he sought. It made him feel alive.

"No, I wasn't there. I would never condone such a meeting."

Justin walked over to his brother. They stood face to face. Justin's blue eyes were as cold and brittle as ice. His face was stern and condemning. Arnold's matching blue eyes were blazing with fire. Tiny beads of perspiration sat on his upper lip. Justin could tell he was struggling to contain himself. "I always thought it odd, Arnold, that Father killed the earl. I didn't know Father was such a good shot."

"You didn't?"

"No." There was no emotion in Justin's words.

"That," Arnold began with frantic spittle raining from his mouth, "is because you weren't close to Father. He never loved you the way he loved me. Never. You can mark my words on that. The only reason you inherited everything is because you were the first-born.

Nothing more than an accident of birth is all you'll ever be able to claim.''

"And that was important to you . . . being loved by Father?''

Arnold's eyes flickered with a distant pain. Justin nearly missed it. "I was loved by him, yes," Arnold said through clenched teeth.

In that split second, Arnold had allowed Justin to see into his soul. Justin had only experienced a similar occurrence with Valentine, when he'd looked in her eyes and saw a bright and loving soul. What he saw in Arnold's eyes made him want to retch. Arnold had been his father's victim.

Justin took a step away from his brother. Standing this close to truth was too brutal, too painful. Suddenly Justin was a boy again, playing with his younger brother, Arnold. Justin remembered how his father would take Arnold to town with him. To the horse races with him. They went to the tailors together and the barber shop together. For years, Justin had felt left out.

But now as he looked in his brother's face he remembered a day when Arnold was no more than nine. They had been playing chess in this very same room, on the floor near the fire. Justin had been lying on his stomach studying a particularly insightful move by his younger brother when their father had come to the doorway.

The man was huge, as Justin remembered him. Indeed, he'd been another two inches taller than Justin was now. He had massive hands he'd used often to slap Justin when he hadn't done what he was told or if his task had not been carried out to his father's specifications.

"Arnold, I'm ready now," was all his father had said.

Justin suddenly remembered the terror in Arnold's eyes. He remembered now how Arnold had frantically pleaded with him. "Tell him we're nearly finished with this game. Please, Justin. He'll listen to you.''

Justin had not understood, but he'd gone to his brother's defense. ''Must he leave, sir? He's nearly trounced me in this game.''

''I'm afraid so.''

''But, sir. You've always told us never to quit a game.''

''That's true. However, I meant card games when one's honor is at stake.''

Arnold had tears in his eyes. ''Please, Father,'' Arnold had begged. ''Not this time.''

''No, Arnold. Or do you want a whipping?''

''No, sir.'' Arnold slowly rose and went to the door. He looked back at Justin still hoping to be saved.

Arnold's voice catapulted Justin back to the present. ''It's time we left, Justin.''

Arnold stepped away from his brother and shoved his hands into his gloves. Then he picked up the box holding the pistols.

Andrew looked at Justin. ''Are you all right?''

Justin had never felt so much compassion for a human being in his life as he did that moment for his brother. Justin was consumed with guilt. Why hadn't he seen it then? Why hadn't he understood? Why hadn't some relative taken him aside and told him that such things could happen to boys? Why hadn't he known there were patterns of recklessness and self-defeat to his father's kind of degradation? Why hadn't the monster come to him instead? He would have fought him off and called up the devil to deal with his father. Then he realized that was precisely why his father had never tried to harm him. Justin was a fighter. Arnold was not. If only he'd been born a god, he could have changed Arnold's fate.

They walked solemnly out of the house just as Valentine opened the door to her room. She nearly flew down the stairs. She was only halfway down the stairs when she heard the horses' hooves on the street.

"No!" she screamed loudly enough to wake the house. "Justin, don't go!"

The butler came running into the foyer as Valentine flung the door open. The carriage was already a half block away.

She slammed the door. The windowpanes rattled.

"Why didn't you wake me?" she demanded of the butler.

"His Lordship wanted you to sleep."

"You mean he wanted me to stay home!" she said, picking up the hem of her nightgown so that she could take the stairs as rapidly as possible.

"Yes, ma'am," he replied.

From the fifth step she leaned over the railing. "I'll do nothing of the kind. Find me a carriage! Now!"

"But, Miss St. James, it's five in the morning. There are no hacks about."

"I don't care if you have to walk the length of Park Lane, get me a carriage!" She bounded up five more stairs and yelled as loud as she could. "Victoria! Aunt Cherise! Get dressed! We've got to stop Justin from being murdered!"

The heavy fog off the Thames clung to the ground like gossamer webbing. The first rays of dawn glinted off dewdrops and cast minuscule rainbows over the petals of the crocus and paperwhites.

It was a perfect day for death, Arnold thought as the carriage crossed Vauxhall Bridge and came to a stop at the designated area.

Justin stepped out of the carriage first.

Henry was dressed completely in white, a trick that

professional duelists used to blend with the fog. If the morning had been clear, he would have worn neutral colors, tans and buffs to blend with the still winter-brown grass.

Henry was the picture of confidence as he walked toward Justin.

"Where's your second, Henry?" Justin asked.

"I don't need one. I have perfect aim. And I aim to kill, or haven't you heard?"

"I heard," Justin said as Andrew stood between the men with his back to the river. Andrew held the box with the dueling pistols out to Henry first. "Let Henry pick first." Justin noted that Arnold had directed his gaze first to Henry, then for a split second to one of the pistols. He recalled that Arnold had been the last one to handle the guns.

Henry took the mother-of-pearl-handled pistol. He smiled sardonically at Justin.

Justin's mind was filled with the vision of Henry raping Valentine.

Henry's eyes were vacant, and when he blinked, Justin noticed the oddest thing. His eyelashes had been darkened with kohl. Then he understood.

He wanted to tear off the bastard's face. Henry was no better than his father had been. Justin had never killed a man in his life, but if ever there was a human who deserved to die, it was Henry.

Justin took the remaining gun out of the box.

Andrew paced off the area. The men were to walk twenty paces in each direction, turn and fire. Andrew found the center spot of the forty-pace area and marked it.

The sun did little to dissipate the fog as it rolled off the river in thick blankets. Justin could barely make out the trees along the street. From this distance he couldn't see his own carriage.

He wondered if he'd be able to see Henry once they'd paced off the distance.

"Gentlemen, are you ready?" Arnold asked.

"Yes," Henry said a bit anxiously. He was ready to smell his smoking gun. He wanted to hear the sound of Justin's body as it hit the ground. He was counting the money Arnold would give him. Then, after he'd talked Arnold into sailing to America with him, he would take the rest of his money and decide what to do with Arnold later.

"I'm ready," Justin replied.

They stood back to back, pistols held upright.

Arnold counted off the paces. "One, two, three, four . . ."

The men were so concentrated on the sound of Arnold's voice they didn't hear the sound of a carriage as it crossed Vauxhall Bridge.

"Ten, eleven, twelve, thirteen," Arnold called out.

Andrew braced himself. He'd never witnessed a duel. He wished he wasn't watching this one.

"Fifteen, sixteen, seventeen."

Valentine's carriage pulled to a halt. Valentine was leaning out of the window trying to find Justin in the fog, but it curled around the trees and shrubs like eerie banshee ghosts.

"Nineteen, twenty!"

"Justin!" Valentine screamed as she jumped out of the carriage.

One shot fired.

A second gun clicked but there was no gunshot.

A man groaned in pain.

Victoria and Aunt Cherise followed Valentine at a distance.

Seduced

Valentine raced across the cool wet grass toward the sound of the shots.

The fog thinned. Justin dropped to the ground.

"Justin!" Valentine screamed again.

Justin reached down into his boot and pulled out the gun he'd hidden there last night as a precaution. He aimed and shot Henry in the heart.

"Justin!" Arnold shouted.

"Justin!" Valentine raced up to him and fell to the ground. Blood was oozing onto his shirt. "Justin, you're shot!"

"I know . . ." he groaned. "What are you doing here?"

"I love you, Justin! Why wouldn't I be here?"

"No," he groaned as a sharp pain shot through his body. He winced and tried to get his breath. "You don't . . . I . . . read your diary . . ."

"My . . . ? Oh, no, Justin, you didn't!" Then she remembered waking up and not feeling the diary in its familiar place beneath the feather bed. That was why the bed had felt strange to her this morning. "Justin, I wrote those things a long time ago. Everything is different now." She tried to help him up. "Oh, Justin, please don't die. I love you."

His eyes rolled in his head.

She kissed him and he felt her tears. It is true, he thought. She does love me. Even if she once meant those things she said in her diary, she doesn't mean them now.

"Help me stand up."

Valentine put Justin's arm around her shoulder and helped him to his feet.

Victoria had reached Valentine, but Aunt Cherise had fallen behind in the swirling mist.

"Henry!" a woman's voice called. "Shoot him! The bastard is still alive! Henry!"

Cherise stumbled in the fog. Then she realized she'd bumped into someone.

"God in heaven! Sarah! What are you doing here?" She seized Sarah's arm.

"Unhand me!" Sarah demanded.

"Not until you tell me why you're here. And why in God's name are you yelling at Henry?"

Andrew heard Aunt Cherise's voice and started running toward her. Victoria ran after him.

In the meantime, Arnold had rushed to Henry's side. He stood looking down at Henry, who was bleeding profusely. His body twitched on the ground like a dying fish out of water. His eyes were wide with terror. His body flopped again and then became perfectly still. His brain was still alive. "Sorry, Arnold."

"Oh, God, no," Arnold wailed.

Justin took Valentine's hand and walked over to Henry in time to hear his dying words.

Arnold's head jerked up to see Justin still very much alive. "You son of a bitch. You killed him!"

Andrew escorted Lady Sarah to the scene with a tight grip on her upper arm. The old woman was stronger and more spry than he'd thought. She yanked her arm out of his grasp.

Arnold looked at her with confusion in his eyes.

Justin was equally as puzzled. "Couldn't wait to hear the details from someone else, Lady Sarah?"

"You fool!" She slapped Justin's arm. "And you fop!" She directed her comment to Arnold. "I knew you'd bungle the whole thing. That's why I was here."

"What?" Justin asked.

Andrew unfolded his hand and presented Justin with a derringer. The gun gleamed brightly as a ray of sun struck it. "She had this pointed at you, Justin, when I got to her."

Valentine was trembling with shock. "What is the matter with you? Must you hate everyone?"

"Not everyone, my dear, only people with the name of Hawkeston."

"Why?" Arnold asked.

"Because your father was a coward. He would never divorce your mother for me. He wanted the money in her dowry more than he wanted me. He told me he loved me, but all he ever did was use me. Because of him and his loose tongue and too much brandy, he told my father that he was my lover. When my father knew I was no longer a virgin, he refused to allow the sons of his precious dear friends in the ton to marry me. I never married because of it. I never had children and I deserved to have a family. I would have been a good mother. Your father was the one who had sons. Sons he abused with his cruel hands and his sex. Sons he never deserved. If I couldn't have children, he shouldn't have been allowed children. I knew I could never rest until the Hawkeston name was obliterated from the earth. I knew Arnold would never sire a child. But Justin. Ha! As long as he was married to his business there was no threat. I'd already set everything up through Henry, who found Crompton to rob your cottagers and ruin your farms. I thought that mess would keep you busy for years. Then you wrote me that you were coming back with a fiancée. I knew then I had to arrange to have you killed. I had to do it before you sired a child.

"Henry was a natural choice because he was the best shot in London." She looked at Justin's bleeding shoulder. "I can't believe he missed."

"If I hadn't realized that Arnold had broken the hammer of my gun, Henry wouldn't have missed," Justin said. "His shot was meant for my heart. I was in the process of dropping to the ground when the bullet caught my shoulder. I brought my own gun. I fired because I knew Henry had marked me for death. He was too smart not to have brought a second gun himself. If Henry didn't kill me, I thought Arnold would.''

''Justin . . .'' Arnold started to explain himself.

''Don't say anything to me, Arnold. I want you to get in my carriage. I've already given Mr. Weems instructions to take you to the coast where he will stay with you until you are on a ship bound for America. I will put money in a bank in Boston for you. There will be only enough to last you six months if you gamble. However, if you can think of a way to earn a living honestly, it will be enough to support you in the style to which you are accustomed while you apprentice yourself.''

''Justin, I want to explain.'' Arnold's eyes were filled with tears of pain, guilt and suffused rage.

''I never want to see you again, Arnold.''

Arnold nodded and walked off toward the carriage.

Suddenly Justin turned and strode after him. ''Arnold! Wait!''

Arnold stopped but did not face his brother.

''I . . . I didn't understand . . . about you. I'm sorry, Arnold. I never knew . . .''

Arnold burst into tears. He was too embarrassed to let his brother see him. He raced to the carriage, jumped in and closed the door. Mr. Weems slapped the reins against the horses' flanks and the carriage vanished into the fog.

Andrew put Lady Sarah in her carriage. As he closed the door, she leaned out the window. ''What is he going to do . . . about me?''

Andrew cocked his head. ''If it were me, I'd throw you to the wolves and never look back. At the very least

I'd alert the authorities. But Justin is more black-hearted than I am.''

Lady Sarah gasped. "What could be worse than being arrested?"

Andrew looked over at Justin who was getting into the coach with Valentine, Victoria and Aunt Cherise. "He'll tell all your friends."

Lady Sarah fell back against the coach wall. "Oh, good Lord!"

Andrew instructed the driver to take Lady Sarah home.

Justin waited for Andrew. "You'll wait here with the body till the authorities come?"

"Yes," Andrew said. "I arranged everything with Captain Pendleton last night. He should be here before too long."

Valentine's eyes were wide as she looked at Justin. Victoria's eyes were filled with as much surprise. "You knew this would happen?" the twins said in unison.

"Not all of it," Justin groaned as he leaned back on the seat. "Lady Sarah was a surprise, but otherwise I knew what was being planned for me."

"How?" Valentine asked.

"When Arnold kept asking me questions about the guns. He insisted a bit too strongly that he clean the guns and make them ready. It took Andrew and me all night to put the pieces together. I suppose I should have seen it coming when I cut off his funds before I left for Venice. But I didn't. My greatest fear was that he and Henry were trying to harm you."

"In actuality, you were just an innocent victim, Valentine," Andrew said.

"Arnold's feud with me goes back to our childhood." Justin groaned. When he peeled his hand away from his shoulder, the blood nearly gushed.

"We've got to get him to a doctor," Valentine said anxiously.

Justin was in great pain as he forced a smile. "A doctor? You mean you didn't bring your needle and thread, Valentine?"

She knew he was referring to the morning after the storm on the ship. "I forgot them," she said to Justin, who finally passed out. "Tell the driver to take us home immediately, Andrew."

Andrew signaled to the driver, who turned the carriage around and headed back toward Vauxhall Bridge and on to Lord Hawkeston's house.

Chapter Twenty-nine

The Hawkeston country manor house had not seen such activity in two hundred years since the birth and christening celebration of Justin's great-great-great-grandfather. And it had never prepared for a double wedding.

Mrs. Foley was given a half dozen assistants in the kitchen to help prepare the food for the wedding feast. Hogs were roasted over open-pit fires. Lamb roasts were stuffed with garlic cloves, and chickens were baked in lemon and wine sauce. Vegetables were cooked and seasoned with cinnamon and nutmeg. Whiskey and Scotch were imported from Ireland and Scotland. Valentine wanted to make certain that everyone had enough to eat for the four-day celebration she and Justin had planned.

Wildflowers from the surrounding hills and valleys filled vases, baskets, pots and urns throughout the house and back terrace. Andrew, William and Justin prepared garden torches and hung paper lanterns from the oak trees that surrounded the manor house.

Everything was fairy-tale perfect.

Valentine gazed at herself dressed in her wedding gown in the nine-foot-high Venetian gilt mirror. She carried a cascade of blush-colored roses and English ivy. Sabrina had done the impossible as far as Valentine could see. The blush silk of the underdress nearly matched the blush of her cheeks.

Valentine couldn't believe she was this beautiful.

Aunt Cherise came swooshing into the room. Her gown was made of springtime daffodil-colored silk with matching yellow organza overskirt. There were chains of ivy, pink tulips, yellow daffodils and deep blue clematis embroidered around the hem. Behind her was Bartholomew.

"Valentine, your guests are waiting," Aunt Cherise said and clapped her hands. There were tears in her eyes. "You've never been more beautiful, my dear."

Aunt Cherise took Valentine's hand and kissed her cheek. Valentine gazed into her aunt's eyes. In the past weeks as Bartholomew came around to see Aunt Cherise nearly every night and share dinner with them or sometimes just converse by the fire in the salon while Justin recuperated from his wound, Valentine had noticed that Aunt Cherise's looks had changed.

She didn't look tired or worried or old as she used to. Gone were the furrows in her brow, the slumped, unhappy edges of her mouth and the tiny lines around her eyes. She had started wearing her hair in a fashionable chignon at the back with Grecian curls around her face. She smiled nearly all the time, and her laughter had become lighter and more carefree.

Valentine looked over at the handsome Bartholomew and realized he had eyes only for Aunt Cherise.

It was odd, Valentine thought. She'd considered 42 years of age to be practically ancient, but now, looking at Aunt Cherise and Bartholomew, they didn't seem old in the least.

"Have you seen Victoria?" Valentine asked animatedly.

"She's as beautiful as you are," Bartholomew said and then laughed. "For the life of me, I cannot tell you two apart."

"As long as Justin always knows the difference, that's all that matters." Valentine laughed along with him.

She took the arm Bartholomew offered her and with Aunt Cherise by her side, she walked out of the bedroom to the hallway where Victoria was waiting.

Valentine gasped. "You're so beautiful!"

"So are you!"

They hugged each other happily.

"Are you scared?" Valentine asked.

"Not in the least. Are you?"

"Months ago I thought I would be. But the truth is, I'm very happy," Valentine said as Victoria hugged her again.

"Did you see what Justin bought for you?" Victoria asked.

"What are you talking about?" She thrust her hand on her hip. "Victoria, if you've spoiled a surprise for me, I'll never forgive you."

"Well, you don't have to wait long. Come see."

They went down the stairs and into the vestibule. William opened the front door and the girls walked out into the glorious April sunshine.

In the drive was a white coach with gold-painted trim. Two white horses with white plumes were outfitted with white leather bridles. On the door hung a piece of parchment inscribed with the Hawkeston coat of arms, and underneath the coat of arms the artist had drawn in black ink the words "Sir Snake."

Valentine, Victoria, Aunt Cherise and Bartholomew all laughed at Justin's joke as they entered the carriage that would take them to the apple orchard.

A canopy of fragrant apple blossoms arched overhead. Each time the warm spring breeze sighed through the trees, white apple blossoms rained down on the two couples being married that day. Seated in two rows of dining chairs from the manor house were Lord and Lady Purdey, Aunt Cherise and Bartholomew, and ten other close friends. Behind them stood over a hundred cottagers, farmers, villagers and household staff.

The minister was from the tiny church in the village. It wasn't every day he performed a marriage ceremony for one of the ton, much less a double wedding. He was more nervous than anyone present.

Valentine recited her portion of the vows facing Justin the way she'd wanted it, just as Victoria faced Andrew. Andrew placed a simple gold band on Victoria's finger. Justin gave Valentine a sapphire and diamond ring that had belonged to his mother.

When it came time for the kiss, both grooms were hesitant and both brides were more than willing.

The guests applauded the marriage, and then everyone went back to the manor house for the wedding feast.

It was well after midnight before all the guests left. Those from London were given rooms in the manor house, and a day of riding and sport shooting was planned for the morning.

With the sounds of laughter and music still playing in her ears, Valentine made her way up the stairs with Justin.

When they got to the bedroom door, she started to

open it. Justin quickly put his hand over hers and stopped her. "Wait."

"You aren't thinking of carrying me over the threshold, are you? Your shoulder will start bleeding again."

"I have a surprise for you." He kissed her on the mouth.

"But you already gave me my fairy-tale carriage, Sir Snake. What more is there?"

"You'll see. First you have to close your eyes." He opened the door and guided her inside. He closed the door. "Now you can look."

Valentine opened her eyes. "Oh my God, Justin! How in the name of heaven did you do this?" she squealed, happily rushing to the Italian gondola in the middle of his bedroom. "Can I get in it?"

"It's anchored with bricks so it won't tip over."

She unpinned her veil, placed it on the fauteil chair that had been shoved against the wall to make room for the boat and climbed into the gondola. Justin had turned away from her, donned his cloak and put on his mask.

"Baldassare!" she giggled.

Justin climbed into the gondola with her. He took her in his arms and kissed her ravenously. Despite his wounds, despite his pain and the strain of the duel, he'd never stopped thinking of the moment when he would make Valentine his own. He quickly unbuttoned her gown with his right hand. When the bodice fell away from her breasts, he pulled the dress down past her waist.

"God, I've waited a long time to do this," he said hungrily and let his eyes feast on her beauty. He took a taut sweet nipple into his mouth and flicked his tongue against it.

He slid his hand underneath her skirts and found she was wearing nothing at all.

"You vixen!" he said lightheartedly.

Suddenly he felt Valentine's legs flex together. She placed her hands on either side of his face and brought his gaze to the level of her eyes. "No," she said.

Fearing that she was still in shock over the attempted rape, Justin realized he was going too fast. It was only natural for her to be frightened.

"Not like this," she said.

"It's all right," he said, starting to move his fingers away from her bud.

Suddenly her hand was on his and she pushed his fingers back where they'd been. "You don't understand at all."

Then she peeled off his mask. "I don't want to make love to Baldassare." She kissed him passionately, her tongue invading his mouth, taking him prisoner. "Nor do I want to make love to Sir Snake." Her fingers raked through the hair at his nape. "I want to make love with you, Justin."

Justin felt his heart explode with love. He didn't care how many gunshot wounds he had. He stood up and peeled the wedding gown from her magnificently formed body. He carried her to the bed. He disrobed and lay next to her.

She touched his cheek. "I love you, Justin."

"I love you, my Valentine."

Justin made love to his wife. He sheathed himself inside her warm, loving walls and covered her mouth with kisses when he broke her maidenhead. He showed her that pain could be turned to pleasure and that he would not let her rest until he'd taken her to the stars.

He told her he would give her the moon and she discovered that in his arms, even that was possible.

They spent hours exploring each other's bodies. He was amazed at her lack of inhibition. She wanted to know every inch of him and what pleasure she could give him. They slept for short periods, rose, lit one of Valentine's scented candles, and made love all over again.

Laughingly she told him that she'd made the candle potion to cast a spell over him and later she'd discovered from the perfumery in London that the recipe the Gypsy Elana had given her was intended to work only on women.

Justin declared that his first and only rule for their marriage would be that she never had less than a dozen of that same candle in the house at any given time.

Valentine told him she loved him at least a hundred times that night.

And at least a hundred times that night, Justin thanked God he'd found his Valentine.

Dear Reader,

I don't know if it's possible for you to have enjoyed reading *Seduced* as much as I did writing it! After thirteen books, I have to admit that Valentine St. James is my favorite heroine of all. Many times Valentine's sense of humor pulled me out of the doldrums. My manager, Charlotte Breeze, and I now have an inside joke about her, and whenever things are not going as well as we'd like, we just say, "Where is Valentine when we need her?"

Because so many of you have followed my career, you are well aware that I have a habit of inserting my favorite recipes into the story line. The stew that Valentine makes is actually one of my favorites, for a Tex-Mex Tortilla Soup. For those of you who love to cook but don't have much time, this recipe is a life-saver, and men adore it!

To request a copy of this recipe, simply send me a

stamped, self-addressed envelope to 5644 Westheimer, #10, Houston, TX 77056 and I'll be happy to send you a copy.

If you wouldn't mind, please include your comments about this story. I have a sequel and a prequel already in mind. What are your thoughts on more Valentine stories?

Fondly,
Catherine Lanigan

Lacey
NORAH HESS

Norah Hess's historical romances are "delightful, tender and heartwarming reads from a special storyteller!"

—*Romantic Times*

Stranded on the Western frontier, Lacey Stewart suddenly has to depend on the kindness of strangers. And no one shows her more generosity than the rancher who offers to marry her. But shortly after Trey Saunders and Lacey are pronounced husband and wife, he is off to a cattle drive— and another woman's bed. Shocked to discover that the dashing groom wants her to be a pawn in a vicious game of revenge, the young firebrand refuses to obey her vows. Only when Trey proves that he loves, honors, and cherishes his blushing bride will Lacey forsake all others and unite with him in wedded bliss.

_3941-9 $5.99 US/$7.99 CAN

A Faerie Tale Romance
The Mirror & The Magic
CORAL SMITH SAXE

Bestselling Author Of *A Stolen Rose*

Sensible Julia Addison doesn't believe in fairy tales. Nor does she think she'll ever stumble from the modern world into an enchanted wood. Yet now she is in a Highland forest, held captive by seven lairds and their quick-tempered chief. Hardened by years of war with rival clans, Darach MacStruan acts more like Grumpy than Prince Charming. Still, Julia is convinced that behind the dark-eyed Scotsman's gruff demeanor beats the heart of a kind and gentle lover. But in a land full of cunning clansmen, furious feuds, and poisonous potions, she can only wonder if her kiss has magic enough to waken Darach to sweet ecstasy.

_52086-9 $5.99 US/$7.99 CAN

Notorious Deception

Adrienne Basso

Young, beautiful, and tempestuous, Diana Rutledge is shocked by the unexpected death of her husband. And a trip to London to set her husband's affairs in order brings even more unexpected surprises for the dowager countess—not the least of which is her introduction to Derek, the new Earl of Harrowby. Dark and brooding, Derek is far too handsome for Diana's peace of mind, and against her will, she finds herself growing attracted to the arrogant peer. But his accusations that Diana is a bold impostor force her to risk her reputation, her heart, and her very life to prove that neither she nor her burning desire is part of a notorious deception.

__3687-8 $4.50 US/$5.50 CAN

Dorchester Publishing Co., Inc.
65 Commerce Road
Stamford, CT 06902

Please add $1.75 for shipping and handling for the first book and $.50 for each book thereafter. NY, NYC, PA and CT residents, please add appropriate sales tax. No cash, stamps, or C.O.D.s. All orders shipped within 6 weeks via postal service book rate. Canadian orders require $2.00 extra postage and must be paid in U.S. dollars through a U.S. banking facility.

Name _____

Address _____

City _____ State _____ Zip _____

I have enclosed $_____ in payment for the checked book(s).

Payment <u>must</u> accompany all orders.☐ Please send a free catalog.

ATTENTION PREFERRED CUSTOMERS!

SPECIAL
TOLL-FREE NUMBER
1-800-481-9191

**Call Monday through Friday
12 noon to 10 p.m.
Eastern Time**
*Get a free catalogue
and order books using your
Visa, MasterCard,
or Discover®*

Leisure
Books